GERMAN REQUIEM

GERMAN

New York

Heike Doutiné

REQUIEM

Translated from the German by Krishna Winston

Charles Scribner's Sons

Library of Congress Cataloging in Publication Data

Doutiné, Heike, 1945–
  German requiem.

  Translation of Wanke nicht mein vaterland
  I. Title.
PZ4.G7394Ge   [PT2664.08]   833'.9'14   75–19335
ISBN 0–684–14373–9

1 3 5 7 9 11 13 15 17 19 C/C 20 18 16 14 12 10 8 6 4 2

Printed in the United States of America

I dedicate this book to the man who said, "I do not love the state— I love my wife": Gustav Heinemann, president of the Federal Republic of Germany, 1969–1974.

Glossary

Abendroth, Wolfgang (b. 1906). Professor of political science. A. taught in the German Democratic Republic after World War II, then joined the faculty at the University of Marburg in 1951. Noted for his works on social democracy and the European workers' movement, A. became one of the rallying points of the German New Left.

Alster. The river that flows through the center of Hamburg, forming the "Inner Alster" and the "Outer Alster."

Altona. A suburb of Hamburg.

"At a horse fair . . ." From the poem "Pegasus in Yoke" by Friedrich Schiller (1759–1805). Formerly learned by heart by most German schoolchildren.

Becher, Johannes R. (1891–1958). Revolutionary German poet who spent a number of years in the Soviet Union during the Hitler era, and after 1945 returned to the German Democratic Republic.

Borchert, Wolfgang (1921–1947). In his brief literary career, B. summed up the experiences of his generation in the war and in defeated Germany. His play *Outside the Door* (1947) records the despair of the returning soldiers.

Britting, Georg (b. 1892). German writer.

"Brown." The color used as a euphemism for Nazi.

Buci. Gerd Bucerius (b. 1906), publisher of the Hamburg liberal weekly *Die Zeit*.

Carossa, Hans (1878–1956). Popular German writer.

CDU. The German Christian Democratic Party.

Celan, Paul (1920–1970). German-speaking poet, author of the famous "Death Fugue," which begins, "Black milk of morning . . ." and deals in highly symbolic terms with the extermination of the Jews.

Django. Hero of "sauerkraut westerns."

Duensing. Police Commissioner of Berlin, inventor of the "liverwurst formation," used against student demonstrators.

Dutschke, Rudi. The best-known leader and theoretician of the German student revolt that began in Berlin during the mid-sixties.

Eichendorff, Joseph von (1788–1857). German poet and novelist, generally classified as a Romantic.

Eisler, Hanns (1898–1962). German composer who collaborated with Bertolt Brecht on several works. Lived after World War II in the German Democratic Republic.

Flechtheim, Ossip (b. 1909). Professor of political science in Berlin. An expert on Hegel and the history of the communist movement, F. was felt to be one of the fathers of the New Left.

Feuchtwanger, Lion (1884–1958). Prolific German novelist.

Galilei. The hero of a play by Bertolt Brecht (1898–1956), *The Life of Galilei* (1939); his fondness for good food and other creature comforts prevents him from choosing to become a martyr for the sake of his discoveries.

"The gentle moon is rising . . ." From a poem by Matthias Claudius (1740–1815), often sung by German children.

Gorm Grymme. Hero of a well-known ballad by Theodor Fontane (1819–1898).

Gretchen. The heroine of Johann Wolfgang von Goethe's *Faust, Part I* (1806).

Gymnasium. The German equivalent of the French *lycée*, it prepares for university studies. The final exam, which qualifies for university admission, is known as the *Abitur* or *Matura*.

Habermas, Jürgen (b. 1929). Professor of philosophy and sociology at the University of Frankfurt am Main. A leading theoretician of Neo-Marxism.

Hallstein Doctrine. Named for Walter Hallstein (b. 1901). Promulgated in 1955, the doctrine claims that the Federal Republic of Germany is the sole legal representative of the German people. Recognition of the German Democratic Republic by third states is to be construed as a hostile act. The doctrine has since been supplanted by Willy Brandt's *Ostpolitik.*

Hölderlin, Friedrich (1770–1843). Famous classical poet.

"Is the black cook there?" A German children's verse.

Jungfernstieg. One of the most elegant shopping streets in Hamburg, situated on the Inner Alster.

Kätchen von Heilbrunn. Heroine of a play of the same name (1810) by Heinrich von Kleist (q.v.).

Kleist, Heinrich von (1777–1811). Brilliant and tortured Prussian playwright and prose writer.

Krippendorff, Eckhart. An instructor at the Berlin Free University who was summarily dismissed in 1965 by the rector (president). K. later became rector of the FU as part of the change of command brought about by the student revolt.

Lantern, Lantern. A well-known German children's song.

Maynard, John. Hero of a ballad of the same title by Theodor Fontane (1819–1898). Formerly learned by heart by most German schoolchildren.

Mozart on the Journey to Prague (1856). A classic novella by Eduard Mörike (1804–1875), a Swabian pastor and writer.

Nolte, Ernst (b. 1923). A well-known German historian, author of numerous works on fascism.

Ohnesorg, Benno. A student killed on June 2, 1967, in a Berlin demonstration against the Shah of Iran. The policeman who killed O. was later acquitted. The incident marked a high point of the student revolt.

Osdorf. A suburb of Hamburg noted for its prison and its cemeteries.

Othmarschen. A suburg of Hamburg near the Elbe, notable for its many villas. Coextensive with Klein Flottbek.

Penthesilea. Heroine of a play of the same name (1808) by Heinrich von Kleist (q.v.).

Pestalozzi, Heinrich (1746–1827). Swiss educator and theoretician.

Peter. Perhaps the head of the Suhrkamp publishing house, Peter Suhrkamp.

Rowohlt. One of Germany's largest publishing houses, located in Reinbek, outside of Hamburg.

Rudi. Rudolf Augstein (b. 1923), editor-in-chief of *Der Spiegel.*

Saint Pauli. Hamburg's red-light district, also known as the *Reeperbahn.*

Skat. A very popular German card game.

SPD. The German Social Democratic Party.

Spiegel, der. A weekly newsmagazine published in Hamburg that imitates *Time* in format but carries more exhaustive articles. One of the few German periodicals that practices investigative reporting.

Spitzweg, Carl (1808–1855). Self-taught German painter who portrayed the world of the Biedermeier in a humorous vein. His most famous work is "The Poor Poet" (1839). Hitler's favorite painter.

Stern, der. Germany's best-known illustrated weekly magazine, published in Hamburg.

Suleika. A figure in several poems of Goethe's Persian-inspired cycle, *West-östlicher Divan* (completed 1820).

Tasso. Hero of Goethe's play *Torquato Tasso* (1789).

Tucholsky, Kurt (1890–1935). A satiric journalist and writer who observed and participated in the Berlin cultural scene during the twenties and early thirties, foreseeing the advent of fascism and analyzing its causes.

"Unmastered past." Unbewältigte Vergangenheit, the standard term used in Germany for the Nazi past with which few Germans ever came to terms.

Wedding. A working-class district in Berlin.

Weinheber, Josef (1892–1945). Austrian poet.

Wellingsbüttel. A suburb of Hamburg.

Welt, die. A conservative daily newspaper published in Hamburg by the Springer conglomerate.

Witz, Konrad (c. 1400–1445). Realistic painter of the German Renaissance.

Woyzeck. Proletarian hero of a play by the same name (c. 1836) by Georg Büchner (1813–1837).

Zeit, die. Liberal weekly newspaper published in Hamburg.

Zweig, Arnold (1887–1968). German novelist who spent the Hitler years in Palestine and later became a citizen of the German Democratic Republic.

GERMAN REQUIEM

Punch and Judy

On the way home she messed up my face. Irma Hoffmann from next door. She herself had a white face. I can still see that milky face before me. Irma Hoffmann from next door shoved me onto the packed snowy incline, and I crashed into the ice at the bottom. Lay bleeding in the snow. And Irma stood at the top and laughed. The more she laughed, the more my blood spurted. My friend, called Irma, whom I got fonder of the more she pushed me onto the snow slide. Just like that, from behind. Bump. I was not allowed to ride her scooter. It's mine, she said, and I stared at her Christmas present, stared at that scooter for a whole year, until I had one of my own. It's mine, I told her. But by that time Irma had a tricycle and could ride faster than I could with my scooter, faster than I could with my sled. Bump, and I went sailing down the death slide, crashed into the wire fence, and Irma laughed until the blood just spurted. My mother wiped it from my forehead. The milky mirror on the kitchen wall was cracked from the war. It had little black freckles. It reminded me of my girl friend's moles. The mirror looked like her back.

I am sitting on the green sofa, the coily sofa at the kitchen table. I rub my heels against its straw intestines. I'm caught on the slit-open belly of the sofa. I snag my stocking on a coil and rip a hole in it and blubber over my bowl of soup. Suddenly puppets pop up. Over the rim of my bowl, inside the window across the way. The ends of Dörte's hair make the puppets dance. Punch and Judy fall into each other's arms, and the policeman smiles. He tumbles over backwards. Irma waves. Irma and Dörte wave from across the way. Punch and Judy come crashing down. Wasn't Dörte Fischer my friend? She lived at Irma's house. She was Irma's friend. If she had lived at my house, she would have been my friend.

SCENE 1. INTERIOR. NIGHT. STUDY. CLOSE-UP: RAINER GEBHARDT AT HIS DESK. Sound on, camera rolling. CLAPPER: TAKE ONE! In two weeks he will be forty-three. Forty-three years old. It's time he thought about himself, came to some conclusion about himself. If he doesn't do it now, he'll never do it. Then all will be lost. Then life is over. The process of decay will begin. CUT! AGAIN FROM THE BEGINNING. ONE, TAKE TWO! He's turning forty-three. For forty-three years he has successfully evaded himself. He has doubled back on his tracks, lied to himself, wittingly and unwittingly. As long as the lie could be maintained. CUT! ONE, TAKE THREE! CLAPPER! Life rolls on. He has fashioned himself an image, but he does not know what it looks like. He covers his face with his hands. He hates mirrors. He has always avoided looking at himself any longer than simple cleanliness required. He has lived toward the future. He has taken whatever he could lay his hands on. He has refused to look back. CUT! TRY IT AGAIN! CLAPPER ONE, TAKE FOUR! He is forty-three now. He wants to start by looking himself in the face. That is a decision. He has decided to decide to make a break. Not away from himself, as it has been for the past forty-three years. But a breakthrough to himself. RAINER GEBHARDT writes on a sheet of paper: Today is February 17, 1968. It is 10:20 P.M.

Hairpins of Revenge
Irma wanted to play dress up. We'll play friends again, she said. We'll play sisters. And my grandmother's chemise petticoats took us under their wings. Those petticoats hung in the tall mahogany wardrobe in the windowless tube of a hallway, hung on long-armed heavy wooden hangers in that mothball fortress, two lofty white vaults of cloth, with lace at the neck and lace lattices along the hem.

A penny's worth of licorice! Herr Dralle, the druggist, counted out squares. Little black squares. His nose was as pointy as his pencil. The hair had abandoned his head in a panic. The nincompoop lines of nonthought had figured themselves deep into his brow, and he counted them up daily like his licorice drops. I said: Herr Dralle, we're sisters now. He looked up. His eyes slithered toward me across the tip of his nose. Herr Dralle miscounted. He took the little silver scoop that was only authorized for raspberry drops and shook licorice drops into the bag. Just like that. And still only a penny's worth. Oh, I see; now how did that happen? he asked, as he painstakingly examined the penny. He always looked at children's money carefully, lest he some day put a hard

2

candy in his cash register by mistake. I see; now how did that happen? My father divorced my mother and married Heike's mother. I took Irma's hand. Yes, now I have a daddy, too. Herr Dralle said, Well, congratulations. He said it with amazement, puzzled, his forehead richer by one more nincompoop line. He stood there in his empty shop. The five o'clock sun had crashed among the Lindt chocolate bars and lay gleaming next to the raspberry drops. Herr Dralle was wearing the sun like a shining band on his hand. Herr Dralle stared after us with reddened raspberry eyes through mirrorlike windows.

Irma wanted to play doctor. Comb, crayons, pencils, a knitting basket full of needles and yarn. She began with the arm. A broken hand. The knitting needle grazed my belly button. Stomachache. Thighs. Irma slipped between my legs and stabbed with her little needle. I screamed my mother to the door. Irma is twisting my arm! I screamed over my scrunched-up skirt—Irma! And Irma, white Irma, stood there and clutched her knitting-needle dagger tight in her fist, holding it out toward my heel-clattering mother like her prey. I had lost the doctor game once and for all. The guardian of my secrecies took the prey out of Irma's hand and sat down at the living room table, a watchtower over my fear. I wish you wouldn't fight all the time, my mother said slowly, as she examined Irma's knitting needle thoroughly to see whether there wasn't a piece of her daughter's flesh clinging to it. And Irma, my childhood torturer, and I stopped playing doctor and began to scrabble around the living room tower, silent and under surveillance. I behind Irma, the hairpin of my revenge, pulled with lightning speed from a side strand, already tight in my fist.

SCENE 2. INSERT. BACKGROUND INFORMATION. MONTAGE of official documents, contracts, vouchers, snapshots, paychecks, medical certificates. RAINER GEBHARDT is forty-three minus two weeks. He is about 5 feet 8 inches, has dark blond hair, still fairly thick, and except for an unpaid mortgage of about four thousand marks has no debts. In 1943 he passed his secondary school final examinations with "satisfactory." The report card can no longer be found. He is married for the third time. He has two children. One from his first marriage and one from his third. He is a Grade 1-A2 employee of a nonprofit organization. He does not know his exact monthly income. It should be about two thousand four hundred marks gross. He lives in the Wellingsbüttel suburb of Hamburg, is a German citizen, has a passport that expires this year and a standard operator's license in a red plastic cover. He has belonged to the Lutheran Church for twenty years and lives in a duplex rowhouse which costs him about four hundred marks a month. His parents are both dead. He has relatives, some of whom he has never met and never wants to. He has others whom he knows but would rather not. He is a nonconformist who owns two cars and is, as his boss Neubüser is fond of saying, uncorrupted. Which is not saying a great deal. He has an orderly job which does not fulfill him. He does not know what his neighbors think of him, since he does not talk to them. He likewise has no idea what his colleagues think of him, since he does not ask them. During the war he spent two years as a soldier and a week in Russian captivity. He has never been seriously ill and at the moment is plagued by an inflammation of the nerves whose cause the doctors cannot seem to locate.

I'm an Egg

Wait and see, Susanna's going to be a prima donna!

A prima ballerina!

Well, you know what I mean.

If you must use foreign words, dear child, at least you could use them correctly.

The old prune! If you ask me, she looks like a stuffed toe shoe.

Susanna, please hand me the hairpins!

Lock after lock is pinned up. She has a little pink train. Mine is black. At least that way one doesn't see the dirt. Now a peck from Mama, and Susanna hobbles ahead of me onto the dance floor. First position! A clean plié, relevé! French for the children's ballet of Altona.

Fräulein Vincenti, all blond waves like an overblown tea rose, claps woodenly with her palms. Be light as a feather, she murmurs, and we try to hold in our soda pop and gumdrop tummies. Across from us Germany's new generation of mothers sits beaming, the Vienna State Opera and the Met in their handbags. Each her own choreographer.

A nice leap, Peter!

Except for my mother, who just views the ballet lessons as a means of getting rid of my old granddaddy gait, except for my mother, who never comes to watch, all the mothers are there, twittering away. Their heads freshly heeled with permanents, always eager for a chat after the lesson, bursting with the future that awaits their little darlings. Perhaps I was only destined to become a feather duster, but Renata will be a butterfly at the very least.

Come children, says Fräulein Vincenti, let's bake a cake! Everybody over here! We swarm toward her on the diagonal. Now you children be the raisins. Roll along merrily. You be the flour, slow moving and lazy. Lisbeth, you must stagger—you're the rum. And Heike—careful, careful! You are the egg. Peter, spread your arms wide, yes, that's good. Melt like butter. And Susanna, you stir the batter good and hard. Gather up the raisins that are rolling off the table, fetch the egg. Now all of you move forward. Remember what you are! None of you want to be caught and baked! Ready, set, go! I roll cautiously sideways, with my legs drawn up. The tricky existence of an egg. If she makes me be the yeast next time, I'll never become a prima donna. The best solution would be to spread my arms wide at the next lesson, play the cake tin and not budge from the spot.

Don't get your little white arms so dirty!

Mother Susanna is directing the show again, asking Fräulein Vincenti in a whisper whether the State Opera doesn't need a flying mushroom or a glowworm. Until now our midsummer night's dream has been baking cakes, but tomorrow, while I trudge along in my blue linen skirt, Susanna will go flying over the roofs of Altona, dressed in organdy and accompanied by her mother on a broomstick, a witch in the fifth position, flying right down the chimney of the Opera. I had better start to pant right away.

Stop that! What do you think you're doing? Fräulein Vincenti, she's spitting at me!

That's a lie!

It is not!

Yes it is!

Dummy!

All right, you go and stand against the wall, Heike! In the corner!

What joy! I've shaken off my eggshells. I hope the bell rings soon and puts an end to the lesson. Then I'll buy myself some chewing gum, licorice, and a red devil, and Susanna won't get any.

SCENE 3. INTERIOR. NIGHT. STUDY. SEMI-CLOSE-UP: RAINER GEBHARDT at his desk, a sheet of paper in front of him. The TELEPHONE RINGS. This telephone that divides RAINER GEBHARDT's day into choppy sections. He picks up the receiver reluctantly. Yes, what is it? Grützmann dribbles into his ear, congeals. Yes, Grützmann, what is it. Grützmann mumbles as usual. Grützmann falters as usual. RAINER leans back, holding the receiver, his excuse, firmly to his ear. Now he cannot go on with what he was writing—he is on the phone. Talking with Hans Grützmann, the doctor. Always with an index card handy. Always one card too many. Now he can ask Grützmann right into the receiver: Yes, yes, what's up? The Republican Club? RAINER has heard of it. RAINER planned to drop in some day. Just to take a look. Just to see. See what's up. Now Grützmann has done it for him. Garrulous as usual. Long-winded as usual. A new steering committee? The old one is incompetent. Stop by some time? At his place? At Rainer's? Why? Oh, he's bringing a good man along. And what for? Grützmann coughs. Swallows air the wrong way. Hans Grützmann gasps for breath. But to get things moving. Even so. That's precisely why. He has to be at the hospital tomorrow until eight, then he'll stop by. With the good man. Grützmann sets a time. Reluctantly. And he won't stick to it. As usual.

Lantern, Lantern

Behind the mahogany wardrobes in the hallway tubes of our labyrinthine old building live the ghosts and the mice. Clap your hands once, real loud. Give a quick, piercing whistle. Whoosh, hold the bowl of potatoes high, take a running start, and career straight ahead. I run toward myself in the mirror, bringing myself the potatoes. The mirror has moles. My skin mists over in the steam from the bowl. Keep going. Past the dressers. One of them has a limp. It lost a leg in the war. Keep going. Is someone standing there? The light bulb dangles from its cord in the shadow of the wardrobe. Grandmother's rows of mahogany. The door. Tenants, lodgers, government-assigned neighbors. My mother hardly knows their names. Behind this cardboard door live Frau Evers and Mother Bläske. They come toward me. They take the bowl of potatoes from me. They untie my apron. They pull off my shoes, my socks, my pleated skirt. They put the bowl back into my hands. My

6

mother is calling me. I run into the living room. I stand tongue-tied in the door, poke out my belly, rub my toe red on my ankle. Say nothing. Am questioned. Why don't you answer me? Silence. My legs hang naked to the floor. I supply the black market, speechless, defenseless.

Behind the doors live the ghosts. I know that, and keep very still. Men come. Many men. They do not ring; they have keys to Frau Evers and Frau Bläske.

I'll kill every one of you!

The moon shines onto my cot. It hangs there high and steep, over the stone balcony that faces north. High and steep over my bed. Fists beat on the door. Like heavy bricks. As if he were catching rats. Catching us.

I'll kill every one of you!

A bottle smashes against the doorknob. Frau Bläske's bear roars into the night, hammers through the wood, stretches out his paws for me. Wants my sweater, my underwear, my clothes, my stockings, and beer. My mother breathes shallowly. Something is flapping behind the pillow-mountains. A heavy thump. The bear has bumped into the sewing machine. The corridor tripped him up. Steps. Whispering. A parcel being dragged along the hallway.

I'll kill every one of you!

The bear is whimpering in the distance. I fall asleep with the moon above me. The corners of its mouth turn down. It gazes down, its woolen cap askew, its skin scarred. Yellow and lofty. Lantern, lantern.

SCENE 4. INTERIOR. NIGHT. STUDY. CLOSE-UP: A COGNAC BOTTLE. A hand moves into focus, grasps the bottle. ZOOM. RAINER GEBHARDT pours cognac into a water glass. He is beginning his decision-making with a game of hide-and-seek. He cowers behind a bottle. He says, Let's start with the essentials. He says WE, and even that is not quite honest. It's not a question of WE. It's a question of I. From now on, no one but I. But I refuses to voice an opinion. I is tired. RAINER GEBHARDT gets up and goes to the window. Looks out. He's been drinking. Drinking because he's in despair. Cannot get his bearings. Can no longer locate himself in the shell he lives in. He is dodging himself. He's almost forty-three. He's dissatisfied. No matter what he does or doesn't do, no matter what he sets out to do—nothing gives him satisfaction. He's searching for something. Something new. Always on the lookout for something new. FLASHBACK. BERLIN, 1946. ACTORS' STUDIO IN DAHLEM. RAINER GEBHARDT practicing a role. After only three weeks he can already see that this was a mistake. But he stays on. Tenaciously. Without alternatives. He tries all sorts of things. He opens a theater that collapses after the first premiere. Built on blind enthusiasm. He discovers cabaret, or rather, he thinks he discovers it. Together with Dieter he founds the SLANDERBEARS. The partnership ends with a blowup. Dieter against Rainer. One hard head against the other. Neither will give in. Rainer pulls out. Compromise seems out of the question. This is the first time he has quit a job. His options will be reduced. But he has nothing more to lose. He pulls out. SOFT-EDGED WIPE. A FEW MONTHS LATER. BERLIN, 1947. RAINER GEBHARDT gets expelled from the actors' studio. For contradicting a professor, for calling him an old fool in front of all the other students. He rejects the life line they want to throw to him. He repeats his charges in front of the entire faculty, including the professor in question. He has to leave. He feels no regret. He begins to write. Hectically, with no concern for technique or dramaturgical principles or style or any of the other things one expects of a playwright. He proves to have been right. He finds a publisher who is willing to print the stuff. Word for word. Without a single cut, a single addition. Which he would not have allowed in any case. He would sooner have given up on having it published. He likes everything he writes. For a year he is riding the wave of popularity in the making. Then the wave recedes. He writes a third play. It is impossible to perform. A publisher in Hamburg suggests he turn it into a novel. Rainer Gebhardt refuses and stuffs the manuscript into the stove. Even now, years later, he is still convinced that it was his best play.

I Am a God of Wrath

Hymn 79, verses 1, 2, and 3. Divine worship for the dolls. My pulpit is a puppet theater that comes up to my knees. I look out at the rows of kitchen chairs, occupied by teddy bears and Steiff animals. Every chair has its stuffed worshipper. Twenty black doll-hymnals, twenty silent singers. Each has his own hymnal in his Steiff paws, his Bible at his turtle feet. Sing out!

    Feed Thy flock, Father, comfort Thy disheartened sinners.

Sing out! He who does not sing will have his head bashed in. I pull out the lashes of the doll I always take to bed with me because she won't pray with the rest of us. Today's lesson is taken from the first book of Kings, chapter I! And when King David was old. Grandmother's worn-out black dress, a pastor's robe for a saint floating above the heavenly rigging-loft of a puppet theater. Lofty and black I preach down to my dolls in their little stockings. Snow white respectably laundered kneesocks and little black felt gloves. Be obedient, be humble, for I am a god of wrath! I hasten up and down the rows, ruler in hand. Check on them, rap their paws, their feet. Pound my dolls' heads down onto the seats until they are lying prone before me, until they bow down before me with their flat celluloid faces.

SCENE 5. NIGHT. HALLWAY IN GEBHARDT'S HOUSE. LONG SHOT. RAINER GEBHARDT GOES TO THE DOOR. A GOOD MAN has arrived. His shadow looms up behind the glass door. GEBHARDT heard the GOOD MAN's steps. He opens when the GOOD MAN rings, standing there glass-ribbed and wood-slatted outside the door. Hello. My name is Böhm. Excuse me for being late. I waited outside for forty minutes. But Herr Dr. Grützmann. May I try to reach him at the hospital? Dr. Grützmann's good man is here. Is here and hangs up his coat. GEBHARDT takes a good look at him, the good man. Blond eyes, blond skin, blond hair. There he stands, rinsed in blond. Two straight blond legs. Filled to the brim with blondness. GEBHARDT thinks: undifferentiated. All one color. GEBHARDT thinks: the gray coat he just hung up is his contrast color. His only contrast. GEBHARDT says, Certainly, right this way, the phone's on your right. GEBHARDT leads BÖHM into the living room. In answer to the man's question, GEBHARDT tells him 47-11-41, and is startled to realize that he knows Grützmann's number by heart. So it's reached that point already. BÖHM makes his call. Leans against the wall. Smiles at GEBHARDT, then at the receiver. Back and forth. HERR BÖHM is practicing a TV charm display, and GEBHARDT thinks: he wants something out of me. He's smiling me into agreeing. He's smiling me soft. And BÖHM says, He'll be right over. He's just getting ready to leave. He sits down in the armchair, the flowered TV armchair with the four shaky legs. One of them keeps breaking off and is always being glued. BÖHM sits there in the glue chair, silent. PAUSE. CAMERA WANDERS SLOWLY FROM BÖHM TO GEBHARDT AND BACK AGAIN.

Tag! You're It!

Rubble wonderland. Racing with the rats, round and round. Away from the bricks. Swinging from the tree with the golden apples, on the path leading from the gate, right behind the bookshop, in the rearview mirror of Raeder's bookstore. He shakes his fist. He shouts down the path. He shouts the roller skates right off our feet. Raeder the bookseller hunts children like rats. If I catch you swinging again! He shouts out the window, red as a turkey. He vomits up his anger. A red face rolls down the path toward us. Beat it! Beat it! Into the rubble wonderland. Into the burned-out Altona Municipal Theater.

The sky dangles into its windows, and you creep through the holes in the sky into the mountain of rubble. Only the camomile and the yarrow have followed you, pitch camp with you. Tag! You're it! Run! Hit the pavement with your knees! Skin them before the others do. They want to catch you, and they'll get you. The tag, you're it can run faster than you can. Is the black cook there? Three times march straight ahead, the fourth time around you lose your head. Run! The police are coming! Run! You're a policeman. Your head falls so quickly into the hands of the robbers. You must learn to run.

SCENE 6. SAME SET AS IN SCENE 5. CLOSE-UP OF GEBHARDT, THEN CAMERA WANDERS SLOWLY TO BÖHM AND BACK AGAIN. GEBHARDT is wondering whether he should initiate a discussion. About the political situation. How critical it is. How complex and multifaceted. A discussion with this fair-haired boy. So he can nod knowingly. And say yes, yes, with great emphasis. Well, leave him alone, GEBHARDT thinks. Let him hang on to his assent for a while. He will need plenty of it for the life of nodding that lies ahead. Let him save it, GEBHARDT thinks and turns on the TV. ANNOUNCER'S VOICE-OVER. Tension increases in the Middle East. This evening the banks of the Suez Canal near the city of Ismaelia were the scene of a three-hour artillery duel between Israeli and Egyptian forces.

President Nasser declared in a radio address that he would no longer sit by while the Israelis. BÖHM yawns. GEBHARDT gets up and goes into the kitchen to fetch beer. That will make him even sleepier. At today's gathering of the Silesian Patriots' League, Chancellor Kiesinger declared. GEBHARDT nods at BÖHM, hands him a bottle and an opener, says, One moment, please, and goes to the door to admit DR. GRÜTZMANN. Garrulous, long-winded Dr. Grützmann. Out of Grützmann-breath as usual. Late as usual. Please excuse me. GRÜTZMANN stands there with heaving lungs. Bowing slightly, he shakes hands. Creeps over the threshold as humbly as on the first day of school. His steps too small. Always one step too many. Too finicky in his haste. Much too finicky. He must know Böhm pretty well, GEBHARDT thinks and closes the door. He turns around. He looks at GRÜTZMANN and BÖHM. Walking toward each other as if they were at a debutantes' ball. In a moment BÖHM will ask Dr. Grützmann for a one-two-three waltz, a four-five-six waltz. BÖHM greets GRÜTZMANN. Two beaming masks, beacons of friendliness glowing behind the façades. Two political Christmas crèches lit by candles. Wine? BÖHM nods. He has already polished off his bottle of beer. GRÜTZMANN nods. Nods with a one-second lag. Waits to see what Böhm will do, his good man Böhm. GEBHARDT goes into the kitchen. Fetches a bottle of Tirolean red from the cabinet. I hope they both get drowsy, he thinks, back in the living room, and sets out the glasses. One, two. I'm not having any. Let's get started. The blond one smiles. Cups his hands. CUT!

Cut It Any Way You Want It

Herr Betje has hanged himself. Downstairs in our house, where the little bar has taken over, a last thread for Herr Betje. Remnants of a large drygoods store, Grandfather's drygoods store, which Grandmother guarded during the war, gun in hand. That is how she scared off nocturnal prowlers, but not Herr Betje.

Apprenticed to my grandfather in 1918, tall, emaciated, black hair combed back, an eye on the daughter of the house. A first abortive love. The business grew, and with it Herr Betje. He advanced, became my grandfather's right hand and thought he should be the left as well. With Verdun in his legs and shrapnel poisoning in his veins, my grandfather died in '45. Herr Betje took over. Thin, hesitant. He had not been in the Party. He had measured out bolts and been rescued from investigative internment by an affidavit from my grandfather.

The main shopping street, Altona's Königstrasse, down which the Kaiser had once passed, was bombed to ruins. But Betje did not want to give up. His drygoods store. He took over the remnant of space next to the bar. He wanted to keep the shop going. In the glass coffins, display cases with fabric flowers, I played dress dummy with Irma Hoffmann. Stiff and posing, with spread fingers, we crouched or stood amidst the flowers and waited for passers-by. If any came, we fled the stage, dissolved in giggles. Betje let us. He swung me through the air with his long, thin arms; he passed me over his fabric flowers, high over the ruins, and set me down among bunches of violets.

Betje had friends, a boyfriend. Small, stocky, full-bodied. His pockets full of money. A black marketeer who would cut it any way you wanted it. The two had known each other since before the investigative internment, since before those times. After all, it was what they had in common that had landed them there.

Betje's stocky friend lived with his sister, and the couple went on vacation with her. Betje overdrew his wallet. Then came the trip to France. Again the three of them. I had enough money along, he assured my mother. I paid for the whole trip there, all the gas, all the hotel bills, and when we got to the Riviera I didn't have enough money to go to the men's room. I had to beg for pennies. I didn't dare mention how much I had already laid out. My friend just laughed. For a good ten minutes he refused to give me money for the toilet. I'm just not strong enough. That sort of thing is too much for me.

It was too much for him. Financial humiliations and physical dependence on the stocky hustler, his poor business methods in a bombed-out area—Betje put an end to himself and his intimate enmity. One day in February, when my mother and I wanted to get into the shop, around noon, we found the door locked. It remained so until it was broken open. There he hung, over his display cases, tall and skinny, the tips of his toes almost touching the fabric flowers. He only had to kick in the glass. He had stretched overnight. Grown much, much taller. He had grown into death. He had leaped into the noose. Herr Betje had hanged himself above his pin-on posies.

12

SCENE 7. INSERT. FREEZE EFFECT, CLOSE-UP: BÖHM'S CUPPED HANDS.
MONTAGE OF SNAPSHOTS, FAMILY PHOTO-ALBUM STYLE. VOICE-OVER.
WINFRIED BÖHM. Thirty-nine years old. Studied philosophy at the Free
University of Berlin. Cherished hopes for a better life. Years as a
teaching assistant. Years of submissive servitude. Promotion to salary
grade 28. Marriage. Two children. A Renault *deux chevaux*. Cherished
hopes of bettering himself. Promotion to salary grade 32. Move to
Hamburg. Probationary year with a newsmagazine. Researching articles.
Writing articles. Rewriting. Revising. Again and again, in hopes of
making salary grade 33. Making salary grade 33 by the summer of '68.
After all, WINFRIED BÖHM is getting older, and the apartment in
Hamburg's Mövenring settlement is not paid for yet. And the wife and
children have not joined him yet. Are still in Berlin. Because Daddy is
going through his probationary year. Daddy is battling for promotion.
Only then, when the goal has been reached, line by line, will WINFRIED
BÖHM's sex life catch up. Come flying to the Mövenring in Hamburg to
build a nest. Only when his promotion report card, the general
evaluation, reads: WINFRIED displayed a cheerful, friendly, and helpful
disposition. His conduct was always faultless. Despite average ability, he
made an earnest effort to fulfill the requirements of the probationary
year. Achievement in OPENING DOORS: satisfactory. FOLLOWING GOOD
ADVICE: satisfactory. FRIENDLINESS: good. ATTITUDE: satisfactory.
ADJUSTMENT: adequate. WINFRIED BÖHM smiles. He dreams of this report
card. He cups his hands and smiles.

God Has a Long Beard
*What place did the children of Israel arrive at on the third day after the
Exodus?*
  The desert.
  Good. And what was it called?
  Sina.
  *No, that's not quite correct. Say it good and loud. And correctly. The
desert was called Sinai.*
  *Sister Anni puts us through our paces. Last time we did a story about
Uncle Moses.*
  *Shame on you, Bert! You know you mustn't eat candy during Sunday
school!*
  Sister Anni is strict. With dark blue wings like the pictures of saints we

exchange. *Or rather, like my cut-out Mary in the paper crèche. All that's missing is the candle behind her Christmas back. I would love to put Sister Anni inside my Advent wreath, next to the dark red little figures that have been riding a sled on a wooden plate ever since I was born. But actually she does not look like my Mary. More like Mary's mother. With her long dark blue dress, her black laced boots, and the stiff, pleated lay sister's cap.*

Now, what did the Lord say to Moses?

My legs still do not reach the floor. I barely grow from one Sunday to the next, even though I inch forward to the very edge of the chair.

The Lord is my shepherd. Let us pray.

God has a long beard. Once I had my picture taken with Him. God was standing outside Karstadt's department store in a red suit and a long white fur cap. Dear God, in three months I will see you again, provided my mother goes shopping at Karstadt's.

SCENE 8. INTERIOR. NIGHT. GEBHARDT'S LIVING ROOM. CLOSE-UP: WINFRIED BÖHM'S CUPPED PALMS. FREEZE EFFECT DISSOLVES, CAMERA TRACKS BACK. OFF BÖHM! BÖHM smiles. He smiles at GEBHARDT and says, It's about—Dr. Grützmann has certainly mentioned it to you already— about our club. GEBHARDT looks at GRÜTZMANN. GEBHARDT thinks about the OUR. What does that mean, OUR? And BÖHM says, I say OUR because Hans and I have joined, have become members in order to bring about some changes. Up to now this club here in Hamburg has consisted of only fourteen people with 1200 marks in debts. The present steering committee members, GRÜTZMANN explains, keep the control in the hands of a small, elite group. They collect dues from other members, who exist only in the files, are not given any say in the club's activities. These activities, GRÜTZMANN says, consist of programs and evening get-togethers, over which none of the members have any control. These activities, DR. GRÜTZMANN says, are cabaret programs, for instance, in rented halls that seat two thousand. And ten people come, BÖHM adds. Politically the club hasn't done a thing so far. But the steering committee will resign if we assume the debts, says BÖHM, says GRÜTZMANN. We have already spoken with the officers, BÖHM says. Herr Hopp is willing. Nice people. Simply ineffectual. BÖHM nods in GRÜTZMANN's direction. We

14

consider it worthwhile. A political base. A platform. A republican starting point. Coordination. Action. People from all walks of life. GRÜTZMANN nods genially at BÖHM. One nod, round trip. The SINGING COMMERCIAL BROTHERS. GEBHARDT would have liked to do the piano accompaniment. Our concern, says GRÜTZMANN. Our cause, says BÖHM. And GEBHARDT, personally indifferent but full of ingratiating courtesy, asks, Does your club have quarters of its own? Wrapped in smoke, GRÜTZMANN sits there wheezing. No, he says, and puffs billows into the air. No, it doesn't, BÖHM says promptly, echoing him in measured tones, thoughtfully. Full of deference. Already worried that it might be Gebhardt who gets promoted ahead of him, one class ahead of him, Winfried Böhm, whose dissertation was stolen from his car, inexplicably stolen from his *deux chevaux*. Would you see to getting a hall, he asks nervously across the table. Would you take on that responsibility, BÖHM asks softly, and GEBHARDT swivels the wine bottle in his palm, and GEBHARDT says, Of course, that should be the first item of business. Actually GEBHARDT does not want to. Actually I'm too old for childhood diseases, GEBHARDT thinks. Let the two of them go ahead. But quarters, GEBHARDT thinks. One really should have quarters. I could certainly find rooms somewhere. He remembers the Easter disturbances, thinks of the demonstrators' trials due to begin in the fall. He thinks of the issue of university reform, of a Thalidomide case coming up, about a broad democratic movement. Without ties to the political parties, free, flexible. Arguments instead of billy clubs. Solidarity instead of hairsplitting. Educating the people. Working at the grassroots. GEBHARDT begins to think in banner headlines, succumbs to wishdreams. He wants to do something, so his children will not ask him, What were you doing in '68? What did you do when a professor told his students, You all belong in concentration camps? When a juror said to a girl in the SDS, You people make a racket like in a Jewish school? When, when, when. GEBHARDT accompanies BÖHM to the door. DR. GRÜTZMANN and BÖHM. GEBHARDT says, I'll be in touch. He says, I'll drop by some time. And he knows that he will. Walking past solid citizens, who shout HIPPIES, MORONS. Who shout, You need a good spanking. GEBHARDT feels anxiety, delicate, physical, lightly dusted anxiety. It settled on his neck when the police horses came galloping up in front of the Opera House, came galloping straight at him. Gebhardt the newspaper reader. From now on he will do more than read the newspaper. Gebhardt the TV watcher. From now on he will do more than watch TV. Gebhardt the head shaker. From now on he will do more than just shake his head. Will do something. With Grützmann and Böhm. But something, at any rate. GEBHARDT catches sight of himself in the mirror. I'm still in good enough shape for meeting the card-file corpses. I'm still young enough for that. I'll be able to swing it.

Cod-Liver Oil and Rat Poison

The stairwell was dark. He stood there like an animal in a hole. His life had written out his death certificate. Mommy, the Russians are coming! Flight to the bathroom. Wooden clogs lost. Pleated skirt caught in the door. My heart in my mouth. Beating against my palate. Hold tight to the door handle. My, but he has a heavy step. Like a bear. What a stumbling and bumbling out there. But why is he crying? No, that's my mother. The keyhole is stiff. Turn the key slowly. Hold your breath. Mouth shut. Tummy in. Open a crack. A squalling heap in the hall. The bear and my mother are lying against each other. No, standing against each other. I tiptoe close. Ouch, my toe! I propel myself along by a hole in my sock, over to Uncle Ernst. What is this Uncle Ernst, anyway? Uncle Ernst is a skimpy bundle of flesh. No, not a bundle. A stick of flesh, much taller than me. Towering above me. With a coat, old green moss, caked with rain. He is coated with earth, my Uncle Ernst, coming back from captivity. He was in the war. He ended up under the revolver of Irma's brother. In captivity. How he eats. Very slowly. He chews like Granny. Does he really have teeth? Yes, he does. He crumbles bread into the soup. Uncle Ernst, the same color from top to toe. White like a kitchen wall with cracks. Uncle Ernst has them, too. A white face with cracks. When you look at him that way, only his forehead is blue, from the eyes swimming in it. Sky blue. They stayed blue even in captivity.

He bartered chocolate for cod-liver oil, Mommy says. That's how he survived. Cigarettes for cod-liver oil, that I can see. But chocolate for cod-liver oil? Here, a spoonful for Frau Ellermann! I don't want any more. I spit it out. I spit out this spoonful for Frau Ellermann. I spit the cod-liver oil in my mother's face. Yellowish guck. It looks like Frau Ellermann's hair when she hasn't washed it for a long time. That's just what it looks like. Not a spoonful! I'm not in captivity. I don't want my

16

bones to get strong. I want chocolate. But Uncle Ernst doesn't want to swap with me. He doesn't have any more chocolate. Ah, but I have cod-liver oil left. The bottle stands on top of the kitchen cabinet, and lower down is the rat poison. Perhaps one should take a lick? A spoonful for Frau Ellermann! Then one would never have to have cod-liver oil again, and Mother would cry and be sorry she hadn't given me chocolate.

My uncle just came home from the war. Irma listens to my account. Her face is white. Maybe she just got out of captivity, too? My uncle has come home from the war, but he still has all his legs! What does he tell you about the war? Oh, all sorts of things. For instance, in the war you can swap chocolate for cod-liver oil. That's great, I'd like to go to war, too, some time, Irma says. She envied me. I could see it in her speechless eyes. She had no Uncle Ernst, not much chocolate, and just like me: lots of cod-liver oil.

SCENE 9. INTERIOR. EVENING. GEBHARDT'S LIVING ROOM. CLOSE-UP: TABLE WITH A BIRTHDAY CAKE WITH CANDLES AND A FORTY-THREE IN ICING. CAMERA ZOOMS OUT AND PANS TO RAINER GEBHARDT AND FRAUKE, WHO ARE SITTING IN THE DINING NICHE UNDER A LAMP WITH A WICKER SHADE AND WATCHING TV. A forty-third birthday. The book is from the book club. He found out about it several days ago. The book he saw on Neubüser's desk. Konrad Lorenz. *On Aggression.* A book for his birthday. Thank you for taking the trouble. I'm glad you like it. Frauke has baked a cake. A marble cake, meant to be eaten. A birthday, meant to be eaten. What's Tanja up to? Tanja's in her crib. We have the whole evening to ourselves. Frauke has given him a tie. The price tag is still on it. Frauke forgot to take off the price tag. We have the whole price to ourselves. Forty-three roses birthday. Darling, I arranged the roses in the vase. What's Tanja up to? Tanja is in her crib. We have the whole evening to ourselves. Frauke has the whole evening to herself. Frauke has been to the hairdresser's. Frauke is all arranged, arrayed. Frauke pours coffee. Later she can wash the cups. Frauke takes his hand, presses it like dough. Here, have another little hand. There's some coffee left. How nice that today is Wednesday. That means that tomorrow is

Thursday. Birthday is off and running. Gebhardt and aggression. The party from the book club. Mail-order birthday. What a pleasant evening under the wicker shade. We have the wicker shade all to ourselves. What is Frauke up to? Frauke's in her little bed. What is Gebhardt up to? Gebhardt's in his little bed. We have the little bed all to ourselves. The price tag is still on it. Gebhardt forgot to take off the price tag. How nice that today is Thursday. That means tomorrow is already Friday. And we have Friday all to ourselves.

Sleeping Beauty Ellermann

I outgrew Irma. I fell into the chalky hands of my teachers, my one-times-one teachers. I was seated according to my marks in dictation. Always in the last row, back where the D's sat huddled together, rivals in red underlinings. I didn't have the commas one needs for a successful life. Frau Ellermann, a Fräulein whom everyone called Frau because she was on the verge of losing her second set of milkteeth, Frau Ellermann admonished, her hollow back proudly packed into her gray jersey dress, the brooch on her collar, green jade. Frau Ellermann, towering steeply, way up there, her head almost grazing the ceiling. At home she ate hay. During class her horse face reflectively chomped the last wisps. And then the dwarf seated himself on a stone. Frau Ellermann dictated the dictation, and my commas crouched down in the spaces between the words at random. Sheltered by my bent head, they hopped across the page toward the next D.

Frau Ellermann. She had long hair. When she was sick one time, we brought her flowers. Flowers from the class. And we saw her hair. Thick brown gray-shot braidy hair. The horse face had stopped chomping. We sat beside her bed, stared at her dry lips. She lay there stiff, like a paper doll. She was wearing her gray dress under the blankets and her hard black leather pumps, under whose soles all the commas in the world took refuge. After five minutes of silence, a whining little woman beckoned us out. She looked like the dwarf that sat down on the stone. Frau Ellermann's mother, shrunk to the size of a thimble. Softly, softly down the hall. Our toes pointing straight ahead, past wardrobes, mothballs, and long flowered silk dresses. Past the moth-balled spring of 1910, which lay in the big chest and slept.

But Snow White Ellermann awoke once more. Probably her mother had kissed her awake, kissed her out of bed, braided her hair, twisted it into a bun, and stuck in the hairpins. For when we sang The cuckoo calls in the woods *for the twentieth time, when we sang,* I am a gay young shepherd *for the twentieth time, in unison, in two-part harmony, Frau Ellermann was back. Towering straight up, her head almost grazing the ceiling. She had become a little smaller, just a wee bit smaller. Frau Ellermann was growing toward her mother. And as she grew smaller and smaller, she taught me personal experience compositions, hacked me in two. My right half sat up front, the part that got a B for content. My left half, the left-handed one, the retrained right-handed one, sat in back. The D in spelling and punctuation sat in the last row. Like the two kings' children in Goethe's poem, the two parts could not come together. I went through school split in two. I hobbled through classes in which the dwarf is sitting on his stone to this day.*

SCENE 10. EXTERIOR. THE YMCA HOUSE ON THE ALSTER. LONG SHOT: RAINER GEBHARDT GETS OUT OF HIS CAR, LOCKS IT, AND ENTERS THE BUILDING. CAMERA FOLLOWS GEBHARDT INSIDE. DOCUMENTARY TECHNIQUE. Green painted stucco work. White curlicues. Palace of Christian youth. Leningrad on the Alster, GEBHARDT thinks and remains standing at the door. He counts off democracy by the number of chairs. A small democracy. With cavities. The fillings are stuck along the wall. Sitting down is bourgeois. GEBHARDT enters the Russian dance hall, greets Böhm. BÖHM is bourgeois. He is the only one sitting, not stuck to the walls, nicotine groomed. GEBHARDT notes the carefully stacked mountain of papers in front of BÖHM. He sees BÖHM arranging lists. Sees him at the head of the table. Blond BÖHM. Stuffed with blondness. So these are the card-file corpses, GEBHARDT thinks. He recognizes a few young film makers with buzzing eyes. Their mouths still show the chalk marks from the last clappers. Mops of curls. Faded jeans. GEBHARDT looks for Grützmann. But Grützmann is not there yet. Late as usual. Drowned in a teapot. Fallen into a yogurt container. Spooned up by Darling. There's Herr Hopp! BÖHM has abandoned his chair. BÖHM has stood up for NIKOLAUS HOPP, the president, the president of this club. GEBHARDT sees a gray tweed suit with a vest and a gold watch chain.

19

GEBHARDT sees HOPP. Glittering gaze. A little mustache under a pendulous nose, beneath a prominent forehead. GEBHARDT is reminded of the Roaring Twenties, of the Great Depression, of speculators with long-stemmed cigarettes. Hopp, he thinks, this Hopp with the glittering glasses, trimmed for betrayal with golden rims, this 1928 tweed coupé, scares me. Behind Hopp's thinning head a jazz band is playing. His debts are dancing the Charleston. He sees HOPP clicking his tongue. He hears him saying ABOUT TWELVE HUNDRED. A practiced wheeler-dealer, GEBHARDT thinks, a rat from Kafkaville. Soft voice, well-mannered hypocrisy, laughing over unpaid bills, perfumed lies in his handkerchief. So his name is Hopp, GEBHARDT thinks. So this is Nikolaus Hopp. SPECIAL EFFECT. NIKOLAUS HOPP IN A TWENTIES-STYLE SUIT IS SUPERIMPOSED, THEN MERGED INTO THE MIDDLE SECTION OF OTTO DIX'S TRIPTYCH "METROPOLIS."

My Father

Things are looking up. Thanks to demolition and the clean sweep. Stone by stone. Person by person. Germany is starting anew.

That man, the one who just drove by in the Opel Captain, that was my father. My father is manager of a bank. My mother only works because otherwise she would be bored. Birgit, look, there goes my father in his Mercedes. Hi, Daddy!

Don't call until the car is already past. Wave when it is almost out of sight. My father is a pharmacist. My father is a judge.

Dear Jürgen, if you come to visit me in Hamburg next week, my father will probably not be there. My father is away on a business trip.

My father on trips. From profession to profession. So Dörte's father is a surgeon? Then my father is a state's attorney. I have a father, too. All children have fathers. The steam shovels lumber up in front of our building. They are moving the rubble, the last remains. The mountains of rubble shrink to heaps, the heaps to single stones you can kick aside. Clear the way! In that new building over there my father has his law practice. No, not on the second floor, on the fifth. Up there, Birgit, the windows with the gray drapes!

Children's birthday. Everyone is invited. Coffee and cake make the rounds, all around the table. Twenty-four children. Twenty-four cakes.

20

Carpets of pastry and whipped cream spread all over the corridor. Just keep on beating with that spoon! Onto the table, onto the chair. A whole apartment of chocolate. An eating competition. Thirteen pieces of cake without stopping, that's the record. Elke Brauer, freckles, with a memory of blond hair and blue eyes, with a fat tummy and chubby little dangling legs that don't have growing pains, still four-foot-six, Elke holds the record. Thirteen pieces of cake cross the goal line first. I am far behind with just eight. And my father? He only eats three. And pours the coffee.

Remember not to say Uncle Ernst. *Keep your mouth shut. Watch out. My mother always says* Ernst. *That goes fine. They do it that way at Elke's house, too. There the father is called Heinz. That works just fine. That's how to do it. Just make sure you don't say the wrong thing. No, I don't have an uncle. But I do have a father. A proper, strong, rich Mercedes father. With a camel's hair coat and a silk ascot.*

That man, the one who just went into the building, the one with the silver tie, Birgit, that's my father. He's an architect and earns lots and lots of money.

SCENE 11. SAME SET AS IN SCENE 10. CAMERA FOCUSED RIGIDLY ON DOORFRAME. LONG SHOT. WHENEVER SOMEONE ENTERS, TRANSFORMER-TRUCK TRACK-IN TO CLOSE-UP AND FREEZE EFFECT. DISSOLVE AND BACK-TRACK TO LONG SHOT. Eleven. Twelve. Thirteen. Seventeen. Eighteen. GEBHARDT is counting, while BÖHM attends to the greetings. BÖHM passes around his friendly smile like a fingerbowl. BÖHM smiles himself from hand to hand. Nineteen. Twenty. GEBHARDT is counting. Twenty-two. Twenty-three. The door feeds the room. They come strolling in, between the ages of twenty and thirty. Hello. They come strolling in, casual and untroubled. What are we going to accomplish, GEBHARDT wonders. They stretch their kneesocks out in front of them. What do we have in mind, he wonders. A political base. A platform. People from all walks of life. But two students plus two students makes four students. Just four students. No civil servants. No office workers. No workingmen. No platform. GEBHARDT thinks, the headstone should be red. Red with yellow stripes. He thinks, the inscription should read Hello. Hello in white toothpaste. He thinks, that will make a nice grave, draped in Indian silk scarves, with a long-haired coffin. Here lies the house slipper of the Republic. But perhaps the headstone could also be blue. As blue as the silk wraparound blouse of the girl next to the man who just came in. Who now takes his place along the wall next to the girl, velvet lined and gray browed. BÖHM whispers to GEBHARDT, That's him. And GEBHARDT thinks, so there he is. A fact. So he really does exist, this Peter Bruhns. Breathes with his stand-up collar, speaks with the velvet lapels of his jacket, gently strokes his right cuff. SLOW TRACK-IN TO BRUHNS. He is served up like an elegant meal, GEBHARDT thinks. He cultivates his forty years hedonistically. Hair gleaming with conditioner. His suit lubricated with subtle scent. GEBHARDT notes a melted mouth, with washed-out points. Its left side dips into a groove. The coarse nose inclines to the right. The eyes crooked, their focus downward. The large protruding ears hold the reins tight. Sharply outlined gentleman's sideburns. An office-nourished upstart who wants to reach the top. But his wrinkles, his drooping face, pull him down. CAMERA NOW MOVES IN FOR EXTREME CLOSE-UP OF BRUHNS'S FACE. FREEZE EFFECT.

Once upon a Time There Was a King

Sugar brought about her fall. She had survived the war, outlived her husband, held on to her bombed-out house, but sugar brought about her fall. My grandmother. With her sky-blue gaze, the snow-white teeth of a young girl, a slow, dragging step, and a wealth of injustices, which she hid in her purse and her bag of candy. Blond hair was preferred. Her inherited line, with blue eyes, small and delicate, received the lion's share.

Here's a mark for you. A pretty shiny mark. But don't tell a soul.

Granny stuffed my little fists with pennies and root-beer candies, she filled my stomach with clandestine pastries, and I was not supposed to tell a soul, certainly not my black haired cousin.

Once upon a time there was a king who had three sons. They were called Franz, Herbart, and Johannes. When the king saw that his last hour, hour, hour . . .

Go on, Granny, I begged from the rug, but her head sank lower and lower, her white hair fell over her chest. She sat there and slept as soundly as if she had fallen asleep in the snow. My snowed-in white haired grandmother.

Granny! Once upon a time. Come on!

I tugged at her dark blue polka-dotted dress. Come on! Read to me!

Her head came up slowly—where are my glasses? But they were still perched on her nose, just waiting for once upon a time. Once upon a time there was a king . . .

Her head nodded. Once, twice, and dropped. Summer and winter, spring and fall. So one of my dearest wishes was to learn to read so I could finally learn how the fairy tales came out, because we never got past once upon a time and there was a king.

Walks with Granny. To the rose garden on the Elbe Promenade. Very slowly. Stop. Catch your breath. Tag-you're-it at a slow crawl. And the slower I went, the more silver-wrapped pieces of Lindt chocolate. I almost forgot how to walk, was always last in races, and did not catch up until later on, without the Lindt squares.

Granny always got up at five in the morning. Every day. Every day since the time certain silver spoons and china plates had not survived the visits of the Evers-Bläske family. She took up her post in the icy cold kitchen, shuffled around lighting the fire, and waited for the thieves and tenants. She sat very still in her chair next to the battered old green plush sofa and waited. Waited for Frau Evers, waited for Frau Bläske, waited for them at six, at seven, at eight, waited for the coffee-making magpies. For Grandmother had the key to the Holy Grail. After her silverware losses, she had collected the remaining keys and now locked up the kitchen every evening at ten-thirty. Since her tenants insisted that the kitchen should be unlocked by six in the morning, she accepted the demand, grimly and with bad grace. She gave out no more keys. She came herself and watched over her possessions. With success. The spoons and forks, the plates and pitchers no longer suffered the fate of the ten little Indians. Once Granny started getting up at five, our well-stocked kitchen cabinet was safe.

Granny also had lady friends. They wore dark blue like her and ate Lindt chocolate, the fine little squares that melted on one's tongue. For instance there was Frau Lobo, who had corresponded with the whole world, even with the Kaiser. My child, that was a man for you! Frau Lobo's eyes gleamed, glittering little pin heads amidst the dark blue. Small and stooped, as small as I was at seven, she propelled herself over the floor, a few carnations in the crook of her elbow.

Flowers for the hostess.

A dark blue hair net bound Frau Lobo and the olden days of the Kaiser together, and as the two old ladies slowly forked cheesecake into their dried-up mouths, it was clear my Granny had company. A visit from an envoy of the Kaiser, Frau Lobo.

And my grandmother knew songs. Ride a cock horse was still going around in my head when we were already singing Swing, swing, come swing with me, my lass. I sang that loud and bawlingly in the hallway when I had been given my swing near the cellar entry. That was my first and favorite swinging song. And when Frau Kimme came for the weekly cleaning of the hallway, the three of us sang it over our Thursday coffee. Frau Kimme was also a friend of my grandmother's. They had met during the war at the little bar and restaurant called The Cask, on the way back from collecting their ration stamps. Frau Kimme received a small widow's pension, and on the way home she accepted my grandmother's suggestion that she come and help out a little in the house. Her husband had worked at the post office. The war had robbed her of her new net curtains. They had been only a week old. A flying shell fragment. What a war! All the curtains in shreds! But nowadays it was worthwhile earning a little on the side again. Frau Kimme. Tall and skinny, with a roomy stomach. She polished off three bowls of lentil soup every Thursday, and still she stayed thin and bony, with a dark red knitted wristlet on her right arm to keep her from catching cold. Her shaved eyebrows were replaced by two thick dark brown pencil lines, her narrow mouth adorned with a red streak. Frau Kimme likewise wore dark blue. I think she was wearing it even before she met my grandmother and decided to become a charwoman.

We suited each other nicely, Frau Kimme, Frau Lobo, my grand-mother, and I. We drank coffee, sang Swing, swing, come swing with me, my lass, and I performed Behold, the moon is risen, all the stanzas and by heart, to general applause. If only it hadn't been for the sugar. I am sure we would still be creeping along the Elbe Promenade together, very slowly, with many stops. But we had a pantry and a coal cellar. The doors to these two areas were side by side in the kitchen. One reached the pantry by ascending many steep steps. One reached the coal cellar by descending many steep steps. Granny liked to nibble. She often disappeared and was found with her fingers in the sugar canister. But Granny, my mother would say, and arm in arm they would descend again. But Granny, I soon learned to say, and made rabble-rousing speeches when I caught her at the sugar crock.

And then one evening it happened. She wanted to lock up the kitchen. We all said good night. And the next morning? The kitchen door open, the pantry door open. And there lay my grandmother, half on the icy tile floor, half on the steps. Fallen, surrounded by her spilled sugar. There she lay, cold and stammering. Ambulance. Hospital. Flower bouquets on Sunday afternoons at three-thirty. The white of her face merged with the white of the pillow. Only her eyes still had their sky blue. They had it even after she could no longer walk. The bones were old and soft. The doctors allowed the leg to grow together crooked. My mother called up Frau Lobo. She came with a few carnations, greetings for my grandmother, and the Kaiser's letters. But my grandmother could no longer follow. She only smiled. She nodded a friendly nod. Like a precious old wall clock her delicate head-pendulum swung back and forth. Evenly, slowly, silently. Ma-me-mi-mo-mu. She's cracked, Uncle Ernst said. There's no point reading her fairy tales. She can't understand them any more.

But I read to her. Once upon a time there was a king who had three sons. And then she smiled at me. I think she did understand me. Certainly she was also anxious to hear the end of the story. For she stared attentively straight ahead, sky blue, and listened.

SCENE 12. INSERT. MONTAGE OF CLIPS FROM A TELEVISION PORTRAIT. TITLE: ONCE AROUND THE CLOCK WITH PETER BRUHNS. SILENT. SOUND EFFECTS. VOICE-OVER. Peter Bruhns. Perhaps forty years old, perhaps forty-one. Somewhere between bombing attacks he graduated from secondary school, between flak and labor service. Postwar theater. Bruhns moved from lesson to lesson. Puppet theater. With his bicycle he black-marketed himself a living. A friend went inside and took care of the job. Peter Bruhns had to push the bike. A friend lured the mice out of their holes. Peter Bruhns had to push the bike. Too scared to go in himself. From lesson to lesson. Bruhns pushed the bike, loaded with stage scenery. The oppressed Bruhns was gathering strength for his ascent. Just wait till I. You'll see. At some point Bruhns abandoned the bike. At some point it became too much even for Bruhns. Now he wanted to. Now he wanted to be Bruhns for a change, become Bruhns, with a student newspaper. It all began with a student newspaper. Today Bruhns buys people—secretaries, apprentices, editors, who push the bike for

Bruhns, always six paces behind him. Always behind him. Girls for six hundred marks. Men for two thousand marks. Bruhns learned his lessons. Bruhns calculates human beings with interest. His magazine can be found on every newsstand. Right opposite *Playboy*. Bruhns has made the magazine what it is. A magazine with naked bosoms, with striptease reports, and lots of socialism. The revolution has slipped down between the thighs. His lingerie editorial board sells political brassieres. VIETNAM on Lolita's cups. STOP THE WAR on Kitten's buttocks. Bruhns once dreamed of a villa and a white Mercedes. Bruhns wanted to become an outsider on the inside. Bruhns has become an outer insider. Bruhns has his villa and a white Mercedes. Bruhns is proud of himself. Very proud. He has printed political counterfeit and no one has noticed. His currency is circulating. The strolling republicans in jeans and kneesocks swallow the magazine like drugs. Revolution between bed and lip. And how could one not go for the combination: thinking of Vietnam while getting laid? Who wouldn't go for it if he is young and bearded and revolutionary in his spending patterns. All for Bruhns. All through Bruhns. LAST SHOT. FREEZE TECHNIQUE AS IN SCENE 11. EXTREME CLOSE-UP OF BRUHNS'S FACE.

Well, Child

Well, child, didn't you bring Frau Evers with you?

A bar in our building, a beer parlor, a den of alcohol. Plunge in and drown. Another beer. One more. Let's have some myu-sick. That plastered flower, the juke box, murmurs its last memories. You hit me like a thunderclap. Frau Bläske swings a mug. Her flowered moiré dress sends an illusion of summery meadows over her skin. A quarry of pores. Wrinkle mountains. Above them a titian red forest of sofa stuffing. And the thick wedge heels with a strap across the bony ankles tap to the beat.

Well, child?

A slobbering ball rolls toward me. A tanker in a storm. A double chin of beer with crumbling teeth and metallic eyes. It must be two beer coasters, I think, and stumble backward, my three bottles in my arms, along with a bar of milk chocolate with nuts.

Egon, close that door!

But Egon, my pursuer, bumps into the juke box, slops all over the floor, dribbles out of my sight. His puddle spreads toward the door. Three steps back. The green wool entrance curtain falls shut behind me. I shove my way out with my hip. The swinging door falls to. And now up the stairs. Eyes closed. Race up the stairs before the light goes out. It only stays on a few seconds at a time, feebly. Someone is standing behind the cellar grille. Someone is sitting in the cellar. Someone is creaking upstairs. It smells of lentil soup and cabbage. It is Thursday.

SCENE 13. INTERIOR. EVENING. GREEN STUCCO WORK ROOM OF THE YMCA. EXTREME CLOSE-UP: BRUHNS'S FACE AS IN SCENE 12. DISSOLVE FREEZE EFFECT. CAMERA BACK-TRACKS AND PANS. To Chicago and back, GEBHARDT thinks, and looks to see if he has a ticket. In his pocket, for Bruhns. For variety. We are a political club. GEBHARDT hears BÖHM speaking. We want to broaden the democratic base. GEBHARDT watches BÖHM. BÖHM, who is talking to BRUHNS, the famous Bruhns, who has also come to save liberty and democracy. Böhm's liberty. Almost as good business as Bruhns's liberty, GEBHARDT thinks, and does a preliminary summing-up. Hypothesis number one: in a political club one can make a name for oneself. Hypothesis number two: travelling salesmen in revolution are well paid. Hypothesis number three: well-promoted illusions improve the image and the sales. GEBHARDT looks over at BRUHNS, who knows what BÖHM is getting at and is totalling up the prospects. BRUHNS takes a running start for the two hundred thousand limit. A naked girl is sleeping inside his velvet jacket. Under his turtleneck is the back door to the place where he will be spending the night. A refrigerator in his heart. A bottle of champagne behind his ear. A box of chocolates in his gaze. I am the only leftist magazine, BRUHNS says. Of course I'm with you, BRUHNS says, and pastes a bosom onto the Vietcong's gun. I'm for the revolution. BRUHNS openly acknowledges his kneesocked readers, and his political men's magazine sells revolution to students in the john, with Ché Guevara on the towels, on the toilet handle. Relax, is BRUHNS's motto. But pay first. We must do something, says a MAN SITTING UP FRONT. We must win over the population, says the MAN SITTING UP FRONT. We must start campaigns, says the MAN. He is wearing a black frock coat, a purple silk shirt. A twenty-eight-year-old man in high black riding boots. A man with his head full of stand-up

27

collars. Full of silk stand-up collars. GEBHARDT gets up and opens the window. GEBHARDT thinks, I am too old for this. Much too old. A whole world war too old. CAMERA TRAVELS OVER GEBHARDT'S SHOULDERS AND PAST HIS HEAD OUT INTO THE DARK REAR COURTYARD. GRAY-OUT.

The Time for Little Red Hearts Is Past

Getting into preparatory school. Entrance examination. The leap into necessity. My mother went to preparatory school. My father went to preparatory school. I will go to preparatory school. The question Why does Jutta Leistner's father drink? *is not a suitable question for preparatory school. If the leap is successful, the father will stop his excessive drinking. The survivors stick together.*

They select the best, my mother said. They select the best, Fräulein Ellermann said. They select the best, I said, and began to eat pastry at recess instead of dark bread. Pastry bought with money I snitched from my mother's purse, secretly, when she was in the kitchen, secretly, when she went to the bathroom. Secretly. Pastry for school. The packet of pumpernickel sandwiches simply got lost on the way to school, dropped by the wayside. Two-marks-forty's worth of honey cake, so their fathers would see me eating it. Two-marks-ten's worth of apple strudel, so their fathers would say, That's a wealthy girl, she would be a good playmate for you. She comes from a good family. You must invite her over some time, Doris. Bring her home with you some day, Waltraut. She has pastry instead of bread for recess. Every day, as much as she wants. She eats apple strudel in school.

Getting into the special preparatory school. Entrance examination. The leap into the group of fathers who pick up their daughters after school, their necks in silken nooses. Upper-class girls from the upper-class school, being picked up by fathers in camel's hair coats, their sleek cars idling at the school gate. A ten-year-old doctor is picked up, an eleven-year-old school principal. And tomorrow a sleek car will be waiting for me. For me and ten slices of honey cake. Examination. Hush. Puella, rusticus, fenestra, porta. Here we speak German, dear children, not Latin. Yes, you there with the blond braids. I can't read your name tag. How do you say door? Well? Yes, Birgit. Door is porta, quite right. Take a breath. Right. Curtsey. Right. Get an A. Right. Say yes. Right.

28

Learn by heart. Right. Wear little white blouses. Right. White kneesocks. Right. And I have gray kneesocks. It all started with the gray socks.

Still, the time of teachers' pets was past. *Gisela Schwalbe, who sat four rows in front of me, who wore little red hearts in her ears, who was always allowed to wipe off the blackboard, who always received special treatment—Gisela Schwalbe's time was past, once and for all. Frau Ellermann was also past, a hollow spine in gray which staked everything on red hearts.* The unfamiliar *Fräuleins* whom one called Frau sorted us according to porta, according to puella. *The red-heart currency was no longer valid. Our intelligence was multiplied by the sort of home we came from. Four times doctor equalled* passed. *Four times warehouse foreman equalled uncertain prospects. And Gisela's father was a warehouse foreman. What an obdurate child! And how bright the Reverend Krause's child was! An amazing memory for Latin. Yes, yes, the child has a future. But please don't disturb us. There's a test going on. No one is to talk at the tables. Here no one wears little red hearts in her ears. Here one speaks only when spoken to. And one is seldom spoken to. We sat there in silence. We heard nothing but puella. We spelled nothing but fenestra. Academic offspring to the front! A slight shoving. Shoving upward. Shoving ahead. Neatly decked-out precocious-ness takes the lead. My father is a doctor. Right. My father is a lawyer. Right. We did everything right. We were so clever. No brats, no boors among us. Dignified. Stiff and clean. Well-bred. The red hearts failed to get their way. Jutta Leistner, the bottle baby, did not make it. Only Irma Hoffmann and I, the doctors' children, we two made it. Irma with her white and I with my gray socks. With gray socks, not quite as good, not quite as right, not quite as smart, not quite as obedient, not quite as white. But still.*

SCENE 14. MONTAGE OF CLIPS FROM THE RUSSIAN FILM "BERLIN" (1945). BEGINNING AND END: NIGHT SHOTS. OFF-SCREEN NARRATION. Somewhere among new apartment buildings, gardens, and a canal. Berlin, 1945. A dead gray sea. GEBHARDT sees it all, but he does not grasp anything. He keeps on fighting. The tanks have holes in them somewhere. In the turret, in the assembly, in the hull. Little round holes. That is what killed them. Now they are burning. Over there something is moving. GEBHARDT shoots. Empties his magazine. He has to hold this position. He must not retreat an inch. Not an inch. Not an inch of territory. Stand your ground. Just another twenty-four hours. Then Wenck's army will get here. Then everything will be all right. Then he will be pulled back. Then he will be able to get a good night's sleep. Just don't lose your nerve. Don't be punk. The Russkies may be here any moment. And they'll polish us off in short order, Lieutenant Heiser says. All up. Finished. Out like a light, GEBHARDT thinks. He is nineteen. As old as the building in which his parents lived, 42 Hölderlinstrasse. They've gone to hell. He can still hear his mother saying, Cut out, son. Cut out while there's still time. Cut out. Just take off your uniform and beat it. Don't lose your nerve, Lieutenant Heiser says. It makes no difference whether they catch you here or a few streets farther on. A few streets farther on. They've hanged a guy there. He deserted. Gebhardt found him hanging from a lamp post. The little scrawny guy. The one from the Reich Labor Service. A few streets behind the main front. The cord had dug deep into his neck. Someone had hung a sign around his neck. I AM TOO COWARDLY TO DEFEND MY PARENTS AND MY BROTHERS AND SISTERS. LONG LIVE THE FÜHRER. Gebhardt saw it with his own eyes. Yesterday, when he was taking the little twelve-year-old whose eyes had been shot out to the first aid station. The guy on the lamp post. And those fellows in the bar. Soused Labor Service and Party bigwigs. They sat in there, puffed cigarettes, and drank themselves into a stupor in order to forget their fear. And he and the others had to stand out here and let themselves be shot at—for those bastards. He stood out here and let himself be shot at. Grit your teeth, Lieutenant Heiser told them. Grit those teeth. Swallow the shit. Everything has to end eventually. Everything. Don't be punk. Take it like a man. Some day Germany will be proud of us. No one can do this like we can. Those guys from the East can't. Not to mention the ones from the West. Berlin. They'll read about it in school some day. They'll write books about it. Books for all the schools. GEBHARDT can't help laughing. What was it Dr. Lademann always used to tell him? Gebhardt, if you can't handle the ablative absolute, how do you expect to manage in life? GEBHARDT is standing guard in falling Berlin. I guess I won't be needing the ablative anymore, he thinks. Or Hölderlin. Or even a teacher. Everything's so easy now. Probably too easy to be taught in school. Long live the Führer? That poor guy was just a kid. You're not supposed to hang children, GEBHARDT thinks. Thinks for a moment, when the firing lets up briefly. And then he thinks, war is rough. War is not for cowards. They hang cowards. They shoot them down. Pow. He learned that in school. In the school of his youth. For the flag is more important than death. Gebhardt stands at his post and shoots down Russians. Shots in the lungs. In the head. Pow, pow! And in between he eats meat out of a tin. Two pounds of pickled tongue. From a provisions warehouse they blew up. Up 'til now the canteen workers got all the goodies. Now the guys who have to face the real filth are getting their share at last. So they can die on a full stomach. Somewhere among new apartment buildings, gardens, and a lamp post.

Private Gallery in a 4711 Cologne Box

Moritz von Schwind. You are looking at a stylized fairy tale world, with a clear spring gushing from a cliff. *I tip onto the outsides of my feet, break off my feet.* Overshadowed by dark pine trees lies a lonely clearing amidst towering cliffs. In the foreground, *I am standing, Sunday morning at ten, taking a somersault into the field of art. My mother urges me from guided tour to guided tour. Turn and turnabout: Sunday school, City Museum, Sunday school, City Museum. I do not get checked with the umbrellas at the entrance. I have to go inside.*

So this is what they mean by cultivation. One progresses silently along a corridor, inhaling deeply before every wooden frame, then exhaling. So this is art. One approaches with well-blown nose and carefully brushed teeth. Aha, a little blue triangle. I've seen this one before, but this time I smell it again through the glass. Beautiful, one is supposed to say when the painting preacher falls silent, this man who has swallowed Rousseau, Velasquez, and Kokoschka, and lives exclusively on art slides. For dessert, canvas with a little whipped pastel. Very interesting, one is supposed to murmur when the official interpreter of Caspar David Friedrich has proved that a ship is a ship.

And now we turn to Max Liebermann's Eva. Note the delicate line. An educated transistor radio stuck onto a gray Sunday suit. When I press his yellow ear I have Radio Velasquez, the Voice of Art. Behind his chin is Radio Cézanne, behind his stomach the Flemish School. Clean the glasses, lick up the saliva. Droplets of explanation-water shower the first row of blind ladies, who hear rather than see the pictures. What do we need museums for? Let's take down the pictures! A button, a microphone can replace Kokoschka's Salzburg. Who, looking at this city, would realize that the poetic and serene spirit of this landscape was recreated by the paintbrush?

One hall after another. The egg carton of cultivation. Section after section. The alarm-system police force keeps an eye on my old granddad's waddle. Don't let the child touch anything. Isn't that beautiful? *Yes it's beautiful.* Start a postcard collection. *I start a postcard collection. A private gallery in a 4711 Cologne box. This child has a future! She drags herself over the carpets. She yawns at the lectures. But soon the moment will arrive. One has only to acquire the taste. The taste comes with boredom. When I get as tall as Runge's frames, I will understand why a cloud is a cloud.*

SCENE 15. SET AS IN SCENE 13. CAMERA TRACKS IN AS AT THE END OF SCENE 13. GEBHARDT CLOSES THE WINDOW AS THE CAMERA BACK-TRACKS. One thousand marks! I'm donating one thousand marks! Behind GEBHARDT's back the auction is beginning. Who wants to buy this nice club? Going, going . . . I offer one thousand marks, BRUHNS says. And GEBHARDT closes the window firmly so the contribution will not fly away. Bruhns, the champagne king of politics. Going, going . . . ! Gone! GRÜTZMANN arrives. Arrives once more. Arrives late. He smiles at GEBHARDT. He shrugs his shoulders. Dr. Grützmann, GEBHARDT thinks. Dr. Grützmann will rake the grave. Late, yet right on time. As far as the future goes, Grützmann is there right on time. When it's all over, he will tend the graves. Talking about politics in a crummy stucco shack like this is bullshit! A junior film maker producing coop-consciousness. CLAPPER 1. TECHNICOLOR UPRISING, TAKE 111. We have a place in a cellar down by the harbor. Why don't you meet at our place? Let's get out of here! Out of the establishment! BÖHM winces. BÖHM looks anxiously at BRUHNS. But Bruhns wouldn't be Bruhns if he weren't familiar with the crooked deals that go on in this city, the crooked little money deals. Contributions from industry. Or perhaps not? Isn't your cellar a suave GET OUT, even though you could get into the establishment at any time, in fact have been in for some time already? And where do your little four- and five-digit sums leave you? BLACK-OUT. Silence. BRUHNS knows all the escape hatches. Even those used by junior film makers. And BRUHNS smiles at BÖHM. And Böhm would not be Böhm if he did not cheer up, blond and

32

cheerful and full of smiles. Question number one. What is the club supposed to be all about? Question number two. What does the club have on its agenda? Question number three. Why am I here? GEBHARDT stands up. He opens the window again. GEBHARDT sits back down. GEBHARDT does not answer. BÖHM tries his hand at ideology. GRÜTZMANN seconds him. GEBHARDT stands up. He closes the window again. GEBHARDT takes a deep breath and speaks to the card-file corpses. Now look. Now look here. A club without headquarters is no club. Nods. The former steering committee presided over a club that did not exist—for a whole year. Nods. Two nods. Without headquarters no place to meet, no base, no club. That's right! Look at Berlin! the COOP-CONSCIOUS MAN calls out, and pulls his fur hat down over his eyes. We need guerilla theater! GRÜTZMANN shouts. Guerilla theater like in Munich! GEBHARDT looks at GRÜTZMANN. Grützmann needs guerilla theater, plural Grützmann, plural WE need something. GEBHARDT flips open a newspaper. The only thing he brought with him. The only important thing for GEBHARDT. He reads out rental ads. He expands on the need for quarters. BRUHNS calls out a third time, for hard-of-hearing revolutionaries, I donate one thousand marks, and the assembled multitude yawns. Either occupy City Hall or have a stiff cocktail. GEBHARDT speeds up. To keep them from falling asleep on him before the club collapses. To keep them from walking out on him when everyone walks out. We will schedule elections for a new slate of officers, GRÜTZMANN puffs. We will recruit new members, BÖHM interrupts. We will, we will, thinks GEBHARDT, and snaps his newspaper shut. We will, we will. But WE left long ago. WE is almost home already. They are talking to a crack in the door. The YMCA director. He is leaning in the door frame. Big, stocky, massive. A bear with a viscous, pupilless gaze. With boiled milk in his eyes. A giant, swimming in white. He keeps a paternal eye on the new undertaking. He pops in again. He places his rooms at their disposal. Once again. And GEBHARDT thinks, skin has formed in his eyes from standing too long. And GEBHARDT thinks, two students plus two students makes four students. GEBHARDT shakes hands with MARQUART. In this very room the workers' and students' alliance failed, the bear says. In this room groups have formed and fallen apart in the space of two times two weeks. GEBHARDT smiles. He smiles and thinks, I am too old for this. Much too old. And the bear looks down at him like a big toy. But, GEBHARDT says, testing him, you put your building at people's disposal. MARQUART holds

33

out his hand to GEBHARDT. Yes, I put my building at their disposal. In spite of everything. Time and again.

Yvonne de Carlo Times Two

My path to school leads through the rubble. Down the path to the gate, past the Scharrer Bakery's ice blocks, past the ice at which the dogs and I lick. Past Irma Hoffmann's back yard. Past the trash cans. One-two-three, one-two-three. The Vincenti school of gymnastics dances a gavotte with the rats, and the children's stones smash against the garbage cans. One-two-three. On and on, diagonally across the ruins. The streets have lost their teeth. Over there one was left standing, hollow, missing a filling, held together by cardboard. A building. And no tree that rains golden apples. Only one survived. The tree in front of Raeder's book shop. Camomile in one's nose and weeds between the toes. My briefcase dangles almost to the ground. No more schoolbag strapped to my back; grade school is over.

Life with a briefcase is beginning, the time of swapping religious pictures from Sunday school, the time of gentle giggles. The time when heads move closer together. Grown-ups? Strange creatures. We used to admire them? Raeder is going with a woman who isn't even his wife. He gives her fur coats. And our German teacher, Frau Kruse, is supposed to have an unhappy marriage, Birgit says. Her parents know the Kruses. That explains why we always have so much homework.

Come on, let's swap movie stars! I'll give you Rock Hudson, because I have two of him, and you give me Yvonne de Carlo. Her name is Anke Gressmann. My high school girl friend. She swaps pictures with me. She has a black bun and I a blond one. She wears wooden clogs and I wear wooden clogs. She eats chocolate-covered marshmallows and I eat them, too. Hand in hand. At the Gressmanns'. Hush! Quiet! Frau Gressmann is playing chess in the living room with a man. He's going to be my new daddy. Anke whispers her mother's life into my ear. My first daddy? They're divorced. Oh, they don't see each other anymore? No. This is my new daddy. And soon we'll be moving. To Bremen!

So far away?

Yes. But I'm getting a horse. And when you come to visit, you can ride, too.

34

Hand in hand. Clogs, bun, and chocolate-covered marshmallows. But all of a sudden Anke isn't speaking to me anymore. I bribe her with four chocolate-covered marshmallows.

My mother doesn't want us to see each other anymore. People on the street turn around to look at you more than they do to look at me. What people? Anke runs away. She won't speak to me anymore. I begin to turn around and look at people on the street. And it's true, some of them do behave that way. Old men with canes.

What are they staring at?

What good-looking clogs!

My legs? Perhaps it bothers them that I don't wear any socks, that I simply go bare-legged? Yes, there are people who turn and stare. Many of them. But why can't I see Anke anymore? And I was also supposed to ride her horse some time.

It's useless. Come over here!

Irma beckons to me across the schoolyard to meet her in the whispering corner. Here we are shielded by the darkness. Here not even a breeze can reach us. Here it is still as a mouse. Here the secrets live.

Hey, that guy with the horse was a con man. The kind that answers marriage ads. Anke won't be coming to school next week. I was over at her house yesterday. Her mother's done nothing but cry for days.

Going home from school, I don't dare to ring the Gressmanns' bell. Because of the people who turn and stare, because of the con man. And there won't be any horse, either. The path to school leads through the rubble. Now Anke wears a black ponytail and I a blond bun. Our ways part. Now I have two Yvonne de Carlos. But we can't trade any more. Anke Gressmann avoids me, avoids me with Rock Hudson in her pocket.

SCENE 16. INTERIOR. EXECUTIVE OFFICE WITH THE DOOR TO THE ANTEROOM OPEN. CLOSE-UP OF KARIN ANDERS, SECRETARY. SHE IS ON THE TELEPHONE. SOUND AT FIRST OFF, LATER CAMERA BACK-TRACKS AND PANS TO DR. CONRAD NEUBÜSER, PERCHED ON THE WINDOWSILL. The Anders girl is getting married. And only twenty. The boy is twenty-two. Bright boy. Good-looking. But still. Karin Anders. Oh well, says Neubüser, Gebhardt's boss. Dr. Conrad Neubüser, sixty years gray. Sixty successful years behind him. For sixty years he has survived, surmounted, surpassed, succeeded. Sixty times yes and sixty times but. But never no. Never no, GEBHARDT thinks. Sometimes second thoughts, but never any first thoughts. He never thinks anything through. Never suspected what was going on, GEBHARDT thinks. Wrote his dissertation on Lessing. Worked for a publishing house in Berlin all through the war and never suspected. Karin, the girl, must know what she is doing, NEUBÜSER says. Says, Marriages are made in heaven. Says, One shouldn't stand in the way of true love. One shouldn't stand in the way of Conrad Neubüser, thinks GEBHARDT. Here he stands, and unlike Luther, he can do otherwise. And basically he smells of shark, GEBHARDT thinks. With gaps between his teeth. His marriage has embedded itself between those inward-pointing teeth, as well as several Karins in the past, who did not get married, but were also twenty, GEBHARDT thinks, and looks over at NEUBÜSER, who slides to the ground and rocks back and forth on his toes. Who says, 'Bye, and, I'm off to the cafeteria, and, Have Karin finish the letters and copy out the feature before she gets too involved in washing diapers. Who says, and says, and leaves the room. He still likes me, GEBHARDT thinks. Even though he knows that I don't think the way he does. The way the others do. The others. We all make our mistakes, Neubüser says. You'll see the light. But we can always use a fresh point of view. In that respect I share your thinking. And soon we'll be sitting amicably side by side, GEBHARDT thinks. He's already waiting for me in the cafeteria. My amicable senior department head with the yellowish teeth pointing inward. Dr. Conrad Neubüser, sixty and gray, at the edge of the proverbial abyss. Marry in haste, repent at leisure. Neubüser knows all about marriage. 'Bye, says GEBHARDT. The letters have to be mailed. And don't forget the feature. 'Bye, says KARIN. Yes, 'bye, GEBHARDT thinks. Marriages are made in ruins. And one shouldn't stand in the way of true ruins.

P.S. Love, Heike

Dear Heike. Back in Essen now I am thinking of you and . . . His first letter. His name is Norbert, and he screws up his eyes when he looks into the sun. Saying good-bye was not easy. He is fifteen, I am twelve. Summer vacation. July and August. Cartwheels and headstands in the sand. Here, hold my legs. Round and round. One, two, around in a circle. How weirdly he looks at my vacation girl friend. I think I'll just disappear. If the two of them want to be alone together. But he's following me. Now we're rid of her, he says. How about a walk along the beach? I nod. I call out to my friend Inge. I call to the neighboring sand fortification for help. Come with us! She doesn't want to. I divert the North Sea with my toes. He trots along beside me, with brown hair stubble, with brown eyes which I simply can't stand. Sentimental deer's eyes. I have lost my tongue. We struggle along against the wind. His back is peeling like a potato.

My name is Norbert.

Bernt would be more suitable. Bernt with the brown deer's eyes.

What's your name?

He asks like in kindergarten, as if he had swallowed a toy of mine. Does he stammer a bit? He is rather small. At any rate one can't look up to him.

Can I see you tomorrow?

Yes, I say, and decide not to show up. We'll see what he does then. He blushes. Heavens, when he shakes hands with me, he blushes. And is still red the next day. There he is, red as a brick, standing by our sand fortress. Not a word about my not coming. He is not afraid of my mother. Pretty cheeky. He simply comes up, says hello, and plops himself down beside me.

How about a walk along the beach?

I nod. I call on my mother for help—come along. She does not feel like it. She acts casual and observes Norbert from behind her glasses like an insect magnified a thousand times. She certainly already knows how big his heart is, whether he breathes properly, whether he has had contagious diseases, whether his parents are both healthy. Our junior marriage can take place. I divert the North Sea with my toes.

What was your name again?

Norbert. Aha. Still the same name. At least he doesn't fib.

This afternoon they're having a concert at the casino. Outside, on the terrace. With dancing. Do you know how to dance?

Past the garbage pails. One-two-three, one-two-three, the Vincenti school of gymnastics dances a gavotte with the rats.

I even know how to be a wave, Norbert.

He does not believe me. So I crouch in the sand and undulate my arms

37

in the air, my head bent deep down to the ground. Keep the back flexible, Heike, keep the back flexible! *Fräulein Vincenti presses my backbone into the sand, raises my chin with her fingertips. Heike the wave, my special assignment from a quarter to five to ten to five.*

Can you dance, Norbert?

He whistles a boogie through his teeth, hops from one leg to the other, takes my hands, folds me around him, then swings me away. And now turn. One-two-three o'clock, four o'clock rock. He orders a Coke for me. Vanilla ice cream. Actually his eyes are not exactly brown, more greenish. And actually the name Norbert fits him very well. With a firm N. And now turn! We provide a running commentary to our dances, count out the beat to our feet. One can look up to him. After all, he's a whole head taller than me.

Vacation. The island is so small that one is constantly bumping into parents. This is Heike. I curtsey to the white haired gentleman. My hair grazes his fat stomach. Feet like paws, a straw hat deep down over his eyes. A big man, a mountain of a man with good-natured eyes, blue water-eyes, a little too watery perhaps for a businessman with no cultural ambitions. The type who never opens a book! And your mother? Frau Möbus, reddish brown hair, Rhineland joy in her bouncy locks. The polylingual nonentity quacks a greeting at me. How sweet, how nice for Norbert. Finally we are rid of our son. And the daughter? She slinks along behind her parents, tall and angular, with saltshakers and the scent of squeezed oranges in her hair. Hilke, the model.

She is only interested in men.

Norbert, the Morse coder. Family history in dots and dashes. She digests me amiably. Run along and take a walk. Dance to your hearts' content, you two. We two. The dunes are high. Just right for cartwheels. Salto mortale in the sand. Down hill. Who can jump the highest, run the fastest? Dune grass. It slices into my calves. Deep concern over every cut. Let me fix it for you. Hand in hand. Two red faces, and we are still red the next day.

Saying good-bye is not easy for him. I buy him a Coke. Perhaps that will help him get over it. I'll write to you, he says. Your address. He writes it down. With pointy green spikes, a fence of letters. Norbert is leaving. I don't feel especially heartbroken. One less playmate. Now there's no need to comb my bangs and drink Coke all the time and eat ice cream. And no need to tramp through the dune grass, which cuts into my legs.

38

Well, see you later.

He edges closer to me. From the side. We are walking along parallel to each other. He touches my shoulder, slows down.

Is there something else?

He stares at my mouth. I bite my lower lip.

Really nothing else?

He stops. He thrusts his head close to mine. I breathe in his breath. I say no. I don't want anything else. I say that so firmly that my eyes glaze over and Norbert goes all foggy. A dissolving spot of color close to my hot face.

Well, so long. I'll write.

He turns abruptly. Norbert goes back into focus, drawing the heat from my face. He takes it with him. I have room again, all the way to the dunes, all the way to the ocean, all mine. No one stands between them and me. Norbert the dot. Gone.

Back in Essen I am thinking of you.

The second letter. What should I write back? I wish you a good math test.

I'm keeping my fingers crossed for you. All the best, Heike.

Or love, Heike? I squeeze a love in.

P.S. Love, Heike.

SCENE 17. FLASHBACK. SUBJECTIVE CAMERA THROUGHOUT THE SCENE. MODERATE SLOW MOTION, ABOUT 32 FRAMES PER SECOND. SLOW, DELIBERATE SHOTS. BERLIN, 1948. GEBHARDT gets married. Then he leaves Berlin. Moves to the country. Withdraws into the mine-strewn garden of romanticism. He can no longer bear literati and hacks. He can no longer bear himself. He wants to live. Romanticism is soon defused. He earns his living as a lumberman. Seventy Pfennig an hour. Then, for months, he travels miles to pick up his unemployment check. He begins to write once more. A novel this time. In his spare hours. And like his last play, a total flop. He tries writing cheap serials. A dead-end street. He gives up writing again. He tries a job as a salesman. A grim period. Almost a complete loss. Hunger. Often he is closer to suicide than to a week's wages. The work is humiliating. Nevertheless he keeps at it. For the first time in his life he understands what it is to worry about money. He adjusts the facts slightly, a common practice among foot-in-the-door men. Several times he avoids arrest by a hair. He lives on credit. From week to week. He switches jobs. Out of the frying pan into the fire. Another dead end. This life is degrading. Furnished rooms. Kitchen privileges. Bathroom privileges. He cannot offer the woman he loves the life she feels she deserves. He washes ashore in Hamburg. There he earns a pittance selling novelties at weekly markets. He tramps from farmhouse to farmhouse peddling shoelaces. Then he draws unemployment again. He is finished. He has failed. In a last-ditch effort he opens a theater. He has nothing more to lose. Artistic ambitions? None. It is a question of bread. A little bread daily. Bread for two. That changes with the first production. Now he has ground under his feet. Unsteady ground, but ground. Hey, you there in the factory. If tomorrow they order you to stop making pipes and pots and to make helmets and machine guns instead, there is only one thing to do: say no! Because if you don't say no, if you don't say no.

GEBHARDT wants to yell people out of their sleep, to jolt them awake. He wants to ignite a fire. His own childhood went up in flames. Now he demands the past. He wants to say no. No. No. No. No to the yes of his youth. He does not spare his audiences' feelings. He wants to perform what he pleases. He dreams up his theater. The seeds of intellectual rebirth amidst an amorphous mass—that is what he proclaims. The first year. Also the second year. A stone that is pushed must roll. The direction is not so important. He gets moving. Gebhardt gets moving. He plays out the drama of his past. He plays war on war. Three years of Borchert's whip. No echo comes. Gebhardt has dreamed out his dream of a renewal amidst the ruins. He cannot hear the no. He has not started any movement. 1956. His first marriage has burned itself out. Love and hate become equally empty. The second marriage, head over heels, brings an opportunity to turn his back on Germany and rearmament. He does not hesitate a second. The betrayed generation, the generation without farewell, lifts anchor. He is on board.

The Snowy Fourth Row

The gray dinosaur slurps me into his gaping mouth and sluices me deep into his stomach. I race across his cold marble palate, his teeth, and along his terraced stone bite. The jaw is big and cold. It is icy. Jonah in the whale. Many thousand little Jonahs a day. Step forward to the slaughter. The teachers write in red blood. Step right into the whale! Step right up! The F has bright red teeth, little red choppers. Stick out your head, dear.

In this room we have German and mathematics. You write cocoa with oh-oh on wide, sea green blackboards. Sixty-five divided by eight. That is something you have to know. There is no getting around it. It doesn't come out even. A life that never comes out even awaits you at the board. A life with John Maynard. Oh, John Maynard, he was our helmsman. A poem, a work of art. What is the poet trying to tell us? Who is Gorm Grymme?

Submit! Laughing at Goethe is not allowed. He is too great, loftier than the steeple of St. Michael's. Goethe gazes down on us from his pedestal. Open your eyes. Learn to say yes, beautiful, profound. Learn to lie about what the poet is trying to tell us, the poet who strangely resembles your German teacher. That is how a poet is supposed to look. Just like that. Probably she wrote it all herself, that stuff about John Maynard. She knows it inside out, this Frau Kruse. She eyes me. She sits in her glasses-aquarium and eyes me. With slightly murky glass eyes. She probably takes me for a goldfish because I float around so silently in front of her. Like the goldfish by Paul Klee that hangs on one wall. The one by Paulie, as Irma always says. Or does she see me as a herring? As a rollmops, an appetizer? She comes to the costume ball as a cat. With her pointed little cardboard ears she ferrets me out, crouches to spring.

How are you coming with your little poems?

She finds me amusing. The longer I remain speechless, the more she grins.

That is quite a distraction, child, a distraction from arithmetic and—well, your spelling seems to be a hopeless case. The cat crouches on the desk, legs dangling. Let me see you write xylophone. Come now, let me see it. Take another piece of chalk. Perhaps that will help. It doesn't help. No kind of chalk helps. But the dictations continue. And the little poems. My little poems. You should learn how to write properly first.

Well, well, a little Goethe in our midst!

Perhaps you should write a poem first and then do the math homework. Maybe that will help.

It does not help. Things go from bad to worse. From dictation to dictation.

Now we are going to write a composition again. That should be something for you. You can make up for your D's.

Frau Kruse. Her blond locks make me mistake her for an angel. Like the one with the blue cardboard robe on our Advent wreath. But she is no angel. She is a dissector. And I am the insect Jonah. In a glass ball. If you shake me, it snows. Then I get cold. I sit in the snowy fourth row. I eat too many chocolate-covered marshmallows and get chubby.

Bad for a poet's figure.

She laughs, laughs until the blood spurts. The red flows over commas, over periods. It dribbles into my little poems. May I return your notebook? That was very amusing, what you wrote.

In the antechamber of heaven, the waiting room of marks, she hands me my little black notebook. The collected works of a twelve-year-old. She stands there with her glass eyes and says Amusing, amusing, amusing. I ease out slowly. Dissolve slowly in the heavenly antechamber.

I wanted you to have it.

No, keep it for yourself. I have so many books already.

The Christmas angel with the blond curls and the black cardboard ears. I think I am shrinking. Now she is way up there. A blond mountain towers above me. I am only as high as her black shoes. Snapping black toes. I scurry under the arch, the heels kick out, and the tower tips. It has bright red arms full of ink. Reaching all the way up to heaven, full of ink. Jonah, the tower cries, give me your black book, I want to eat it up! Page for page. And the commas, one by one, line by line. And finally the periods. Bigroundfatblackstuffed periods. Jonah, the tower cries and reaches into my mouth with its arms. The corners of my mouth rip, the red paws are pulling on my tongue, drawing out John Maynard. Oh, John Maynard, he was our helmsman. He was our helmsman, was John Maynard. What a long tongue I have. It stretches all the way to the teachers' lounge; it stretches across the schoolyard into the classroom. And over it John Maynards are running, shouting, waving their arms. They are innumerable. They row with commas and pilot with periods. With fat round stuffed periods.

You recited that well. Poetry seems to suit you.

I may sit down now. The bell rings for recess. The cat leaves the room through the window.

SCENE 18. INTERIOR. NIGHT. LOBBY OF AN OFFICE BUILDING IN HAMBURG'S BUSINESS DISTRICT. LONG SHOT: GEBHARDT STANDING IN FRONT OF THE BUILDING DIRECTORY. BEHIND HIM, COMING FROM THE STREET, BÖHM ENTERS THE PICTURE. Hello, Gebhardt! This way. BÖHM holds the elevator door for him. BÖHM presses the button. A fantastic building, BÖHM says, staring at the flickering floor numbers. Yes, Bruhns has it good. He has it made. Sixth floor. The door is already open. Bruhns has put the office at their disposal. The main office. His main office. For Conference Number 1. For the bigwigs' conference. I invited Dr. Raake, too, BÖHM says. He invited Dr. Raake, too, GEBHARDT thinks. All the too's will come this evening. All the distinguished too's. Well, quite an office, eh? BRUHNS shakes hands with GEBHARDT. Here we're going to get what we want out of them. GEBHARDT observes BRUHNS. A dancing bear, always going around in circles. Roundabout his big main office. GEBHARDT pushes his way over to BÖHM. And BÖHM pushes toward Grützmann, who is on time today, because the meeting is at Bruhns's. At the great Bruhns's. Interesting. Interesting. Yes, a magnificent room. Grützmann has to get onto the steering committee, BÖHM whispers to GEBHARDT. Grützmann has to be included. Because Grützmann is supporting Böhm. Because Grützmann nods obligingly for Böhm. When Böhm smiles, Grützmann says yes. GEBHARDT has noticed that Grützmann always says yes for Böhm. Böhm is somewhat pallid. Böhm is vacillating and cautious. Böhm is friendly and smiley soft. But Grützmann is his intensification. He is even more Böhm. Böhm-times-two. And Böhm-times-one knows that. Böhm-times-one knows where to find Böhm-times-two. Grützmann has to be included. There's a corner left over by the desk. Here, by the window. Shove over! GEBHARDT shoves over. GEBHARDT moves over, for the card-file corpses are arriving. They come rolling into the editorial office. Carload by carload. Last stop club. All out. GEBHARDT cannot keep track. GEBHARDT does not know any of them. They are between twenty and thirty years old. Their hair allowed to grow out for the new election. Their nails polished for ousting the original officers. The forty-year-olds have stayed home. The forty-year-olds are reading yesterday's politics in today's newspapers. The forty-year-olds have broken their necks. For at thirty you've reached that point. And at forty you've had it. Oh, what a joy is life. At the office. Let me recommend the Wiener Schnitzel. And another Wiener Schnitzel for the lady. Nothing but Wiener Schnitzel for the rest of one's life. At forty one tips generously, GEBHARDT thinks. Paying off one's funeral. Work bears down on one. And another Wiener Schnitzel for the little girl. Bravo. The peaceable forty-year-olds have stayed home. Have become bosses. At the top or in the lower echelons. Have become underlings. At the top or in the lower echelons. Bent back. Bent head. Bent thoughts. GEBHARDT stands up, makes the rounds once. Nothing but young folk. GEBHARDT sits down again. GEBHARDT thinks, nothing but young folk. All Bruhns readers. All gullible young people. Orgasm and repression. Student revolt and sexual revolution. Bruhns revolution. That sells well. Revolution in bed. An overslept revolution. And Bruhns is raking in the money. Bruhns is drawing up the balance sheet. Isn't this a fine big office? Yes, it's a fine big office. We'll wait another fifteen minutes. Okay. We'll wait another half hour until everybody's here. Okay. BÖHM thinks about GRÜTZMANN. And GRÜTZMANN thinks about GEBHARDT, who always sits there so strangely and doesn't say anything friendly. Not at all like Winfried Böhm. The good man Winfried Böhm. We'll wait a bit longer. We'll wait another few minutes. We'll wait another ten years, GEBHARDT thinks. By then I will be in my fifties. And what if we wait another twenty years? GEBHARDT stands up and forces his way through to the door. CAMERA ZOOMS TO LONG SHOT. GEBHARDT DISAPPEARS INTO THE CROWD.

How Does a Kiss Like This Taste?

Departure nine-thirty A.M. I am visiting Norbert in Essen. Mother takes me to the train station. Be careful—you know what I mean. And I haven't the faintest. Met at the station by his mother. Fall vacation in the city's garden belt. Big bright white rooms in a brand new house. A balcony reaching out into the apple trees, a guest room built into the clouds. I see sky, sky, and more sky. We have a Mercedes like this, too, I say. We drive into town for a stroll. Coffee and crumb cake round off the days. Up in the attic we manufacture death masks. Norbert in plaster. That suits him. The stony face, the strange, compelling sternness, obstinacy, with a vein in his forehead that swells when I say no, when I refuse to let him press me up against a wall.

Plaster suits him better than life, I decide, and stop breathing when he thrusts his head toward me, his hands glued flat to the wall. A slow

44

pursuit begins, interrupted by shooting at sparrows and a blond hair in a colored glass bottle. He has pickled me in alcohol. For dessert. I love you, he says suddenly, drops his plaster mask to the floor, and descends on my mouth. If my mother only knew. And Frau Kruse. I open my eyes. He has little blackheads on his forehead. Very tiny. His eyes are closed. He bends so far forward that I have trouble keeping from suffocating. How does a kiss like this taste? It tastes of plaster and a bit of apple juice.

SCENE 19. SET AS IN 18. CLOSE-UP OF A POSTER WITH A PORTRAIT OF CHÉ GUEVARA, OVERLAID WITH PORTRAITS OF THOSE PRESENT. Give me one student, six feet by twenty inches. To paste on the wall, in the following colors. Red. Blue. Black. And forest green. They look like posters, GEBHARDT thinks. They imitate Ché's beard. And Fidel's cap. The more advanced ones the cigar as well. They wear Mao's jacket and the GIs' jeans. And their heads are full of the Latin reading exam, German punctuation, or English for English majors. STOP THE WAR IN VIETNAM. MAKE LOVE. Girls to the front. One student, five feet four times Penny Lane. For mounting on the wall. Net stockings up to the neck, patent leather boots up to the chin. We want a new world. We want. We want. We will. We must. Do something. But what? But when? GEBHARDT counts the trenchcoats. He also notices a few styles of the day before yesterday. There are still some who are beardless, with clipped nails and brushed hair. They are here, too. Republicans who have gone astray. First Castro Street to the right, second Youth Fashion Street to the left, and then straight ahead to Bruhns. They are here, too. They do not feel comfortable at the scrubbed, shiny tavern tables habituated by their party fathers. They've had their fill of beery singing.

BÖHM claps excitedly. A Bonnie-and-Clyde cap cuddles up to a Guevara beard. BÖHM wants to get started. A Guevara beard cuddles up to a Bonnie-and-Clyde cap. BÖHM wants to welcome the important guests. Herr Dr. Raake. The well-known editor Herr Dr. Raake. Editor-in-chief Herr Dr. Raake, who is also here. Come straight from his big publishing house. The famous Dr. Raake in a fine brown tweed suit, with brilliantly polished glasses. With chalked white leisure-teeth. With hair in the prime of life. Herr Dr. Raake, who has taken up young people. Revolutionary youth. In words and pictures. Yes, the man in back there is Dr. Raake. The one you always see on television. Whenever you switch on the TV, Dr. Raake is speaking. GRÜTZMANN's palms feel hot. What will Dr. Raake think? Will he help oust the old steering committee? And what about when the new slate is elected? And the debts? What will Dr. Raake say to the debts? The debts incurred by the old steering committee? Will Raake make a donation, too? And will he join the steering committee? Will he allow himself to be nominated? And if so, what will Dr. Raake say then? HERR DR. RAAKE says GOOD-BYE. BÖHM raises his hand. GRÜTZMANN raises his hand. GEBHARDT raises his hand. And RAAKE hurtles away. Sleek, well-lubricated, elastic. He takes his trenchcoat. He leaves the petty details behind. He has swallowed his speech, the speech he could not deliver. Not even on Channel Three. Not a single spotlight. And the office is smaller, too. Much smaller than Raake's. And he still has some business to attend to. Way off in a back street. You know what I mean. And Winfried knows. WINFRIED BÖHM knows. One less democratic luminary. GRÜTZMANN has risen to his feet. He signals to Böhm. And BÖHM signals back. He cannot understand GRÜTZMANN. And Dr. Raake, travelling salesman for extraparliamentary opposition, enters the elevator and presses the G button. G like German National Television.

Grown Tubby under the Cross

First comes a sweet crumb crust. On top of that a layer of chocolate cream, prayed smooth. Then come the candied relatives, spread over nougat chairs, slightly glazed between lemon cream and chocolate shavings. Finally a fragrant meringue roof to protect everyone from hell and the devil. And on the very top, in pastry heaven, a mouth-watering cherry, sits our minister. I am wearing my dark blue dress with a corsage of lily-of-the-valley pinned piously at my waist. They let me carve my confirmation. Bake, bake, bake a cake, the minister fluted, and one by one the family display pieces appeared. Today they are performing a baptism with coffee. Jesus issued invitations to afternoon tea, and all came.

Let us love Him, for He loved us first.

Pastor Zimmermann summons all the cookies to prayer. Amen, say the cake forks. *Bon appétit, says Pastor Zimmermann, and stuffs his large, gold-capped mouth with hazelnut cream and Black Forest cherry torte. He is sitting next to me, the dear communicant, who has learned Holy Writ by heart, catechism-hour by catechism-hour. He stuffs his big black robed stomach with a generous last supper. Yes, thank you. Another piece of cream-and-honey cake. Ah, but these lemon cookies are good. He is pouring in the food. His consecrated belly, a vast black inkwell, overflows our table. Do not covet thy neighbor's cake or anything that thy neighbor has, I think. I, a freshly confirmed Christian whose newly minted genuflection collapses amidst the whipped cream mountains of a family coffee klatsch.*

It was a nice ceremony, Zimmermann says, A good ceremony, if I do say so myself, and he brushes his slightly flushed forehead contentedly with his nougat-fed hands. He is close to retirement. He has grown gray in the service of Christ. He has grown tubby under the Cross. His temples have grayed over the Word of God. Now it is time, it is time, he sighs, For a younger man to take over.

You are the last one to be confirmed by me, my child.

Yes, you are the last one he wanted to confirm, Aunt Meta echoes and looks at me with big Dodo Knows Her Own Will *eyes. A book for girls twelve years and up. On my gift table. A book from Aunt Meta about pretty, spirited Dodo, whose pluck and good humor stand her in good stead and who in the end becomes a fine wife and mother. May Jesus attend you in fulfillment of your duty, Aunt Meta has written in under the title. In purple ink with festive confirmation curlicues. Your loving. Aunt Meta has laid her book beside the* Big Book for Girls *by Rosmarie Schnittenhelm. With 442 illustrations and 16 tables. For from today on, everything is supposed to be different. If one wants to blow one's nose or sneeze, one uses a satin handkerchief with a blue crocheted border. One eats with a golden cake fork, from Aunt Waltraud. One wears three amulets around one's neck. One from Aunt Berta, one from Uncle Ernst, one from Uncle Gustav. And one reads books with titles like* The Poet Hears the World's Heart Beat, Life Grows More Beautiful, Anne, *or* My Daughter Lisbeth.

A rich assortment of gifts, Pastor Zimmermann comments, and looks over at the carnation-decked confirmation cart. I have a little something for you, too. A little poem. He drawls the words out comfortably, in a singsong, as if he were reading the Christmas service.

A poem, Reverend Zimmermann?

Aunt Meta, who garnishes the minister's right hip like a well-groomed, well-draped lump of yeast, Aunt Meta claps her hands. Hush! she cries. Hush! Reverend Zimmermann wants to recite something! A poem! And Zimmermann smiles. God-the-Father Zimmermann heaves his belly away from the table. Pulls out a slip of paper and carefully unfolds it. Reads it over once more, silent and solemn, with slightly reddened watering eyes. Then he stands up, massive as a sacred mountain, and gazes gravely around the table until everyone has choked down his mouthful of cake, until everyone has stopped breathing. Now Zimmermann takes a deep breath. Pumps the whole room into his stomach, and with a freshly waxed and polished voice, his eyes fixed on the ten commandments of his sheet of paper, begins to proclaim the eleventh.

Title Solemn Moment.

This young child of man . . .

Zimmermann clears his throat. Bends his reddened coffee eyes closer to the verses. This young child of man . . . *he repeats and looks around the table furtively to make sure that no one is secretly chewing Black Forest cherry torte.* This young child of man, *he repeats once more myopically, and almost swallows his slip of paper, to which he clings like a drowning man.*

This young child of man/raised up by God's own hand/gentle as a summer wind/now enters into Life's great land. *Pause. Lovely. That's the first verse. Aunt Meta begins to rummage in her pocketbook. A pencil. A pencil, she murmurs, I must take this down, it's so lovely. But Zimmermann continues. Pays no heed to Auntie's pencil excavations. Propels himself briskly into the second lyrical verse.*

God's love on high/gives strength and delight./T'will show her right paths./Parents praise His might.

I glance over at my mother. She is sitting there at the far end of the table, her face turned toward her knees, quivering slightly, with laughing shoulders.

Dear girl. *Zimmermann looks up, turns toward me with thumping poet's heart. Looks deep into my Christian eyes before he continues, heavy lipped, and repeats,* Dear girl. Blessings to you on your confirmation./May your parents' hearts and the love of the Lord/be with you all the days of your life./On few—*Zimmermann raises his right hand. Raises his hand to show God the Father he knows the answer . . .*

48

On few, he repeats sententiously, such gracious blessings are poured. Bravo! Aunt Meta exclaims. Bravo! And I, knowing my own will since Dodo, stand up. Offer Zimmermann my hand. Curtsey. Say thank you. Thank you very much, Reverend Zimmermann. And sit down, to become a fine wife and mother. Perhaps for Frank, who was rubbing my leg with his toe under the table while I recited the seventh commandment.

SCENE 20. SET AS IN 18. ON THE EMPTY SCREEN A CLOSE-UP OF A HAND APPEARS FROM BELOW. THEN A FIST. CAMERA WIDENS OUT SLOWLY. MORE AND MORE HANDS AND FISTS APPEAR. TONE REMAINS OFF UNTIL THE CAMERA REACHES LONG SHOT. My name is Lammers. Twenty-two years old. Member of the League of Socialist Students. I nominate myself. My name is Langhoff. Nineteen years old. Bookstore apprentice. I nominate myself. My name is Dr. Frenzel. Thirty-one years old. Doctor and psychologist. I nominate myself. The antiauthoritarians are electing their authorities. GEBHARDT likewise nominates himself. Although he is no longer thirty. Although he is not a cofounder of the Berlin Republican Club. Although he does not belong to the Berlin SDS and did not even write his dissertation under Abendroth. The way Frenzel did. Little scrawny flesh-carved Dr. Frenzel of the antiestablishment who studied under Abendroth. Under the magic formula with the big A. In Frankfurt, in Bochum—Abendroth. Even in Kiel, dissertations under Abendroth. What is a bookstore apprentice, a business school graduate, in comparison with one of Prof. A's professional Ph.D.'s? The card-file corpses will select their favorite brand. The top ten in the juke box. Hands up for the political hit parade. Votes for Dr. Frenzel. One, two, three, four, forty-one, fifty-two. Votes for Helmut Fromm. SDS. Dissertation under Prof. A. Votes for Frau Frenzel. Berlin RC. Dissertation under Prof. A. Votes for Winfried Böhm. Newsmagazine. Direct line to the press. Forty-four, forty-five, forty-six. Dream of all German literature students. My vote for the press. My vote for Winfried Böhm. From Berlin. From the Berlin RC. He knows them all personally. Dr. Meschkat. And Dr. Krippendorf. Hands up. You can vote for this Gebhardt, too, for all I care. He's in radio, after all. After all. The semester babies raise their hands. Raise their fists. GEBHARDT counts forty fists for himself. But GRÜTZMANN doesn't make it. Böhm-times-two, minus Berlin, minus Abendroth, minus SDS, minus the press—that doesn't draw. Average guys don't get elected, GEBHARDT thinks. And the business school graduates should be dumped. For here only the elite are nominated. The dream of a successful career. None of these young people will take up an ordinary profession. Here everyone plans to become at least a film director or an editor-in-chief or a professor. Here no one plans to become what he will become: an average salaried citizen, like Böhm, like Raake. Like me, GEBHARDT thinks. Like me.

Floor Wax and Lentil Soup

Norbert is visiting me. Actually he would just as soon settle in. In six months we'll be able to see each other every day, anyway. In six months I'll be around all the time. In six months we're moving to Hamburg. Norbert smiles triumphantly. In six months when we move here on business. In six months, hotel guest Norbert, with his mother and father piggyback. Norbert from the Imperial, where they are staying, where they are planning their move, the Möbus family, this business-busy family. So Norbert from Essen is moving. With the villa and the Mercedes, with the fashion model and a view of the Alster. They'll be living by the fairy pond, with willows on the shore and a new villa.

We are walking through the streets of Altona now, going to my place. This is the moment I have been dreading. I feel embarrassed for all the rats and garbage cans and rubble of Altona. We have a bar downstairs in our building. How am I supposed to explain that to him?

You know, Norbert, our Mercedes is at the garage. That's why we have to walk.

I say it very slowly. Even more slowly than I am walking. I wish I could stop dead, not budge from the spot. But perhaps my father is home.

Why are you stopping?

He's in a great hurry. He's dying of curiosity to see where I live.

Do you sometimes help your father in the pharmacy?

In the pharmacy? But my father's a lawyer.

That's impossible! The little vein swells in his forehead. That's impossible! You said he was a pharmacist.

50

I never said anything of the sort!

He can tell I'm lying. And blushing. Norbert doesn't look at me. Norbert asks no more questions. And I go all hot and a little faint. Like on my old scooter, I can't seem to steer clear of the lamp posts. I bang my shoulder hard against the iron.

You're crying?

Where am I supposed to get a father from?

Is your father dead? he asks. My head droops to his shoulder. No, not dead. Missing. But my uncle is back. And soon my father will be coming back from Russia, too, I'm sure of it. I'm positive. I'm not crying. See, I'm not crying. Everybody has a father. I want to have one, too.

Then take mine. I'll give him to you.

Father for sale. Used father, in excellent condition. Sliced or in a chunk. Norbert has two hundred pounds of father at home. A big 220 SE father who never opens a book. A heavy bundle of father, good-natured, with boorish rages. The girl friend gets a box on the ear, too, when the son gets home late. Norbert has too much father. And I? I don't have so much as a spoonful.

This is where I live.

We are standing in front of the building. Our building. It reeks of beer. The day before yesterday someone stole the door handle and smashed in the windows. Covered with cardboard. The stairwell a dark hole. Gloomy. Worn. Floor wax and lentil soup. I bring Norbert to a home without a Mercedes and without a father. No camel's hair coat, just a paralyzed old grandmother who smiles all the time, heavenly blue. My mother works all day. But she will be back at four if too many patients don't come. I put on the whistling kettle. The tiled kitchen breathes icily. Come in here, I say, and lead him into the little room where Granny is not sitting. With the stone balcony. We are very quiet. We don't know what to say to each other. Here to the north the sun is not shining, but Norbert screws up his eyes.

Look, another D!

I fetch out my old composition book from the briefcase and display my collection of failures. Poor choice of topic. Read through Irma Hoffmann's composition and correct the awkward expressions in your own. Your corrections for the last composition still contain some errors. Kruse.

Norbert remains silent. Ma-me-mi-mo-mu echoes across the hall.

51

Uncle Ernst is giving a lesson. In the room with the paralyzed old grandmother he is giving a speech lesson.

He's an actor, Norbert. He's doing his voice exercises.

What theater is he with?

None, at the moment. He always sleeps late, doesn't get up until around three. A real laze-a-bed.

Norbert laughs.

A few days ago Mother dragged him out of bed. She yelled, Here I am sweeping up the dust under the sofa and you just lie about. Enough is enough! Since then he's been practicing.

Ma-me-mi-mo-mu. Concert in the hall. As one young actor leaves, the next is already on the threshold. Norbert's path crosses Herr Carstens's. Norbert does not want to be an actor. Norbert does not even want to stay for a cup of tea with me. Norbert has to be somewhere in a few minutes. He leaves our house. He clatters down the worn steps like a garbage can.

SCENE 21. NIGHT. FOUR-ROOM APARTMENT ON THE TWELFTH FLOOR OF A MODERN STUDENT DORMITORY. POSTDOCTORAL TEAK DECOR. CLOSE-UP OF A BATTERY OF BEER BOTTLES AND A SAUCER FULL OF CHANGE. Let's have another beer at Dr. Frenzel's. Another beer for the steering committee. When the steering committee meets, Irene Frenzel collects small change. Ten Pfennig C.O.D. for every cookie. Ten Pfennig due for every sip from the bottle. The Frenzels play host to the group. The Frenzels, calculating hosts, cash in on their guests. GEBHARDT looks at BÖHM, and BÖHM looks at IRENE FRENZEL, and IRENE adds up the assets and the debits. For when four come together, we serve cold beer. And Helmut Fromm is still not here. Not a very good rhyme, GEBHARDT thinks, but better than nothing. He begins cleaning his nails. Running the nail of his middle finger under the edge of the others. No one will notice, and it helps kill time. One can do all ten fingers and still find that Helmut Fromm has not arrived yet. The handsome Ph.D. candidate Helmut Fromm, who speaks of the mind of the masses and how it must be reached through a learning process. GEBHARDT decides that Helmut Fromm is not coming. Valentino Fromm, with his black belladonna eyes and the white silk scarf knotted around his Adam's apple. I have a house that would do, BÖHM says, and

52

opens the official meeting. It is located. BÖHM sketches out the future of the club with delicate little pencil strokes. And then here at the corner. DR. FRENZEL bends forward and watches BÖHM drawing. He looks like a whitewashed Rumpelstiltskin, little and withered like a prune, GEBHARDT thinks, and notes down addresses. Body-building studio at the Holsten train station. One could remodel it. Four-room apartment on Tesdorp-strasse. Small and expensive. A villa on Rothenbaumchaussee. That would be the best, of course. IRENE FRENZEL leans against the teak desk, bottle opener at the ready. IRENE FRENZEL likes that idea best, of course. This magnificent piece of architecture that Gebhardt has come up with and already visited and viewed. A late nineteenth-century villa. Near the university. Parquet floor in the ballroom, with a view of front and back gardens. Rothenbaumchaussee. Excellent part of town. First and second floors, with balcony, for a gentle little political reception—that would be pretty grand. Rent one thousand six hundred. Silence. Rent one thousand six hundred, everything included. Silence. Rent one thousand six hundred per month. Hm. Rent one thousand six hundred without any transfer-of-lease payment. We could swing that. Rent one thousand six hundred with use of cellar storage space. That would be handy. The only other tenant a tax consultant on the third floor. And he is not there in the evening. IRENE FRENZEL pokes her glasses up her nose. Focuses her cashier's eyes straight ahead. That would be an ideal tenant. A tax consultant who would not disturb anyone because we would not be around during the day. A tax consultant whom we would not disturb because he would not be there in the evening. DR. FRENZEL says nothing. BÖHM puts down his pencil. GEBHARDT ponders a feudal villa future. Like in Berlin, he thinks. Fancy, but purely for strategic reasons. Perhaps that would appeal to the workingmen, too, IRENE FRENZEL says. I mean, better than something in a working-class district. Frau Frenzel marches off to war. Frau Frenzel marches off to the dustcloth war. GEBHARDT has a vision of her riding off on a wad of steel wool. It will be her villa. Tomorrow she will buy the chandelier. Tomorrow she will lay out the Oriental runners. Tomorrow she will issue invitations to a formal dinner. Workingmen like to get out of their dreary surroundings now and then. It's a central location, after all. And then close to the university. GEBHARDT adds up points. Highly polished plus points. Just wait until the Frenzels move out of their four-room apartment into the nine-room villa. Out of their rent-free faculty resident's apartment with the paid-off bookcases and the mail-order decor. Into the parquet castle of a political career, so they can get used to living in a villa early. Rent one thousand six hundred. BÖHM calculates membership dues. With one hundred republicans. With two hundred republicans. Not to forget the donations. Rent 1600. Silence. 1600. Silence. Rent 1600. Hmm. Rent 1600. We could swing that. GEBHARDT has visions of smoked salmon and Guevara. One thousand six hundred. That just might be what we are looking for.

Dew-Drenched Steps of the Privileged

For rent. For rent. We're moving. We're renting. My mother says, I've made up my mind. My mother says, I have an apartment lined up. My mother says, It's in a green belt. I know the green belt she means, the green belt where we'll be renting. Finally. A parklike area where everything is high-class and expensive. An area that will make Irma Hoffmann jealous. An area as if made for long Sunday walks, with lovely houses. Yes, that's the area. I skip my flute lesson, take the train to Klein Flottbek, clutching my ticket in my hot little hand.

I take the train to the green belt. Home. I'm moving. We're moving. No more bar, no more cat. The apartment has a broad balcony that looks straight into the sun. No more tubelike corridors, only bright, light, new rooms. And one for each. For each of us a door that can be locked. For each. Something of my own. No one will come pounding on the door, startling us, murdering us. Moving. Moving away. Away from Irma Hoffmann. Everything new. Different, the very best, in Flottbek. Here the children ride bicycles. I will have a bicycle, too. Here the children carry tennis rackets. I will have a tennis racket, too. Here the children wear jodhpurs and riding boots, the mothers wear jockey caps and fresh furs, and there are no rats and no ruins. There are only gardens and houses and much visiting back and forth. Here Norbert will visit me, and even Frau Lobo's Kaiser. Here one need not be embarrassed. Here one can live, may live, must live.

Flottbek. The path past the old farmhouse with its thatched roof. Then left along the Jenisch Park. This will be my new route to school. At ten to eight, five to eight. Soon I will be able to look out over the golf course. During recess I will watch real golfers. This is my new school. Long and low like the ice blocks at the Scharrer Bakery which the dogs and I used to lick. *This will be my school. Slabs of glass amidst the evergreen, with an inner courtyard and plantings. Just follow the wall, past the farmhouses. This is where I am going to live, among the beige-lined turtleneck fathers, the forest-green mothers, the portly gentlemen.*

Flottbek, dew-drenched steps of the privileged. A golf club slung over my shoulder. A slow, easy gait; a light, well-shod gait. For rent. For rent. Soon the moving vans will roll. Perhaps in as little as two weeks, perhaps even in ten days. Silvery gray hair with a dash of violet speeds over the tennis court. Distinguished graying temples ride past my window over the polo field. We. I. Tomorrow. A few stations farther on the same line that goes through Altona. Many ruins away. Central heating.

Bring me the milk!

My mother calls from the balcony that faces north.

How did you like it out in Flottbek?

My mother lures me across the corridor, the dark, black-stuffed corridor. The wardrobes' hunchbacks loom out of great mountains of shadow. The cats threaten. They don't want me to run away, with the hot pitcher of milk, my handwarmer, held tightly. Light switch. Light switch. High on tiptoes. It must be here somewhere, very near. Actually I should put down the milk, but something is standing behind me, silent, breathing. Flottbek, I think, Flottbek. Out there the light switches glow in the dark, illuminate the hallway.

Good evening, a voice says. Good evening, Frau Bläske says, and my heart stands still, then races away, throttling me with its thumping fist. I shiver with fear when Frau Bläske begins her slippered dance across the hall, when she comes flying toward me, without light, breathlessly moving in. For rent. For rent. No, Flottbek does not exist. For rent. For rent. The only thing that exists is this corridor, and it is endless.

SCENE 22. FLASHBACK. THROUGH A CLOSE-UP OF GEBHARDT'S FACE, FADE IN A WHITE DREAM HOUSE BY THE SEA, SURROUNDED BY PALMS. DOCUMENTARY CLIPS: LIMA, PERU, IN ANTISEPTIC HOLLYWOOD STYLE. IF POVERTY IS UNAVOIDABLE, IT SHOULD BE PORTRAYED AS PICTURESQUE. Peru is a great experience for Gebhardt. For the first time since the war he has something like a sense of home. This country does not have his youth on its conscience. This country is made for living in. Peru means

55

an escape from his cellar-theater life, in which he went without warm meals for three years, washed at a sink, worked, worked, worked, smoked the audience's butts, always surrounded by creditors, never with a penny for himself. There are directors who claim they cannot live without the theater. Rainer Gebhardt can. Basically he soon got sick of performing other people's plays in order to interpret into them what he wanted to say. And the interpretation was all that mattered to him. Not art. Not theater. The theater to him was never more than a potential weapon. It proved itself inadequate, and he dropped it. Without regrets. He left Germany without saying good-bye. He does not want to return. He sees the reemergence of fascism in rearming Germany as a real threat. The crucial date will be 1956, he thinks. Because there was a rat gnawing at everything they called democracy. He remembered the rat from the ruins. There it had grown thin. Thinner from famine month to famine month. But now it was recovering and fast becoming roly-poly. And it had given birth. To baby rats with a lot of catching up to do. Gebhardt had never paid much attention to politics. He did not have any arguments to offer. But he had a horror of rats. And so he left this country, without ties, without a home, without farewells. Peru means a plush apartment house, an exotic life of blue sea, palms, gleaming new car, and all almost without transition. Gebhardt moves in a dream. He begins making movies. He wants to do something. Anything, because the sea is getting too blue. He begins with a small American company that makes documentaries and shorts. He learns the art of cutting. He learns about editing. He learns about film. In half a year he is out again. Against his will. They tell him, You don't believe in the company. They say that to him, who once believed in a regime! Gebhardt cannot believe in companies anymore. And now he is out in the cold. That doesn't matter. It can't hurt him financially. Gebhardt takes up photography again. Reluctantly. The profession irritates him. But to maintain his standard of living all he has to do is work for two weeks now and then. Neither he nor Julia, his second wife, aspires to anything more in this climate. The only question is, for how long. If he had wanted to, he could have been in Lima to this day. As a photographer or god knows what. Gebhardt begins to write again. He begins to read. He is growing impatient. Not much comes of either activity. There are parties. Bullfights. Trips. Lazy baking on one of the west coast's most beautiful beaches. Gebhardt tries acting again. A German-American amateur group. The days get bluer and bluer. Pass in dalliances, drinking, playing
56

poker. The days bog down in social life. Gebhardt sees no end in sight. Then a letter arrives from American friends. It calls the idyllic life into question. Suddenly. At last. The friends are in Ibiza. They suggest he follow them there. And Gebhardt, restless like Julia, agrees. Back to Europe. To this day it is unclear to him why he actually left Peru. He can find scraps of motives. He wants to catch onto them. But not now. Not today. For he has a thread to take hold of. An external thread which is unravelling his life's pattern. The wrecked areas of his life. He goes to Ibiza alone. Along with Peru he renounces his second wife. If there is such a thing as malicious abandonment, this is it. He is simply cowardly. He explains his behavior when he reaches New York. By letter and by telephone. Months later he meets Julia in Paris. They go to Ibiza together. In the course of the year they get used to living apart. Ibiza. Months of intense studies. A slice into vacation flesh under a blue sun; it has cut its way into Rainer Gebhardt's mind. He wants to know whether or not. To write or not to write. He tells himself, you will make a decision a year from now. He works with self-discipline, following a plan. He buys books. Sets up a schedule. English. French. Spanish. History. Philosophy. Excerpts. Notes. He goes back to school, his own school. Then his money runs out. He is still living out of Julia's bank account. It's up to him to take care of himself now. Earn a living. Faced with the alternative of going to Los Angeles or back to Germany, he chooses what seems more logical. Chooses financial independence from Julia. In the fall of 1960 he arrives in West Berlin with ten marks in his pocket.

I Cry over Alaska

I have stopped writing. My narrow black notebook is in the bookcase. Behind the volumes of Kleist. Now at least it can't be seen. Kleist curlicues goldenly away, bound in leather, and I no longer have any inspiration. I am no golfish anymore. My color has faded. The cat has bitten the fish in the neck. Now it lies on the sand, stinking slightly. The aquarium has been pushed over, and blood is dribbling into the water. What a lovely broken neck!

The pronoun with self. I defend myself. In German a comma precedes because. With transitive verbs, the object is in the accusative. I study grimly. No, I don't want to recite poems anymore. I can't get past John Maynard. Get stuck right in the first line. John Maynard, he was, was

*. . . The record has a crack in it. It sticks. I repeat and repeat. I can't
absorb anything anymore. The cat slinks around me, spits red blood into
my notebooks and growls.*

*Your oral performance used to be better. Now you barely open your
mouth. What should I give you?*

*What should they give me? A D? An F? Well, in that case I won't pass.
What difference does it make. What difference does anything make. It
does make a difference. I fetch out my notebook from behind Kleist. My
narrow black notebook. I had wanted to give it to her. And now? All I
can do is cry. Loudly. Great big tears. For hours on end. At the drop of a
hat. On command. Over every comma. Over every awk. for awkward.
Crying is one thing I can do. Good and loud. Right into math class and
geography class. I cry over Alaska and over the square root of two.*

*His arms are yellow up to his neck. His head is white, burned-out
ashes. An ashtray. And in the intervals between classes he inhales the
Reemtsma Tobacco Company. He coughs. He chokes at the blackboard.
He smokes the package as well, and is done in by the cellophane.
Smoking mathematics. Our smoked homeroom teacher. Weak, addicted,
affectionate. He showers me with butts of pity.*

Your witty poems. Let me take a look at them.

*He wants to help me and has already adopted the language of the cat.
He succumbed soon enough to the uniform language of the antechamber
to heaven. For a cigarette bummed from Frau Kruse he is ready to find
my poems witty and amusing.*

*I have stopped writing. I no longer have any ideas. I am collecting
movie stars again. I believe in Rock Hudson and Yvonne de Carlo again.
And in between I pick up my D's, round-bellied and chock full of
misunderstandings. I stuff them all into one-two-three o'clock, four
o'clock rock. Stuff my rage into my feet and into movie schedules. I do
badly in geography, in biology, in art. I fail in the subjects of silence.
Unsatisfactory in religion to finish me off.*

SCENE 23. MONTAGE OF FILM CLIPS FROM THE HEYDAY OF THE
EXTRAPARLIAMENTARY OPPOSITION. COMMENTARY ADDED IN THE FORM OF
CAPTIONS. Recruit. Recruit. Recruit. Recruit. Gebhardt is collecting
signatures. Signatures that will draw members. Printable signatures.

Prominent signatures. Dr. Frenzel sets out in one direction, Dr. Grützmann in another. Call ahead. Ring the bell. Wipe your feet. Hello. You're a republican, too, I believe. Hello. You are committed to making democracy work, too, I understand. Good morning. You are dissatisfied that everything, that things are, that the total picture.

FOR WHERE DOES ONE GO IN THIS CITY, OF AN AFTERNOON, OR AN EVENING, WHEN THINGS HAVE GOTTEN OUT OF HAND? WHERE DOES ONE FIND OUT WHAT THE NEWSPAPERS DON'T REPORT? WHERE CAN ONE OBTAIN LEGAL RECOURSE AGAINST THE RULING COALITION'S ABUSE OF ITS POWER? WHERE CAN ONE EXCHANGE POLITICAL EXPERIENCES AND INFORMATION? WHERE CAN ONE RECOVER FROM THE LETHARGY WHICH HAS BEEN SPREADING EVER SINCE PASSAGE OF THE SPECIAL EMERGENCY POWERS BILL? WHERE DOES ONE GO WHEN THE POLICE INTERVENE AGAIN, WHEN THE NEO-NAZI GERMAN NATIONAL PARTY'S ELECTION RESULTS CAUSE HEADLINES AGAIN, WHEN ANOTHER DEMONSTRATOR IS SHOT, WHEN FASCISM TAKES HOLD IN YET ANOTHER NEIGHBORING COUNTRY, WHEN POLITICIANS BEGIN ALLUDING TO THE VOLK AGAIN? WHERE DOES ONE MEET WHEN A DEMONSTRATION IS IN THE OFFING AND IT BECOMES ESSENTIAL TO ACT QUICKLY AND WITH COMMON PURPOSE? AND WHERE DOES ONE MEET ON THOSE SEEMINGLY CALM, QUIET DAYS WHEN ONE HAS NO SPECIAL PRETEXT? AT SOMEONE'S APARTMENT? IN THE MAIN AUDITORIUM AT THE UNIVERSITY? IN A BEER PARLOR IN PÖSELDORF? THAT DOES NOT QUITE FIT THE BILL. WE NEED A PLACE FREE OF CLUBBISHNESS AND PROGRAMMED ACTIVITY WHERE THOSE OF US WHO ARE NOT REPRESENTED IN PARLIAMENT CAN MEET. PEOPLE WHO HAVE A POLITICAL ROLE TO PLAY AND WHOSE INFLUENCE COULD INCREASE CONSIDERABLY IF THERE WERE A PLACE WHERE THEY COULD MEET INFORMALLY AND CONFER, A CUP OF COFFEE TO THEIR RIGHT, A BOTTLE OF BEER TO THEIR LEFT, A STEAMING POT OF ONION SOUP IN THE KITCHEN IN CASE IT GETS LATER OR EARLIER THAN ONE HAD PLANNED. ALL THE IMPORTANT POLITICAL PUBLICATIONS SHOULD BE AVAILABLE. THERE WOULD HAVE TO BE ROOMS FOR DISCUSSIONS ON POLITICAL ISSUES AND FOR PREPARING CAMPAIGNS AND ACTIONS. ONE SHOULD BE ABLE TO DUPLICATE INFORMATIVE MATERIAL THERE AND BE REACHED BY TELEPHONE. AND THERE SHOULD ALSO BE A BOOKSTORE. THE KIND IN WHICH ONE FINDS WHAT ONE IS LOOKING FOR. ONE COULD INVITE GUESTS THERE. GUESTS FROM ALL OVER THE WORLD WHO ARE COMMITTED TO THE SAME DEMOCRATIC VALUES AS WE ARE. IN SUCH A PLACE REPORTS COULD BE PRESENTED, READINGS AND DISCUSSIONS COULD TAKE PLACE WITHOUT THE USUAL RITUALS, WITHOUT RENT FOR THE HALL AND OFFICIAL PERMITS. PERHAPS NOT ONLY WRITERS, JOURNALISTS, STUDENTS, MINISTERS, TEACHERS, SCIENTISTS, TEACHING ASSISTANTS WOULD COME, BUT MORE AND MORE SHOP FOREMEN, PROFESSORS, WORKINGMEN, HIGH SCHOOL STUDENTS, UNION MEMBERS, WHITE COLLAR WORKERS? PERHAPS SOME DAY EVEN DISSATISFIED SOCIAL DEMOCRATS, POLICEMEN, AND MEMBERS OF THE ARMED FORCES.

PERHAPS ALL TOGETHER WE COULD FIND A WAY TO RESCUE OUR DEMOCRACY,
DESPITE THE EMERGENCY POWERS LEGISLATION AND THREATENING
ELECTORAL REFORM. IN MANY CITIES SUCH A PLACE ALREADY EXISTS. NOT IN
HAMBURG. THAT HAS TO CHANGE. FOR THE PAST THREE WEEKS WE HAVE BEEN
WORKING TO CREATE SUCH A CLUB. A HOUSE HAS BEEN RENTED. IF YOU DROP
BY 95 ROTHENBAUMCHAUSSEE SOME EVENING IN THE NEXT FEW DAYS YOU CAN
TAKE A LOOK AT THIS CLUB. OF COURSE RENT AND REDECORATING COST
MONEY. AND SINCE WE WANT TO REMAIN INDEPENDENT, WE ASK EVERYONE
WHO, LIKE US, EXPECTS THE CLUB TO PROVIDE A VALUABLE INITIATIVE
TOWARD PRESERVING OUR DEMOCRACY TO CONTRIBUTE ACCORDING TO HIS
ABILITY, WHETHER IT BE A FOUNDER'S DONATION OR MONTHLY DUES OF AT
LEAST TEN MARKS, PREFERABLY BOTH. IF WE ARE ON THE RIGHT TRACK, OUR
CITY WILL BE POLITICALLY MORE ACTIVE BY 250 SQUARE YARDS AND IN A FAR
MORE HOPEFUL STATE.

Christopher

I have met Christopher. The commuter Norbert, Essen-Hamburg-Essen,
is forgotten. Christopher. Our friendship is as old as my new skates.
Children's exchange in the Planten un Blomen Park. Thirteen- and
sixteen-year-olds conclude marriage contracts. Skate a few rounds, Tölz
Athletics Club against the Füssen Athletics Club, brake sharply, yell
Hello, kiddo, and yank the ponytail until the kiddo yells. These are the
cavaliers of the rink, waiting for their victims at the Coke stand. I have
just come out on the ice, ankles wobbling wildly; the skates looked much
more reliable under the Christmas tree. And already someone has me by
the hair. A little striped woolen cap with a hockey stick trips me up.
Behind him his gang is yodelling. The loudspeaker bawls out one-two-
three o'clock, but I don't manage to get back on my feet until the skating
waltz is spraying from the speakers. How can one possibly go skating
with a ponytail? No sooner am I standing than the striped cap is there
again. Bump, I land hard on the ice. Boiling. With tears in my eyes. I
could bite the snow. You idiots! I yell at the top of my voice, and stay
sitting, while the gang of wool caps circles around me, skate blades
flashing. A paleface up against the totem pole. My tears are carefully
observed. The blades scratch past my legs, making the ice fly. But there is
also a chieftain. He was standing off to the side and had his eye on his
victim even before the attack. He is very tall and slim. He looks like a
whippet we studied in biology. His head pushes its way to the front. He
halts the Hottentot dance. He comes up close to the little wool cap and

60

says, Out of the way. *I don't know what gang this chief belongs to, but at any rate he is much respected. He extends an arm to me. Feeble and frozen, I prop myself up on my skates. He says, See you tomorrow at three. That's all he says, but he smiles like Tony Perkins, smiles like my bubble gum cards. He is simply heavenly. Compared to Norbert, that little block, that little blackmailer, insistent, with daily letters but still not even a head taller than me. Compared to Norbert, this new boy is really terrific. Big, slim, casual, with the charm of an easygoing sophomore.*

Tomorrow at three. My legs are as soft as the jellybeans that are sticking to my pocket lining. Tomorrow at three. Christel Ostermann, the classmate whom the cat favors because her sister three grades above us always gets A's, Christel Ostermann offers me aid and comfort. She is a Cover Girl makeup expert. Good in school, her face scrubbed white and childish, she slinks silently from class to class. But after two in the afternoon, while the teachers are bent over our notebooks, dreaming of happy children who play catch and help mother dry the dishes, Christel's life begins. High life she calls it. She lives not far from me. In a towering apartment building Christel makes herself up for the boys on the block who haunt the entrances from five o'clock on. With jangling bicycle bells and raucous horns. Christel knows what has to be done. And our shared afternoon goes on and on. A black mascara applicator circles before my eyes. Yes, that's how you do it. Shut that eye now. See, I'm putting on blue shadow. Men go for that. We'll leave your mouth pale. Give him a chance to look for it. Christel is in the know, so much so that it is three-thirty before I reach the rink, as a redskin.

The wool cap from yesterday greets me respectfully with raised hockey stick. It sees, as I do, the chieftain circling toward me.

Hello, my name's Christopher!

He takes my hand and holds onto it. I learn to skate hand in hand, always in a circle. Day after day.

What's my name?

How old am I?

Just turned thirteen, but going on fourteen.

Snowball fights with Christopher, tests of strength. Let's see who gets knocked down first. Gets his head held down and snow slapped in his face.

Stop it! Let me go!

That's just what he had in mind. He grabs every chance to put me out of breath. Then he forces quick kisses on me. On my nose, my ear, my red ruffled fists. His mouth does not miss a thing.

He is sixteen, has two brothers and a sister, all about ten years older. That's what causes his stutter. Them, the Cabrios of the family.

When people ask my father why he always goes places on foot, he always says, I have three children who've had an education, and one still in high school. They're my cars, television sets, and washing machine.

Christopher's father, a professor of zoology. He lived in the back room in a big old apartment. I never heard him say anything or come in—just go out. Father lived for himself, separated from the corridor and from his family by a curtain. But that did not seem to bother anybody. The rest of the family had enough problems with themselves. Then there was the sister. She was an interpreter in Erlangen and translated all men into a pronoun that expressed possession. She was plump and loud, with a vulgar laugh and plenty of champagne in her hips. She began every party tipsy with an I-don't-know-what-I'm-doing air and got what she was after. The two brothers, partly black haired, partly bald, smaller and more wiry than the latecomer, were full grown Ph.D.'s. They had good man-to-man discussions, and Christopher learned to say r three times and s four times before he got a word in edgewise.

From the time we first met, we stuttered in unison. He infected me with it. We forgot about the brothers and the sister, and about Norbert, too. Norbert was still writing letters, but I hardly answered. There was just one thing he still had to see: our new apartment. Our new apartment in Flottbek.

What's all this about Christopher?

He had guessed. I misspoke myself, gave myself away, and half intended to do so. But Norbert wanted all the cards on the table. His next visit to Hamburg came at Whitsuntide. The day of decision had arrived. In a sentimental hour with lots of Coke and jellybeans, I promised Norbert to stick by him. He had appealed to my conscience, and I realized with remorse that he had priority rights.

Nevertheless, a duel proved unavoidable. Norbert, armed with a can of pineapple chunks, Christopher with a bottle of currant juice. And I equipped with all the subtleties of makeup and a pale-painted mouth. Rendezvous: the Othmarschen train station. Right away one of my little green strap shoes broke. Both of the boys tried to knot the broken strap.

In vain. So I continued on one leg. And I managed somehow. My petticoat rustled with every step like a stack of tissue paper. My cavaliers kept a tight grip on their can and bottle. Down the street, lined with villas. I felt like Yvonne de Carlo. Gardens, trees in bloom, and two duelling partners. I with my broken shoe in my hand, not letting either boy carry it, for fear of giving either one a premature advantage. We reached the house. A dried-up spruce tree on the ridgepole and a smell of stone and mortar, paint and varnish.

Let's do it in the kitchen, I said. Small and controllable, a room for a triumvirate, suitable in size and potential.

Well, we have gathered here to reach an important decision.

Norbert started to set things up, and Christopher played dumb, grinned, twisted his mouth sarcastically, looked down at Norbert, who was puffed up with rage. The vein in his forehead betrayed him. He was trembling, the can of pineapple still clutched in his arms. He burst out, She made up her mind a long time ago! That was against our agreement. And besides, I had changed my mind during our walk after all.

I choose Christopher, I said loud and clear. I knew it was treason, but it was too late to switch now. Christopher was so much bigger and more suave, more casual. He had an aura of movies, bubble gum pictures. Besides the two of us were so successful as a pair. The two are so sweet together! Passers-by had never said that of Norbert and me. Norbert. Good Heavens, his vein! It was thick and angry and blue.

Well, here's to the decision!

Christopher decided to open his bottle of juice. What could Norbert do but contribute his pineapple? Six golden chunks for each and fifteen swigs from the bottle. Back to the station. Silent march, three abreast. I was still hobbling. Except that now I hobbled at Christopher's side and he was carrying my shoe.

SCENE 24. INTERIOR. DAYTIME. DARKENED CUTTING ROOM. GEBHARDT IS SITTING NEXT TO A CUTTING GIRL AT THE CUTTING BENCH. SCENE BEGINS WITH A LONG SHOT. LATER TRACK-IN TO PROJECTION SCREEN. FRAME-FILLING. Is that the third reel? Yes. The sequence after Ibiza. I put the material together chronologically. To the extent that was possible. To the extent that is possible, GEBHARDT thinks, and nods. All right, let's run it through. West Berlin, fall of 1960. Gebhardt still has ten marks in his pocket. He stays with one of his former actors. Who has changed his profession, is seldom at home. Has become a high-class male prostitute. Gebhardt eats one cooked meal a day. He gets a bowl of pea soup for forty Pfennig at Aschinger's. Searching for work. Old acquaintances prove useful. He writes scripts for the SLANDERBEARS. He meets cabaret artists and does some directing again. Ends up again right where he never wanted to be. But directing is the only thing that seems to be available. Okay. All right, all hands on stage. He lives on two hundred marks a month. He owns one pair of pants, a turtleneck sweater, and a six-year-old raincoat. He feels free, because he sees some options. He writes for RIAS, Radio in the American Sector. He works as a ghostwriter for television producers. He gets out of cabaret work. An opportunity for opening a theater presents itself. This time with fifty thousand marks' backing. This time with culture-loving bankers behind him. He has the choice between theater or television. In between, a divorce. Another marriage. He goes to Hamburg with his third wife. He breaks into television. A former classmate from the actors' studio gets him a job as production assistant. It promises money and seems solid. After six months, his first contract as program writer. An area to himself. An area to burrow his way into. Without regard for others' areas of expertise. After only a year Gebhardt is stopped dead in his tracks. His actors' studio colleague has remembered machinations from the old days. Has remembered a certain professor, a verdict, Gebhardt's inability to compromise. Hintze, the friend of Gebhardt's youth, begins to look to his own safety. Gebhardt, the Trojan horse, is shifted onto a siding. Hintze hopes he will show remorse, do penance. But Gebhardt refuses to be forced to his knees. He switches departments. Out of sheer stubbornness. Out of curiosity as to what will come next. And because his days are numbered in any case. But here, too, he finds little empires. Established long before his arrival. Jealously guarded. Protected against interlopers. Gebhardt tires of fighting. He retreats. He waits for a moment to prove his mettle. To prove he has ability. Some kind of ability. CAMERA WIDENS OUT TO LONG SHOT. THE REEL IS FINISHED. THE CUTTING GIRL SWITCHES OFF THE TABLE AND TURNS ON THE LIGHTS. That's it, she says. Yes, that's it, GEBHARDT says. Let's go get some lunch.

64

Smoothly Ironed Children

My room. My own off-yellow room with off-yellow built-in closet. With a view past nature preserve signs to flawlessly brushed polo ponies and neatly weeded polo players. My window with its view of the polo field and high-carat gardens. Once upon a time I did not know what polo was, but today I live next door to the ponies. My school is a mere twenty minutes' walk. The golf links are a mere twenty minutes' walk. The tennis courts are a mere five or twenty minutes away, depending on the club you pick. One chooses between golf or polo and picks a tennis club to match.

I am looking forward to school. Tomorrow I enroll. Tomorrow everything will change. I am rid of the cat. I look Frau Dr. Rautenfeld in the eye. Principal's office in Flottbek.

Hello, dear, she says, and looks up at me with studied friendliness. She must have read a bad evaluation of me. Beaming unnaturalness holds my hand in hers, many seconds too long. My hand goes all moist. And still she holds on to it.

Don't worry; we'll get you straightened out.

She accompanies the words with an emphatic left foot, which goes up and comes down with an energetic thump. She is very floor conscious. Small and stocky, she stands before me, legs slightly apart. All the transitions in her body are buried in fat. There are no ankles, just leg stumps. No wrists, just arm sausages. No neck, just a double chin that overflows onto the shoulders. Her hair is combed back straight. Little gray brown frizzles, like the stuffing of our old sofa. Everything pulled severely to the back, gathered into a little bun. Comb it straight back and pull it tight. A couple of waves wander loose over her head. Not produced by hair curlers but by silver clips which one snaps into the wet hair like combs. Skeptical waves, without the sparkle and enjoyment needed for a new hairdo. This hairdo is already a hairdo for the grave. The eyes watery, without pupils, coated with a glaze of fat. Her gaze looks a little like the carp we have at Christmas, malevolent and slippery. The mouth—wide, a single line. She had a carp as a grandparent, I am sure of it. No ring, but a string of pearls around the chins, a gathered brown silk dress, garnished with Frau Ellermann's pleats across the bosom and an inset of the same material. The back round, almost hunched, broad shoulders. Almost a gnome.

My dear, she says. Now I am going to take you to meet your new classmates. Like a stumpy little tugboat on the Elbe she chugs off on her round, clumsy wedge heels. What weird shoes. The shoe seems to have relinquished its characteristics as a shoe and turned into a kind of foot. Awkward, clubbed, like a swollen water blister.

Frau Dr. Rautenfeld. How weird. I have to run to keep up with her, she moves so quickly. Past the glass display cases, the sacred corridor cases set aside for art. Just look at these lovely drawings, she says in passing, and does not look herself. 8A is written on a little plastic door plate, and underneath, Frau Dr. Müller-Hintze. With a dark brown pageboy, long bangs, and too tight skirt, makeup in her pores and a bright red mouth. One set of trimmings, still available for the marriage market. Glaring red fingernails, a yellow middle finger. She breathes at me, and I find myself in a smoking car. Perhaps she also tips the bottle now and then. Her voice drags. Turned down from 45 r.p.m. to 33. Aha, you're the new girl. Well, all right. There should be a desk free in back. All right, you can sit down. All right. Well.

She smiles at the blackboard. But what are you going to do for me? They are having English. The girl beside me is eating a salami sandwich. In back someone is writing a letter. In front of me girls are whispering. All right, that's enough, quite enough, comes the voice from the board, dragging and stale.

All right, let's have it quiet now. Quiet, please!

My new class. Kilts and pageboys. Pretty knitted sweaters. No city or rubble faces. White collars peeping out of V-necks. Snowy white cuffs. Mothers who starch and iron their little girls smooth for school. Which ones look as if I might like them? Maybe that girl two rows in front of me with short brown bangs and a flat white face. Like a white Japanese. She also seems to be pretty cheeky.

I can't follow you.

She says that in English and grins. Frau Dr. Müller-Hintze goes all helpless. Did the girl really not understand, or is she pulling her leg? Better explain once more. All right, Judith. Aha, so her name is Judith. One row in front of me someone turns and smiles at me. A little pug nose in glasses, knitted into a chubby pullover.

That's Helga Petersen. Aha. I try to find out the names. What is yours? My neighbor hands me half of her second salami sandwich.

My name's Hannelore.

Hannelore!

The voice comes from the front of the room. What did I just say? Whispering.

Come, children, that will do. Hannelore!

Hannelore does not know. I'm disappointed in you, comes the plaintive voice from up front at the board.

You said you wanted to make a special effort after Easter. Considering that you're repeating this grade.

Frau Dr. Müller-Hintze. So she talks to people about repeating grades in front of all the others. Not entirely harmless. One has to be on the lookout. She's certainly the type to bear a grudge. Doesn't ask much of herself; comes to class poorly prepared. But demands proper behavior of others. Which girls does she like? I see, the class president and Annette von Steinhoff. The most childish ones, the littlest ones are her favorites. She has something against young ladies. *She's keenly aware of them as competition, my new homeroom teacher. You'd do best to braid your hair into thick blond plaits and wear a checked peasant dress to school. She's also our German teacher, Hannelore whispers. I realize that myself before long. Our very first composition has repercussions.* How I Help Mother Around the House. *Like a fool I write the truth. How I still like to play, and my mother does not fuss much over housework. My first D sits pouting in my briefcase. But who gets a B? I see, all the girls who write about Mommy and Daddy and vacuum cleaning, about stirring cake batter and cutting out cookies. I can do that, too.*

I learn how to lie. The cat broke my resistance. I intend to make it this time. I don't want any more wobbly D's. I describe our mobile, which hangs in the living room, swinging gaily in the breeze as if the bright little fish were frolicking in the bright blue sea. *That gets me a C. The cigarette addict prefers nonsmokers. The alcoholic prefers ginger ale. I increase the* Momsie *quality of my compositions and continue to get my C's. Keep it nice and babyish, don't grow up, celebrate the birthdays backward. By the time I get to age 5, I'll be earning B's.*

SCENE 25. DAYTIME. CORRIDOR. HUMANITIES TOWER OF THE UNIVERSITY OF HAMBURG. CLOSE-UP: NAME PLATE WITH THE WORDS "PROF. DR. PANTENBURG, OFFICE HOURS MONDAY 11:00–1:00." CAMERA WIDENS OUT AND PANS. ON A BENCH, FACING THE DOOR, SITS RAINER GEBHARDT. NEXT

TO HIM THREE STUDENTS, ALSO WAITING. GEBHARDT'S WATCH READS 11:42. GEBHARDT STANDS UP, GOES DOWN THE CORRIDOR, STOPS IN FRONT OF A BULLETIN BOARD, READS THE NOTICES TACKED UP THERE. Gebhardt knows Prof. Pantenburg. Has known him for a long time. From many parties with tipsy champagne glasses. May I introduce you? Professor Pantenburg. How do you do? You know, I recently reviewed. Aha, you're with a newspaper? Radio. I see. Well, then. Gebhardt knew Pantenburg. The historian Pantenburg. Knew his well and his then and his pro and his con and his reputation in professional and nonprofessional circles. A troublemaker. Gebhardt's boss Neubüser poked a pretzel stick down his steamy radio-throat. Always us. Always us. And it hasn't even been determined who is to blame. Hasn't even been determined, I tell you. And Gebhardt looked over at Pantenburg. And he stood there, his shoulders drawn up almost to his ears, smiling broadly like a Japanese lantern-moon. Well, then, Gebhardt knew Prof. Pantenburg. But Winfried Böhm insisted they had to get professors. Winfried Böhm called up every day and said, We've got to get him. He's prominent. He'll draw many others. Progressive and well-known. The students will come if we have him. And so Gebhardt was here, because he knew Pantenburg, because he had met him so often among the canapés. Because that was a good sign, as Böhm always said. A very good sign. You are invited to join by. But there were only five definite. Still only five. Pantenburg was to be the sixth. GEBHARDT RETURNS TO THE BENCH, WHERE FIVE STUDENTS ARE NOW WAITING. HE SITS DOWN AGAIN. Office hours from eleven to one. Do you want to see Pantenburg, too? Neatly lined up on the bench. If my paper is good, I'm in business. He always does most of the talking. Just listen and take it all down. That'll get me an A. And make sure to quote from his books. Everything okay. GEBHARDT stares at the door. The door is still gray. GEBHARDT stares at the little plate. The words are still there: eleven to one.

Between Two Crows
I come home. Moving van in front of the house. The new tenants. Moving into the ground-floor apartment. I unlock the door. Stick my briefcase in the corner.
    What's for lunch?

68

My mother is already home from her office. She is crying. I ask, What is it? Granny is dead, she says. I found her this morning, when I went to wake her. I didn't want to tell you before you went to school.

Granny is dead in her bright new little room. With the cheery lilac curtains with dark blue and red checks, an abstract design. I picked out the curtains for her myself. Everything was supposed to be nice and modern. And now Granny is dead. Without telling us beforehand. I'm not allowed to go into her room. I'm hungry, but my mother is crying. So I cry, too. Granny simply fell asleep.

She didn't suffer.

Is that an excuse for simply upping and dying? We sit facing our balcony, with its view of the nature preserve. The mood holds us prisoner. We cry away the hours. Nightfall. The walls put on dark mourning clothes. I daren't switch on the light. Now we will have to wear black, and it's spring, too. Spring without Granny. I wanted to show her the new cello I've gotten so I can play in the school orchestra. Tomorrow I have my first lesson.

The doorbell rings. Go to your room, my mother tells me. I creep away behind the keyhole. The hallway is lit up. Two men in black top hats, in proper stiff evening dress. They leave again, then come back. They are carrying a black coffin, which they deposit in front of the mirror. And Grandmother? They carry her out of the little room, place her in the open box, which stretches its mouth wide. Now they stand in the hallway, take off their top hats, fold their fingers over the brims, and stare at my white grandmother. What kind of faces do these men have? I can only make out one of them. His face is as white as my grandmother's, with death-smoothed lids. Perhaps he is already dead, too?

My mother stands there between two crows. My mother weeps into the silence. It looks as though they are counting to one hundred, like when one cannot sleep. Now they put on their hats, bang the box shut. Out it goes, piggyback. And one of them comes back again. It is the white face. He shoves his chalky hand through the door, he tips half of his top hat through the crack in the door. Bang, the door shuts. Grandmother is going off to a banquet with two escorts in evening dress.

SCENE 26. DAYTIME. SET AS IN 25, EXCEPT THAT NOW SEVEN STUDENTS ARE WAITING. CAMERA AT EYE-LEVEL GIVES CLOSE-UP OF THE DOOR, WHICH IS OPENING. Professor Pantenburg will be here momentarily. A narrow, gold rimmed glasses-wearer is playing house-of-horrors, and peeks briefly out of the partly opened door. He just heard a car drive up; this is his big scene. Open door. Speak your lines. Close door. Hey, he's coming. Man, I'm going to drop dead of starvation in a minute. Well, the old guy was here first. In that case I'm splitting. GEBHARDT stands up. GEBHARDT, the old guy, straightens the creases in his spine. GEBHARDT follows PANTENBURG in. The solid plantation owner Pantenburg, who carries his briefcase like a riding whip and holds a Scotch glass like a Bible. I'm so busy, so busy, the professor murmurs. Please sit down. And GEBHARDT sits down and thinks of *Alice in Wonderland* and of the rabbit that runs after the alarm clock. Pantenburg is still speaking with his back. He is shifting books to the windowsill. From the desk to the windowsill. Well. You see, all this on my desk. All dissertations. All dissertations. And at home I have my new book. You know, I've been working on it for five years. Five years, and still I haven't had time to finish it. Well. GEBHARDT wonders how to broach the subject. Should he start with we-already-know-each-other? Or of-course-you-remember? But PANTENBURG is sitting now. Spreading and comfortable, he sits massively in his chair and looks at GEBHARDT for the first time. You're here about your paper. No. GEBHARDT takes a breath. The small amount of air left over after the professor has filled his great lungs. No. GEBHARDT does not mention that he knows him from hours among the Scotch glasses. But, PANTENBURG is already exclaiming, and blowing pipe-brewed clouds into GEBHARDT's face, we know each other! He stands up. He rolls around the curve of his desk. Yes, of course. Well, how are you? What brings you here? Well, let me hear. PANTENBURG rolls hastily back the way he came. Pipe in mouth, he runs both hands through his gray, water-combed hair. Ah, I'm glad to hear that. Yes, please. It's about. GEBHARDT feels like a travelling salesman. Political Club in black or brown. In leather or in cloth. I have read your books, GEBHARDT says. I would like to invite you to participate. To join. PANTENBURG puffs. A good idea. Really most welcome. You're absolutely right. The established parties leave much to be desired. As a free human being. Have you spoken to Professor Schlesselmann? I see, he's not interested. Well. And I see you don't have any of the historians. Just a medical man and a professor of education. PANTENBURG glances over

70

the list. The list of signatures. You are invited to join by. The Republic is at stake, PANTENBURG comments. Democracy, and in this country of all countries. You're right there. It always came from above. Was always forced on us. Never grew organically. Aha, Hesse hasn't joined. Nor has Jäger. Well, as I mentioned, my new book. And then the dissertations. These things keep piling up. They keep piling up, I tell you. But if you would give me a progress report now and then. I'm really very interested. Very interested. And now you must excuse me. There are students waiting out there. And, GEBHARDT thinks, please let me know when democracy fails. That really interests me, RAINER GEBHARDT thinks. Forty-three-year-old Rainer Gebhardt, who knows Professor Pantenburg and his books. And Professor Pantenburg's office hours. Democracy from eleven to one, and an hour late.

Summer Comes on Wings of Chanel No. 5

They carry the coffin past the moving vans. My white grandmother leaves the house, and two of the living dead move in. Into the ground floor, the new neighbors. A shiny, black winged hearse parks in front of the house. A coffin with windows. A Cadillac with dark gray curtains. The Menzel family is moving in, with built-in music by Handel, she as a teak sideboard, he as a Venetian standing lamp. Frau Menzel. She offers me her arm, she strikes out with her golf club, she rides three times around the house on a tennis racket, and her husband counts the rounds. Her camel's hair coat smells of her perfume. Summer comes on wings of Chanel No. 5. The stairwell stuffs a perfumed gag into my mouth. I stumble over porcelain table settings, Chinese teacups blocking the stairs. In the corners the cake forks rattle, the golden spoons.

The house is filling up. Persian lambs, silver foxes, stoles from the golf club, the tennis club, the riding club. Chatter chatter. While the men are off making money, the women chew ladyfingers. Stand back, swing! The little ball flies into a friend's open mouth. At golf teas the ball always goes into the hole at the first try.

He is losing his hair, while she grows younger and younger. He spends his days in the safe, getting paler and paler. Soon he will have exhausted all the air. She breathes it in, pumps herself up, gets fuller and more leathery, more and more snow-tanned. And on Sundays over tea in the garden they both sit silently, stirring the stillness. He keeps his eye on her. He knows that otherwise she will swallow him up, pop! Just a moment's concentration on his cup, and Herr Menzel will disappear.

In the fall they go home, to a villa in Liechtenstein. Hello, Herr Menzel says, We're leaving tomorrow. Hello, Frau Menzel says, We're back. Two vacationers return to their vacation. The black angel is with them, brilliantly waxed, admired by all the savages glued to the garden fence. What wouldn't they do for a car like that, a coffin with windows! I daren't even ask. They wash the Cadillac with their tongues, lick the back window, polish the stern with their lips. Even if it doesn't belong to one, how beautifully it gleams.

Did you ever meet my grandmother? I ask Herr Menzel at the garden gate. No, he says, but take a look under the car. There are so many people lying about. I can't keep track of names. If you find her, say hello to her for me. All the best to your Granny. Herr Menzel, the stock-broker, tips his hat like a Chinese teapot. With softly grating lid he heads for the vault. Departs for his four-hour workday.

SCENE 27. EXTERIOR. DAYTIME. DOWNTOWN HAMBURG ON A SATURDAY ON WHICH STORES STAY OPEN LATE. GEBHARDT OUT SHOPPING. SUBJECTIVE CAMERA. LONG FOCUS. CLOSE-UPS OF INDIVIDUAL FACES. ADD OFF-CAMERA NARRATION. Gebhardt knows Professor Pantenburg. Gebhardt knows why Professor Pantenburg cannot do anything for them. And why Dr. Raake cannot do anything for them. And Peter Bruhns, the publisher Peter Bruhns, who welcomes every new idea and hails every new concept. And finds fault with every new idea and agrees on ideas, and weighs ideas, and outweighs ideas, and is working for his emancipation and that of his readers. Away from political parties. Away from the hypocrisy of political caucuses, Professor Pantenburg declares. Pantenburg the freethinker. The democrat who unfortunately cannot do anything for them. Who at the moment cannot get involved. Because he is finishing a book. Because he is not finishing a book. Because he is supervising dissertations. Does not get to supervising. Because his children are sick. Because his children are not sick. Because he has a cold just now. Because he does not have a cold just now. Because he is preparing for a class. Because he has cancelled a class. Because he never gets around to preparation. Because his wife has to go to the hospital. Because his wife is not going to the hospital but his parents-in-law are coming for a visit. Because his parents-in-law are still there. Because Professor Schlesselmann is not joining. Because Professor Schlesselmann is not interested, but knows Herr Dr. Raake, who unfortunately cannot come because a writers' congress is taking place. Because no congress is taking place. Because he has to go to London. Because he has just gotten back from London but has to fly to Milan tomorrow, to recover a bit from London. Because he is putting together a book. Because he is not putting together a book but is writing a preface. Because he is not writing a preface. Because he is editing the afterword. Because he is not editing an afterword. Because he just got engaged yesterday. Because he is dissolving his engagement tomorrow. Because his father just died. Because his mother lives with him and needs a little company in the evenings. Because his mother has to go to a health spa. Because he is fetching his mother from her trip to the health spa, where he meets Peter Bruhns, who unfortunately cannot do anything because he is over-worked. Because he is not overworked but has to husband his small amount of free time so he will not overwork. Because the April issue is not ready yet. Because the April issue is ready, but the May issue has to be put to bed. Because tomorrow someone is giving a party. Because there was a party yesterday. Because one cannot go out every night. Because one has something every night this week. Because one cannot support every new movement that comes along. Because one has to support so many things. Because one really should relax occasionally. Because one never gets a chance to relax. Because he is suing for divorce. Because his wife is suing for divorce. Because he is spraying bugs in the garden, so they will not eat up the rosebushes. Because the rosebushes have been all eaten up. Because he is just leaving for Kampen. Because he has just returned from Kampen and is leaving again for Kampen. Because his house is being painted and is not being painted and is being painted again. Because his daughter was not promoted in school. Because his daughter was promoted but might not be. Because he, like a hundred thousand others, is an independent person with a mind of his own. A person who thinks for himself and, like a hundred thousand others, affirms democracy. Who affirms freedom as he should, who affirms the free democratic legal system of the affirmed Federal Republic. But, like a hundred thousand others, is too cowardly, too lazy,

73

too indifferent to make a personal commitment to this affirmed affirmation. Because he, like a hundred thousand others, did not believe in it yesterday, does not believe in it today, and will not believe in it tomorrow.

Black-Stamped Relatives

Telegrams of condolence. I can already recognize them by the cancellations. Printed-matter letters. Black borders. Our apartment, our lovely new white-plastered apartment, is turned into a rectangle of mourning. Thin black lines frame my off-yellow walls. We live in our condolence telegrams.

No one says a word. No one wants to talk to me about death. As if it weren't interesting to talk about how a person dies, and of what, and why. My black-stamped relatives appear in telegrams. I pry them out of the mailbox one by one. They sit in the living room weeping. You poor child, they say, and stroke my head. In school I don't get a single D. I even get a C-minus on the math test. A death like this gives one a new lease on life. People have to be friendly and patient, even if their name is Frau Dr. Müller-Hintze and they catch the child whispering. In fact all of them are so gentle with me. A death like this certainly sets one apart. Otherwise they would not be so considerate. Everything is permissible: doing badly on tests, not learning the vocabulary, making mistakes at the board. All is permissible, except for one thing: asking why Grandmother died, asking how they were sure she was dead, who closed her eyes, Mother or the gentlemen in evening dress? After all, one has seen movies. And how about the cremation? Is the coffin burned along with the body? Well, asking shows a lack of tact. There's nothing to be done. So I prolong my mourning period into the summer, into the fall, and comfort myself with many fat little C's.

SCENE 28. INTERIOR. TOWARD EVENING. IN THE EMPTY, PAMPERED ROOMS OF A LATE NINETEENTH-CENTURY VILLA. LONG SHOT FROM ABOVE. DOLLY OR CRANE IF POSSIBLE TO GIVE THE IMPRESSION OF A GUIDED TOUR OF A CASTLE. GEBHARDT leads the way through the rooms. Leads card-file corpses through rented rooms. You are invited to join by. You are invited to join by all those who never come because they are much too busy inviting you to join. They invite everyone to join in order not to have to participate themselves. All those who do not possess fame and fortune trot along joiningly behind GEBHARDT, to be there when the walls are painted. Here on the left you see an office. And here on the right another office. And here you see the room where we will hold our meetings. Aha. Well, well. Lovely. Aha. Lovely. IRENE FRENZEL hurries on ahead of GEBHARDT. She flies through her villa. She is dreaming of well-sealed floors. Of a parquet republican club. She is dreaming of Karsten Neitzel, the mascot Karsten Neitzel, who is paying for it all. Paying for the sanding and the sealing and the removal of a partition to enlarge the meeting hall. Paying and paying and paying. The mascot Karsten Neitzel. The scrawny little mascot who is paying for everything. And suddenly the mascot appears. Races noiselessly through the rooms. Eighteen ounces in faded blue jeans with a fringed bald pate. Suddenly it appears, in its shrunken woolen shirt, with shrunken armlets and leglets. Neitzel, the millionaire mascot, with bad political digestion, who is paying for everything. Neitzel goes along, is with them, dragging his inheritance, a food chain, along behind him like a tricycle. And on the left you see. And on the right you see. Biehl would like to live here. Irene has already found a caretaker. The student Dieter Biehl, who is opening and closing the doors. The student Dieter Biehl who will be taking his exams next year and can live for free in the villa if he receives the mail and answers the telephone. If he locks up and keeps an eye out and maintains lists of who is meeting on what day and at what time. Biehl would do that. IRENE FRENZEL pokes her glasses up her nose. Focuses her bookkeeper's gaze straight ahead. IRENE introduces DIETER BIEHL. The student caretaker Biehl. With scrubbed ears and brushed teeth, with clean polished feet and disinfected mind. Biehl. How do you do. I'm Joachim Schuster. And this is my wife. How do you do. My name's Neitzel. How do you do. My name's Gebhardt. Aha, you're the president. I'm Dr. Hauswald. I'm Matthias Hauswald. Pleased to meet you. My name's Frenzel. Hello. Pleased to meet you. I'm painting the left wall. Hello. My husband will do the windowsill. Hello. Pleased to meet you. BIEHL is scrubbing the floor. Scrubbing it clean. As clean as himself. BIEHL is doing the housecleaning, catching the last dust loiterers with his sharply faceted spectacle-gaze. Hello. Nice to see you. Hauswald is spackling cracks with Irene. Hello. How are you. Good to see you. The word is getting around that people are fixing up a building. That people are setting up a club and have free beer. That there will be free beer at the grand opening. A club where there will be free beer. Beer for joining. That will be fun.

C-G-C-G-C-G

I have already advanced beyond the first few notes and am scratching out an étude. I saw my cello apart, to the tapping foot of my teacher, Prof. Maurer. Dull, snow-white wisps of hair, a Henry the Eighth of music. A massive monster, sprung from my English book, Prof. Maurer, with slightly moist mouth. A slobbering lout. Slimy eyes, the eyes of age. Everything is moist and bleached out. He sits, a massive heap, on my rocking chair. The chair most likely to support his weight.

In sonorous Viennese he loosens his shoelaces to ease his poor swollen feet.

Professor Maurer refers to himself in the respectful third person plural. At the beginning of the lesson he speaks his magic word: untie ze shoelaces. Moaning and groaning like an old locomotive. His high-laced old boots squeak. Then bump, back into the chair.

Vell, let's hear you now.

The old Maurer-locomotive starts up. The flapping patriarchal boots beat out the time with their heels. Hammering in step, I march across the strings until the professor falls asleep. And he always does fall asleep. Half an hour of lesson, half an hour of nap. His head rolls onto his chest like Grandmother's. The mouth dozes off between chin and double chin. Unrhythmic snoring in D-minor. At last, I think, and spend the substantial rest of my hour on C-G-C-G-C-G. If he happens to wake up, I simply fall into a chord and play forte. Zere, you see, he says, pulling himself together in his rocking chair. Ve're getting zere. So, do zis piece again for ze next time, and ze Mozart a bit more lifely, if you don't mind. Then the Herr Professor tips forward again.

Ach, zese shoelaces!

Groaning, he wobbles forward on the chair runner and looks up at me glassily, his back bent. Oh, all right, let's help the old fellow wrap his footsies into his boots. He smiles gratefully with his two mouths, heaves himself awkwardly out of the chair, which I hold for him, to keep it from suddenly rocking backward and playing leapfrog with my teacher.

Herr Professor readies himself for departure. He seizes his big cello, which he never takes out of its case but always lugs panting around with him, in case a duet. Well, Küss die Hand, he says with a heavy sigh. Auf Wiedersehen. Wheezing he departs and rumbles down the stairs, bumping into the railing a few times with his cello, and thunders away in a final mighty chord.

SCENE 29. INTERIOR. EVENING. DR. FRENZEL'S APARTMENT IN THE STUDENT DORMITORY. CLOSE-UP: A SHERIFF'S BADGE, WORN BY JÖRG FRENZEL (7). CAMERA WIDENS OUT TO MEDIUM SHOT. JÖRG IS PLAYING WITH HIS BROTHER PETER (5): COWBOYS AND INDIANS. OFF-SCREEN NARRATION. Böhm demands a private meeting. The steering committee simply has to get together. Frenzel demands a private meeting. The steering committee simply must come together some time. Grützmann demands a private session. The steering committee, of which he is not a member, the steering committee, to which he was not elected, the steering committee to which Böhm on his own initiative secretly adds Grützmann, this steering committee simply must meet one of these days. Basic principles have to be defined. Another beer at Dr. Frenzel's. Subject: the Hamburg Republican Club. IRENE FRENZEL lines up the coins, because they are discussing what will happen when the club no longer exists. When the society has come of age. When everyone has a say in how things are run. What then? What do we do then? We have to formulate a plan for eternity. For what comes after eternity, after the Great Revolution. For whatever has a future after eternity. For a learning and developmental process for later on. They are discussing what comes AFTERWARD, even before the club has any members. Even before a single study group is functioning, the issue of AFTERWARD has come up, the AFTERWARD that comes after AFTER. GEBHARDT begins to go over his one-times-one. GEBHARDT states that a REPUBLICAN CLUB is first and foremost a republican club. And DR. GRÜTZMANN nods. And DR. FRENZEL nods. But afterward, says BÖHM, Afterward, when one plus one makes one hundred, then one will have to, then one will, then one should. Hands up! JÖRG yells. I'm going to shoot you dead, PETER yells. And afterward,

FRAU FRENZEL says. Go stand in the corner, PETER yells. Pow, you're dead, Gebhardt, JÖRG yells. And after the future, GRÜTZMANN says. Bang, bang, JÖRG yells, and reloads with building elements. Come on, Gebhardt, die! little PETER shouts. Oh, let the children, DR. FRENZEL says. Oh, let them, Irene, DR. FRENZEL says. And IRENE FRENZEL, who opens bottles, who murmurs hush, and quiet, watches over her children, counts up the children between the coins. Her children. Her two from Sheriff Bonanzaland. And afterward, says BÖHM. Afterward, when everything and everything. War! PETER yells. Let's play Vietnam! Irene, you don't want to suppress their natural impulses. Look, Daddy, I just shot Jörg! And if in addition to antiauthoritarian day care centers we have antiauthoritarian schools. You're dead, Jörg! Your leg's been shot off! And when this repressive structure is finally replaced by antiauthoritarian universities, well then. Daddy, I'm going to shoot you, too. You're a capitalist. When the children no longer. When the children are free. Now all the capitalists are dead, Daddy. When the children are finally their own masters, well then, DR. FRENZEL says, and gathers up all the corpses his sons have shot, Well then, everything will be different. Completely different.

The Business on Page 174
Jutta Sass did not play hookey. Cut out before lunchtime—we don't feel like taking gym. Jutta Sass did not play hookey. Jutta stayed and conscientiously delivered her situation report. Jutta Sass wore tightly laced shoes, dark blue pleated skirts, and blue and white striped blouses. A blue ski jacket with stitching, her hair cropped short like a boy's, light blue eyes with glasses, and a forceful heroic nose. Jutta Sass specialized in Siegfried and the ballads of Conrad Ferdinand Meyer, and our religion teacher wept an accompaniment. And Atli's goblets echoed, heavy with wine. Jutta echoed the Germanic heritage. She spent her afternoons buried in Bender's German Reader, in volume six with Gutrun and Gunnar.

Religion class with Frau Friedrichs—an ode to Wotan! Frau Friedrichs and Jutta rode their steeds up and down the great table—onwards, knights! I once wanted to be an actress, Frau Friedrichs confessed, and tossed her white head, bristling with wild locks. Small, stocky—she could only have taken on dwarf roles or tree stumps if she had not become what she did—religion teacher at the old Germanic assembly ground, the thing. And they sliced Halli's heart from his breast. *Jutta recited, her eyes glazed. Our hearts thumped when* Atli returned to his home and gloated over the hoard. *Religion class bogged down among shield maidens and treasure troves. And when Frau Friedrichs departed to devote herself to other classes, when the time came to change homeroom teachers, Jutta's heart broke, and Jutta Sass and Fräulein Religion were found at the classroom door in each other's arms, dissolved in tears. Frl. Friedrichs moved on with clanging of shields and inebriated senses to blooming new children, and Jutta Sass circumspectly began to love the new religion teacher.*

For Jutta Sass loved all her teachers. No matter who it was, no matter who left the school or moved on to another class, Jutta wept and never played hookey. Except for one day. Frau Dr. Müller-Hintze rustled into the room, put one red-lacquered finger to her mouth, and said, Hush, children. Jutta is going to be coming a little late today. Her father, well, children, I might as well tell you, her father has been arrested. But it doesn't mean anything. Why? That's what I would like to know, too. Probably something to do with the war. So be nice to Jutta when she gets here and don't ask her any questions.

So when Jutta got there we were nice to her and didn't ask any questions. She sat there, her eyes all red and her glasses misted over and her long nose rubbed sore, and Hannelore whispered to me, Do you think he was a looter during the war? And Judith said, You don't have to whisper. He was no looter. Why don't you ask your parents when you get home.

When we got home we asked about the war, but no one knew anything. No one knew what Sass had done. But page 174 of our history book told us what our parents wouldn't tell us, what no one would tell us. Our assignment was to read pages 172 to 176. Frau Plath, our history teacher, with black locks and a red mouth, a misshapen Madonna with a cherub's face and the body of a giant, Frau Plath, a mountain of a centaur, gave us another assignment and kept silent. For the past three years she had towered over us, stood at the blackboard like a monument, and kept silent. I adored her. Her face reminded me of the December picture on my wall calendar. She looked like the stained glass window of the Madonna in the Cathedral. I never tore off that picture. The

*Madonna lasted through March with Frederick the Great, through the
summer with Leipzig and the Belle-Alliance. She was young, perhaps in
her early thirties, and from day to day we guessed her to be younger. She
stood there silent before us, and when she spoke, she chattered
nervously, her face bright red. She stumbled over the battlefields at
Verdun and Langemarck, then fell silent again. Frl. Plath. The more I
adored her, the more I wanted to put her on the spot. The more I
enjoyed hearing her stutter and stammer—first one had to back her into
a corner, and when she went down, floundering in red, gallantly come to
her aid.*

*Pages 172 to 176. Her hands folded, knotted behind her back, in her
green and blue checked dress, she stood there before us and asked,
Would anyone like to say anything about this? Judith and I had
prepared something. This business on page 176, this business with the
Jews. Judith raised her hand.*

Beginning in 1941 several million Jews in Germany and the occupied
territories were arrested and for the most part brutally murdered.

Why?

Frl. Plath hesitated. Does anyone know the answer?

I raised my hand and waved it stormily.

*No, Frl. Plath, we want to know what you think! How many Jews
were involved, and why does the book say, Most Germans did not learn
of what was going on, and the others heard only rumors?*

Frl. Plath blushed again. Well, I think—she hesitated.

*How could one not notice that people were being hauled away? Judith
shouted. You couldn't help seeing something like that!*

*Frl. Plath had her pretext now. Judith, don't interrupt! How can one
have a grown-up discussion if you're going to act this way?*

*Frl. Plath wiggled out of answering and quickly followed up with an
order.*

Jutta, please read us the last paragraph on page 175.

Jutta straightened her glasses on her nose and read aloud.

At the Nuremberg Trials an American judge came to the conclusion
that the testimony of those involved in the terrible mass liquidations
showed that in all likelihood no more than one hundred persons in all
had had knowledge of the matter.

*That's a complete and utter lie! Judith could not be stopped. She
yelled at Jutta, poor Jutta, who had only read the paragraph aloud. She*

shouted at her, That's simply not true! If you look in the Putzger Atlas on page 121 you'll find the camps! Dachau, Flossenbürg, Auschwitz, Gross-Rosen, Maidanek, Sachsenhausen, Oranienburg, Ravensbrück, Bergen-Belsen, Neuengamme, Esterwegen, Osnabrück, Theresienstadt, Buchenwald, Stutthof. Judith read them off from a crumpled slip of paper, a list of names that I was unfamiliar with, had never heard.

Only a hundred people knew about it? A hundred? How can one tell such lies? How about the transports? And the shipments? And the guards? The gassing? Everyone was guilty, come on, admit it, everyone!

Frl. Plath remained silent. She always remained silent. History class with her consisted of silence. But since I had arranged with Judith to support her, I shouted, That was mass murder! At that moment Jutta Sass suddenly jumped up, without asking permission—for the first time ever. If she hadn't done that, if she hadn't suddenly exclaimed into the silence, That was right, Jews are nothing but animals—we would never have found out why Jutta Sass's father was behind bars.

Oh, I see, they're animals. So my grandparents, my family are animals?!

I stared at Judith. Why should they be animals?

If we hadn't emigrated, your father would have liquidated us! And here I was feeling sorry for you. I thought you couldn't help it that your father was a butcher. I never told anyone about it, not anyone in our class. But now I want everyone to know: you come from a family of murderers, and you're no better than they are. I'm never going to speak to you again!

Jutta Sass began to blubber. Her seat near the window grew damp. Jutta was comforted by the girl next to her, with an arm around the shoulders and pats on the cheek. Judith began to blubber, too, out of rage. I put my arm around her to comfort her. Come, come, Frl. Plath said, It's ridiculous to get so worked up. Girls, it's nothing to get so excited about. You see, you're not ready to discuss a topic like this.

Frl. Plath murmured her way to recess. She noted down in the class logbook: A discussion on the Jewish Question. I read that to Judith the next hour, and we almost burst laughing. A quiz on the Jews, Judith chortled. Hey, listen, all of you! Who's the smart one who knows what Theresienstadt is? Judith put us through our paces. She stood on the desk, the geography pointer in her hand, and indicated Jutta. You there, please take a stand. You see, it's impossible to discuss a topic like this

with you! She clasped her hands behind her back, and we, the chastened,
confused class, laughed at Judith Zabori and were relieved when she
imitated Frl. Plath, because we did not understand that business with
Theresienstadt.

Pages 176 to 179, a new assignment. There was no going back now.
Confusion spread in concentric circles. We sat there in the classroom
separated into groups, Jutta-comforters and Judith-comforters. The
subject of Auschwitz was pushed aside—we'll come back to this two
years from now. *And way off in the distance echoed our history teacher's*
voice, stammering and chattering—something about aerial bombard-
ments and capitulation. *Jutta and Judith never again said a word to each*
other. That was hard on Jutta. She was the one who always wanted to be
liked, who loved all her teachers, who never played hookey, who obeyed
everyone, who said hello to everyone. For Jutta never wanted to have
enemies. No enemies.

SCENE 30. INTERIOR. EVENING. GEBHARDT'S LIVING ROOM. FRAUKE AND
RAINER HAVING DINNER UNDER THE WICKER LAMPSHADE. SCENE OPENS
WITH AN EXTREME CLOSE-UP OF FOOD AND THE EATING PROCESS. Why
does it always have to be you? Frauke has bought liverwurst again.
Fresh, creamy liverwurst. Gebhardt would like to spread it on the table.
It would do the table good, GEBHARDT thinks. A spread table. At your
age. I'm beginning to find it embarrassing, FRAUKE says. She finds it
embarrassing, RAINER GEBHARDT thinks. My wife with the well-groomed
embarrassment. What will Neubüser think of you? You're making a fool
of yourself, FRAUKE says, wicker-lampshade nice, wicker-lampshade
cozy, with Tanja in her little bed. Fills the beer glasses. Rinses the beer
glasses. You don't have to dry. Put the butter in the refrigerator! Go sit
in the living room. A good thriller. You have to relax now and then,
FRAUKE says. Go ahead and relax. You can't do anything about it,
anyway. Ripe for decay. At forty-three. Escape to the family in a duplex
for four hundred marks a month. I don't understand you. These study
groups. All right, all right, I'm finished. But why does it always have to
be you? Now she's going to pour me a sherry, GEBHARDT thinks. Now
he's supposed to make himself comfortable. You'd be better off in a
political party. Things would run all right without you. Without me,

GEBHARDT thinks. She'd like it best without me. And besides, you're not twenty any more. Leave such things to the young people. Too old, GEBHARDT thinks. Already much too old for demonstrations. Much too old for a new start. Three marriages too old. Would you like a sherry? He drinks a sherry, makes himself comfortable. Dozes off watching the thriller. Should we see what's on Channel 2? No? How about Channel 4? Frauke's channel. Frauke's domestic soap opera. She has to tell him. It's all Grützmann's fault. He got you into this. I know how you dislike parties, but those were different times. You were just a kid. Not your fault. That's got no bearing on the situation today. That's got a great deal of bearing on the situation today. A great deal! GEBHARDT shouts. His youth is preying on his conscience. He doesn't want to get hung up on words. Wherever one goes. No, whatever one does. How long ago was that? Do something, weary between gross and net. At your age. For the length of a sherry. A few wrinkles old. Always on the defensive. Frauke and Tanja. A family. His usual patterns of thought. Always you. Always him. On square wheels. His love rolls on square wheels. His profession rolls on square wheels. A future, his future. On four rolling squares.

People–That Was the Essence of the Past

Judith Zabori. So my girl friend was Jewish. Zabori. The name had a ring of thousand-and-one nights to it, a ring of caravans and samovars. And they had slaughtered several million Zaboris. In Bergen-Belsen, Neuengamme, Ravensbrück, Flossenbürg, Theresienstadt. I had copied all the names from Judith's crumpled slip of paper and spent the whole afternoon looking them up in Diecke's World Atlas, page 140, Southern Germany and the Alps. Here I found Dachau. But Mauthausen was not near Linz where it was supposed to be, between Hunsrück and Greiner Wald. How difficult it was to make anything out on these maps, with their innumerable tiny names and innumerable crisscrossing red lines.

The administrative borders within German territory as of Dec. 31, 1931, officially established between 1945 and 1950, await permanent rectification in subsequent agreements. *That's what it said. In red under the map. But I couldn't find Bergen-Belsen and Neuengamme on page 130, North Germany.*

Do you know exactly how many Jews were killed during World War

II? I asked my mother. I asked my mother, and she did not quite know what to say. My mother had never mentioned anything about Jews to me.

Why do you ask?

She said that falteringly, uncertainly, almost in a bit of a panic, and put down one of the medical journals she always read after supper.

Six million.

She did not wait to hear why I asked. I think it was six million, she said briskly, and became a little wavering around the eyes. She blinked more quickly than usual.

You know, we had four Jewish girls in our class.

My mother began to talk. I didn't even have to ask her. She talked as if she had been waiting the whole time for me to ask. Pent-up excitement dusted her face lightly with flush. She sat there facing me as if she were at a ball and a rejected suitor were just walking away.

One of them was called Rita Neumann. She was very musical. Everything by heart—fantastic. Her father was a doctor.

My mother. She did not look at me as she spoke. And when she did, it was briefly, hastily, somewhat awkwardly, as if I had asked about some very intimate matter, as if she were committing an indiscretion.

And the others? I gave her little nudges. What about the others?

Then there was Käthe Levi. She was especially interested in literature and very gifted. A very, very pretty girl. She lived in a house on the Elbe Promenade. You know the one. Where the kindergarten you used to go to is.

Go on!

I kept pushing her. Trying to shorten the gaps in between. No faltering, or her story might come to a standstill. And I had to hear everything.

Käthe's father was a lawyer. And Judith Frank? She was very sensible and intelligent, too. Her father was a gynecologist in Altona. You know that house, too. That's where your pediatrician, Dr. Kaiser, had his practice until he died.

Strange. We had kept our house on Königstrasse. And Irma Hoffmann's was still standing, too. But in these other houses, which had not even been bombed, strangers were living.

Dr. Frank was a rabbi, by the way. The family were Zionists. Very pleasant people.

My mother added details, bridged the gaps. Perhaps my magnetic attention was what made her falter and hesitate. Probably my head was buzzing too loudly. My questions suddenly embarrassed me. I put on an air of elaborate unconcern. The tension was so great, so strangely vibrating. Like on a hot summer day when one squeezes one's lids shut to prevent everything from going black before one's eyes.

And the fourth girl?

That was Else Gold. I never got to know her at all. She belonged to the lower class of Jews. She did her homework all right, but she fitted into the picture of what used to be called a dumb Jew.

Now she spoke faster, no longer harassed by my questions. Hastened on, as if she wanted to reach a certain point in her narrative. Her head bent forward, out of the circle of light from the standing lamp. And behind the light she grew calmer.

I graduated in 1928. After that I didn't hear from anyone. The whole class got scattered during the war. I did see Rita Neumann once more. She had married a Jewish doctor and was passing through on her way to Berlin. Her husband had been reassigned. Jewish doctors were only allowed to practice at Jewish hospitals. After that meeting in Hamburg we never saw each other again.

A long passage. My mother spoke slowly, without faltering, almost as if she were reading it off. The fewer questions I threw in, the calmer she became. I only gave her little shoves, cues like Did you have no idea of what was going on? *And the story went on, with deliberate haste. I was happy just to be talking with my mother, although I myself couldn't picture what* what was going on *actually implied.*

What was going on? *Of course, officially I knew about the Kristall-nacht. My mother. My own mother had been there* when things like that took place; *she had lived through the Kristallnacht. Had experienced that. I simply couldn't imagine what people had been like in those days. If indeed there were any people who were alive in those days. And now my own mother had been there. Just like that, and was saying,* I never heard anything about physical abuse. I suppose they only did that at night. Besides there were no Jews in our building.

But who had done such things? And without asking my mother?

Well, there was always some kind of rowdyism going on. From the Kapp putsch on, windows were always being smashed. In those days there was always a bit of revolution brewing.

She was born in 1908. So, '18, '28, '38. The Kristallnacht. *She was thirty. Back then. And now all that was almost twenty-five years ago.*

Maybe your father knew something.

She could still remember quite clearly. She did not have to grope for words. Around 1939 or '40 he was sent to inspect something. Beforehand he had to swear an oath. He was not allowed to talk about what he had seen. But afterward he told me, I never want to become a judge. That was all.

My father. That sounded very grim, very mysterious. So sinister and murky. A war thriller, I thought. With secret missions and enforced silence.

And then?

Don't keep asking and then! *I'm telling you.*

What was going on in Poland? I asked quickly.

In Posen, my mother said. It was in Posen that I first saw something. Around 1942. Your father was an antimilitarist and was declared only partially fit for active duty. At first he wasn't drafted but was assigned to an economic task force working on questions of food supply.

My father was an antimilitarist. He was against the war. So my father was in the Resistance, the one that wanted to avert war. In our history book it said that the Resistance included persons of all classes, professions, and religious denominations. It is the moral justification for the continued existence of Germany. *And my father belonged to it. He was there.*

What were you doing in Poland, I asked. My mother looked at me quizzically. Perhaps she thought I wasn't understanding her. And yet I understood everything.

What was going on in Poland?

Behind our building there must have been a detention camp. Somewhere behind us people were living in a camp, because one morning, very early, I happened to glance out the window. And saw people being led out of the camp to work. I heard the tramp-tramp of the marching column. That is probably what had woken me up. I saw prisoners, and Jews wearing the star. In front and behind and on both sides were Nazi guards. The way it normally is in such columns. We went and looked again and again, and it made us sick.

I was listening to my mother's composition on What I Saw, *and I could not give it a grade. Yesterday Judith talked to me about concentration camps. Did you ever see one of those?*

One can't discuss such topics with you yet. *At this point Frl. Plath would have broken off the discussion and made me wash down the blackboard or water the begonias. But here I was at home. Here I received an answer to my question.*

People didn't know anything about concentration camps in those days. At least I didn't. Just once I saw people lying higgledy-piggledy in a railroad stock car with their arms and legs all mixed up. I just happened to see that from my window and realized that human beings were being treated like cattle. That people were treating human beings like cattle.

People. *I had heard that word often enough. People meant someone who did or said something and was called* people. *People was someone who knew something, or who claimed to know nothing.* People *was the essence of the past. But the more I asked who* people *was, the closer I came to narrowing down the concept.*

Judith thinks everyone knew about the ghettos.

A few seconds passed. I didn't look up. My second hand circled once more before she answered.

In Posen I heard that there was a ghetto in Warsaw. People told me that the ones who lived there had their own form of government, their own factories, and could make a living for themselves. I never was much of a newspaper reader. I hated Hitler simply on instinct.

One time I went to the Ernst Merck Auditorium with Wilhelm Rabe. He was studying medicine with me. That was when I was still a student.

I nodded. She had mentioned Wilhelm Rabe in other stories. He was one of the ones who were determined to marry my mother, a fixture in those funny courtship stories I kept after her to tell me. But today I was not interested in hearing about Rabe.

What did Hitler say?

My mother smiled. I really don't remember very clearly. In those days I was a confirmed pacifist and pan-European. After Hitler's speech I remember commenting to Rabe, That man's a plebeian, never mind his racial theories.

I was never active politically, my mother said. That was out of sheer humanism that I made that remark. Sheer humanism, she said. And I listened raptly.

SCENE 31. INTERIOR. EVENING. FIRST: BIEHL'S ROOM IN THE LATE NINETEENTH-CENTURY VILLA. LATER: LOUNGE, STAIRWELL, AND LOBBY. CLOSE-UP: BIEHL IS ON THE TELEPHONE. Telephone. Telephone. BIEHL's voice is quivering. BIEHL exclaims, They're here already. They're taking the cases of beer. BIEHL, disinfected Biehl, cries, They're ripping off the beer. They say, Paying is bullshit, capitalist bullshit. BIEHL, the caretaker Biehl, can't explain who THEY are. Telephone. Telephone. BIEHL is trying to rescue the grand opening and does not know how to go about it. His broom can no longer stem the tide of cigarette butts. The parquet floor is being turned into an ashtray. The butts linger on the chairs. Biehl is dreading eight o'clock. Biehl is scared of eight o'clock. What will Dr. Raake say? Dr. Raake has nothing to say. The only one who shows up is GEBHARDT, around seven-thirty. Gebhardt is the only one who can come and say something. Gebhardt is the only one who turns up to count the empty beer cases and the tipsy strangers who yell, HI, SQUARE, who crowd into the back rows and yodel and shout. My father says, Call the police. BIEHL passes on the advice. Neatly polished parental advice from the neatly polished front row. For there sit FATHER and MOTHER BIEHL like brightly polished apples and enjoy the nice club with its freshly painted white walls. And enjoy the floors which Mother Biehl scrubbed clean for today's grand opening. The grand opening of the Hamburg Republican Club, which they came all the way here to witness. To which all the people in the front rows have come. Have come for their first session in the front rows. People without party affiliation. The parents' generation in the front rows. Here for the first time. The republicans are here, WINFRIED BÖHM says, and smiles encouragingly at GEBHARDT. Let's get started. Yes, let the shit roll, comes a voice from the rear. GEBHARDT looks at his watch. Dr. Frenzel is not here yet. And Helmut Fromm has vanished. Hasn't been seen since his miselection. And Oskar Negt isn't here, either, the grand opening star for the new club. And the other speaker, the man from Berlin, is also missing. Well, let's get started anyway. BÖHM has set up a table, a little steering committee table. BÖHM claps his hands. BÖHM claps in the direction of a LITTLE MAN, who comes creeping in on tiptoes. Who whispers, I'm from the German Press Agency. Could you wait a second. I just wanted to. He whispers to GEBHARDT, We received an anonymous telephone call. Someone said all hell was going to break loose here tonight. The whole shebang is supposed to blow sky-high. I just wanted to warn you, whispers the

LITTLE MAN and disappears among the rows of chairs, behind the back rows. On behalf of the steering committee—Idiot! On behalf of—Fuck off! On behalf of the steering committee—What do we care about the steering committee! I would like to—Let's cut the crap! Welcome you—Sieg heil! Sieg heil! Quiet! FATHER BIEHL shouts. Let's have it quiet back there. Get back to the cemetery where you belong, someone yells back. Old asshole! It gives me great pleasure to—Like hell it does—see that so many of you are here tonight—Yeah, we don't turn down a free beer—and I would like to—Hey, what would you like to do, old windbag? OSKAR NEGT and the other SPEAKER FROM BERLIN slip through the partly open door. With them the pale HERR FRENZEL. They slip onto the window seat behind GEBHARDT. And they hear about the study groups that GEBHARDT wants to set up. A study group on the church—Get thee to a nunnery, old boy—a study group on democracy—He's never heard of Mao, this bourgeois shithead—a study group on the reactionary German National Party—What about socialism, huh?! Quiet! FATHER BIEHL exclaims. Let's have it quiet back there! Yes, I mean quiet! What did you come here for, anyway? And in the back of the room the beer bottles begin to fly. It begins to rain broken glass. And without the second speaker from Berlin, from the Berlin Republican Club, from legendary Berlin, where everything is different and better, and without Oskar Negt, and without the front rows' resistance to the back rows, the two speakers would never get a word in edgewise. Good Lord, what a bore. NEGT is delivering his report. Wow, it hurts me just to listen. NEGT is addressing himself to the subject of VIOLENCE. Man, let's go to the flicks. NEGT begins to count empty seats. Man, let's split. And OSKAR NEGT, travelling salesman in revolution, with his light hand luggage, scares away the happening-socialists and argues with the empty seats. Here's someone who's staying. And over there's someone. Only the front rows are still full. Down in front, where HERR and FRAU BIEHL are sitting, the NONPARTISANS, who have questions to ask. Who want to ask questions about the student revolt, about everything. Who want to keep asking questions until one A.M. The travelling salesman packs his bag. The discussion dismisses its listeners. Caretaker BIEHL hands out brooms, for heaps of ashes are left behind for FRAU BIEHL to scrub away. And beer bottle shards are left behind for HERR BIEHL to sweep up. And large bills are left behind, plane tickets for the speakers, which Dr. Frenzel pays out of the first membership dues, without asking Gebhardt. Without even asking. Because Frenzel, whitewashed Frenzel, feels that discussion-democrats cannot be expected to come by train. Because Frenzel, the Dr. med., feels that progress flies. And who will pay? The little club that up to now has lived exclusively on Karsten Neitzel and on thousands of marks promised by the political play-bunny Bruhns, who has long since forgotten them.

This Decadent Coca-Cola Life

Class party. The girls' high school of Klein Flottbek is sending its tenth graders out into the wilderness, under the supervision of Frl. Plath. The eleventh graders from St. John's boys' high school have issued an invitation—for the first time.

Good heavens, our girls!

Frau Dr. Rautenfeld, the frog, trundles across the hall. Our German class ends early. Frau Doktor is addressing us. Of course she is wearing her brown gathered dress again, the one with the inset over the bosom. The wrinkles in her brow ripple threateningly, her skeptical waves roll even more skeptically over her head, but God is with her and her girls.

This is your first such invitation, children, and I—new paragraph, gulp, deep gaze into the eyes of the class president—I am happy for you. Don't let the fact that I am talking to you this way worry you unnecessarily. Even deeper gaze into the representative eyes of the class president.

Young men nowadays . . .

Hannelore starts to giggle. Frau Dr. Rautenfeld folds her fat little hands over her fat big belly.

Yes, Hannelore, your giggling shows how little you understand. And that is precisely why I am here.

Our principal, an official amoeba, divides before our very eyes. Four Frau Dr. Rautenfelds surround our class. From every side of the square they wobble vehemently, threatening to divide further. Young men nowadays, intones the chorus of amoebas, Young men and young women nowadays are often somewhat careless. Frl. Plath, perched on the windowsill with the begonias at her back, blushes for us.

And therefore I ask you just to behave the way you usually would. A party like this can be great fun if one knows how to approach it properly.

90

Words full of veiled threats. Every sentence coyly old-maidish, every one ending with Girls, I'm counting on your good sense; please justify my faith in you. I find the whole thing comical. Frau Doktor has probably never seen a man close up, but she's a great one at issuing warnings, as if she were constantly involved in tricky situations herself. And yet every day a white haired, gold rimmed lady picks her up after work, her Herr Dr. Rautenfeld. Why doesn't she warn us against that?

O wilderness! If we hadn't subjected Thornton Wilder to a grammatical X-ray in English class, verily, we would have no idea that love even existed. Tender transparent love in the present tense. The boat house on the Alster has been rented, and while the gentlemen spend the afternoon tossing horseshoes and stringing up Japanese lanterns, we girls drown in eye liner. Here Norbert and Christopher don't help a bit. Here we are out strictly for conquest, with white ruffled blouse and gray bolero suit, with a high waist. The red one would be more becoming, of course, but who wants to go down a grade in German and history? Distracted and no longer as attentive as when one wore the gray dress!

We all meet on the train. In the smoking car. With crossed legs and hair teased into beehives. Watch out—a draft! Hang onto your hair! A breeze is blowing in from the Alster! Off we go, to the party lit by Japanese lanterns. The Amazons of the class are girding themselves for battle. Conversations falter. Everyone is talking to someone else for the sole purpose of being seen talking. Eyes wander.

What did you just say?

Hey, are you listening to me?

Everyone squeezes onto the few chairs in the narrow space around the dance floor. In the room next door, brighter by three red bulbs, Frl. Plath sits in her washed-in-from-the-street centaurian black and talks to Jutta Sass. Well, of course that's a possibility. One gallantly renounces young men nowadays and sits chatting with the teacher. Such episodes are remembered and can convert many a C-minus into a brave, hard-working-girl C.

May I have this dance?

The first dance. And it would have to be the blond boy with the delicate silver wire-rimmed glasses, the schoolboy de luxe model, whom I had picked out right away, Plato in his heart and a Coke in his hand, leaning against the wall near the dance floor, smiling distantly. Floating high above the clouds of our vulgar enjoyment.

I just happen to be here. Actually I never meant to come.

Exactly what I had guessed. That made him a very special catch. Sensitive as a pinwheel. Blow hard, so Plato will turn nicely.

Do you like to dance?

He looks at me like Diogenes, searching for someone. I feel small and stupid. Thanks a lot. Bump, here I am, back in my seat.

He was something!

Hey, how was it?

You hit it off?

My classmates buzz around me excitedly. And what about him? He is drinking a glass of Coke, absent-mindedly leaning against the record player. What could he be thinking about? The market place in Athens? He's thinking about himself. Time is reeling itself in on the record grooves. Margot is still sitting, but my sensitive Plato has already become a tipsy Plato. He staggers across the tiny floor of the dance beat, hurls himself at his classmates' partners, and exclaims, A kiss! Come on, honey bee, let's go!

Margot gets her first dance and outdoes us all. The wallflower striptease begins. Shoes go flying into the corner after the first steps. Stockings after them. Don't look! Unsuitable for children. And then lights out. The slow, sticky honey-dance, barely flowing past the light switch. Click. Now only one little red bulb is still lit. Necking alarm. I didn't know one could get drunk on Coke. But now I know.

None of the girls are still sitting, except in the room next door, one hundred watts brighter, where Jutta Sass and Frl. Plath are still enthroned, deep in conversation about God and punctuation. My partner kneads me violently. Come on, he whispers, It's party time. Uninhibited upperclassmen with sweaty palms and glassy cow eyes. Hannelore has already let down her hair. A dissolved fancy hairdo eddies around a pimply youth, smaller than she, but clinging. Margot swirls by barefooted with Plato. She has been transformed into an ashtray. A tin container is balanced on her head. The transition to this decadent Coca-Cola life is taking on Frisco-like features.

Look—Frl. Plath! The first dance before midnight. A black shadow glides into the room and obscures the last light-bulb sun. Danger! Kisses break up. Bodies separate. Hands unlink. Respectable distance. And one, and two. Madonna Plath tries to do the shake. On wobbling wedgies. She tries to remodel her 1945 fox trot into today's steps. She

92

*smiles helplessly down at her dwarf, an eager, dance-crazy mole with a
black Beatle mane.* And turn. *With arms close to her sides, shoulders
hunched up, hem slightly crooked, and pursed dark red smear of a
mouth—our classroom angel's erotic qualities turn us to stone. Plato
sobers up and begins to think about the market place in Athens again.
Margot is back at her chair, and I next to her, well kneaded. Clear the
floor for Frl. Plath and her Beatle!*

*He has put on a boogie record. Rapid, hurried steps. When he looks
up at her between two revolutions, the centaur blushes, and her street
stars shine like in the United German Film newsreels. Slowly the hips
begin to swing, gigantic, mighty centaur hips. They reach out, extend
toward the little benches and chairs, sweep the floor clean.* And one, and
two. *Her black skirt finally extinguishes the light.* Step one, step two.
Heavy menacing heels trample us off to bed. Twelve-thirty, one-thirty.
*Frl. Plath's red Madonna face goes down, and above our heads, stars
with slightly crooked hems appear in the sky.*

SCENE 32. INTERIOR. EVENING. BIEHL'S ROOM IN THE LATE NINETEENTH-
CENTURY VILLA. THE STEERING COMMITTEE OF THE REPUBLICAN CLUB IS
SITTING AROUND A ROUND TABLE. SCENE OPENS WITH AN EXTREME
CLOSE-UP OF A PAPER NAPKIN WITH SCRIBBLINGS ON IT. I'm curious to see
what the others have come up with, DR. GRÜTZMANN says. I myself didn't
get around to it, DR. GRÜTZMANN says. Unfortunately. Busy at the
hospital. Same here, says DR. FRENZEL. Ten weeks, says FRENZEL. Awfully
tight schedule, says BÖHM. You know, my probationary year, says
WINFRIED BÖHM. I jotted down a few points. On my napkin, during
lunch. Well, fine, says GRÜTZMANN. Go ahead, let's hear them, says
FRENZEL. And BÖHM reads off his menu to the assembled multitude.
BÖHM declaims: Admit difficulties honestly. Avoid traditional solutions.
Avoid going from impractical theory to untheoretical practice. And,
BÖHM says, that's it. A basis at any rate, FRENZEL remarks. That's
something. Your last point—a starting point for discussion at any rate,
IRENE says. As a program for the club. A challenge at any rate. That's
right, says GRÜTZMANN. And Irene has a good newspaper article she
found for us. Already run off, says GRÜTZMANN. Why don't you read it
aloud, Irene. Why doesn't she read her Meschkat aloud, her Meschkat

93

who has done all her thinking for her, GEBHARDT thinks. Who has done all the thinking for the entire steering committee. Although Frenzel had insisted. A program for the club, GRÜTZMANN had said, That's essential. That we've got to have. A program with a firm theoretical base. In ten weeks' time, Frenzel had said. That should give us all plenty of time. But a busy schedule at the hospital, and in general. Ten weeks. Everyone has time enough. But a busy time with the children. Oh, well, and that's why. Why doesn't Frenzel read his clipping aloud. Why don't we all read our napkins aloud. Why don't we, GEBHARDT thinks, and hands out copies of his program. Quite a massive document, says IRENE. I'll look it over tomorrow. I'll get to it tomorrow first thing, GRÜTZMANN says. Too much work, FRENZEL groans. I really meant to, too. They really wanted to, too, GEBHARDT thinks. And now I have done it for them all. And now the only choice they have left will be to accept what I have taken off their hands. Because tomorrow and even ten weeks from now, GEBHARDT thinks. Well, says FRENZEL, I think we should go over Gebhardt's proposal point by point and jot down the aspects we don't like; that way we'll spare ourselves unnecessary work. Yes, as a basis it sounds pretty good to me, says IRENE, And perhaps we could add on Böhm's point. Include it, says GRÜTZMANN. Quite right, says FRENZEL, A program like this has to be carefully thought through. We need a concrete proposal. It would be best if Gebhardt submitted his proposal for criticism. Yes, that seems the best approach to me. And we can add any new ideas that come to us, says FRENZEL. Add them onto the program, says IRENE. Okay, says DR. GRÜTZMANN. In two weeks, says BÖHM. In two weeks, GEBHARDT thinks, in two weeks Grützmann will be curious again to see what the others have come up with.

Entombed among Whole Notes

Old Vienna-in-exile is dead. Deaf-Beethoven dead. A little black-bordered card, May we have the honor, in deepest sorrow. The Maurer Family, C-sharp minor.

Isn't it awful?

My music teacher Frau Meiners blinks at me, and the school orchestra begins to tune up. Our beloved teacher. Three cello children have lost their father.

94

The funeral is on Tuesday. I'll take you along. Frau Meiners begins to cry. Hot warm mother's tears. She loves all life. Frau Meiners has two children and a good husband. She wears bright checked skirts and a heavy dark green sweater. Petite and blond, she stands there before me and weeps in syncopated time. Ritardando with loudly overflowing bursts of tears. I like her weepy tears, so I launch myself into the flood. My windshield wipers are not functioning properly—the heavy sweater goes blurry.

They say, Frau Meiners croons, They say he was talking animatedly with his brother about Beethoven just before he was run over, before it happened. Yes, his last discussion was about Beethoven. The witnesses confirmed it.

And his brother?

In serious condition, but he survived.

So there it is, Beethoven dead. My music teacher moons tearfully at me. What a way to die! *She will pick Telemann for her own last hour, of that I am sure.*

Three girls behind, and in front Herr Wulf from St. Christian's, the conductor of the young people's orchestra. And off we go.

Such lovely ladies, and all for a funeral!

He turns his dignified head to the back seat. Frau Meiners smiles lugubriously. Conductor Wulf pats our knees and calves with funereal sympathy. Parked VW. Chapel G. Death stalks in black Weltschmerz hats and black veils.

Hey, I'm missing a math test.

Ute, my cello sister, jabs me with her elbow. That's great, *I whisper back, and pull out my handkerchief.* He was a true and loyal friend to all of us. *A loyal friend entombed among whole notes, round flower notes, empty at the center, wreath music.* Vell, do ze funeral again for ze next time, and try to make ze death a little more lifely, if I may say so.

Above us in the choir loft an Ave Maria wails forth. He would have undone his shoelaces and fallen asleep at the sound of so much artistry, the art he called martristry when dilettantes choked Bach with their violins. But the mourners are wailing martristry tears. The Ave scratches out the last notes, and then comes the procession through the cemetery walks. Solemn steps past box-hedge nature with stiff top hats.

Those are his poor dear wife and his poor dear son.

Graveyard affection bursts forth. They shake hands. They fall into

each others' arms, aunt after aunt. Henry the Eighth is dead. We are
shovelling him in. My regrets, I say. Scatter-sandedly I look down on his
box. Auf Wiedersehen.

SCENE 33. INTERIOR. DAYTIME. OVERFLOWING CAFETERIA; GEBHARDT
STANDING IN LINE WITH HIS TRAY. THE CAMERA FOLLOWS HIM AD LIB
UNTIL THE END OF THE MEAL. Gross, net, GEBHARDT thinks. The moment
has not yet arrived. Not up to today, at any rate. Basically it's all one to
him. What he is doing contradicts what he wants. Gross, net. Gross, net.
Contradiction after contradiction. The world is too large and Gebhardt
too small. The options incalculable. As incalculable as the things that are
available. And his limbs as dwarflike as his stomach. As Gebhardt's
digestion apparatus. Starving to death between gross and net, in
gross-and-net pablum because he does not know what to eat next. He
would like to cut himself into a million I's. Gobble up everything that
presents itself, that is worth gobbling up. He would like to be in Paris,
Rome, Barcelona, New York, Hongkong—all at the same time. He
would like to speak every language, to cross every street, gobble up
everything. A gigantic eye. Omnipresent. Everywhere. The sheer impossi-
bility of it. Attempts at compromise. But travel is not the answer. Travel
means being en route, being a stranger, a guest. Gebhardt would rather
feel at home. Not just look at things from the outside. Always on the
outside. Travel is just a fraud that sells well. Changeable wallpaper. And
you never really understand what you are seeing. You collect impressions, that's all. You are a hungry man eating his way through the ads in
a lavishly illustrated glossy magazine. What is real? What exists? Two
days in Grenada? Nothing. A dream on full pension. A carriage ride.
Merely a confirmation that you have been there. But what do you really
know about Grenada? What have you really tasted? Nothing. Snapshots
for an out-of-focus album. That's all. And it's the same with people as
with countries and cities. There are plenty of things you can have. A man
can have a hundred women. A woman can have a hundred men. And
what's left is not even a snapshot. You never really understand. A life.
Your life. You haven't even had one. A snapshot. He hasn't even had
one. The world is a funhouse. One of those rooms full of mirrors, one of
those fifteen-cent mazes you find at amusement parks. You pay your

money—you can afford it, after all—and wherever you go, you bump into yourself. A thousand paths beckon. A thousand delusions. There is only one path that seems to lead anywhere, and you grope your way along it. And in the end you are outside again and have still seen nothing but yourself. Gebhardt is perfectly aware of that. If he were in Valencia tomorrow, the next day he would be longing to be in Damascus, or back in Lima. Everywhere. Nowhere. At home everywhere. Gebhardt knows all that. But it's still useless. Embrace the entire world. He knows how the experiment will end. There is only one path. Only one. The path of substitution, which leads away from the physical. Which leads along the mental tracks of dusty bookshelves. Encyclopedic prospects of partial success. Thinking takes place independently of space. Knowledge can be taken in at a glance, like the glass cases in a museum. Time to abandon the kind of life that one takes hold of, that one licks with one's tongue, measures with one's hips. Time to turn to dry leaves. Easy to come by, for lifeless objects can be stored readily. If only one could be consistent. Then all would be well. If only Gebhardt could renounce life. But it exists, breathes rhythmically, and compels Gebhardt to sustain a beat he cannot keep up with.

Strawberry Fields at My Back

Exchange student. My first time farther away than two streets to the left and the first right. My first time farther away than Essen. My first time. Keep your eyes, ears, and nose open—they speak English here. Not just from eight to eight-fifty; here they speak English, sleep English, say hello or say nothing, stroll or read English. London. A soot-covered wedding cake. A tower of turrets and Thames, courtyard gardens and sixpence, please. I measure the town on foot. I pick flowers in the park and books in the libraries. Good heavens, it's a hot summer, and the city is a stone desert. Melting in London. Not a tree, a child, a car—only wads of newspaper and stone, and the madness of similarity. Everything in duplicate, everything the same, a drunken city in one hundred editions. The city is a long, an endless park, an endless Thames, an endless Big Ben, with a crooked map. That building over there is the Royal Concert Hall. I brush the dust from my lips. I am dirty, bedraggled, dusty; I have been transformed into Eliza.

She calls me love. *Thin as a rail, with gray threads wound tight around her pointy head. She calls me* love *and adores Shakespeare. The school's tennis courts lie before me.*

Just choose. What would you like to do?

No, I'm not Prince Hamlet. We're under milkwood. Every morning we pray for three-quarters of an hour that God may save the Queen.

Just choose. Poems or drama, art or music.

Going to school without coercion. How hard that is for me. And I feel lost in the libraries. I only know my Hamburg books, and they were all from some list I had been given. At home I couldn't go astray; everything was neatly selected and lined up. But here? What does England mean to me? A step toward freedom. I'm grown up. I don't have to curtsey anymore, to smile, to say yes. I learn to say no. No—that's London. It consists of baklava, dripping with honey, and foaming tea-rose cider.

Take whatever you need.

I learn to take whatever I need. School is a university of freedom, a bowler of amiability. And how do I feel? As happy as the pigeons in Trafalgar Square. I get fed. And when I'm no longer hungry, I fly away.

How shocking! Her name is Christine Keeler, and she leads into temptation. The BBC boasts of its telescopic vision. And Minister Profumo steps in the direction one usually steps in England—down. What do you think of all this? The cocktails are poured higher, the voices foam a little louder, and the scandal tonics are handed around. In my family's park, in the house of the Commander of Kent, the horsey society whispers, with horses and strawberry fields at its back. And a German girl gets handed around. How nice to see you.

I was over there once after the war.

Aren't you ashamed to be German?

Laughter. It was only a joke. But we do hate the Nazis, you know.

Hello, Heike!

That's Michael coming for five o'clock tea. He comes high on his horse, to see Michela, the daughter of the house. He will stay late, as usual. And Michela's parents will be out visiting friends, as usual. And that night there will be shouting and a my daughter scene with doors banging and a crisply toasted good morning the next day. A reproach to me. I should be having an affair, too; perhaps that's it. Then Milady would not have to weep her society tears over these premarital evenings.

98

You see, we don't approve of such things. We care about our daughter.

How's medical school? I ask. I ask that every time Mike comes, high on his horse. We have nothing to say to each other. We always ask each other the same questions. Soon he will be a doctor, with a rich inheritance. Soon she will be the doctor's wife, Mrs. Michela Doctor; the rings have already been purchased. Just the last hurdle of her graduation, and the moment will have come. He smiles at me. He dashes into the vast kitchen, dashes through the rock garden into our palatial kitchen, a house in itself, with a suite of back rooms. Milady is brewing the tea, and in an instant Michela is hanging on his neck with affianced eyes. She is dreaming of babies and caresses. I go to fetch the cookies. The chocolate ones, Michela calls after me. I turn around, Of course, and Mike says, I'm coming, too. I'm thirsty for something cold. He smiles at me. We have known each other for months, smile distance at each other. Two in the pantry. He pushes the door shut with his foot. Does he want to nibble sugar? He pulls the big silver canister with the chocolate cookies down from the shelf for me.

Here's the cherry juice.

He takes the bottle from my hand and pushes me up against a shelf. A kiss, he says. Mike, we hear from outside, Come quick. Coming, he says, takes his cherry juice and a kiss, and goes. Goes where one usually goes in England—back. To Michela and Milady. And the tea is sweet and the sun is warm, and before us spreads a park of a garden. Mike smiles at me and holds Michela's hand. I keep out of his way. I don't want to see him.

Listen. Time passes. With Sinbad the Sailor and Captain Cat. The spring days of under milkwood pass amidst essays and grades. Grades for Germany. For a few wandering waves of hair, for a brown gathered silk dress, for a clubfootlike girls' Germany. Soon I have to go back. But for the moment I am still playing the cello in English and singing Heigh-Ho the Giant in the choir. How would you like to go to a party?

My English cello sister pokes me with her elbow. That'd be great, I whisper and climb to gigantic soprano heights. Heigh-Ho.

Into the country by car. Around eight o'clock. The party is taking place somewhere beyond Hollingbourne. An architect's family with a country house set in a half-abandoned garden and a son being groomed for Cambridge. What a house! This is where Anne Boleyn was caught hiding out with her lover and executed by Henry the Eighth. England's secrets are whispered into my ear amidst murals painted by the family

99

and glass mosaic inlays on tables and chests. And as I am on my way to the mirror, between two dances, two parents approach me in the hallway and invite me to visit them. You seem to like music, says a small gray haired gentleman with a mustache and a French smile.

This is Miriam, my wife.

Somewhat hesitantly I shake hands with her. She reminds me of Madonna Plath, without the centaur's body: black haired, delicately friendly. And this is Lawrence.

I turn. He strolls slowly out of the room where the party is going on—brown curls, corduroy gait, beige and sheepish.

We would like you to join us for a concert.

Aha, the son of the house. I hadn't noticed him up to now. I had said hallo to everybody, and they had all gone fuzzy among the hallo's. Why are these parents approaching me? I don't know them. They don't know me.

He told us about you. They explain it to me between Handel and Mozart. In the balcony at the concert hall. What a strange Lawrence. At the party he did not say a word to me. We do not even know each other, yet he sics his parents on me, and I say yes. Actually it was the father. He complimented me, invited me, wooed me for his son. And Mrs. Miriam smiles, and Lawrence's brothers and sisters climb oaks and beeches with me. Penny is eight and John has just turned twelve. I am seventeen, Lawrence nineteen. Ouch! Damn these branches! We skin our knees in Anne Boleyn's park.

They come for me every day after school. Not for cocktails and horseback riding. They invite me to home concerts, to help them paint murals on their walls, to go to the theater—resounding rhetoric on Shakespeare's all-the-world stage. And at my side Lawrence gradually learns to talk. He reads Mansfield stories aloud to me. He paints pictures for me. He buys me ice cream, flowers. Kent is an endless park, an endless stroll, an endless conversation. Lawrence likes to hear me talk. It's the first time anyone has wanted to listen to me. To hear what I think, what I like, the first time anyone has wanted to read books to me, to do everything in my company. Without any sort of coercion. With the generosity of one in love, Lawrence spins me into his web. With his brown curls thrown back, love falling down onto his neck.

Tomorrow, before you leave, we're having company. A Polish girl who's visiting the Smiths.

She is blond, a relative of the Smiths from next door, the woman a blue-flowered chatterer, the man a quiet pipe smoker. We are sitting in the Smiths' garden. Lawrence and I and the Polish girl Jovana, who is searching for summer in Kent. She does not speak to me except to say hallo. Then she talks about Poland, which seems to consist only of school and art class, clothing and pocket money. She has steel blue eyes. She looks past me, through me, under me, to the side of me.

And how are things at Dachau?

She says this suddenly, as she is leaving, after the good-byes and handshakes. She speaks fluent German.

I'm going upstairs now.

She drops my hand like a piece of garbage. Lawrence is staring at me. Mrs. Smith has no idea what is going on and just gazes on the scene through green eye shadow.

What do you mean, Dachau?

Jovana bears down upon me, her head very close to mine, her eyes ready to spring.

I hate Germans, especially you!

She says this loudly, in English. Not another word in German. Only loud, hard, cutting English.

I know all about your cities. I know what the real capital of your country is! It's not Berlin or Bonn, it's Auschwitz! Your parliament convenes in Maidanek, in Theresienstadt, in Oranienburg. Don't look at me that way! You come from Nazi country, from murder country!

It wasn't me! I didn't do it!

I shout at her. I scream at Jovana. I shout back. I didn't do it!

I want to spit at you, little Nazi!

Jovana turns and runs into the house, and I begin to sob, right in front of blue-flowered Mrs. Smith, Lawrence, the English tea setting. I have a Jewish girl friend, a Jewish best friend. I have Judith back in Germany. I didn't do anything!

Lawrence puts his arm around me, comforts his sobbing Germany. He brings his weeping Germany to the train station. I travel back to Auschwitz, to Maidanek and Oranienburg. With Shakespeare in my suitcase and many exams passed and my poems printed in English in the school newspaper. I return. I would rather stay in England, but they send me home. They simply dismiss me.

SCENE 34. INTERIOR. DAYTIME. OFFICE BUILDING IN DOWNTOWN HAMBURG. LONG SHOT. A REVOLVING DOOR THROUGH WHICH GEBHARDT ENTERS THE LOBBY. THE OFF-SCREEN NARRATION BEGINS. GEBHARDT GOES TO THE ELEVATOR, RIDES TO THE FOURTH FLOOR. HE HAS TO PERSUADE THE RECEPTIONIST TO LET HIM WAIT. A SECRETARY APPEARS. HE FOLLOWS HER DOWN LONG CORRIDORS TO HERMANN KNAUER'S SMALL OFFICE. Böhm has made an appointment for Gebhardt. Böhm himself plans to drop by. Böhm plans to drop by from his probationary-year office. Taking the elevator to the fourth floor. And then the first door on your right. And please get the receptionist to announce you. And then down the hallway, for he is ready to contribute something. Böhm has taken the plunge. Böhm has revealed the secret path to his boss. Böhm has made an appointment for Gebhardt with *his* newsmagazine. Böhm has asked for an audience. Böhm has acted. Even though Böhm is still in his probationary year, he has acted. The carpet is soft and the Scotch is hard. HERMANN KNAUER asks the gentleman in. The chair is hard, and HERR KNAUER speaks softly. Speaks a soft, fluid German. HERMANN KNAUER invites the gentleman to have a seat. And BÖHM slips into the room late. Late by a few minutes of audience, he cautiously sits down on a folding chair and holds his breath, for his superior has asked them in. Well then. RAINER GEBHARDT begins. CHEERS! Rainer Gebhardt has the floor. Rainer Gebhardt wants to reduce the number of undecideds. Rainer Gebhardt wants to win them over to democracy. Wants to transform them into republicans. The lukewarms. It is a matter of the lukewarms, who never join any political party. Who vote every four years on command. Who have still not grasped that democracy is not simply a layer of paint under which the termites can continue to gnaw away. KNAUER listens. His white brushed curls crisp gently over his head. Perhaps Knauer has already reached fifty. Perhaps Knauer was involved at one time. Was also an active democrat at one time. Was also ready at one time, and in the process has turned fifty and become managing editor of a magazine that has educated and investigated and informed, in an effort to make republicans out of those who just read the newspaper all the time and nod knowingly. And say, Yes, yes. And say, Tut, tut. And say, That's bad, very bad. Who after twenty years of the magazine still just read the newspaper and never lift a finger. Read the newspaper and say, That's bad, very bad. Another attempt, says KNAUER. Another attempt to stir up this mass of apathy. Another idealist, KNAUER tells

102

GEBHARDT. Forty-three-year-old Gebhardt, who at eight shouted DEATH TO THE JEWS and now would like to do something. Something that would amount to more than just three square meals a day and seven hours of sleep. But go ahead and try, says KNAUER, Go right ahead, and withdraws into the citadel of his years. His fifty years. His managing-editor years, taken up with yes-yes people and bad-bad readers, and print-fixated democrats, who read and read and never lift a finger. A little contribution to help launch the project. GEBHARDT thinks, a little contribution for people who want to do more than just read. For people who want to learn democracy. A little club democracy. Well, a little contribution to help you get started, KNAUER says. Yes, a little contribution, says GEBHARDT. And the managing editor with the hard Scotch offers three times six hundred marks. Offers six hundred marks for each month. Offers three times six hundred for the beginning. And WINFRIED BÖHM, who has not drawn a breath for ages, sits there white-faced on his chair and learns what it feels like to suffocate. Three times six hundred. What do you think? And what do you think of this club? And the whole undertaking? What do you think, Herr Böhm. WINFRIED BÖHM lays his palms together. The managing editor is asking him a question. The teacher who will promote him from Class 34. BÖHM chokes on what is left of his schoolboy throat. BÖHM, always exemplary in behavior, rasps out, I don't have an opinion. I am an employee here. I really can't say anything. The thirty-nine-year-old schoolchild Winfried really can't say anything. The thirty-nine-year-old republican child doesn't want to say anything at all. He just wants to sit there quietly. A cheerful, friendly disposition. And KNAUER pulls out his checkbook. And KNAUER thinks about the yes-yes people. And KNAUER writes out three times six hundred, and glances at RAINER GEBHARDT in between. RAINER GEBHARDT, who is thinking that one should establish a republican club to win Böhm over to the Republican Club from the Republican Club.

Now Jus' Repeat after Me, Honey
. . . at a horse fair, perhaps at Haymarket . . .
  Please say Haymarket more emphatically. Go on!
  . . . where other objects are transformed to wares . . .
  Wares! Let's hear the w clearly! Go on!

. . . a hungry poet brought one time . . .

I guess I had better read it to you myself. Listen carefully, now! Peg-a-sus in yoke . . .

The room resounds. Vera Zirkel, the German and history teacher of Class IIa, is reading aloud. By herself. That she insists on. She always begins by saying, You, let me hear you read, using the informal mode of address although everyone else uses the formal with us by now. But soon she asserts that she had better read it herself, either as monologue or as dialogue. And if we are reading a play, Vera takes all the parts, becomes the embodiment of the play. A play with sixty-four characters. Vera could handle that with her left hand. *I guess I had better read it to you myself.* Zirkel—a circle that encompasses the world.

I hardly knew her before my trip to England. Occasionally I would see her creeping along the glass connectors, the type of person who looks very tall sitting down, with stumpy legs, long arms, and in her right hand the largest and heaviest briefcase in the entire school. A stone of knowledge that dragged along the floor. A longish face that grew longer and longer from all the briefcase-dragging. A little black knot of tightly drawn-back hair—that was Vera Zirkel.

Now I had returned from England. Centaur Plath was gone, and Vera Zirkel sat towering before me. A melancholy bogey man, I thought, or a lizard. A melancholy bogeylizard with hairy, large scaled skin.

Now jus' repeat nicely after me, honey.

A buddy? A colleague? Her little black-dotted pores, each spiked on a dark hair, eye me suspiciously. Chalk-white flabby folded skin, like a loosely stretched clothesline. Like two or three clotheslines with a face hung out to dry. Frau Dr. Zirkel.

My first composition for her. *Lying is permissible; lying is never permissible. Discuss and contrast these two contentions!*

She uses the formal mode of address only when standing at the blackboard. In private she likes to slip into Low German dialect. And she has cut off her bun! She's become a Beatle, with long black bangs, puffed out around the ears. A squashed, aging Beatle. And I, honey, am supposed to find the Golden Mean in the topic she has set us. Am supposed to come up with some juicy composition platitudes. I decide to write what I really think. *Heavens! You can't say that! There are no wholly unambiguous concepts.*

D!

Off I had gone to England with a good centaur report card. Qualified for the student exchange by many B's and a big fat A in German.

D!

How easy it is to slip and fall. A change of teachers equals a change of grades. But no one admits that fact.

No, this is objectively wrong, my dear. One really cannot assert that. There are some concepts that are clearly unambiguous. For instance loyalty and truth and maternal love. Think of your dear mother. No, objectively one really cannot assert that.

Frau Dr. Rautenfeld shows me very subjectively to the door.

Does Frau Dr. Zirkel know that you are here to see me? No? You mean to act behind her back?

She looks at me witheringly. Legs spread, stocky, floor conscious.

I just wanted to ask . . .

No, my dear, that is sneaky. Hush! Don't start crying again! You must start to work on yourself now. England does tend to bring out the worst in young girls. I'm crossing my fingers for you.

I see brown gathered fingers. Good heavens, how tearful and streaky faced I look. To the teachers' lounge. Yes, that's the solution. Hello, Frau Schopek. Curtsey. Hello, Frl. Stiller, called Frau Stiller. Curtsey. Curtsey. Yes, thank you. Thank you very much. Thanks ever so much. Yes, I'll wait here. Yes, yes, yes. I'm not grown up. I have to curtsey again, smile, say yes. I learn to say yes again. It is two-thirty. The others went home long ago. I am still sobbing, am sobbing again, will sob some more in a moment.

Fräulein Plath, look, please read this.

She sits there facing me and reads.

I just don't understand, Fräulein Plath!

Madonna Plath reads on and keeps silent.

You were the only one of my teachers for whom I could write. Express my own thoughts. You see?

Frl. Plath sits there and keeps silent.

You should speak to Frau Dr. Zirkel for me. Just this once. You don't think this composition is so bad, do you?

She nods, strokes my hair, and keeps silent.

Frau Dr. Zirkel won't discuss it with me. She simply says, Don't get hysterical over your D! Look, this is Jutta's composition. I copied out the beginning special because it's a B. Look! Lying is bad. One should

105

always speak the truth, even in life. *That's so banal! Please, Fräulein Plath. In life—what's that supposed to mean?*

Frl. Plath sits there and keeps silent.

Please, speak to her just this once. I did so much better for you. If I get a D in the course, I won't pass, and then I'll have to quit school!

Good luck, says Frl. Plath, called Frau Plath, and shakes hands with me. I have to go now, says Frl. Plath, called Frau Plath, and says not a word. On my way home I hear her behind me. Her heels clattering. She crosses over to the other side of the street in order to pass me.

SCENE 35. INTERIOR. EVENING. FOUR-ROOM APARTMENT OF DR. FRENZEL (SEE SCENE 21). SCENE OPENS WITH CLOSE-UP OF A BATTERY OF BEER BOTTLES AND A SAUCER FULL OF CHANGE. Run politics up the flagpole. Lower politics from the flagpole. The actors are coming. They are already at the door. Crowding in beside each other, behind each other. Come in, come in, enter the bottle citadel, the hall of teak delights. Where we can have privacy. Be by ourselves. In an appropriate setting. IRENE FRENZEL has waxed and polished everything. Hair curled, dress ironed. HERR DR. FRENZEL has tidied up, his children in bed and his television feet tucked into warm pale yellow woolen socks. The little plate for beer dues stands ready on the pretzel-stick table. Come in, come in. The calculating hosts cordially invite you to join in peanut chat. A rolled R, a throaty K, are already seated. They call for a hissing Z, for Zambia, Zeppelin, Xylophone. And even PETER SEEBERG has come, straight from the City Theater premiere—furrowed with effort. His hair is receding from sheer intelligence. Even HELMUT DONNER has put in an appearance today. A television bust between Schiller and Brecht. Always ready to come at you through the tube, to take a friendly chunk out of any text you hold out to him. Come, Sultan, eat! Helmut Donner, a white giant's head. An expandable balloon into which any author can pump his texts. IRENE FRENZEL pokes her glasses up on her nose, directs her cashier's gaze straight ahead. And GEBHARDT thinks of role-playing exercises. A step to the left and a step to the right. For the royalties with Stalin for Kennedy against Ché, and vice versa. HELMUT DONNER speaks out in favor of street theater. HELMUT DONNER says, I'm for it. We must support the young people. And PETER SEEBERG nods his head from side

106

to side. And the acting students hold their breath, because the big star is nodding his bald head, while the beginners rush to get chairs and pillows for Peter Seeberg, so Mirabeau can sit comfortably. I don't know, I don't know, the great Seeberg says, Whether we shouldn't keep out of this after all. Whether it isn't better to leave it to laymen, to school kids and students. Whether we wouldn't do better, much better. And GEBHARDT already knows that SEEBERG is for others' doing something, for others' doing everything, all those others who are not called Seeberg. Who, to be sure, is also for youth, because youth happens to be in. Because youth is so charmingly youthful. Who would also, but. Better to stay here and keep out of it. I don't know, I don't know. HERR SEEBERG looks over at the students, who are sitting in a circle on the floor. And HANNES PECHSTEIN, the young spokesman, chief of the tribe of acting students, Hannes Pechstein calls out, Even so, you should do something. You especially, Herr Seeberg, should get involved. GEBHARDT knows Hannes Pechstein. RAINER GEBHARDT knows why Pechstein is so bold, so eager today. Hannes Pechstein works for radio occasionally. Hannes Pechstein occasionally reads Rainer Gebhardt's scripts, which Rainer Gebhardt occasionally gives him to read. And because Gebhardt occasionally employs him, Hannes Pechstein is occasionally employed. Street theater, HANNES PECHSTEIN says, Street theater is the only true theater. It's theater not just for an elite minority, but for the amorphous masses, the man in the street. It challenges him to think, to discuss, to act out. The open street should be our favorite stage. That's where we can still accomplish something as actors. And PECHSTEIN looks over at GEBHARDT. And GEBHARDT is supposed to think, what a bright young man, eager to become involved, involved in my cause, in his cause. And GEBHARDT thinks, four whole hundred marks. And tomorrow I'm dropping my membership in the club. And the day after tomorrow Pechstein will follow suit, already believing in the day after the day after tomorrow, just as boldly and just as decisively. And will speak out against the meaningless street theater project, which only produces self-gratification, which is only seemingly revolutionary and helps no one. And then tired old Seeberg will turn out to have been right after all. Just as all tired and cowardly people always do—they always prove right, because they never get involved, and those who do get involved don't get involved either. And GEBHARDT looks over at SEEBERG, this hero by Aimé Césaire's grace, who fights evening after evening for the liberation of the Congo in return for a nice check. And evening after evening incites the public against exploitation and colonialism, and all for a measly five thousand marks a month. And he hears SEEBERG saying, We won't get anywhere by approaching people on the street if they don't want to have to think anyway. SEEBERG takes a deep breath, and SEEBERG exhales his deep breath. And HELMUT DONNER is already thinking about tomorrow. HELMUT DONNER already has his doubts, and is not coming out so strongly in favor of street theater. Not as strongly as before. With fully inflated principles. With a sharp Z, a clear A, a hard T, and a brief D. And that's the cue for PECHSTEIN to get out his sentence, All right, we'll do it on our own. And the flock of young acting students nods. Their Hamlet curls fall crisp and lean over their Beckett brows. The girls' Ophelia locks glide lyrically over their Saunders shoulders. And IRENE is already passing around a list. And IRENE is already nodding encouragingly to PECHSTEIN, for PECHSTEIN would be someone she could take an excursion to the Baltic with; the boy is really fantastically good-looking. And HERR DONNER exhales his theatrical breath. HERR DONNER collapses smoothly and agilely, and dissolves. GEBHARDT hears him slither through the keyhole. And SEEBERG murmurs, I admire young people. Especially our rebellious young people of today. And SEEBERG strokes his bald pate, winds his watch punctually, assumes the perpendicular. Good-bye, good-bye. I have to be at a rehearsal first thing in the morning. First thing. First thing. Bye-bye. And there are two names on the list. Two for Gebhardt. Hannes Pechstein and Susanna Pechstein. For what does man live by? But the others will think it over. And if they have not died, they are living yet. Thirty-four, says IRENE. Well, thirty-four at any rate. And DR. FRENZEL arranges empty bottles in the case. GEBHARDT knows that in a minute he will total up the take. In a moment it will come out to exactly twenty-seven marks twenty. Twenty-seven marks twenty, FRENZEL calls into the kitchen. And IRENE, who is already rinsing her glasses, calls from amidst the detergent billows to GEBHARDT, Bye, your Pechstein is cool. He'll do all right for himself. Yes, GEBHARDT thinks, and presses the button for the elevator, he'll do all right for himself. This is Channel 3 with its series "Current Events: Discussion, Analysis, Commentary." Today's installment by Rainer Gebhardt is entitled "Revolution in the Sign of a Consumer Society." Narration by Hannes and Susanna Pechstein.

108

An Oven for Bad Students

The Rolling Stones are blaring out of every powder puff. Saturday night at the Rock Barn with Christopher. Located in St. Pauli, the red-light district. In hell. An oven for bad students. The good ones stay home and help mother wash the dishes. Keep on running. Beat with soul, and a necking signal when the light turns red and the band dissolves in music. We react like robots. When the light goes white again—mouths apart! Our feelings are painted by the changing lights. I want to be an actor, Christopher groans in the hot, sweaty, comfortable rock crowd. Simple. I'm giving up dentistry. He wipes the first-semester sweat from his brow. An electric guitar is summoning him to art.

But what about your parents?!

What?

Your parents!!!

We shout happily at each other. We are doing what most people gave up long ago—talking to each other. We shout old-fashionedly instead of just jerking our arms and legs dully and silently around the room. We are out.

All around us Daddy's well-behaved little boys are hopping up and down, enjoying their liberation. They are pounding the brain out of their legs, trampling their complexes underfoot. Their preferred partners seem to be sluttish salesgirls with mountains of teased hair, their bosoms ordered from the catalogue. They are silently ecstatic. The institutions of higher learning are mixing with the masses. Here Plato gives way to Coke.

What about your parents???

Today our parents are not holding office hours. Have a good time. They provide us with three square meals a day. Zippadeedooda. We are in. They pour the syrup of selfishness into our little sugar mouths. Be my sunshine, hippadeeyaa. They are fattening us into young people who will do their bit and frolic obediently in the space between Troll's Latin Grammar and Bartels's The Major Powers with plenty of yeah-yeah-yeah. You're a love of mine. The band is playing a slow number now. And to keep from melting in each other's arms, we sit down for Coke and Cheese-its.

An actor. What a strange goal in life.

What do you mean, goal in life?

I mean, always dissembling.

How so? It's better to do it professionally than to do it without getting the applause you deserve.

How so?

Well, we have to stoop and duck constantly. First in school. You kowtow your way through to graduation. Then you have to lick your professors' boots. You push and shove your way over corpses, making sure to remember to invite your professor to dinner, just so things work out well for you.

I don't get it. What do you believe in then?

What do you believe in?

Well, I believe one should . . .

. . . lie as honestly as our parents? With Nazi underwear and postwar street clothes? I tell you, the thing we West Germans need is to take a firm stand against Communism. And meanwhile forty million people are starving to death in any given year. Great, isn't it? What a life!

Christopher must read the Spiegel. I'm sure of it. Frau Dr. Zirkel always says that people who read the Spiegel do nothing but criticize, drag everything in the mud.

Say, do you read the Spiegel?

What do you mean?

Just that. And besides, there's no point.

In what?

In being an actor. You still won't get away from all those things.

But at least I won't be deceiving others. Only myself. I'd rather be Prince Hamlet in Nowheresville than a dentist in Hamburg who fills the holes in old Nazis' teeth so they can march off to the East again with their golden crowns flashing.

But . . .

That's the truth! Do you think they don't have something special in mind when they say areas under Polish administration and refer to Berlin as the former capital of the Reich? Do you think they say East Zone just for fun? Why do you suppose they refuse to recognize the Oder-Neisse Line? They all want to go back. Reunification with jolly postwar flags. A nice little third world war. I prefer to pull my support out from under this scarecrow country and be happy Horatio. And what do you believe in? You just want to have it good.

Ultraviolet shirts swirl in the draft from the door. Let's shake, cries a black curled monster in a gold silk suit with a black patent leather gaze.
110

And Christopher Bond and Heike Lane, twisting in the Rock Barn, admit that they don't believe in anything. Perhaps in themselves, but even that is uncertain.

SCENE 36. INTERIOR. EVENING. IN THE LATE NINETEENTH-CENTURY VILLA. A SMALL MEETING ROOM, LARGE ENOUGH FOR TWENTY TO THIRTY PEOPLE. CAMERA FROZEN. LONG SHOT, VERY HIGH ANGLE. ALL THOSE IN THE ROOM, ABOUT TWENTY, ARE SITTING MOTIONLESS, LIKE FIGURES IN A WAXWORKS. DURING THE NARRATION MORE AND MORE FIGURES LEAP FORWARD IN A FREEZE-FRAME EFFECT, SOMETIMES SINGLY, SOMETIMES IN GROUPS. WHEN ONLY FOUR ARE LEFT IN THE ROOM, THE FREEZE-FRAME TECHNIQUE DISSOLVES INTO MOTION. TO hear them talk, they're all with you. The blond guy, who sends his regrets. Alex Sommer, who simply doesn't show. To hear them talk, they're all IN. All the students are IN. Two hundred students are IN. Two hundred fifty members are IN. Today they're giving a Godard at the University. Today the LIVING THEATER is in town. Tonight I have a date with a cool chick. Out. Out. Out. Frenzel sends his regrets. Grützmann can't make it today. Böhm sends his regrets. Ever since they've had what they were all asking for, the study groups, all of them have been sending their regrets. In-in. In-out. Out-out. Drop in and drop out. Two weeks ago there were two. The two from the time before. Tonight there are three. But the two from last time are not here. And the three from tonight will not be here when two people come two weeks from now. Then the two and the three will no longer be here. Study group on unions. Established by special request. My name is Gebhardt. Pleased to meet you, I'm Henning. My name is Stiebler. Pleased to meet you. I'm Armgart. GEBHARDT doesn't know any of them, and none of them know Gebhardt. Gebhardt does not have to make excuses for Böhm. Either for Böhm or Frenzel. That's not necessary. And next time Gebhardt won't explain why Stiebler is not there. Stiebler or Armgart. That's not necessary. Perhaps some time. And Dr. Hauswald will come, too. Workers and students, students and workers—that's the main thing, says Dieter Biehl, who isn't here. We have to start with fundamentals, says Herr Sommer, who is away this week. They mustn't be allowed to draw even farther apart, says HERR STIEBLER; They mustn't be allowed to batten on their troubles by

111

communicating with each other. Like the SDS, says HERR ARMGART. Like students in general, says HERR STIEBLER. That's our chief problem: students and the working population. Yes, that's true, says HERR ARMGART. Yes, certainly, says HERR HENNING. Really true, says HERR HENNING. I'm from Kiel, says HERR HENNING. I'm studying sociology and history. This is my first time at the club, and I speak on behalf of my fellow students who unfortunately couldn't be here tonight. But they think the same as we do. Just the same. CUT.

Zir & Kel

She lives on Schlüterstrasse. Right around the corner, Hamburg's Chamber Theater rings with cries meant to drown out the shame of Marathon. She lives in a tall apartment house with high turn-of-the-century windows. Frau Dr. Zirkel, with a little strip of garden out front and a wrought iron avenue. She lives in Hamburg's Berlin, with children rolling hoops and velvet curtains hoisted in honor of Bismarck.

I know the house well. Many's the time I've slunk around my homeroom teacher's building. Baumgart, Wiese, Liebermann. Porcelain cupids stretching their fat little dust-gathering fingers through Florentine drapes. The family of Prof. Kneibel has its windowsill decorated. I know the house well. I know my way around it. For the past two weeks Vera Zirkel has been storming into the classroom with Persian battle cries. Here we have the Chamber Theater of Marathon. The cry rings down Schlüterstrasse, The army of the Persians is destroyed. And she plays all the parts in all the plays for as long as they remain in the repertory. At the moment she is Atossa.

The Persians are coming, I think one afternoon at four. A paperback classic is firmly clamped under my arm. I left it on my desk in school. And since you live so near, you might as well bring it to me, honey.

A telephoned order. I don't live nearby. But I come up the lofty, cold old staircase. With steep temple steps. A heaven-and-hell mystery play. It goes dark again. I cautiously feel my way toward the light button again, before Frau Bläske catches me. And another floor. The light only stays on a few seconds. Dr. Zirkel. A little card. A thumbtack name. Zir/kel. Divided in two. The bell hisses like a cat. A shuffling of feet. I clutch the book in my hand. A narrow crack in the door. Atossa blinks at me from beneath the chain.

112

Hello, Frau Dr. Zirkel.

Good, good. Come in, honey.

She opens her chain. Entrance gratis. A hexagonal lobby, bald, unlived in, cleared out. She's been planning to move for the past fifty years. The walls are already peeling away. Cold electric wires, the innards of a ceiling, and no lighting fixture. She plucks at my coat sleeve. A hopping, leaping little dog out for a walk with mistress.

Well, I suppose he's waiting downstairs with a bouquet of roses.

No, I say, and stare into an empty, hollowed-out room.

When I was young, it had to be roses.

She pulls me into one of her cavernous rooms. Some day her black turtleneck will draw her into the ground. My teacher, with blue embroidered harem slippers. She leans against the wall. Living room, I suppose one would call this. Parlor. Frau Dr. Zirkel has invited me into her parlor. With bare walls and narrow strips of light. Last crevices of daylight, shining steeply through drawn, mouse-gray curtains. There is not quite enough material to completely cover the windows. A fragile, creaking wicker chair. I sit down. We want our good old Kaiser Wilhelm back. The rolled up, dark red sausage there in the corner. There might be a Kaiser inside, with muttonchop whiskers and stand-up collar.

How did you spend your Easter vacation?

I ask into the silence, hoping that Frau Zirkel can be found somewhere within it.

I drew the curtains and draped covers over the mirrors. I lay in bed until school opened again.

In bed. That must be that looming, high-legged oak monster in the corner, surrounded by teacarts stacked with books. The light is growing dimmer. Bit by bit I take in the room. No pictures, no shelves. Might there be cats slinking around, too?

Well, is he waiting downstairs?

Who?

Your sweetheart.

No, I say, and accept a cardboard cookie. On my left the outside of the wardrobe is hung with clothes. Zirkel underwear on a line from the door hinges to a hook in the wall.

Frau Doktor, do sit down.

Only now do I notice that the room contains but one chair, and I am sitting on it.

Never mind, honey, comes a hoarse croak from the wall. I'll just lean against here. That works fine.

Those teacarts must be very practical?

A meager conversation.

My library is next door.

I tiptoe after her. Into the teacart room. And there is a cat here, and teacarts piled high with literary freight. Like railroad cars parked on a factory siding.

My movable bookshelves.

She giggles. She plucks at my cuff. She does not invite me to take off my coat. She reaches for my hand, pulls me across the leached vestibule into the clothes room.

This is more practical. I can get at everything more quickly. That's better. Before I get the wardrobe open. Do sit down. That's better.

A guttering light appears. A three-bubbled standing lamp spreads its forty-five-watt brilliance through the Zirkel chamber.

What do you plan to become when you're older?

She sits down in the wicker chair. Now I am standing facing her, looming like a giant.

And the longer I look at her, the glassier her eyes become and the more drooping her mouth, her clothesline folds.

Maybe a doctor, I say with forced cheerfulness, to give myself courage.

I adored art history, she says. Twelve whole years I devoted to it. It was the exams. I always had to leave my seat before the walls fell in on me, the ceiling. They were racing toward me, faster and faster.

She bangs her elbows on her tile table. The cookies begin to jiggle.

It was the walls. Thank you for visiting me, child. I know you don't like me.

No, I say, and look down at a little hunched-over frog with chalked lids. The place seems empty. All that lives here is Zirkel. Zir & Kel, a fragmented image. I hand her the book.

Oh, you can keep it.

She crawls out of her chair.

It wasn't very important.

Once in the bare hallway, she pushes me out the door. With a bye-bye, honey, Vera the Circle slips the chain back into its groove.

114

SCENE 37. INTERIOR. EVENING. IN THE LATE NINETEENTH-CENTURY VILLA. A SECOND WORKROOM THAT HOLDS TWENTY OR THIRTY PEOPLE. LONG SHOT FROM EYE LEVEL. CAMERA, BEHIND GEBHARDT'S BACK, TURNING EXTRA-SLOW, 16 FRAMES PER SECOND. AT THE END OF THE OFF-SCREEN NARRATION, WHEN ALL TWENTY HAVE GATHERED, CUT AND NORMAL ROTATIONAL SPEED. Gebhardt has invited them as representatives of the church. He has invited them so they can form the study group on the church. So they can launch a common undertaking of brotherly love. The twenty one-shoulds, if-one-only-coulds, if-one-only-hads. The progressive men whose names everyone mentioned. Whom Böhm had jotted down in his address book. All of whom Frenzel knew by name. Whom Biehl had summoned telephonically. And all of whom have put in an appearance. All twenty of them. It is impossible to overlook, RAINER GEBHARDT is saying, The role the church could play within the extraparliamentary opposition movement. First of all because it does not harbor any aspirations to political power, but is concerned rather with the self-realization of the individual within the community. And second, because it constitutes an oppositional force within any system of government, thanks to its purely humanitarian ideals. GEBHARDT is lecturing. Lecturing on basic principles. Lecturing before spiritual shepherds, nineteen Protestants and one Catholic. Twenty individual cornerstones, twenty rocks of faith are sitting in a circle, dangling their legs. Six smoke pipes. Four are wearing jeans and colorfully embroidered linen shirts. To make sure no student misjudges them. To make sure that youth does not lose its faith, the REV. FERDINAND is chewing gum, popping it in his high holy mouth. A cool club, ONE OF THE PROGRESSIVES comments to GEBHARDT. Some cool cats you have here. He yanks up his progressive terry socks. He has dolled himself up youth style, is wearing an Indian silk scarf tie. And on the street in front of this swinging club stands a white convertible, crying for its daddy, who is playing church again today. Progressive, brightly colored terry church. One suit. Two suits. They all sit there mustering each other, with nothing to say. Is there more beer down cellar, FERDINAND asks, and GEBHARDT says, It's a question of expanding purely religious issues to take in general social issues. GEBHARDT is blowing conversation into the circle. Round and round. From chair to chair. DR. BÖRNE will only smoke Juno tobacco. DR. BÖRNE has brought his own Juno along. Dr. Börne knows what he likes. Dr. Börne likes Juno. DR. BÖRNE smokes Juno and looks down contentedly at his shoes. His brilliantly polished shoes. His high-salaried alligator shoes. The employees are here, GEBHARDT thinks. The employees of the Cross. Christ's sales personnel. The administrators of Christ's blood, sweat, and tears. It is a question of returning to the best tradition of Christianity, the revolutionary tradition of the church, GEBHARDT says. And the Holy Twenty stare straight ahead. Over the mouths of the beer bottles. Over the bowls of their pipes. And the REV. FERDINAND chews out, That's right. Yes, it's nice that we can all get together like this. Yes, it's a great idea, nods rolypoly DR. BÖRNE. Rolypoly little Dr. Börne, who makes everything into something nice. Who whispers, Damn, my stomach's growling. Who would so love to have a second dinner and is already secretly readying knife and fork to carve up his comfortable chair, to consume a delicate upholstery fricassee. Who would just love to polish off the whole study group, putting on even more pounds. For every pound is a pound for Christ. And if the REV. BACHHOF had not come, with his narrow, restless head, always circling, always circling with his service under his arm, I want to assure you right now, over the phone, I'll bring my service when I come on Monday, and if the REV. BACHHOF were not here, VIETNAM, BIAFRA, AND THE THIRD WORLD: WE WORKED THIS UP IN THE CONGREGATION, WE CALL IT AN INFORMATION SERVICE, and if BACHHOF did not have the text in his hand, and if BACHHOF did not pass the scripts around, LADIES AND GENTLEMEN, WE HAVE INVITED YOU TO THIS SERVICE SO WE CAN PONDER THE CAUSES OF POVERTY TOGETHER, and if the REV. BACHHOF didn't say, Solidarity with the world is solidarity in poverty, and the middle-class church lives beyond its means anyway and consumes more wealth, labor resources, and money than others have access to, if this BACHHOF did not swear up and down that almost all of Europe has fallen into the church's cheese-baited trap, And now we're in there, envied for the cheese but actually the ones who're trapped, if this minister did not explain unmistakably that The efforts of the progressive church capture the essence of that much-abused concept of revolution, since they aim for a revolution of awareness, a revolution that nowadays in the industrialized countries is the only possible preparation for an as yet unscheduled social revolution, if BACHHOF did not say all this, GEBHARDT would not be able to go on speaking to this circle of salesmen, with Jesus in their samples cases, stainless and durable and available in several price ranges. CUT.

116

Cornelia Thiele

Almost twice as tall as I, twice as blond, twice as slender. Cornelia Thiele, six seats away. A face knocked together out of bones, with a high, prominent Irma Hoffmann forehead. Large-pored complexion, clusters of blackheads, furrowed by a mighty nose with flared nostrils, cut across by a narrow mouth with engraved lines at the corners. Cornelia Thiele, with blond, freshly washed hair and a plastery dusting of makeup: a ceramic angel. Cornelia Thiele with stringy, unwashed hair, combed behind protruding ears or pulled up in a bun—a menacing Widow Bolte, the wicked mother-in-law of German fairy tales.

Cornelia's parents have money. She lives surrounded by a park, perched magnificently above the Elbe. Cornelia owns this and owns that and owns even more. Carpets from Persia, a marble fountain, a tea service from China, parklike grounds, statuary classicism. Cornelia the villa child also owns a mother and a brother, just by the bye, in addition to the Greek vase over there. Massive, gilded rights to all that is choice and expensive—that has been Cornelia's birthright from her first silken cradle howl on. Only three things stand in the way of her many-carated future as a society witch, dripping with jewels and destined to choke to death on a cocktail cherry: her persistence, her courage, her intelligence.

Why Cornelia contradicts, questions, and refuses to give in, why she is not poodle jolly and mink happy like her classmates, content with every C, satisfied to get by, slip through, squeak by with a D, why Cornelia is disruptive and asks Frau Plath what her opinion is and questions Frau Dr. Zirkel about her past when Frau Doktor calls the Russians animals, rushing from one world war to the next and speaking as if it were just the Russians, always the Russians involved, why Cornelia asks and asks and asks, questions the silence out of every classroom cranny and every teacher brain—I can find no explanation for this phenomenon, neither behind the wall tapestries nor at the bottom of the marble fountain of the Villa Thiele.

Cornelia's audacity has something lord-and-masterish about it, something plantation-ownerly, something ruling-classic. I have read Uncle Tom's Cabin and know that Cornelia cannot stand little Toms. Pariahs from employee families who have wandered by mistake into elegant Othmarschen. On these classmates Cornelia does not waste a glance. I don't understand how you can make friends with such simple girls, she scolds me on the way to school.

117

As the daughter of a doctor, I am accepted, but after me, the daughter of someone with a university education, Cornelia draws her recognition line. Anyone on the other side—well, of course one speaks to her, but Danger, pariahs! cautiously, distantly. The same class in school, but not the same class. Here Cornelia makes sharp distinctions. And even if I, already a junior, still do not know the difference between a Chinese teacup and an ordinary water glass, it is also true that Cornelia is right when she exclaims with her piercing smile, You know perfectly well what I mean!

I do know. I can guess what she means. But since I do not acknowledge this what, we never become best friends. Altona, rubble and camomile, rats, and the stench of beer from the little bar are still too firmly implanted in my front-lawn consciousness. My childhood hangs in giant spider webs behind the villa ghetto. I have had more dealings with water glasses than with Chinese teacups. I share neither Cornelia's scorn for pensioners, gardeners, hairdressers, and postmen, nor her unconditional admiration for nouveaux riches mansions, with bundles of stock certificates in the bookcases and carnations in the buttonholes. And nevertheless: Cornelia and I fight on the same schoolroom battlefront. I do not respect her pride, but I do respect her pluck. We make common cause against prefabricated opinions and teacherly megalomania. I am friends with her qualities, not with her views. I divulge to her teacher conversations which try to win me over in the hallways with dear child. I reveal to her that Frau Dr. Rautenfeld called me to the teachers' lounge and said, You're such a nice girl, you can get the class on your side, you can isolate Cornelia. I betray Frau Dr. Rautenfeld. I betray her to Cornelia, and Cornelia betrays her to me. Cornelia. You're such a nice girl. You can get the class on your side. You can . . .

Judith moved to the island of Amrun while I was in England, and now that Judith and I can no longer read history books together, Cornelia is the only one who joins me in asking difficult questions, in showing resistance. We work together. We decide that the Russians are not animals. We determine that Jesus, Son of God, is a man. We wander up and down in front of the bookcases in her villa. We compare the myths of various peoples, and Cornelia notes down Hellenic influences, Arab influences. Cornelia sketches out a system of coordinates. Cornelia and I compose a lengthy polemic. And since we know that our seventy pages will never be read, we record the text on tape, dividing the speaking parts

118

between us. Our efforts are in vain. Our critical examination of various religious dogmas disappears into the stomach of Frl. Friedrichs, called Frau Friedrichs, who has returned to us with clamor and inebriated senses, with hoyotoho and Wotan. She thanks us most cordially for our little project. Then nothing more is said. And the more often we inquire, and we inquire every time class meets, the sharper Frl. Friedrichs hones her shield of Christian faith. She, a Christian Wotan with actor's failure and a Biblical thing, is not willing even months later to tell us what has become of our bound text and our tape. Probably she devoured them both secretly during Holy Communion, for often when I see her in profile I think I can detect a tape reel, somewhat undigested, under the jersey swaddling of her stomach.

Soon we are forbidden even to inquire. Soon Frau Friedrichs threatens with thundering dispensations, and if Cornelia did not introduce the little cue word lawyer and plunge the whole school into icy terror, we would lose our privilege of sitting beneath Wotan's gaze. Telephone calls, letters, warnings. Not for nothing is Cornelia's brother studying law. Not for nothing do our mothers fight, the legal sword between their teeth. Not for nothing do a few grim letters guarantee us our impious, inalienable places in the class. And when the controversy finally blows over, everything is the way it always was. The Russians remain animals, and our joint project, which was supposed to be discussed in class, never sees the light of school. God Friedrichs remains unshaken, ensconced behind shield maidens and under the wings of our dear-girls amoeba. One crow does not peck out another's eyes. Amen.

SCENE 38. INTERIOR. EVENING. IN THE LATE NINETEENTH-CENTURY VILLA. THE SAME ROOM AS IN SCENE 36. THE FOUR MEN ARE STILL HOLDING THEIR MEETING. CAMERA, SET UP IN THE CENTER OF THE TABLE, PANS AT CLOSE-UP RANGE FROM FACE TO FACE. What is important, says HERR HENNING, is that the extraparliamentary opposition should become actively involved. That workers be brought together at meetings in the plant. That one get discussions going during the lunch break, so the workers' problems can finally be formulated accurately. HERR HENNING is making a speech. We must avoid taking a purely negative position, the STUDENT remarks. We must see that worker participation in decision-making becomes a reality, the STUDENT comments. The student from Kiel. Where of course things are not perfect yet. But still. Still, HERR HENNING says, We have one worker already. He's been coming for a whole year, HENNING says. Of course we haven't managed to get inside the plant yet, but our man is trying to persuade a few of his fellow workers to join us. Of course without success so far. But still. Still, HERR ARMGART says, You have a worker already. The contact, HERR HENNING says, Between us and the workers is the crucial matter. The real crux of the matter is to get workers interested in social questions, in their own situation. And we have to go about it in a practical fashion. Get away from theory. Theory doesn't interest the workers. That's true, says ARMGART. That's what I always say, too. Practice, practice. I'm a member of the factory's labor-management committee. We do everything in terms of practice. Perhaps, HERR STIEBLER says, One could start systematically approaching the worker comrades in their bars. Simply strike up a conversation with them. I always do that after work. I sit there and discuss various issues with them. It's better than handing out leaflets, HERR STIEBLER says. Leaflets only provoke the workers. And FELLOW WORKER ARMGART adds, Well, let's face it, Willy, you never get anywhere with your bar sessions. That's been so for years. I know the set-up too, you know. You bitch about things over a beer, but back at the plant no one opens his mouth to complain. You don't either, says STIEBLER. This is our study group on unions, GEBHARDT thinks. Two fellows from a labor-management committee and a student from Kiel. How much longer are you going to be here, DIETER BIEHL calls through the partly opened door. I'm just asking so I'll know when to lock up here. Another hour, GEBHARDT calls to him. Maybe another hour or so. And GEBHARDT asks STIEBLER about his factory; what factory are they both from? And STIEBLER, Herr Willy Stiebler, says softly, for both of them, We'd really rather not say. We just dropped by here. We just heard something about the club. And we just think that in general, not just in our plant, the workers should be drawn into the discussion. That's right, HERR HENNING says. The issue is to activate the masses in their own interest. That's what we're all concerned with here. We have to find really good people in each plant who can pick out the abuses. Who can really go at things from within the plant. And of course not working against the unions, but rather in concert with them. And how is that working in Kiel, ARMGART asks. Well, HENNING says, That's a long drawn-out process. The bosses keep a close eye on the people in their plants. Informants soon have the rug pulled out from under them. And besides, it's not possible to keep your anonymity. Yes, yes, says STIEBLER, That's just how it is. Yes, yes, says ARMGART, But it's not just a question of wages. It's a question of working conditions. And our worker comrades should also know what's going on in Greece, and right here with the German National Party and the recurrence of fascism. I thought that here in the club one could work out some form of organization for inside the factories. Rethink everything. That's right, STIEBLER nods, All these things have to be rethought from scratch. The way it looks now, we'll never get moving. CUT.

The Chipo Is Watching

We are raised to be little informers. She calls out your name. She says, You were whispering again. She gives you some assignment as a punishment. She makes you come up to the front of the room. Now you have to keep your eyes open. Who else is whispering? Barbara was whispering. Barbara gets an assignment as a punishment. Barbara comes up to the front of the class and stands at the board, her eyes scanning the room, suspecting everyone. She will manage to pass her punishment on to someone else. Soon she has caught the next victim. Lie in wait, denounce. Petra stands in front of the class and keeps her eyes open. Dorothea was just whispering. The next victim assumes her guard post. The Chipo is watching you, the Children's Police. And meanwhile she sits there and corrects papers, distributes punishments and corrects our errors. A teacher, our teacher. In The Spirit of the Times *she crouches at her desk, volume seven, and corrects* Man and His World *on page 96 of the* German Reader.

What did it imply when Jovana said I exterminated Poland? It implied a punishment. Man as a creature of orderly structures. *Copy three times! Now it's my turn. Track down, denounce, Auschwitz's barbed wire between my teeth. I bite in. Punishment. Cornelia has been caught, too.* The magic of personality. *Copy three times!*

I roam around with a long, pointed stick. I got it from my teacher. A long, pointed park custodian's stick. With it I spear leaf after leaf, person after person. The people collector takes aim. Stab away. Slit-open schoolgirls. She sits there and corrects papers. Her red blood drips over

121

the edge of the desk. She is sitting in a pool of blood, brooding over the origins of the Prussian state.

Nervous grass—*what kind of expression is that!*

But I didn't make it up! It's by Georg Britting.

Then put it in quotation marks!

Now it's no longer considered wrong. Now it's by Goethe, Schiller. Now it's all right. I copy page 220. Freedom—Folk—Fatherland. I am writing out my punishment.

Homeland, *I write,* Homeland is a word created by the genius of our language, *I write,* a word that does not exist in other languages, a word that awakens entirely different emotions from the passionate word Fatherland. *I am punishing myself out of our reader, punishing myself adult, dragging myself out of hot water into* German Life and Letters, *into the* Reader for German Secondary Schools. The Chipo is watching. Watching over The Ponies, *watching over* In Spring the Jolly Peasant, *watching over* Lakonia, Land of the Spartans.

I learn to structure everything. I break things down, reader-style. My left-right, text-illustration pattern arranges Eichendorffian autumn days, Novembers, winter landscapes. Rilke's panther takes a bite out of my briefcase. He is looking for Franz Marc on the far left. Lie in wait. Denounce. The panther leaps, his eyes wide open. The next victim of a whispering punishment. I'll tell on you! You'll have to copy that out! And between Frederick the Great and Bismarck's tariff policy, I write off The Temporal, the Eternal Flame *of my high school. Dante's divine unsatisfactory D-plus comedy. A little green caterpillar creeps out of the ear of my marks machine, and the panther would gobble it up if our police-chief teacher did not crush it with an A. Now the panther's skin is hanging on the wall of our classroom to dry, right next to* Nation and Mankind. *We are drying out the moral imperative of Kant, slaughtering Josef Weinheber's* The Grass. *Carossa's* Old Well *is already dry and tough. Next week we will roast it and hang Goethe's* Dedication *on the empty meathook.*

SCENE 39. INTERIOR. NIGHT. IN THE LATE NINETEENTH-CENTURY VILLA. SAME ROOM AS IN SCENE 37. THE MINISTERS ARE PREPARING TO LEAVE. SLOW MOTION AS AT THE BEGINNING OF 37. THOSE STILL SEATED, IN THE END ONLY BACHHOF AND GEBHARDT, MOVE WITH EXAGGERATED

SLOWNESS. I think I'd better be going, says A GENTLEMAN UPHOLSTERED IN BROWN and picks up his hat and coat. And when THE REV. BACHHOF says, It's not primarily a question of social conflicts, but of conflicts of conscience, HERR DR. BÖRNE also takes his leave. HERR BÖRNE says, I'm really happy to hear all this. Your idea about the information services, Mr. Bachhof, is really most interesting. Really most interesting. That is something one should try. And DR. BÖRNE says, Please excuse me now. I have a funeral tomorrow. I'll certainly drop by again. And he says good-bye and leaves. The next time we'll discuss all these matters more thoroughly, chews THE REV. FERDINAND. Who is to work on putting Bachhof's proposal into action. Who is going to try out these new services on his congregation. Mr. Bachhof is right. It really is a question of sharpening the Christian conscience. That's what I always tell the young people I am preparing for confirmation. That is our most pressing task as Christians. And BACHHOF nods and adds with brightly polished annunciation eyes, JESUS is our great ethical opportunity. Like a bird, GEBHARDT thinks. He is like a bird. And continues to the last item on the agenda. One person in isolation, GEBHARDT says, can easily be silenced. By the congregation as well as by his superiors. The kind of information service the Rev. Bachhof has in mind constitutes a deliberate provocation. And that is only the beginning. If you really want to choose this course, you have to display solidarity. Only in that way will each individual have any prospects of success. That's correct, says THE REV. FERDINAND. I really consider that significant in the case of the information services. We should discuss that more thoroughly, too, next time. And secondly, says a GENTLEMAN who up to now has not said a word and now also stands up, And secondly I propose that we examine the legitimation of political parties that lay claim to the word CHRISTIAN. That is long overdue, says the GENTLEMAN who up to now has not said a word and now goes, never to return. This whole progressive Christian elite, which draws a tidy salary for amiable kindliness and has found itself a warm, sunny spot where it can act on behalf of its fellow human beings who support the Church with their taxes.

Genius in Suspenders

Ta-tum, ta-tum, ta-dum-dum-dum, dum. *He has wild white hair. Ta-tum. A red-pored nose. Tum. His name is Rehbein, and he is a licensed music teacher. Two, three, hold! Too short gray pants. Too short striped socks. Always a funny hunk of flesh exposed, a naked horizontal stripe. Every inch the maestro. Herr Rehbein is fiftyish, married, and ringlessly blissful. A genuine artist from a martistry catalogue for thirteen marks seventy-five or a bit more, with a loud Colgate smile and gold chromed tooth. His right hand buried in his wild hair. He sweeps it back like Karajan. A genius in suspenders. The cello children have a father once more. Not a professor, to be sure, but certainly a gentleman.*

Yes, yes, that's it. He leans over my shoulder and strokes my hand. A very good C!

Until I notice that it has nothing to do with my C. He also strokes me at F and G. Altogether, he does a lot of stroking, avalanche style. He must have eight hands. Every day there are more, and they seem to be everywhere.

Today I am making up the lesson I missed yesterday. At his house. I cello away amidst doilies and potted geraniums, while upstairs a monster stamps and shouts Karl Heinz!

Leave me alone! I'm working!

He rips open the door and bawls up the stairs. Leave me out of it!

Bang, the door slams shut. He beams at me. He digs his hands spontaneously into my hair. That was very good, smacks Teacher Rehbein, You deserve a kiss for that. A nasty wet kiss on the cheek. A snapping turtle kiss. My stomach turns over. With difficulty I free myself from the tentacles he has wrapped around me. But Rehbein is not one to let himself be deterred. He moves in again. If he were not the school's official cello teacher, warmly recommended by Frau Meiners, I would smash my cello over his white head. But the cello belongs to the school, and even a genius in suspenders is not worth 2000 marks.

Again his hand is in my hair.

This Christmas for vacation a group of us are going skiing.

I don't look up. I have already learned that it is wise not to look at him. If I do, he becomes indiscriminately active. That sounds nice, I murmur, and practice a syncopated passage with grim determination.

Why don't you come along. We can get a tan together.

He crouches down and stares at me from below with a grin. His doggy

124

tongue flips over his lips. *Teacher Rehbein, the court cellist who can teach one so much. Whom Frau Meiners swears by, counts on, insists upon. All the cello children have a lover again.*

Please, don't. No, please!

I barely manage to escape. Good-bye. He throws his arms around me. To get rid of him I would have to give up cello or tell Frau Meiners the truth. But I don't dare. How can I tell her that Herr Rehbein caresses the little fingers of his girl pupils as he shows them the positions on the strings?

Isn't he good? Ute whispers to me at recess. I nod wordlessly over my cheese sandwich, and ask her if she is going away for vacation.

Yes, skiing with a bunch of teachers from Altona and a few girls from school.

A cut-rate trip with loud guffaws, a gold chromed tooth, and eight hands.

Isn't that nice? Ute asks.

SCENE 40. INTERIOR. NIGHT. IN THE LATE NINETEENTH-CENTURY VILLA. SAME ROOM AS IN SCENE 38, WHERE THE FOUR ARE STILL MEETING AND THE CAMERA IS STILL WANDERING AT CLOSE-UP RANGE FROM FACE TO FACE. What we need, HENNING says, And urgently, is a utopia. A concrete utopia whose strategy we work out together. So that some day the people will not only have a say in running their affairs, but can determine everything for themselves. What nonsense, says HERR STIEBLER. Utter nonsense. Just try telling that to the workingman. Try telling him something about Greece. Or about the German National Party. You're not going to get the workingman on your side that way. Not that way. But a utopia, a utopia ruled by self-determination, says ARMGART, That would be quite interesting. If you, Herr Henning, would tell us something about it next time, two weeks from now. The sociologist HENNING pulls fuzz off his sweater. The historian HENNING runs his hands through his hair. And says, You know I live in Kiel, as I said. I live in Kiel and won't be able to be here next time. I'm afraid I can't make it next time. You know, classes and work and so on. That's too bad, says STIEBLER. Really too bad. But, as I said, it's primarily a question of social policies. Perhaps they should be given priority. The question of wages and the business with the students. That's right, says ARMGART, Perhaps one could. Perhaps students could get into the factories some time. Like in France, HENNING says, Like in France: that's how it will be here soon. It just requires a little consciousness raising. We just have to chip away a little at the general lack of awareness, and everything will take care of itself. Then we'll find the solidarity we need. Maybe, STIEBLER says. I tell you, there's a lot you can do at the bars, after work, just sitting with the fellows. He's been sitting in there for over ten years, drinking his beer, ARMGART says, supplying a footnote. And as STUDENT HENNING waves and calls, See you, comrades, STIEBLER, Herr Willy Stiebler, is already making a motion that Rainer Gebhardt should draw up the minutes. That Rainer Gebhardt, who has been taking notes on everything, should have them mimeographed for next time. Just in case something comes up. In case anyone can't come. For it might happen that. And one can never know. In case two weeks from now, before the next meeting two weeks from now, Stiebler or Armgart should call to say he can't come, and Dr. Grützmann unfortunately can't make it either, then at least there should be minutes available. Minutes for the next meeting, in case no one is there.

Clouds around Our Hips

Amrun. The dune grass draws back for the slash. Blood on the beach, scratched feet. My fluttering hair banner indicates the wind direction. Clouds hang down around our hips. Water gurgles between our toes. Amrun in autumn, a blur of oil-color gray, a sky smeared by a giant thumb. The last tourists left with the high tide, leaving behind coffee rings in the cups and hairs under the bed, apple cores in the wastebasket and corn pads on the chair leg.

Amrun. You get onto a train in Hamburg, your fall report card as a ticket, your reward in your wallet, but no youth hostel card in your pocket. That means a no at the hostels, means soaking-wet hitchhiking, being washed away on country roads. That means spending the night at the rescue mission in the railway station, sleeping, unwashed and in your clothes, in a dormitory with only a woolen blanket for a cover.

Husum, spoken with a sharp s, a sharp, fishy s. It would have been more sensible to wait for the next bus and check the schedule, instead of simply turning up here. *The woman who runs the rescue mission comes slurping over with a pot of hot coffee. A stool by the stove. Husum blanket distribution, neatly folded like a handkerchief. I avoid thinking of Theodor Storm, Husum's native novelist. I feel outcast enough as it is.*

Finally on board the ferry, chugging, swaying, fragile, with screaming seagulls that zoom in to attack floating sandwiches like jackals, finally on board the ferry—salt on my lips, clothes flapping, launched toward the freedom of the dunes.

Judith has a red nose, cold hands. She is hardly in the mood for a welcoming celebration. Hello, she says, and thumps me on the shoulder with her arm, a branch broken in the storm.

Let's stop off at Thesa's bar first.

Cobblestones. A village for dwarfs, with crooked little houses. On the left, feeble-minded Carla weaves one rug after another. On the right is Thesa's red light bulb bar, with juke-box atmosphere and yellow dotted curtains. Thesa, a blond, washed-out creature without eyebrows, has bought everything she could think of that would not go together. Oriental-type carpets from a licorice bag, checked tablecloths, dotted curtains, and many abstract designs. All this Thesa is throwing open for next season. Cheers, Frisco. Chic, neat, crazy, cool. The conversation builds toward a climax—delightful. Thesa, whose mother was from Vienna before she fell into the hands of a Cap'n from Steenode, Thesa defines her abstract dotted and checked future with delightful. And her chalky white sun-shunning North Sea hand comes down in an affirmative slap on the green gold worked plastic back of her egg-form chair.

Everything from the teen magazine Bravo.

I nod admiringly. Eighty different magazine suggestion columns have been merged into one ice cream parlor-chambre séparée checked reality.

After our ice cream see-you-soon, we strike across the bicycle path, a narrow track through reedy underbrush. We greet the sea again. Judith going on ahead, dragging herself up the dunes. Two puffing suitcase porters trudge down to the beach. Swept empty. A sandy ironing board. No one to the right. No one to the left. Into the naked October waves. I do it for Judith's sake, and she for mine. And if a strange man had not suddenly popped up in the distance, we might both have frozen to death in the waves, from sheer bravado. But the seducer out of a Scandinavian movie, who is out looking for girls bathing in the nude, is frustrated in his Amrun adventure. We are already stuck into our clothes like salt herring by the time the stranger appears on our part of the beach. Judith gives the orders. With both hands gripping the handles, we run a little in that direction. Toward the house with a thatched roof back there!

SCENE 41. EVENING. THE MAIN AUDITORIUM OF THE UNIVERSITY OF HAMBURG. ALL SHOTS FROM THE DIRECTION OF THE STAGE. A SING-OUT-GERMANY AS OFF-CAMERA BACKGROUND, OCCASIONALLY MOVING INTO THE FOREGROUND. CLOSE-UP: RAINER GEBHARDT. LATER OVERLAID WITH SHOTS OF AUDIENCE. Why don't you go, Neubüser said. They're supposed to put on a pretty clever show. Go and see if there's anything in it we can use, Neubüser said. In any case I'll have it video-taped. An assignment for Gebhardt. An after-work show. According to the program, MODERN YOUNG PEOPLE. According to the program, GOOD-LOOKING LADS AND MAIDENS. There's certainly something in it, GEBHARDT thinks. There's everything in it for us. For a starter they're singing the national anthem. BLOOM IN THE GLOW OF YOUR GOOD FORTUNE. They are singing, and the whole audience is standing. Next to GEBHARDT. In front of him. Behind him. All standing, surrounding the sitting GEBHARDT like a Teutonic forest. Sixteen hundred tickets sold, standing in the glow of their good fortune. Lay sisters in their habits. Venerable white manes. Whole herds of fifty-year-olds. Multitudes of mastered past. Multitudes of unmastered future. Spotlights shine out. Television cameras whirr. The clever show. One hundred fifty SING-OUT STUDENTS clap their hands, swing their arms. THE GREAT SPIRIT. HE CREATED A PEOPLE, STRONG AND FREE. UPRIGHT LIKE CEDARS. STRONG AS BEARS, HIS PEOPLE! One hundred and fifty SING-OUT STUDENTS clench their fists and cry, COME ALONG! ALL ABOARD! READY FOR TAKE-OFF! Not again, GEBHARDT thinks. Republic. Third Reich. Over and over again, GEBHARDT thinks. Republic. Fourth Reich, underlaid with a rocking beat. Well, says Gebhardt's NEIGHBOR ON THE RIGHT. Well, says Gebhardt's NEIGHBOR ON THE LEFT. Well, they BOTH say, That's really something. That's snappy. That has a good beat to it. GEBHARDT breaks out in a sweat. Chorus-boy Gebhardt, Rainer of the Mozart Chorus in Berlin, capital of the Reich. Brown shorts. Black neckerchief. And the hundred and fifty are singing, THE EARTH HAS SUFFERED MUCH. BUT IN MAN, IN ALL MEN, GLOWS A SPARK. THE SPARK OF GOD, WHICH MUST BE FANNED TO A FLAME ONCE MORE. Bravo! shouts THE

128

MAN ON GEBHARDT'S LEFT. Bravo! Applause to accompany the ride through the House of Horrors. Future on, future rolling. Flags, torches, triumphal processions. GERMANIA, O HOLY WORD, ECHO OF INFINITY. Past on, past rolling. Freedom: a skeleton. God: a cardboard dummy. Fifty Pfennig for the ride. GEBHARDT leafs through his program. Leafs his way into the past. LOVE FOR THE FATHERLAND. ABSOLUTE MORAL STANDARDS. Words, words, words. The girls in red, yellow, and green jumpers with white blouses. WHY DOST THOU STAND AND HESITATE STILL? GEBHARDT is standing there. GEBHARDT is hesitating. The boys with dark blue blazers and red ties, rock-booted and spurred. LOOK INTO THE DISTANCE. A THING OF GREATNESS IS YET TO COME, NOT YET IN VIEW. A thing of greatness, GEBHARDT thinks. A thing of greatness. Death to the . . . , Gebhardt yelled. Jews, screamed his troop. And now a hundred and fifty are singing an accompaniment. A hundred and fifty are shouting, TO THE EAST! TO THE EAST! THAT IS THE LAND TO WHICH MY SOUL IS DRAWN. With rock 'n' roll in their knapsacks this time, GEBHARDT thinks. With rhythm guitar this time. And up there in front they are singing, LET THY HEART BE YOUNG. TAKE COURAGE. DO NOT DESPAIR. THEY SAY, THOU WILT NEVER WIN THE BATTLE. HEED THEM NOT. COURAGE COMES ONLY TO THE BOLD. He who would conquer the world with a clap of thunder, GEBHARDT thinks, must not wait for another to be the lightning before him. Lightning war, GEBHARDT thinks. One must simply be bold, GEBHARDT thinks. A pop-art army with marching faces. Total song. That's really something. Just listen to that. And Gebhardt, Youth Squad Leader Rainer Gebhardt, is marching through the Berlin of his childhood. When Jews' blood from our knives does spurt. MIX ON FOCUS PULL.

He Wishes Me a War
The room is small, like a bar of Lindt chocolate, panelled with bookcases, surrounded by built-in shelves. There are three wobbly chairs and an enormous desk. Blocking the bay window are chests of drawers, stuffed with newspapers. And facing a newspaper mountain sits Herr Dr. Zabori. His untamed wiry black hair puffs up around his outsized head. He is wearing one of his short sleeved sport shirts, from whose brightly checked holes plump child's arms protrude stumpily, with little fat blobs at their ends. The body stocky, the legs crooked. The briefcase he always

lugs around with him is the match of Vera Zirkel's in every respect. Today it lies looted next to his desk, its contents spread out in the form of books and towers of clippings. Wherever one looks, books, books, books. If one sliced open the master of the house, one would probably find books inside, nothing but books.

I know I ought to say something. He is looking at me, slightly magnified by his glasses. How fine it's hidden from the world, that Dr. Zabori I am called. I ought to ask him something, now that Judith is outside playing with her little sister Andrea and Frau Zabori is indulging in an afternoon nap.

It's about the Jews, I say. Are you still having your problems with that Frau Zirkel? he asks. What do you learn in that school of yours, in history class? What are they teaching you, child?

They are teaching me that Rome and Sparta, that the ancient Germans—The Germanic Heritage, starting on page 1 of our textbook. But the business with the Jews—Frau Dr. Zirkel always says it was less than six. She says the concentration camps were set up as reeducation centers. Jews, asocial elements, and criminals were all in there together.

And communists.

He thrusts his head forward over the tea mirror in the cup. He squeezes lemon into the mirror. He says, And communists. I am a Jew and a communist.

Communist. A communist! No one has ever explained to me what a Jew is, but I know what a communist is from civics class. He compels the individual to accept his system. He is brutal, warmongering, an enemy to the working class, and ruthless, because he does not have a clear conscience. And the East Zone is a concentration camp, because we are the only ones who live in freedom. A communist. A communist sitting there listening to me? He stirs up his tea. He stirs it out of the cup. A communist, who is not listening to me. He stirs with closed eyes. He's asleep. No, his head is pulling him down.

Herr Zabori, I say. He stares at me. Yes, he says, with blue rimmed spectacle eyes. Yes, he says, how old are you now?

I'll be nineteen next month.

Herr Zabori smiles. With a flat, pendulous mouth, down which his smile slips. Worn down from much talking.

Nineteen next month.

I seem to upset him. Why does he keep stroking his five-fingered comb
130

at nervous intervals through his long hair, checking his forehead on the way?

I was not much older than nineteen when I emigrated to England, the only member of my family who did.

He wants to answer my nineteen years. He stops stirring. He leans back in his wobbly chair. He folds his plump hands over his short legs. Dr. Zabori in response position. Of my family, of my whole family, not a single person survived. Auschwitz settled its accounts with humanity in Germany. It's true that I came back to Germany, but I am leaving again.

So you are a refugee?

He laughs at me. My poor child, he says, How they've muddled your little head. Here, have some more tea.

Child! He always calls me child. I no longer dare ask him about the Jews, ask the communist about the Jews.

But why do you want to leave Germany again?

He hands me a newspaper from the desktop mountains. German Nationalists' and Soldiers' News. A red headline at the top: "The Fraud of the Six Million Jews." And underneath it an election slogan: "Crush the Left Wherever You Find It." The Voice of the True Germany—The German National Party. I look at Dr. Zabori. I learn that Germany is reawakening again. I follow Dr. Zabori with my eyes as he wanders over to a blind spot in his bookcases. He pulls something out, unrolls it. He says, This is a map of Germany. And these are the territorial goals of the First World War, the Second World War. And these are the territorial goals for the third war. Not a world war, child, but a war. His chubby little finger traces out areas for the child, moving always in a circle, always in a circle. He says, There has been no peace treaty signed. We don't accept a policy of renunciation. He says, Anticommunism, the system that is heir to Hitlerism, aims to recapture all the lost territory. In our governmental machinery, fascist resistance fighters are conspiring to destroy the Federal Constitution and our postwar democracy. He says, Take a good look at the weather map on television. Then you will see how big Germany really is. Home to the Reich, my child. Home to the Reich with a lightning war, and this time only in the East, not in the West. They will make up for Hitler's only tactical error. And you will live to see it.

He talks like the Delphic Oracle, I think. He sees everything pessimistically, I think. He wants to rob me of my pleasure in life. He wishes me a war. *Doesn't Vera Zirkel always say that the Russians are animals who will rape any woman they come upon? Doesn't my civics book say that* the recovery of the lost homeland is a goal of such formative influence that it can establish moral standards and give shape to personality? *Communists are criminals. That's what I learned. And Dr. Zabori, as a Jew and a communist, is doubly criminal. What would Vera Zirkel say?* How fine it's hidden from the world, how fine it's hidden from the world. *Dr. Zabori wants his newspaper back. Dr. Zabori says,* Tomorrow there will be two million voting for the German National Party, and the day after tomorrow four million. *But there is one thing you must realize,* says the Jew and communist, folding up the Fraud of the Six Million. *One thing is very important. The danger doesn't come from the German National Party. It comes from the center. From those who call themselves democrats but are busy establishing legal fascism. And if you ever poke your head out of your schoolbooks and learn to read a newspaper properly, make sure you direct your opposition against the fascism of the center.*

I cannot answer him. I am incapable of understanding. My head is turned upside down. My hair is growing into my shoulders, my neck pointing up in the air. He is talking about Portugal now, about Spain, about Franco, with whom we are allied. He talks about Guernica and the Legion Condor. He tells me about a Munich agreement which is still legally valid. He rattles off history to me. Once upon a time. *And between* once upon a time *and* once upon a time, *there is me. Born late, plunked down in the cease-fire zone, I, the child, forgot how to mistrust. Or rather, never learned to mistrust. Now the child is learning, on an island, instructed by a double criminal. The child hears history being recounted, learns that the title of her civics book,* Freedom and Responsibility, *is incorrect. That freedom is responsibility, that there is no* and. *The child learns that there are racial and religious minorities. Oppressed, liquidated, beaten down. Hitler's gas ovens. People deprived of their rights. Murdered Zaboris. They would have gassed Dr. Zabori, torn out his teeth.* He digs his hand into his hair. Yes, it is still there. Still there. *Lampshade Zabori. Judith often uses that term when she's calling her father. Where's Lampshade Zabori?*

Lampshade Zabori is sitting here, facing me. Dictating a future to the child. Dictating the information that in the name of anticommunism one dictatorship after another is seizing power. You must learn that anticommunism does not constitute freedom. *Learn to see. And I am supposed to learn to see.* He tells me that with his back. Dr. Zabori is cramming his map back into the crowded shelves. Deliberately, straining up on his toes to reach.

So things are not simple anymore. The West good and the East bad. My math problem does not come out evenly anymore. Dr. Zabori brings the six million Jews into my calculations. A whole six million. Six whole million. The child will soon witness a war. A third war. The child will be attacked by a map. He tells me this, Lampshade Zabori does, and rubs Pomerania from his hands. And then he tells me, on tiptoes, on his little island in the North Sea, that I will perish at the hands of the freedom hecklers. For a map. The child will perish.

SCENE 42. FLASHBACK. MONTAGE OF DOCUMENTARY CLIPS FROM THE DAYS OF THE THIRD REICH. SUBJECT: THE HITLER YOUTH. Gebhardt has a bad memory. Does he not want to remember? Or is he not able to? Has he repressed too much? Or is he simply forgetful? He has always admired people who can remember precise details from their youth. Clearly delineated events. His own youth resembles a fog. What does he remember? And which memories are really his own? It is pointless to proceed chronologically. But as well as he can remember, his youth was closely linked with fascism. There were summer excursions, camping trips, mass rallies, Whitsuntide outings, call-ups of the militia, trumpet marches, organized sports, piping, braids, uniforms, song fests, flags, music. Gebhardt comes from the lower middle class, the pillar of reactionary politics. His father was one of many children. Twelve live births. Grandfather had still been a member of the working class. Had struggled up the social ladder by sheer determination, with Grandmother on his back and suspicious rustlings in one lung. Gebhardt only saw him once. He was six at the time. Grandfather seemed like a fossil to him. An old man who hardly spoke, having been buried twice down in the mine pit. Surrounded by the familial halo of the honest man whose greatest moment had been when the Kaiser shook his hand. Gebhardt's father had been a soldier. A volunteer in the First World War. That gave him a martial air. Especially with his Iron Cross. He had worked and starved his way through the university. A dissertation on Gottfried Wilhelm

Leibnitz at Berlin's Humboldt University. With a Ph.D. he tried writing. Miserable, derivative attempts. Then he succumbed to the enticements of Gebhardt's mother and in a fit of weakness and coerced decency married her; Gebhardt was already two years old. After that his life was over, his little struggle for happiness lost. To be father and husband without a profession was unthinkable, so he became a pharmacist. He never really understood why. For a while, during his university days, he must have sympathized with communism. Once he had hinted as much to Gebhardt. By the time Rainer came to know him as a father, he was already a Nazi. Very early Gebhardt began to go his own way. His parents were preoccupied enough with preventing the final wreck of the marriage, already leaking from a thousand holes. Probably Gebhardt served as a kind of moral caulking. At age eight, even before Hitler's seizure of power, he was already wearing a brown shirt, marching through the streets of Berlin. Something he nowadays tries in vain to understand whenever he meets up with eight-year-olds. Gebhardt's parents approved of his choice. Not surprisingly, since his mother spoke of the FÜHRER with gleaming eyes; she had met him once in person in Munich, amidst the beer steins. And his father wore the uniform of the SA, with ceremonial dagger and an increasing glitter of stars. His evening duties for the Fatherland probably suited him just fine, for they gave him the opportunity several times a week of getting patriotically drunk and frequenting ladies of ill repute with fellow party members. At least that is how Gebhardt's mother viewed the situation. In grade school Gebhardt was one of the best. For years he brought home exclusively A's and B's. That changed dramatically when he entered high school. Learning became a grim chore. And Gebhardt hated chores. Service in the Hitler Youth was no chore. That was something he did of his own free will.

The Resurrection of Wilhelm Zabori

A night spent in the gabled room under the eaves. A wooden staircase outside my door creaks me to sleep. The wind spears the thatch on its horns. Now we are bobbing over the sea. And out the kitchen window, from amidst red checked curtains, topple plates and cups, forks and knives, and fat, squashy fruits, glass-coddled strawberry preserves.

134

Something is dripping out of the house's kitchen pocket, dripping toward Dr. Zabori. I recognize him by his measled tie. Dangling around his Adam's apple, a self-knotted noose. The resurrection of Wilhelm Zabori. He hops across egg cartons, whitely rounded wave bridges. Now the hanged man leaps onto the water. With gnawed-off bone paws he stands there firmly upon the sea. He opens his jaws wide. He licks up his blood. Then thrusts his skull toward the jam, which drips his hollow places full. The soft fruits dribble down his breastcage from rib to rib. They bubble along his backbone. We must resign ourselves to their not being strawberries. The best thing is to attack. *Vera the circle as squadron commander. With a piercing whistle, on duty, cap on head, she scurries up the wall of my room.* How is my composition going? *She takes the Munch reproduction off the wall. She beckons to me.* I can't come. My hair gets tangled around the bedpost. Our house has tipped over. Help! *She reaches for her revolver, which she carries behind her ear, like a grocer's pencil. She shoots my hair apart. Now I hustle up the wall, scrabble out onto the balustrade. I did not know there was an airport behind the Munch. Silver birds are parked there. They sway gently back and forth. A mobile with graded wings, with red, washed-out F's under a steel blue sky. Blurry colored bubbles are flying around. Those are gallbladders and hearts. Frau Dr. Zirkel whispers to me,* Now I'm going to shoot down a stomach. *It spurts and bursts apart.* The beautiful blue sign-heaven, *I shout, nauseated, and cover my face with my hands. Evening is coming, Vera says,* The blood is draining away. We're ready for take-off. *Now we roll down the runway.* We're flying off to war, *says Frau Dr. Zirkel and slides under my arm and along my hip to the airport.* You're losing your cap, *I call, and regret that I have no whistle.* Listen! I'm going to let myself slide through the opening. I'll bring you your cap right away. *Slowly, in a descending circle. The fall rips my jaw open. My teeth fall ahead of me, and behind me the planes are droning. We're turned around, Frau Zirkel calls,* You stole my cap. *She flies ahead of the birds, an airplane behind her ear. She comes humming toward me. I am falling in great swoops. A cemetery and no runway. Then I shout,* It's because of the cap. *My left leg is foreshortened. It reaches only to my knee. They're shooting at me. My bloody leg stump melts. A bullet is dripping at the back of my head. I'm falling, softly and bloodily. And beside me glide the pencils. A bomb-filled sky of metal. Soon I will hit bottom. The spears of the crosses cannot reach me. An*

army is moving toward me. And on the bombers' wings my teeth are
already growing, like mussels on the shore. With bloody crawling
stomach I think: I must get to the cap. I must throw it at them. I stick
fast to my wounds. I'm not strong enough. I thrust my head deep with
fear into the slime of the innards. They're coming. I hurtle through
bloody ground into cold, flowing water, with cold, flowing hair, my shot
hair. There is a gathering-in, before the pencils strike. Gathered-up hair
is knotted fast to the bedpost. I knot myself fast in my pool. I wipe the
water from my brow. With the motor vibrations of my hand, my head
lands in whirling circles. On a wobbly night table. With oil paint behind
my eyes. But the sky is gray. An endless, gigantic aircraft carrier. It must
be getting on toward four. I think of the six million. For if one counts
Herr Zabori out, it is six million.

SCENE 43. SETTING AS IN SCENE 41. OUT OF MIX ON FOCUS PULL. CLOSE-UP
OF GEBHARDT. OFF-CAMERA SONG. TAKE HEART. DO NOT GIVE UP.
Gebhardt took heart. Gebhardt did not give up. Gebhardt learned to say
yes, to shout yes, to roar yes. Yes to the bitter end. Until everything
shattered. MANY PEOPLE WOULD BE HAPPIER, WOULD BE MILLIONAIRES
TODAY, IF YOU HAD TAKEN MORE OF A RISK AND HAD HAD GUTS, IF YOU
HAD SAID YES. Yes, yes, GEBHARDT thinks. YOU, MAN AT THE MACHINE,
GEBHARDT thinks, YOU, MAN AT THE MACHINE, WHEN ORDERS COME
TOMORROW, SAY NO. FOR IF YOU DO NOT SAY NO, IF YOU DO NOT SAY NO.
Gebhardt learned to say no. He learned to search for his mother with the
bombs falling all around. One early morning in June of 1945. With a
letter in his hand. Her last letter. And someone looked out of an upstairs
window. Whom are you looking for? Oh, she's not alive anymore. Good
God, are you the son? And GEBHARDT, the son, is sitting in the twelfth
row, sitting in the packed auditorium in the twelfth row, and the one
hundred and fifty on the stage rap out, FOR THE DAY IS COMING, FOR THE
DAY IS COMING, WHEN MILLIONS WILL MARCH WITH US. WHEN MILLIONS
WILL MARCH WITH US, GEBHARDT thinks. Father didn't have any millions,
GEBHARDT thinks. Father didn't even have a pharmacy of his own. But
when the millions came. But when he marched off with the millions.
When the millions dealt with the Jews, he got a lease. Father got a lease
to a Jew's pharmacy. GERMANY, MY FATHERLAND, WHITHER GOEST THOU?
136

One hundred and fifty SING-OUTS stretch their hands toward the sky. One hundred and fifty from the Mozart Chorus stretch their hands toward the sky. One hundred and fifty SING-OUTS sing, Freedom is not in vain. One hundred and fifty Mozart singers sing, To freedom we devote our lives. Special bulletin. Special bulletin. Father marching through the apartment with a frying pan. Father marching around the living room table with a frying pan. Father singing at the top of his lungs, France will yield to our victorious blows. Father is still singing, GEBHARDT thinks. But we are still around, too. Stand up. Hands at your sides. Recite out loud. Recite Tucholsky. LADIES AND GENTLEMEN, WE ARE STILL HERE, TOO. YOU OPEN YOUR MOUTHS AND SHOUT, SHOUT IN THE NAME OF GERMANY, SHOUT, WE LOVE THIS COUNTRY—ONLY WE LOVE IT. BUT THAT IS NOT TRUE. IT IS OUR COUNTRY, TOO. Good God, are you the son? There's something in it for us. For Wotan is galloping across the stage, the blue flower of Romanticism behind the crooning rhythm guitars. FOR THE DAY IS COMING, THE DAY IS COMING, WHEN MILLIONS WILL MARCH WITH US. Dr. Rindfleisch is no longer marching with us, GEBHARDT thinks. Our family doctor, Dr. Rindfleisch, of whom mother whispered that he was a Jew, but a decent one. Dr. Rindfleisch is no longer marching along. Neither in spirit nor in any other columns. He marched along thirty years ago. Marched along with millions. Six million. In those long ago days, when we were all marching along with millions.

Only a Rally

He is back in Hamburg. The first few semesters of studying dentistry in Heidelberg to satisfy his father sped by. Christopher has become Hamlet to the bone. He has discovered his smile and his physical possibilities. His shiny dachshund hair is brushed into a Mortimer. His twenties lie before him. The actors' studio in Hamburg lifts the lids of its drama pots so he can peek in; Medea offers Tasso half of her frankfurter. And Christopher, young and heroic, a modern Caesar, forgets the stammering of childhood in the arms of Juliet.

We quarrel more and more often. All he wants to do is talk about himself. I am bored to death by diction and role-playing techniques. He does not want to hear about school, and when he walks beside me, a smiling Colgate advertisement, vibrant and filter-conscious, a darling of

137

older ladies and stagestruck young girls, his casual naturalness makes it evident that his world, at least, is very much a stage. Every time he jumps onto a streetcar, it's a fencer's leap. Every time he reaches into a candy bag, he is a dying swan. Christopher: a Romeo in third position. Had he not invited me to an election rally in the Planten un Blomen Park, I would not have gone. But he made the telephone wires buzz.

A party rally; Chancellor Erhard will be there. I need it for facial expressions and gesture.

All right, I'll come. Come to one of the smaller meeting halls, to the wooden benches in the gallery. Election rally. With stiff back and nothing to lean against. Down in the hall security men with arm bands, boxer types with smooth red faces wreathed in fat, masses of calm. On the podium tulips bloom, and down in the front rows sits the chosen audience of politics. Wrapped in clouds of smoke, the foggy aura of fifty- and sixty-year-olds. Two wooden rows in front of me, a young, long-haired back. And farther down a girl in a red sweater. But otherwise, wrinkle upon wrinkle. Ashy, unaired faces.

And then he arrives, working his way with his big cigar down the center aisle. Past stormy applause to the podium, where certain noble spirits have already taken their seats. Local functionaries, forty-year-old neophytes, who rise as if they were in school, hands rattling, behind in their schoolwork.

Bravo!

Behind me, in front of me, massive bellies wave a bare-fisted welcome. Facial expressions? Mass meeting of thundering aggression. Silencing the opposition. I dare not turn my head, because if I don't clap—look! We've had enough of you, Erhard!

Two rows in front of me. And Christopher's sturdy neighbor battles his way past the massed heads and yanks her hair. A girl turns around.

Enough of Erhard?! Watch it, you bitch!

He braces one leg in a space between the hips of his close-packed comrades and spits in the young woman's face.

I'll beat the daylights out of you!

Christopher stands up. Skinny and cowardly. In a high, mannered voice, a soft Please, stop it. The security men are on their way. I daren't say a word. Who's in the majority here? Someone's going to be beaten up.

A security man grabs the offender by the arms. Panic. Stampede.
138

Leave the old man alone! *And while in the balcony brute force prevails, down below the rows of seats are clapping* Welcome, *clapping at the word* reunification, *licking the boots of business and economic power. Who is in the majority here? Abandoned by youth, the grandfathers are roaring out their stale opinion.* No experiments! *The fathers come armed with stick and fist, to voice their hatred of the long-haired youth. Why are there no young people here? Why am I afraid to ask a single question? Why am I petrified of this political men's club? What do I have to fear? It's only a rally, after all. The girl squeezes past me, wiping the spit from her face.*

You bitch! Bravo Erhard!

If I don't clap along, the man next to me will beat the daylights out of me. My first election rally is sending shivers of physical terror down my spine. I clap. I don't know a thing about Erhard, this movie figure, this television creature who comes on at the press *of a button. I don't understand politics, have no idea of the Christian Democrats' platform. But here I sit, jammed in between Christopher and two fists, and clap out of pure fear. Clap my way backwards out of the rally by the emergency exit. I clap my way past the security men to freedom.*

SCENE 44. INTERIOR. NIGHT. GEBHARDT'S BEDROOM. CLOSE-UP: A GLOWING CIGARETTE. GEBHARDT IS SMOKING. OFF-CAMERA NARRATION BEGINS. GEBHARDT SWITCHES ON THE NIGHT TABLE LAMP. FRAUKE, HIS WIFE, IS SLEEPING. GEBHARDT SWITCHES THE LAMP OFF, GETS OUT OF BED, LEAVES THE ROOM, SHUTTING THE DOOR SOFTLY BEHIND HIM. HE GOES DOWNSTAIRS TO THE KITCHEN, POURS HIMSELF A BOURBON. TAKES THE BOTTLE WITH HIM INTO THE LIVING ROOM. PLOPS DOWN IN AN EASY CHAIR AND DRINKS. Martyrdom on. Martyrdom rolling. A leap into asceticism. For people like Gebhardt—a leap into the desert. One way of being consistent. Gebhardt doubts whether he is strong enough. To say what he thinks. To pull out. He dreads solitude. Withering up. He is addicted. He must withdraw from his fixes of LIFE. Slowly. With utmost concentration. All his energies focused on one point. Shake off the dependencies that frazzle him. Deep breathing. Give up narcosis. Alcohol only quickens the metabolism. Breathe out. Break the dependency on the morphine of mechanical work, regulated frenzy. Gebhardt knows a way.

The escape into illness. Put the body out of commission. Fall out of the race to neatly lined-up nothingness. Dry out. Shrivel up. Unsensuous people have an easier time of it. If you are sick, your path is smoothed without your having to lift a finger. To him, that means hell freezing over. But he will find a way. He must find one. He is choking on life. And every choking fit affects innocent bystanders. He is not irresponsible. His cowardice results from his sensitivity. He does not want to cut the deck. He feels pity when he has to cut. Not pity with himself. Pity with the innocent. With those who have bet on him without knowing what card he has up his sleeve. Gebhardt is no card cheat, but he is fast becoming one. A person who does not want to get hurt had better know a lot about him. Must remain extra watchful. Must never sleep. His exterior is deceptive. But has any woman between bed and door, any woman at his side, across the table from him, ever taken the trouble to find out more about him than was immediately necessary for her own purposes. All of them called their own indolence, their egotism, their deep beauty sleep *trust.* How simple and self-gratifying. Raise your right hand for the First Commandment. I will trust you. Raise your right hand for the Second Commandment. I will not think about you. Raise your right hand for the Third Commandment. I will not question myself. I will not question you. I will not even try to perceive the changes in you. I will trust you until death do us part. First wife. Second wife. Third wife. Not one of them ever noticed changes in him. Except perhaps for a new haircut or a clean-shaven chin at an unaccustomed time of day.

Decimals in the Wastebasket!

The first time I saw him, small, black haired, imperious, he was standing in the classroom door. He called out challengingly, Where is the editor-in-chief? *The first time I looked at him and called out even more challengingly,* Come on in, it's me you're looking for, *he forced me to lower my head, forced me with his flat, ink-black eyes, screwed into his face like gleaming metal snaps. He looked at me until I lost the battle of the eyes and lowered my gaze. A rumor had hastened on ahead of this new ruler. Stubborn, energetic, argumentative. A math teacher who let fractions and square roots perish amidst the chalk dust. A teacher who tossed the decimal system into the wastebasket and threw the textbooks at the heads of the prerecorded textbook-teachers.* We have to learn to think mathematically and get away from this business of memorizing formulas.

In front of their own classes he offered to tutor the old and younger math teachers after school. He refused to give homework assignments out of the dusty old books. He demanded discussion and debate, attacked the student government as an incubator for infant retirees. He got in his licks, and refused to accommodate old maids with red ink noses who tried to talk about education with this newcomer, this assistant teacher. We were told that he had come to us from the university, and he was the only teacher of whom I could believe it. The rest of the school's faculty must have washed ashore somewhere sometime, secretly, by night, clinging to a heating coil. He came by day, bearing a knife, and slashed his way through the cream-no-sugar of our spinsterish waxworks with its cracker-and-cookie dummies. He rapped their drowsy humdrum on its cupcake knuckles. He knew too much; it was best to avoid any sort of shop talk. The womanly hearts beat reluctantly faster—a man, at last—and the classes of girls glowed red.

The first time I saw him, black hair thrown back—indeed, everything about him was black—the first time he hastened toward me with beetling black eyebrows, he hesitated. Hesitated at me, when I bent my head. *Yes, what can I do for you?*

We stand there facing each other defiantly, without speaking. I had taken over the school newspaper, a sheet halfway between tabloid and crêpe suzette. *See if you can do any better,* the editor had said, and tossed her eight-page kitchen edition at my feet. So I took on the editing job, wrote a thirty-five-page dotted i, wrote twenty pages all by myself, designed the cover, drew up a table of contents, and modeled my lines on Brecht, not on cake-mix recipes and kitsch. *Young girls nowadays.* The official amoeba folded her fat little hands over her big fat belly. She crouched there in her malicious brown silk folds and called her girls to an accounting between tabloid and kitsch. The principal's office demanded an expanded editorial board. The principal's office demanded teacher censorship. With hunched little shoulders the principal's office demanded hunched little confessions. It threw out a sharp, pointy metal comb which caught my girl right in her opinions, combed them through, swept them aside. But then something took up a position facing that blob of protoplasm, something black, something energetic, something defiant.

Someone asked Where is the editor-in-chief *and took over as faculty adviser. Herr Dr. Siefert did not walk his student newspaper on a leash. Herr Dr. Siefert walked on the grass himself. Herr Dr. Siefert supervised. He supervised to see that no one supervised.*

SCENE 45. INTERIOR. EVENING. OFFICE IN THE LATE NINETEENTH-CENTURY VILLA. BACHHOF IS STANDING NEXT TO GEBHARDT, WHO IS SITTING ON A DESK AND DIALING A NUMBER ON THE TELEPHONE, OF WHICH THE CAMERA GIVES AN EXTREME CLOSE-UP. Study groups within the congregations. Common channels for information and publication. BACHHOF is standing next to GEBHARDT. GEBHARDT is reading through BACHHOF's minutes. The minutes from last time. The first minutes. The last, GEBHARDT thinks, as he dials Börne's number. No, I'm sorry, the Reverend Börne is not at home. The Reverend Börne left a message for you; he says unfortunately this information service is not going to work out. He says his congregation is not yet ready for it. But perhaps in two years. In two years, GEBHARDT thinks and distributes copies of the minutes. Minutes for twenty empty chairs, while BACHHOF says, I just don't understand it. Börne too. The REV. BACHHOF sits down. Chair space 4b. A study group for chair space 4b. We've never suffered from a lack of ideas, only a lack of people, the REV. BACHHOF says, and falls silent. Starts his study group by himself. And GEBHARDT thinks, this movie house is going to close. This film, DEVELOPING SOLIDARITY IN POVERTY, OBTAINING A PURIFIED CHRISTIAN ETHIC. The film cannot run because the theater has gone under, GEBHARDT thinks. Only one mark in the cash register. One solitary Bachhof mark. It's depressing, says BACHHOF. Why depressing, asks FERDINAND. The REV. FERDINAND, who strolls in at this moment. Easy, slouching, taking it slow. Eighteen excuses late. And a whole DEPRESSING too early. Why depressing? FERDINAND asks. Only three left, GEBHARDT says. Only three people came today; it's just unbelievable, says the REV. BACHHOF. We wanted to discuss the service. We wanted to do a dry run. That's not so tragic, FERDINAND says. Let's go downstairs. Let's join the others. And BACHHOF says, No, let's wait a bit. Another twenty years, GEBHARDT thinks, a year for each. He telephoned twenty. And twenty said they would come. Eighteen have stayed away. Only Bachhof and Ferdinand have come. The REV. FERDINAND, who says with a smile, But

142

there are many more besides these twenty. Many more ministers who will say yes, GEBHARDT thinks, and who will not come. Too cowardly to try out a new form of service. I'm sure many of them will join us, says FERDINAND, who smiles for twenty, who says, Let's go downstairs. Let's see how the study group on the press is coming along. And BACHHOF is looking at his pocket calendar. BACHHOF says, It was today, wasn't it? Today is the fourteenth, isn't it? It was supposed to be today? And GEBHARDT says, as the REV. FERDINAND is already on his way down to the press, Yes, today is the fourteenth. And it's not a mistake. None whatsoever. It was supposed to be today.

Suspicion for Fifty Pfennig

June 17: German Unity Day. Officially proclaimed paradox. Open the gates. *Undo the Second World War. We salute our brothers and sisters in the East with bouquets of yellow tulips and go to memorial services. The Munich Pact lies on the ceremonial altar. We condemn the Russian barbarians who raped Berlin. We solemnly recall our German unity in the Greater German Reich.* Deutschland, Deutschland, über alles. *We wear black pleated skirts and starched white blouses. In our heads gurgles the Etsch River, and our teachers row their boats across the Belt River of civil service loyalty.* We are hungry, hungry, hungry! *Undo the Second World War, ye powers of the earth. Look down upon singing German school girls and their ironed-out teachers. Take pity on fifty-five million dead. Give us back our Buchenwald near Weimar.* Brothers, join hands now together. *Buchenwald and Dachau, Bergen-Belsen and Sachsenhausen are inseparable.* Split in three? Never!

Napalm war in Vietnam. June 17 has many siblings. The dotted i, *our school newspaper, types busily over curtseying, kowtowing teachers' hymns, with generous retirement-pension tears and law and order in their buttonholes. The napalm war occupies our pages. Gardening, needlework, cross-stitch in egg soufflé and crested impotence give way to the truth. A newspaper begins to take a stand. It punctuates the legal holidays with question marks. A newspaper begins to fight. Children who are kept in ignorance, under tutelage, in prejudice, take the floor. Suspicion for fifty Pfennig, available in the schoolyard, in every classroom, under every desk. But in the teachers' lounge silence reigns.*

They sit there in their drawers, in their file folders, our cowardly little teachers. They do not ask. They do not look. They read nothing, hear nothing. They avoid discussions. They scurry under the floorboards. They scurry away. But suddenly you stumble into a pit trap, impaled on a sharpened bamboo D; your blood is drawn off. They slit open your composition, in revenge for page 15. They stab you silently from the rear. The connections are woven behind your back. In front of you you see only bare, gray façades, blocks of silence. But a C-minus for Angola rubs your backbone raw. And as you run past, the editor-in-chief for Vietnam, they hurl grades at your vertebrae. They are waiting to stick your head on a pole. They stab at you until you forget how to walk upright. But they do not talk to you. They nod at you. They smile at you. Friendly murderers.

SCENE 46. INTERIOR. EVENING. LOBBY OF AN ART CINEMA. LONG SHOT. AMONG THOSE WAITING ARE GEBHARDT AND FRAUKE. THE CAMERA PICKS THEM OUT. Early April. A quarter of a year wasted. Three months of NEW YEAR are past. He had resolved to start a new life in January. Not much has come of the resolution. Fragments are floating in the soup, flotsam and jetsam. He is getting old. Lazy. Is he growing tame? He is afraid to lose what he has. What he has in the way of bedtime with wicker lampshade and Christmas star. No, he is not afraid. But he does not do it. So he is afraid of the decisive step. The step out of the full cookie jar. Some day he will have to take that step. There is no avoiding it. One step. His foot out of the nest. He does not want to hang a noose around his own neck. The foot must move. Life has become insipid. His marriage has become insipid. One dull, the other trivial. He is suffocating in this knitting-and-slippers life. His third marriage is jogging along in indifferent coexistence. The mumble-jumble of body warmth. Hardly even that any more. Constant repetition of a deathly boring ritual. The days come. The nights go. Gebhardt is drowning in monotony. He is not prepared to accept this as final. Salary scale 1A2. Profession 1A2. Standard of living 1A2. Everything standardized. Everything monotonous. Everything inconsequential. Happy are those who demand nothing more from life. He demands more. Antonioni is the key. But the popcorn chewers don't understand him. How could they? Wedded to their salary and their three meals a day, they keep looking for themselves and their own retirement prospects in Gebhardt. For them there is no bridge. Neither to "Red Desert" nor to "The Silence." Gebhardt has seen the Bergman three times. He is seeing the Antonioni for the third time. He sits through their celluloid. Both have their fingertips on the anxiety pulse of the times. Both pulsate with almost inaudible yet penetrating anxiety. Gebhardt pays three marks fifty for this anxiety. He saves the program. He feels as if he were surrounded by Neanderthal men. The red desert is already inside him. He knows that nothing will change, that nothing can change unless human beings are changed. The popcorn chewers will bleed to death. Program buyers, too. That is inevitable. GEBHARDT stubs out his cigarette. He had resolved: a different life, starting January 1. And he is still smoking. A habit. He hasn't even licked that in these three months. Not even one lousy habit.

Seize an F by the Tail

It is not a table leg. It is soft and flexible. It slithers up and down my calf. It presses into my knees. It comes as a leg and as an elbow. It strokes and plucks the skin from my hands. It is white and black haired. It pokes its head over my shoulder. Decimals begin to dance. My writing peters out. My forehead pounds my voice in two. I cannot follow the text any more. My skin comes to a halt. My back begins to hum. The encroachment arranges tutoring sessions.

I had cheated. I had cheated myself into an F. My C-minuses began to waver. Final exams, the noose of terror, began to tighten slowly around my neck, and at that point a colleague offered to loosen the noose. My faculty adviser for the dotted i. He sits there with our editorial team amidst chocolate bars and sourballs. He gives me a free hand. He prolongs meetings. He gives me the go-ahead. He invites me imperiously into his car, and his trip home expands into hour-long loops. He saves me for last. He drops off all the editors, except for one remnant. I'm that remnant, stiff and reluctant, invisibly chained to this car, which honks and opens, carries me and waits for me, and blocks off avenues of retreat if a meeting is cancelled, if the war of the eyes does not take place.

It was not in his class that I cheated. But he seizes my F by the tail. He offers himself. Colleague to colleague. My aging teacher is content with the arrangement: let the young man take on the task. A good way to be rid of the problem, the F's, the questions. My old teacher is exhausted. His mouth droops. The folds in his brow sag down over his eyes. He himself has trouble with the decimals, needs tutoring. Why should he object to my having extra help?

My colleague offers himself. My advisory teacher spins a net of logarithms around me. For two hours at school he stares away my last certainty with his ink-black eyes. Two afternoons at school, in empty, June-brown classrooms, with rapid blackboard steps. He never sits still. He paces me up and down. We start lessons at home: morning lessons, afternoon lessons, evening lessons. Outside instruction, impossible at school, takes place at home. A teacher edges in closer, rearranges his times. When my mother leaves the house in the morning, he is already on the doorstep, smilingly wishing her good office hours, and shutting our door behind her with a swift push.

My assignments.

Edge closer. Check them over. Edge closer. Two seats at right angles at the table merge into one bench. He edges toward my hip. My breath begins to pulsate into my hands. This is my teacher. A grown-up man. A creature to whom one is supposed to curtsey in the schoolyard, whose assignments one fears, a god of marks who marches off to war against the children, armed with red pencil and chalk. He has a family, two children, is untouchably adult, ought to stand in front of me and dispense instruction. A creature that belongs to a superior order of things, an unreal being. He ought to be unapproachable, this Herr Doktor Teacher, this colleague, this pedagogical co-conspirator from the teachers' lounge, from the restricted area behind closed doors.

And now he puts his hand on my neck, strokes up and down, up and down with his index finger, until the arithmetic goes to my head. I can no longer keep track of the transitions, no longer know when it all began. This stroking, gently slithering finger rubs away all awareness of time from my skin. A red, throbbing eternity behind my eyes. Everything stretches into the distance, prickling and hot. It does not want to stop. It clings to me and won't let go.

Please leave. It's seven already. My mother will be back any minute.

Anxiety takes over. Suddenly I am anxious. Anxious and afraid of this aroused whatever-it-is, this unbridled passion, this never-let-me-go, this persistent contact. The corridors at school are full of him. No matter

146

where I go, he is coming toward me, greeting me, turning to look after me, opening the door of his car, his arms, his mouth. I try to conjure my mother behind all the doors, into the next room, into the window niche, behind every curtain. I wish someone were watching me, that he knew someone was watching me, that he would give up, give in. But he edges closer, rearranges his schedule further, until she leaves the house. Yesterday he invited me to his house. Right after school, in his car. He lives on the outskirts of Hamburg. Where it becomes green, sparsely settled, lonely. I dare not say no. My mother finds him pleasant. My math work is improving. And when I hear other students talking about him, respectfully and gushingly, I feel a caressing finger on my neck. Up and down. And I do not say no.

SCENE 47. EXTERIOR. DAY AND NIGHT. WAR MEMORIAL ON HAMBURG'S DAMMTORSTRASSE. AN OPTICAL SKETCH. ADD OFF-CAMERA NARRATION. My glass house is fairly safe, GEBHARDT thinks. He thinks that every day as he drives past the massive granite square. He can allow himself that thought, when he sees the high-rise buildings, the Botanical Gardens. Well-maintained, he thinks then. Streets and people and houses. Well-maintained and safe. He also drives past it every evening. When everything is safely lit up. Movie or the opera, whichever. Maybe a pizza afterward. Just as you please. Safe. Maybe this or that. And the voice on the radio can be switched off. Who wants to hear about Hué after *Aïda*? Just stick to a routine, RAINER GEBHARDT thinks. Keep going as before. Don't rock the boat, he thinks, and drives past the gray stone block again, on which soldiers are marching endlessly, round and round. On and on through Hamburg. Through thick and thin. Stoney faced in perpetual unmoving motion. Calling out GERMANY MUST LIVE, EVEN IF WE MUST DIE. Calling that down the busy shopping streets. Calling it into Mrs. Consumer's shopping bag. Calling it into the business offices. Calling it out to Gebhardt every morning. The password for the day. The password for the evening. Decorated with wreaths. Never smashed. Never dismantled. Simply still there. Between mini and maxi. GERMANY MUST LIVE, EVEN IF WE MUST DIE. Between the Alster Pavilion Restaurant and the Soapbox Green. Between high-rise buildings, streets, the Botanical Gardens. Even if we must die, GEBHARDT thinks. Germany.

Somewhat lethargic, GEBHARDT thinks. War is still marching in place. Around and around in a circle. Still there. We're the ones who leave our war standing, GEBHARDT thinks. Preserved as a historic monument. Our form of total war—for borders in ruins and refugee children, who live out their future amidst provisos. Amidst wreath-decked provisos. Germany must live, even if we must die. Still there, RAINER GEBHARDT thinks, still there when I drive home every evening. When the cannon fodder drives home every evening. Certainly. Still there. Just as you please. With ice cream in his stomach. *Aïda* in his stomach and intermission champagne. Champagne between the intermissions. Between the first and second act. Between the second and third act. Germany must live, even if we must die. It's still there, RAINER GEBHARDT thinks. It sweetens the intermission for us. Between high-rises and gardens, movie and opera. Around and around in a circle. Clearly visible and well-maintained. And relatively safe. Well-maintained and preserved as a historic monument.

That Would Be Something

It costs eighty Pfennig and takes twenty minutes. The ride by elevated into town. Up the steps to the station. One should try it at five in the afternoon, when the trains run every few seconds. Liquidation sale of humanity. Rush hour.

He lets me wait at the ticket counter. Brings the line to a standstill. He is on the phone, this little counter tyrant. He keeps me from making the next train. It is five o'clock, and he is king. With a white, unaired face and a squashed right index finger. Handling too many tickets has made it atrophy. And we stand in line and wait. Grumble, but under our breath. Not daring to make a fuss. Knocking on the glass, infuriated, but gently. It is five o'clock, and we will put up with anything. The fat housewife behind me. The high-stilted secretary. The many men, anonymous beneath their hats. Chubby little overtrained thinkers with brightly polished spectacle-ideas. Round heads, long heads—they all put up with it. We stand there. A little dyed-in-the-wool telephone tyrant brings us to a standstill. We look at each other. Infuriating, we whisper, until one person takes his one-mark piece between thumb and index finger. The slender gentleman with distinguished gray-streaked hair. I'm in a hurry, he exclaims, and stirs up a tempest. He actually dares to pound on the glass. The ticket counter roars at us. He shouts his daily routine into our faces. I'm sick and tired of this, he shouts, I'm not going to let myself be pushed around. He blows his staleness through the glass. Dusty, sour staleness. Clouds of dissatisfaction. He's had it. He's through. He's fed up. Yes, that's right. Things used to be different. No discipline anymore. Bunch of lazy bastards. Proletarian scum. Like the Pollacks!

Finally I'm in my train. Stuffed to the gills, locked in. If these people don't get a vacation tomorrow, they'll all be raring to march off to war. That man there, behind the newspaper. Overfed, drowning in fat. The corners of his mouth knot the slobby fat under his chin. Everything about him sags. He crouches behind his paper, cramping his spongy white fists around it. Sixty years of saturation. The Great Years. In those days he had different boots on. In those days his arm was raised high, the corners of his mouth turned up, and the flags waved aloft. In those days he had a part in a murder mystery. Now he is reading an account of a murder. Drinking the blood from the pages in thick red letters. He's putting new wine in his old cask. Fed up. He's fed up with reading. With his life, stuffed to the gills with office and commuting, the old lady always on his back. She looks like that one over there. Rigid backbone. A gum tree from top to toe. Grown straight up with very little water, German and erect. She rubs the sleep of prejudice from the corners of her eyes. But a dark, soft gray speck remains stuck to her cheek.

Smoking car. Irritable. With hands folded. Go ahead and sign. Put your name on the list. The nose gives it away. Just phone privately, that's all that's necessary. With him I'm on shaky ground. He is so young and polished, so pudgied in the direction of thirty, so elusive and slithering. An overgrown young man. A reliable man. Chewing his conscience, he earns his young pockets full. All right, here goes. Let's take a body count. We don't worry about a thing. Snap, open your compact. Powder your nose into the metallic reflection. Just keep an eye out. In gray, in blue coats, knotted into a head scarf, we just keep an eye out, with button earrings and gold fillings in view. Watch how he twists her leg out of its socket. Simply forces it back. Farther and farther, until the bones snap.

The man behind the newspaper turns a page. If I stepped on his foot, he would kill me. If I stumbled against her when the train lurches, she would slit me open with the feather on her hat. I'll powder it over before

149

it bleeds. I won't look in that direction. Anyone wearing a gray or a blue coat doesn't look in that direction. Only he, young and agile, would pull me up by the hair and rub me raw on a soldier's locker. Something's in here, he would say. And my neighbor, the emaciated past with needle-thin long fingers, would take a poke. Would turn the eye around once, like a key in a keyhole. Poke it out. Slowly. That would be something. That's something one could do. They've been waiting for this. Only the slightest offense, and behind the newspapers, behind the eyeglasses, war would break out.

They would leap out of their coats. They would burst out of their tight collars, fed up with peace, their overly substantial lunches slopping in their bellies. They would jump off the armistice train. Free again at last. Free for anything. These discontented train riders. This sixty-year-old, fifty-year-old, forty-year-old, thirty-year-old sour residue at the bottom of the seats, Germany's dagger between their teeth.

SCENE 48. INTERIOR. DAYTIME. GEBHARDT'S LIVING ROOM. FRAUKE AND GEBHARDT BENEATH THE WICKER LAMPSHADE. SILENT BREAKFAST. AUTOMATIC GESTURES. CAMERA OPENS WITH EXTREME CLOSE-UP OF THE EGG WHICH GEBHARDT IS JUST BEHEADING. OFF-CAMERA NARRATION. He seldom lies. But he keeps many things to himself. Less a weak character than a permanent sensation of impotence. Why should he try to explain things that will only be misunderstood anyway? He dreads the future. He admits that. The more one experiences in life, the more one's sense of responsibility grows. One reins in one's feelings. One starts to weigh priorities, to prevent nasty smash-ups. The ringed person across the table changes from an object into a subject. Love is no longer a thing unto itself, but a mixture of cowardice, stupidity, and yes, yes. Fat and comfortable. Forty-three years old and a cripple. Frauke spreads his wings on his bread. The leg irons are clamped shut. Soon she will switch on the current. Hold tight. There, it's over. If he were consistent, he would put a bullet through his head. Right in front of this soft-boiled egg. Just like that: pow! Plop into this vacuum-cleaned morning. Do something meaningful. Though it is questionable what meaningful means. But the signposts don't permit tepid compromise. They point either toward him or away from him. Coffee with cream and sugar and

150

some whipped cream of marital bliss. He does not have to choose any more. He has already chosen. Eat. Chew. Eat. Chew. He can no longer give up the habit. Down the gullet. Down, down, down. Submerged in the garbage pail of life. A reptile stranded on a chair, still eating. Out cold. Between knife and fork. Position: lost. Inhale. Exhale. That uses up time and energy. That's fine. Things will go downhill more rapidly. Downhill into the trap of steady income and the good life of total dependency. For who has enough in reserve to be able to afford freedom? On the last day of the month he is always broke. What if he were fired tomorrow? That would be just fine. He could sell his belongings. An old vw worth not even a thousand marks. An electric sewing machine. Two Persian lamb coats. Added up it comes to about four thousand. He doesn't own anything beyond himself and his daily quotation. What does he have to lose? What to defend? Freedom? No. It's best to admit right away that it's a phantom of freedom. Freedom? The jester's freedom to think what he likes. Perhaps even to say what he thinks. But that's as far as it goes. It would be suicide to draw conclusions from his thoughts. GEBHARDT GETS UP, GOES INTO THE HALLWAY. FRAUKE HELPS HIM INTO HIS COAT, GIVES HIM A PECK ON THE CHEEK. GEBHARDT STEPS OUT OF THE HOUSE. The witching hour, he thinks. He lets the witches dance. He dances with the witches. GEBHARDT WAVES, GOES TO THE CAR, UNLOCKS IT, WAVES ONCE AGAIN. Witching hour, GEBHARDT thinks. Punctual. Every hour on the hour. THE CAR DOOR SLAMS SHUT. CUT.

Authorities Subject to Recall

His favorite color is gray. His favorite drink is water. There are no pictures on his walls. If there were a law that one had to have pictures, he would get it changed.

She could be about forty. Or thirty-five. Or forty-five. She will always look the same. Smiling broadly, a chignon at her neck. Broad and flat. A sturdy, friendly puppet in sensible flat laced shoes. If there were a law she had to be that way, he would get it changed. How did he come by her? She must have been slipped inside something else, like a piece of blotter in a notebook. Now she flattens out his life with her iron. She smiles. Her flat puppet face smiles at me.

She's in the dark. She wants to be in the dark. I'm going to save her marriage.

This is the fourth time I've been out here already, the fifth time. Squalling children. Two little boys wrestling. Walls and toys. No boxes, no fans. Just heaps. Dolls and balls. Walls smeared with finger paint. Do what you want. Go ahead. Hurl yourselves down on the floor. Bang your heads against the wall, you three- and five-year-olds. Do what you feel like. And jump on your Daddy's back. He likes that. That's the only thing he does like. These dragging, screaming, kicking children in the kingdom of the bare walls.

She cooks for me. She goes into the kitchen. The children play, rumpling up the rug. The father reaches for my knee. Slinking hands. In these furnitureless rooms, there is a lot of space for the attack. And she is glad to facilitate it. She leaves the room more and more often. All her pretexts can be found in the kitchen. She invites me again and again. A Ph.D. in mathematics, a colleague of her husband's. Drowned in instant pudding, missing in broiling, fallen on the field of baking. She invites me to join them for vacation. In Italy. As a sort of daughter. And he reaches deep down my dress while she is putting the children to bed.

In a spanking new apartment house I set forth to learn what fear is. Behind the wheel, on dark, wooded back roads, the air freezes my voice, frosts it over. Fear flowers on the windows. Wood road. Stop. He moves in for a bite. He slips through the openings in his coat. He unbuttons.

I'll get a divorce. I want to marry you. Be with you. All night long sinks its teeth in. Hands want to stay all night long.

I'll get a divorce.

Divorce. Separation. Break off. Leave the country. I am supposed to caress a yes to that, to kiss a yes. I am not supposed to slap a no. A gray episode down a wrong path. Then flight from the car, in any direction, mindlessly. The return. Furious, biting, weeping, caught and hauled in. My vanity, my schoolgirl fortress, has long since been taken by storm. This teacher melts into my ears. Stops up every orifice with his divorce. Pours out his family life over me with watery kisses.

My admiration for stubborn, energetic, argumentative dissipates in the face of this bundle of uncontrolled flesh. My teacher, I think. This is my teacher, who betrays grades and homework assignments between kisses, betrays his family, betrays himself. Who edges closer to me with every day that passes. State of siege.

I stop going home alone. I invite Cornelia to dinner. I go home with Hannelore. I find seconds and thirds. I don't go to his house anymore. I fall sick and wiggle out of his invitations. I fetch my mother and seat her at the table between us. Now I can't make it at five anymore. At five I invite girl friends over and scrape away at my cello.

He was not the first to inject seduction into a shared activity. He was not the first grown-up to mistake my body for the task at hand. He was not the first. What sort of a creature is a teacher, anyway? Simply an age gap. They are more vulnerable than I had thought. They peep out of all the cracks. They are unsheltered. And their security is merely freedom subject to recall. The burrow has many exits. These fathers of families. These hallowed adults. Gods to children. How can they fail to fail us, when given the chance? Authorities subject to recall. Monitors subject to recall. Teachers subject to recall. The fathers of my classmates. Fathers and their overweight families. The dull, unaching wounds of everyday routine. Every glance sets them afire. They remain steadfast only if temptation remains static. They can't restrain themselves. They should be grateful that habit has a firm grip on them, that they stick to the bottom of the pot with their lunch. They should be thankful that they can move into prisons with nervous front lawns and pudding-stirring neighbors. Otherwise they would end up in the gutter. Languishing wretchedly among the dogs and cats. Raping every blade of grass. Scalping every child.

SCENE 49. DAYTIME. BIEHL'S ROOM. DIETER BIEHL IS SITTING AT AN OLD TYPEWRITER. CLOSE-UP FROM BIEHL'S PERSPECTIVE: MEMBERSHIP BLANKS, TO THE RIGHT OF THE TYPEWRITER. BIEHL IS TRANSFERRING THE DATA ON THEM TO THE INDEX CARDS, WHICH HE ARRANGES IN A FILE BOX TO THE LEFT OF THE TYPEWRITER. BIEHL has set up shop. APPLICATION (a) I declare myself prepared to support the club's endeavors to the full extent of my ability. BIEHL hands out membership blanks. APPLICATION (b) I request admission to the Republican Club but cannot become an active member at present. BIEHL answers the phone and studies for his exams. APPLICATION (c) I share the goals of the Hamburg Republican Club. BIEHL records the applications. BIEHL fills out little file cards. BIEHL paints the old furniture green. BIEHL tends to the meeting rooms. BIEHL sets up a schedule. Name. Address. Telephone number. Occupation. BIEHL keeps track of the members. There are already over two hundred, BIEHL says, And I don't know most of them from Adam. Hardly one of these people ever puts in an appearance. At least not for the study groups, BIEHL says, and pours tea into GEBHARDT's mug. They love to turn up for the plenary sessions and exercise their right to vote. Remember our grand opening. Half the people there just came to rip off the beer and sprawl all over our chairs. And they weren't even members. BIEHL is worried. BIEHL is having second thoughts. Law-student examination thoughts. BIEHL studies every day from eight to three. It will pay off. His law degree should be a highly polished summa. BIEHL works at the club every day from 3:00 to 11:00 P.M. That, too, should pay off. The club should also turn out to be a brightly polished summa. If it were up to me, BIEHL says, If it were up to me, we'd check membership at the door. Yesterday that fellow Denicke was here. Never lifts a finger. Just talks. Rants on about Schrader and keeps asking about the bookstore. He claims we forced him out. He claims we didn't want him. He claims we manipulate the membership. At the next plenary session—I dread to think what will happen if he brings his whole gang. We won't have our club very long. BIEHL places the cookie tin on top of his Civil Code. BIEHL chews his neatly brushed nails. Biehl comes from a well-scrubbed house. Dieter Biehl, with the protruding teeth. With the little rabbit teeth and the quick, piercing eyes behind the shining glasses. DIETER BIEHL invites GEBHARDT for Saturday tea and thinks caretakerly thoughts. Everything looked so promising at the start. But these people really don't do a thing. Don't even pay the dues they voluntarily agreed on. But they want a club. And it's up to us to scrape together the rent as best we can. Revolution and socialism, but they can't even bring along a chair. My car is outside, GEBHARDT says. There are twelve chairs at the University Hospital in Eppendorf. We can pick them up any time after five-fifteen. BIEHL puts a second kettle on to boil. Biehl, who rents a station wagon and combs the streets for chairs at the beginning of the month when the bulk trash is put out. BIEHL brews another pot of tea. Just as long as the lords and ladies can sit comfortably. Just as long as we see to getting the place furnished. Damn, it's already become standard practice. Agenda. Statement. Counterstatement. They won't even pay dues, yet they blather on about changing society. BIEHL fetches his card file. Thumbs through the alphabet. Recites his file out loud. Dues delinquent. Delinquent. Still delinquent after three

154

warnings. Delinquent. Delinquent. And so on, and so on. BIEHL pours out a fourth round of tea. BIEHL says, I don't plan to grow old here. Democracy is all well and good. But who ends up sitting here and doing all the work? Just us. Five of us slaving for two hundred. We do the dirty work. And what about the others? No, BIEHL says, Pretty soon this fire will go out. One more year, says BIEHL. I'll stick it out one more year. Then I'm joining the establishment. The establishment, says BIEHL.

Whoever Risks, Loses

I want to leave school. She told Hannelore's father that his daughter should not associate with Cornelia. She told him that Cornelia looked like Ilse Koch, of concentration camp fame.

But please don't do anything. Please don't tell anyone.

Hannelore has a C-minus in German, tottering on the verge of a D. Hannelore does not want to take any risks, for in our class the Nazi principle of kinship jeopardy prevails. Frau Dr. Zirkel sticks to her guns. The Russians are all butchers; they rape our women. Cornelia and I declare war. The spirit of contradiction, the guilt of Auschwitz, demands to be heard. Zirkel chooses a frontal defense. Yesterday she made an appointment to have us examined at a mental hospital. The doctor calls us in the afternoon.

A school scandal? We rush from pupil to pupil. We collect boycotters. We collect signatures. We collect against the old order. Without success. The D in math keeps Annette in line, prevents her from speaking out. Many weak C-minuses are bobbing on heavenly C's, thanks to the childish feeble-mindedness of Vera Zirkel. If anything happened they would plummet to a D. Too many know their grades. They muddle through by avoiding trouble. They progress by standing still. They don't want to change the status quo.

And a brown gathered silk toad keeps silent. With protective plump arms she lovingly shelters her raving child. She waters down the depression of a sick woman, who was in a mental institution years ago because the walls were closing in on her. Why do we have this woman as a teacher? The school board replies. The superintendent of schools speaks the magic word: teacher shortage. The school board hangs up. My mother's medical vocabulary fails her.

And Vera sings Tristan *to us. Wagner as a seated giant in German class. Arias on stumpy legs instead of the First World War. History class is redirected, drowns in overtures. Vera sings. Sings us the* Meistersinger *and Siegfried. Lessing's* Nathan the Wise *is shoved into a drawer. And with it the Weimar Republic. We push it under the carpet, under our desks. We don't learn to read such things. But we learn eagerly what Lessing was wearing when he hastened across Hamburg's Lombard Bridge, his coat flapping in the wind—the velvet morning coat and the buckled breeches; we listen giggling and rejoicing to descriptions of Marie Antoinette's gathered bodice.*

Hail to Hans Sachs! Hail to Nuremberg's faithful Sachs! *She braces her leg against the chair and throws up her arms for the final chorus, while the populace waves hats and handkerchiefs. The curtain falls on our history class.*

I want to leave school. Or get another teacher in place of Zirkel. This can't go on. We all know that. And we complain peevishly to other teachers, threatening mutiny.

Since we feel a mighty urge to increase human well-being. *Cicero's political theory is drowned out by whispered reproaches. But Cicero keeps silent, lets us struggle on with the translation. One crow won't peck out another's class. Except for one. Surrounded by India ink and charcoal one exceptional teacher, a married woman, our art teacher, admits to us that Zirkel is ill. A breakthrough. The only one. But it, too, is stopped by the wall. When she asks for a hearing in the principal's office, she is urged to transfer to another school. School spirit must not and will not be disturbed. To be sure, we have eccentrics here, pathologically depressive exceptions, but so long as they don't hang pupils in the broom closet, fiddlesticks, childsticks.*

Frau Doktor trips along ahead of me. Chirping softly like a cricket in the grass. Twittering and trilling. But we won't do anything. And in the corridors Frau Dr. Rautenfeld besieges me to exercise my influence on Cornelia— It will be to your advantage, you'll soon see. *And down the corridor she lies in wait for Cornelia and promises her better grades if she can persuade me to desist.*

You're a sensible girl.

I'm a sensible girl. We're both sensible. There's no call for leaving school. One can whisper everything away. And then the parents are telephoned, and sensible parents give in. And sensible children remain in the Zirkel circle.

156

Three names languish on signature lists. Corruption of the youth. Right now nothing is at stake. Not family and children, not career and salary. A C is at stake, an undeserved C-minus, a mere grade. And history and German. Two grades. And a homeroom teacher. The worm of grades gnaws at our youth, bends our knees, eats away at our backbone. Corruption of the youth. We adapt. We are born senile. Little adults. Little tricks, running around the schoolyard and brooding over their own security. Whoever reaches security first is king. Whoever risks, loses.

SCENE 50. INTERIOR. DAYTIME. IN DR. HAUSWALD'S LIVING ROOM. CAMERA OPENS WITH CLOSE-UP OF A COFFEE TABLE, SET FOR THREE, WITH MOUNTAINS OF PASTRIES; THEN LEAPS TO THE WALL OF BOOKS, WANDERS ALONG IT, LINGERING OVER TITLES, EXAMINING THE ENTIRE INTERIOR OF THE HAUSWALD APARTMENT BEFORE IT RETURNS TO THE TABLE AND THE THREESOME SEATED AT IT. They barely manage to survive in their professions. Just barely, DR. HAUSWALD tells GEBHARDT. Dr. Hauswald, the gymnasium professor. Matthias Hauswald, the vacation-time collector. The display case undertaker Dr. Hauswald, who numbers stones and animals under glass. But politically, says DR. HAUSWALD, Politically these people are dead. Work ends at suppertime. Then it's off to TV-bed. I don't need to tell you these things. And from thirty on, they just want their peace and quiet. DR. HAUSWALD extends his legs under the table. Legs which reach all the way to the classics. A volume of Cicero. A butterfly in aspic. A volume of Cicero. A stone from the Dolomites. A volume of Cicero. A rusty coin. He fulfills my stereotype image, RAINER GEBHARDT thinks. His glasses are collector-bright. All that's missing from this room is a piano. A Sunday piano to be dusted. To be dusted by Camilla Hauswald. The tea-pouring, cake-baking, five o'clock powdered-nose housewife. How nice of you to come. FRAU HAUSWALD, a forty-year-old marriageable girl. An overage girl from Revlon country. In woolen A-line dress with a bow in her hair. Frau Hauswald oils her velvet propeller. She circles for a landing in the kitchen, to brew well-washed tea. For another pot and yet another pot. How nice you finally could come. How nice to have you here. We usually just have Matthias's pupils. The velvet bow whirrs. FRAU HAUSWALD touches down. She descends from the ceiling and lands on the deck of her rosebud-pampered sugar bowl. Yes, we have many counselling sessions here. With young people and lively discussion. DR. HAUSWALD fills in. Fills in for his Camilla. And GEBHARDT thinks of anise-flavored cookies, anise-flavored cookies that have been stirred up by hand and cut out and baked by hand, all by hand, from scratch. GEBHARDT thinks, tea times have made him political. Cookies have opened his mind. Discussions and afternoon tea for young people. Perhaps that's it? And GEBHARDT thinks, how good that Frauke isn't here. Otherwise she would be sitting cheek to cheek with Frau Hauswald. Sentence to sentence. Gossip to gossip. And Frau Hauswald would have another excuse for not listening again. And Frauke would have another. Another and yet another. For not hearing, for not seeing. Because women when they get together with other women. Like at every party. Like at every meeting. Always side by side. I always use King Arthur's. Woman next to woman. Is that really silk? Oh, how nice to have you here. But you should have brought your wife. If I had a gun, GEBHARDT thinks, one shot through that little mouth. And then anise cookies on top. And the big ribbon. Mustn't forget the bow, thinks RAINER GEBHARDT. The big bow is important, GEBHARDT thinks. And FRAU HAUSWALD cuts chocolate eclairs in half. And HERR HAUSWALD says, I used to be interested in nothing but Cicero. I took refuge in my books. Just look at those shelves. They contain only the most ancient past. Only the most ancient past, laughs CAMILLA HAUSWALD, the spokeswoman for the kitchen. And one of those who read Cicero because he reads Cicero. Who learns English because he also, he too. Always tagging along. Tender with the tender, strong with the strong. One of those, one of the many thoses of whom GEBHARDT has had his fill. His husband-and-father's fill. When he thinks of Irene Frenzel, who engages the speakers in serious conversation, only to take excursions with them to the Baltic the next day. When he thinks of Frauke. Of Frauke, who. All right, says GEBHARDT, Let's go over the whole business once more. One thing is clear: so far you're the only teacher in all of Hamburg who has been willing to conduct discussions with school kids at the club, who finds time for this study group, who makes any effort. Come now, go easy on the praise, says HAUSWALD. This study group on the schools is very tricky. How am I supposed to help these kids? They come from all different schools and for the most part they are so beaten down that they consider wearing blue and white terry socks and a red shirt a drastic expression of protest. Actually, says

158

HAUSWALD, The only one who talks is Lohmann. Only Lohmann, from the student council. He's the only one who talks about giving pupils a say in running things. And the others sit around in a circle and don't say a word. And I sit in a circle with them and describe my school to them, and suddenly one of the boys says, My teacher's a Nazi. And suddenly another bursts out, They censor our newspaper. We have to print it secretly now and sell it on the sly. And the class president is going to be replaced day after tomorrow because he was caught handing out leaflets outside our school. And then I sit there, says DR. HAUSWALD, And we don't accomplish anything. We don't get beyond general resolutions and lists of demands. Yet HAUSWALD still considers the project important. He still wants to try to construct a model for democratic schools, a joint creation of pupils and teachers. Because in spite of, and especially in spite of, we must all pull together. And when HAUSWALD says that, while Hauswald is speaking, GEBHARDT thinks, he is a thoroughly decent man. A good German gymnasium professor. Infused with classical learning. And yet he is more than a good German gymnasium professor. For there's a mite more understanding in him than the usual nature club urge that finds release in vacation hikes. DR. HAUSWALD retracts his legs. DR. HAUSWALD says, Actually it's all since Berlin. Or rather, since that student. In front of the Opera. It began with my simply trying to become better informed. I started to read the foreign press, to discuss it with my students. Actually all since the student business, says HERR HAUSWALD. HERR DR. MATTHIAS HAUSWALD. And the tea holds in its five o'clock coziness. And the cookies stand at baking sheet attention. And the volumes of the classics stare in yellow amazement. Stare yolk yellow out of their shelves. Amazed at their gymnasium professor. Gymnasium professor Dr. Hauswald, who set forth to learn what democracy was.

Pedagogical Doves of Peace
Wow, is he good-looking. A Roman numeral two on the right and left halves of his collar. They call that collar insignia. Aha. Frau Doktor blushes. This handsome young man wants to say something to you, girls.

This good-looking guy. Saturday we'll take the bus to the barracks. To the officers' training academy in Osdorf, for vol-au-vents and uniforms.

We'll sit there, chosen by lots. With fluffy, freshly washed hair, each waiting for the good-looking one. Waiting for the party to begin, with pretzel sticks and young soldiers. Our school gives us its blessing.

I used to have handsome suitors like that, too, says our little Vera, hoping that every one of us will be able to press an ensign to her bosom. *The two senior classes are invited. The soldiers have issued an invitation to the dance.*

You lucky girl!

Yes, he really is good-looking, is called Klaus Werner, and pays court to me assiduously. He pulls my curls, blows my bangs up while we dance, plays gentle summer breeze, and grabs hold with a pincerlike grip. He wants a kiss on the ear straight off, between fox trot and rock 'n' roll with collar and tie. Muted Beatle guitars, modern but restrained, suitable for older gentlemen as well. Between let's go and electric waltz, one-two-three, one-two-three, wine glasses tinkle and candles flicker on the tables. Snowdrops and anemones hold a rendezvous. Spring comes in uniform. And vol-au-vent and lettuce leaf rise respectfully when an older gray spectacled man enters the hall, both hands raised in greeting.

Our colonel!

Elegantly custom tailored, with epaulets, armpatches, and braid. On his sleeve a bird, an eagle, is embroidered. Flying through two narrow golden rings.

Airplanes wing on their way. Winging toward the sun. Already Samos lay below to their left. Icarus, he calls.

The auditorium is dark. We gaze into a steel blue sky. The silver birds of the troop fly onward, into the light. Homer. That's how soldiers are educated, with Samos below on their left. A film for the upperclassmen. The introduction and conclusion spoken by a young soldier, himself a gymnasium graduate. Education-proud, he lets that fact slip out. He knows what a gymnasium stands for. The army summoned him, complete with his liberal arts education. And Icarus, Icarus came. Ready to serve for two years now. And teachers and schoolgirls gaze with him into the light of this flight. I see, I'm supposed to get used to the sight of the uniform. This film is obviously not shown at a girls' school for recruiting purposes. Slow-motion romance of war without conflict. I see, we're supposed to develop into good soldiers' wives, good officers' widows. Thank you; I already have one at home—my mother.

Please be seated, lovely ladies!

160

We sit down with the colonel. The uniform buttons glitter. Quick glance in the mirror. Nose powdered, lashes mascaraed twice over. Politely drilled cavaliers, ready with wine glass and dance steps.

Here's your chance to make your fortune.

Klaus Werner is already an ensign second class. He is still hesitating. Perhaps he'll commit himself for life soon. Perhaps the army will pay for his university education. Who knows. May I have the pleasure?

May I have the pleasure, into the sun. Our side's losses—none. The army builds men. Rewarding friendships in a man's world. *Who wants to join the soldiers, with fathers fallen and relatives gassed? Homeland, needful of defenders. Now I begin to probe. Now I force discussion on the stillness. Now I say, The real job of soldiers is to wage war. Why do you show us romantic falsifications like this film? A kitschy image of martial peacetime?*

Icarus, our gymnasium graduate, remains silent.

I read somewhere that the libraries of the Federal Army still contain many books from the Third Reich. And every fifth soldier votes for the German National Party.

I rattle off my newspaper knowledge. The introducer of the film remains silent. My schoolmates remain silent. My teachers remain silent. They are all sitting in the back row, these pedagogical doves of peace. And they remain silent. Stare at me as if I were insane, a nuisance, a spoilsport. Yes, I want to spoil this war for you. I don't want to join the soldiers. I don't want to fall in battle like my father. Missing. Fallen. Go find your fathers. Collect them from the last few wars. Sort out their bones. You saw Hamburg in flames, not I. You described fleeing from the East, the horrors of war, not I. Why don't you say anything? Why don't you comment on Samos and the sun? Why don't you demand to see the truth? Show us the atrocities in Vietnam or somewhere else, not the merry bomb life of Homer. Show us the horrors. Help raise our consciousness; we don't need technicolor dreams.

But we dance and eat pasties. He tucks me under his chin. An enterprising type. My man in Hamburg. *The talk of the class next day. Our men. Our side's losses—none. Order, industry, cleanliness. Klaus Werner has lofty goals. And in the schoolrooms sit the brides of tomorrow and learn reading and writing for the letters to their husbands at the front.*

SCENE 51. EXTERIOR. LATE AFTERNOON. HALLERSTRASSE SUBWAY STATION. SCENE OPENS WITH A LONG SHOT; CAMERA THEN PICKS OUT JÜRGEN KRANZ FROM AMONG THE PASSENGERS COMING UP THE STAIRS AND FOLLOWS HIM TO THE LATE NINETEENTH-CENTURY VILLA AND INTO BIEHL'S ROOM. He must buy his clothes in the children's department, GEBHARDT thinks. He rents his suits by the day from Rasch's Toyland. He has the famous turtle trademark inside his shirt, and his skin is flesh color from a spray can. Gebhardt bets three 16-ounce steaks with Biehl that Jürgen Kranz is made of celluloid and sleeps in a doll carriage at night. The famous Jürgen Kranz. Recommended by Frenzel. Size four. He gets around. A man worth cultivating. A man of importance. He knows everybody, says Winfried Böhm. He'll get us money. He knows how to go about it. JÜRGEN KRANZ knows how to go about it. He has just come from Rudi's. Comes straight to BIEHL. Dwarfs up to Dieter Biehl's desk. I've just been to see Rudi. A cup of coffee for me, too, please. Everything's hunky-dory, he exclaims. Ten thousand. Just have to finalize the deal. And tomorrow I'll stop by to see Buci. He's already promised me eight thousand. My old friend Buci. I'm hot on the trail. He's been hot on the trail for weeks, GEBHARDT thinks, and stirs his coffee. The only thing is, where's the trail? I went to see Schlesselmann, JÜRGEN KRANZ exclaims from the floor. JÜRGEN KRANZ laboriously scrambles up on the sofa, thumps his fist on his attaché case. On his black, mysterious box, and exclaims, Everything's hunky-dory. Schlesselmann is willing. Soon he's going to work something out with Pantenburg. He promised me his cooperation in no uncertain terms. This very day. This very day, this very morning, GEBHARDT thinks. He is always saying this very. And BIEHL says loudly, That would cover the rent for two years. We could use that. And the rest for office supplies. He also went to see Bruhns, GEBHARDT thinks. Who just happened not to have his checkbook on him. He certainly intended to. The thousand which he meant to give eight weeks ago. In a week our coffers will be overflowing, JÜRGEN KRANZ exclaims. I already have an appointment with Peter. He already has an appointment with Peter, GEBHARDT thinks, and with Buci and Rudi. He knows everybody. And he borrows money from me for his streetcar fare. The money he simply forgot to put in his pocket when Rudi's chauffeur came to pick him up. Just for today, KRANZ says. I'll get it back to you right away. In a few weeks we'll be swimming in money. Then we'll expand, RAINER GEBHARDT thinks, and then Gottfried Pantenburg will show up here, and Professor Schlesselmann. Then all two hundred of us will fly to Rio. With Rudi, Buci, and Jürgen Kranz, so our piles of money don't gather dust. For Herr Kranz already has a new appointment to see Hopp, GEBHARDT thinks. And Herr Hopp is a man worth cultivating.

Checkpoint Face No. 110

Class 13a, herded together in a place they call Berlin. Berlin, the former capital of the Reich. The last flea in the hide of denazification. Tour of a trademark. No man's land of a legend. They stripped off the Berlin bear's Nazi-brown pelt. They are supposed to be my brothers. They divide everything up. They string barbed wire around its middle. One side has the head, the other the legs. And they march. March on the head and think with the feet. March on the feet and have no head.

We travel by train and elevated railway. There and back. There and back. The graduating class's trip to Berlin. Look, there's a watchtower, I exclaim, and wonder, what will Berlin be like? More cosmopolitan than Hamburg, that's clear.

I look closely at the clothing.

A large, comfortably equipped prison.

The train stops at Büchen. A poster proclaims, Life itself is at stake. Never again must Germany cause a war. What are you doing? *Slogans on a red background. What is Vera Zirkel doing? She has forbidden us to talk. The monsters are coming. Border controls. The cleaning women have striped socks on. Identification check. Checkpoint face no. 110, white, lean, elongated. The train halts in Schwanheide. Here lips are lipsticked. The black-tarred ashtray opens its jaws to receive candy wrappers. We are riding through East Germany, museums and Konrad Witz in our hearts, Lukas Cranach in our eyes. Fields of flowering rape plants. Birch forests. Tall telephone poles.*

Are you curious about the Wall?

Naw. It's just a bunch of stones.

Still, you should see it. It gives you a funny sensation.

Funny sensation? Eggshells and sandwich bags spawn pretentious conversations between Büchen and Potsdam West.

Our first evening in Berlin. Askanischer Platz, the square near the old Anhalt Station. Blooming barbed wire and a sea of weeds. Memories of

163

1945. I follow paths cracked and crumbling. The scent of camomile, which luxuriates in the crevices, reminds me of childhood games in the ruins. We are housed at the Dunant Red Cross Hospice. *From the window of our room I stare out into a stony crater with eighteen garbage cans.*

SCENE 52. INTERIOR. EVENING. A PIZZA PLACE. CLOSE-UP: HANDS PUTTING A COIN IN A JUKE BOX. CAMERA WIDENS ANGLE. HELMUT FROMM IS STROLLING BACK TO HIS BAR STOOL. CAMERA WANDERS AIMLESSLY, DISCOVERS GEBHARDT, CLINGS TO HIM. Gebhardt eats here quite often. Dinner from the juke box. Between the end of his working day and his night shift at the Republican Club. He quite often sits in this Italian joint, which is always running down the top ten. Here he eats his recovery ravioli. Between seven and eight at the pizza bar. Tonight HELMUT FROMM is here. GEBHARDT has not noticed him yet. He glanced cursorily down the bar when he came in. The people bore him. Stuffed yes-men. If the food tastes good, everything is all right. And if FROMM did not yell TWO MORE BEERS into the silence between two recorded hits, GEBHARDT would not even have noticed him. So there's Helmut Fromm. No, I'm just his mother. No, Helmut isn't back yet. What a pity, he just left the house. Yes, he did get your letter. Certainly, Helmut will call you back. Oh dear, Helmut hasn't called you yet? No, Helmut is in Bochum this week. So there's Helmut, GEBHARDT thinks. Six seats down the pizza counter. With his wife or girl friend. Wearing the brown vest he wore the day the steering committee was elected. The double-breasted velvety vest. He's studying in Bochum. Under Abendroth. And under Marcuse in Happyville. Fromm, the elegant junior sir, who plans to drop by some time. Who analyzes and differentiates. Who has mastered the vocabulary that got him elected unanimously, only never to appear again. Getting elected is what counts. Knowing how to make speeches. About irresponsibility. About the fraud perpetrated by the political parties. About politicization of the masses. About a flexible attitude toward the future, when everybody, when everything. While Dieter Biehl is scrubbing the floor. While Rainer Gebhardt is drafting a letter to the membership. Licking two hundred stamps. Copying out two hundred addresses. Ten-Pfennig printed matter practice for the club's theoreti-
164

cians. For Helmut Fromm, who hopes to drop by soon. Who hopes to drop by some time next week, because ten weeks have passed during which he did not drop by. For the card-file corpses having elected him is quite sufficient. After all, Gebhardt and a few others attend to the work. Some sort of time-consuming dull work. Instead of discussing every imaginable issue. Instead of analyzing and differentiating like Helmut Fromm. Six seats down the counter. With wife or girl friend. HELMUT FROMM noticed him long ago. He grins in GEBHARDT's direction. From bar stool to bar stool. He raises his beer glass. He drinks to Gebhardt's health. No, Helmut isn't home. What a pity. Just left the house. What a pity. GEBHARDT pays. GEBHARDT takes his coat. He has to pass by the six stools. Well, how's things back at the ranch, someone calls out. How's it going? I'm going to drop by soon. And GEBHARDT, errand boy Gebhardt, the forty-three-year-old stamp licker, walks out on his practice-oriented fellow steering committee member. Walks past HELMUT FROMM without a word, past this elegant young Helmut-man, this political showman, who plans to drop by some time. Like so many others. Who will perhaps drop in once over a period of weeks. Yes, Helmut will call you back. You know, he has to get out an important book for Rowohlt's summer Contemporary Issues list. Didn't Helmut tell you? No, Helmut is in Bochum this week. The Republican Club there just elected him to the steering committee. You know, the boy is so active in politics. No, no, I'm just his mother.

You're My Own Sweet Girls

We're not going to take the Communists' trains! They'll keep us there and not let us out.

Museum Island, East Berlin: one of the items on our endurance itinerary. But Vera loses her nerve.

No, how can I watch out for a whole group!

She runs down the steps ahead of us and whimpers in the dining hall. I'm so alone!

Over the soup Hannelore whispers, She was in a mental hospital twice, and once she abandoned a class half a year before graduation. Nerves.

As Hannelore is giving away the secret, Frau Doktor exclaims loudly, Look the other way! I'm going to lick off my plate! And Frl. Plath wrinkles up her composition nose. As chaperone for our sister class she sits there silent and slightly wrinkled.

Plath, my zipper is stuck! See if you can get it open!

Graduating class trip. In Berlin with our teacher. A calibrated program that lacks any unifying principle. Every building is a museum. Every post office is suspected of having architectural merit.

I'm so sorry that I can't tell you anything about it. But you're my own sweet girls!

We suffer neglect and the strictest supervision. The only safe time is mealtime. And after dinner, stuffed with liverwurst sandwiches, pop into bed at six. Quick, before the Russians come to get you, into your nightgown.

Plath, get into bed with me!

The teacher-style double room begs for a good-night kiss. She speaks tenderly of Ingrid Plath, her dear little rabbit. *While tea is being poured she rubs purringly against Hannelore's pot arm. She nestles her head against Margot's angora sweater and growls. She leans up against everyone. She puts her arms around my neck. Good night. She stares after me, eyes moist.*

No one's interested in my old backside!

Her toothbrush under her arm, she stumbles to the bathroom and gurgles Tristan. Frau Dr. Zirkel does not speak to us. Discussion is forbidden. Orders are orders. She crawls through all the museums. Berlin, one big gallery. The site that makes Berlin interesting—the Plötzensee prison—is off limits. Everything one could possibly want to see is on our itinerary. I'm not responsible for anything else.

We troop from bus to bus. Frau Dr. Zirkel refuses. She trudges home, whining that there is nothing more pitiful in the world than someone who is abandoned by her friends. Frau Dr. Zirkel bemoans her fate. And Dorothea takes pity on her feet. Dorothea goes with her. In a flash Frau Doktor wipes away her tears and hisses at the red traffic light. Head raised in tomcat pose, she miaows at the intersection, miaows until the light turns. Frau Doktor, the cat at the pedestrian crossing. Back at the hospice she finishes off Hannelore's sundae. You're still full from lunch, girls, right? She feels over Sabine's stomachache. Slowly, over all the hills and valleys, her fingers stroking and caressing until Sabine's head is ready to burst.

Now I'm going into the dark. Six o'clock. Bedtime begins. She is already sitting there in the bedroom. In the bathroom Madonna Plath is giving away secrets. Zirkel never opens the window. She crouches on the bedsheet. Unaired, full of wrinkles. She sits in the darkroom with heavily draped windowpanes and develops herself.

You there, with the red bow!

Overnight she forgets our names, plucks timidly at our nightgowns, gives the morning a slap on the behind and scolds.

Tomorrow we're off to the Commies on the Museum Island! My, am I petrified!

Frau Doktor butters a roll for her breakfast.

Ute has such pretty legs! Luscious calves!

Lascivious cuteness. Our teacher. Miaow, miaow. Our teacher in Berlin.

SCENE 53. INTERIOR. EVENING. IN THE LATE NINETEENTH-CENTURY VILLA. A ROOM TEMPORARILY USED AS A STOREROOM FOR FURNITURE, PAINTING EQUIPMENT, AND PLASTERING TOOLS. FREEZE EFFECT: "FAMILY PORTRAIT" OF THE ROSA LUXEMBURG GROUP. SPECIAL EFFECTS TRACK-IN TO SHOW THE FACES. BACKTRACK AND DISSOLVE INTO MOVEMENT. The Rosa L. Group is here. The Rosa Troupe, which drinks up whole cases of beer—paying is capitalist bullshit—and dabbles in revolution. Loud, young, with pop-art beards. GEBHARDT remembers. Shut your trap, you bourgeois motherfucker. Sieg Heil. Sieg Heil. Up yours, old blabbermouth. I'm from the German Press Agency. I've heard that tonight. Tonight this place is. GEBHARDT looks over at BIEHL, who is leaning against the door and demolishing his nails. GEBHARDT looks at BÖHM, and BÖHM looks at GEBHARDT. GEBHARDT hopes that FRENZEL is getting ready to say something. But FRENZEL is shrinking visibly. FRENZEL is getting smaller and smaller. The next time GEBHARDT looks at him, he will scurry away through the keyhole. Will you be able to set up the bookstore? No. Can you at least pay some of the rent? No. Can you? No. No. No. They loll opposite GEBHARDT, BÖHM, FRENZEL, and KNOPKE, scrawny little Attorney Knopke, and say no. The bookstore people. They loll about on boxes and paint cans and smear the paint splatters around with their toes. You know how high the rent is, GEBHARDT says. We need every penny we can get. If you could just contribute something in the beginning for rent and current expenses. A hundred marks, or fifty. No, says the ENGINEER OF ROSA L., We don't make that much. Our bookstore won't bring in that much. HERBERT DENICKE, a thirty-one-year-old belated prophet with long black wavy beard and gold wrinkled patent leather vest, the locomotive of Rosa L., says no. And his THREE BRIGHTLY PATTERNED BOXCARS likewise say no. In a sonorous Rosa chorus. No, our store won't bring in that much. How about getting a loan? KNOPKE asks. Yes, what about a loan? BÖHM echoes. I could call Vessel. We've tried that already. It's useless, says the BRIGHTLY PATTERNED TRIO. A rich publisher like that isn't going to give us a thing. Absolutely useless, LOCOMOTIVE DENICKE says. We won't get a penny out of Vessel. He won't lift a finger for us. In spite of all the pseudo-leftist books he puts out. DENICKE is painting his nails tile-blue with his index finger. Good. Okay. That takes care of a beautiful dream. DENICKE is smearing paint all over his hands now. Now it's the others' turn. It's obvious you need money here. So you have to take Schrader. Can't be helped. CARETAKER BIEHL nods with satisfaction. He has finished his meal. Of the three possibilities, the first fell through because the book dealer turned them down, the second has fallen through because Rosa L. can't swing it, and now the third possibility can move in, for two hundred marks' rent per month, financially sound. BIEHL is happy, because the business with Nikolaus Hopp has not yet been taken care of. On the contrary. The 1200 marks' worth of debt has metastasized. In the meantime it has become 3000. We need every penny, GEBHARDT says, Otherwise we'll have to close up shop here in a month. And to forestall any emotional response, GEBHARDT details obligations and debts. Debts incurred by Herr Nikolaus Hopp. Who lied to us, says little KNOPKE. Who never kept written records, says FRENZEL. Who must be called to account, says BÖHM, At a plenary session. Day after day the bills keep coming in. The unpaid bills incurred by Nikolaus Hopp during the amateurish early days. All right, then, says DENICKE, and withdraws his foot from the pool of blue paint. All right, then, say his FOLLOWERS, and haul themselves to their feet. Think it over, murmurs DENICKE. And FRENZEL, shrinking Frenzel, who is getting whiter with every day that passes, DR. FRENZEL answers, Yes, we'll think it over. Because basically we would much rather have you. And as far as leftist literature is concerned, we're also much more progressive. We know that, says DR. FRENZEL, composing a farewell chorus. For Frenzel

168

does not want to spoil things with the antiauthoritarians, certainly not with Rosa L. And when BIEHL has already gone off to get his broom to sweep up the ashes and butts, WINFRIED BÖHM admits that Dr. Frenzel is right. Winfried Böhm is already afraid of the group. Böhm has visions of smashed beer bottles and organized terrorism, and admits that paying rent probably is capitalist bullshit. I wish you wouldn't be cleaning all the time, says BÖHM. Put down that stupid broom, FRENZEL says to BIEHL, and offers GEBHARDT his hand. His good right hand. His vacuum-cleaned little hand, waxed daily by Irene Frenzel. Gives GEBHARDT his good right hand and says, Think it over. Best to get Fromm in on the decision. He wanted to stop by some time anyway. His mother told me that yesterday. Some time, GEBHARDT thinks. When the last wall is painted and the debts have become negligible, then Helmut Fromm will come flitting in to decide that Rosa L. is much more progressive and politically relevant than the sober Schrader bookstore, which can pay two hundred marks a month in rent. Only two hundred shitty capitalist marks.

Baedeker and Lunch

Please note the contrast between the Great Elector and his slaves! They writhe on the ground. While he exudes calm and majesty from atop his horse. Marcus Aurelius's horse served as the model for all the horses of the Renaissance.

The cue word is Charlottenburg. The Orangerie of the past. Culture rammed down your throat. Visit to the Tegel Palace. Closed to the public today. What a shame, she forgot to check up. Now she pulls out her Baedeker, and standing at the barred gate reads us the section on the Tegel Palace. A real live palace in Berlin. Two curlicues further down the page her voice loses its fervor for art. Her stomach is calling.

Let's go to a café for pastry and look for bridegrooms for ourselves! On Berlin's Lake Tegel. I sit there in the milky light. The land droops down into the water. The wind is mowing the reeds. Ships lie at anchor in green jade. The water sways the tree trunk. A motorboat comes foaming up, a green wake flying behind. Lake Tegel and raspberry pudding. Around the café table leaves rustle from the previous fall.

School seniors rushing through the Dahlem Museum. Allotted time: one hour. Back at twelve. Lunch. I dash to the first floor, the second. I witness the execution of a wealthy inhabitant of Genoa, who dies in his ruff collar as if screwed into a vise. Van Dyck. Paints eyes that kill by sheer penetration. A mouth without sweetness. A leg grows out of the brown of the ground. Goya. Ten minutes left. I dash along, fly down the stairs. I see my first El Greco. Five minutes of Mater Dolorosa and me, alone together in a gallery. I hang there in my skin frame and stare at her. A green cloak over her shoulders, a white veil about her head. The mouth, chestnut brown, is the same color as the hair. The hands, folded into a brooch, hold the cape together and divide it into two green fans to either side. Past Oriental carpets, interwoven tendrils of flowers and hunting scenes. A face dies, hanged by the hair.

My classmates are waiting, postcard-grumpy. Waiting for me in the lobby. I join the trotting herd. I march along, surrounded by overfeasted eyes, dulled by one hour, hurrying to lunch, the immutable mealtime. School has become a little-girl dress, too short, above my knees. Squeezed into it, I continue to grow, bursting out of every opening. Soon I will slip out of the dress, change my skin. But for now I am still crushed into the crowd, wearing my number. Every morning I put on my little-girl dress, which confines me almost to the point of immobility. Baedeker and lunch. Berlin, the former capital of the Reich. A sandbar in the red sea. That was before our time. The way everything was before our time, before Frau Dr. Zirkel's time. How could it have happened? How? From the meathook of forgetfulness drips the blood of my questions.

SCENE 54. INTERIOR. NIGHT. CROWDED OFFICE IN THE LATE NINETEENTH-CENTURY VILLA. GEBHARDT AND BIEHL ARE MIMEOGRAPHING. CLOSE-UP OF THE ANTEDILUVIAN MIMEOGRAPH MACHINE. BIEHL is cranking the handle. The meeting resulted in. BIEHL says, This damned thing is sticking again. BIEHL is running off a letter. And GEBHARDT is collating. Sheet after sheet. The last fifteen are no good. We might as well throw them away. Now GEBHARDT is cranking the handle. The following proposals were presented. GEBHARDT says, This stupid machine is sticking again. RAINER GEBHARDT is running off a letter. And BIEHL is collating. Sheet after sheet. I think we should run the whole thing off again. Our Raake donation is conking out again. Is calling for its daddy again. GEBHARDT

170

cleans his blue-inked hands. The following issues were raised. The following topics were discussed. Now BIEHL is cranking the handle again. Cranking the wheezing box. Cranking this groaning mimeo machine. For the young people from an underground publishing house. BIEHL is cranking away, cranking out letters. GEBHARDT is collating again, piling sheet on sheet. You're going about this all wrong. ALEX SOMMER paces the office. There are many things that need drastic improvement. ALEX SOMMER says, The whole principle, especially the publicity angle, hasn't been thought through properly in the total context. One should appeal much more vigorously to the average citizen. And it is especially important to approach Professor Pantenburg. I see a lot of possibilities there. He sees a lot of possibilities, GEBHARDT thinks. The work for you and the leftism for me. He sees many possibilities, RAINER GEBHARDT thinks. He says, It's a nice, progressive, pleasant atmosphere you've got here. He paces the office to see if the square footage he's paying for with his contribution is really adequate. He paces while we work, GEBHARDT thinks, to see if we are really keeping busy. And HERR SOMMER says, There are so many opportunities. It's just a question of exploiting them. And BIEHL cranks away. Cranks out letter after letter. And GEBHARDT licks two hundred stamps. And HERR SOMMER says, More work should be done at the base, at the grass roots. And BIEHL folds letters. And GEBHARDT sticks the letters in the envelopes. And BIEHL cleans the machine. And HERR SOMMER says, Böhm agrees with me completely. And GEBHARDT takes two hundred letters to the post office, and BIEHL begins to sweep the room. The work for you and the club for me. And BIEHL sweeps up Herr Sommer's ashes. And HERR SOMMER tosses his cigarette package onto the heap. And while BIEHL is drafting the schedule for the coming week, ALEX SOMMER groans, Out of cigarettes again. Hell. What a nuisance. And strolls down the steps. And calls back up the stairs, There are many things that need DRASTIC IMPROVEMENT.

In the Cold Kitchen of Freedom

A star shines over this building. Not a celestial body. It is the Mercedes star. Inner courtyards, cafés, terrestrial pleasures. 2142 marks. Eighteen-carat gold. Egyptian jewelry for tomorrow. Daring dresses blowing in the autumn wind. Berlin white beer lapping in everybody's head.

Ain't this terrific?

Americans drinking amber colored beer, chewing the words of their mother tongue. In front of Café Kranzler a Pietà takes shape in chalk on the sidewalk. Beatnik girls in black pants and pink sweaters lean against the flower boxes in front of the Kaiser Wilhelm Memorial Church like twins. Café Zuntz. Gypsy cellar. Advice on makeup. What cosmetics does one use in a divided city? *Between Elizabeth Arden and Max Factor people are eating pastry in display houses of glass. I walk among them without broken panes, without loss of blood. I meet beatniks with a pacifier in their mouths. Berlin's Kurfürstendamm covers the territory between St. Pauli and the Jungfernstieg in Hamburg. Here one can become an addict, on this milk-and-honey street in a tuberculous city. Bacterial greenhouse climate.* If the dead cells are expelled by coughing, a cavity forms.

Twilight of the gods in a legendary frontier city. In the cold kitchen of freedom. I burden my memory with the Memorial Church. Root and branch of the zero hour. Stepping across round flagstones set in pebbles, I approach Jesus, the larger-than-life Jesus at the Iron Curtain. Someone has placed withered roses in his hand. His halo is replaced by a neon advertising sign. Over Jesus's head run the moon-color letters, Europe's Most Elegant Styles—Visit Arndt in Berlin.

The ghosts of Berlin which plagued me in history class, which plagued me in civics class, place their arms around my shoulder. The Communists say, Persevere in the East Zone. Deprivation of freedom, three-way partition, never. Soviet-occupied. *Those offspring of the Great Times, the small times, rustle over the Kudamm, arm in arm with myths and symbols.*

Two illusions cheek by jowl. We visit the Wall, which divides them. A bus makes its tourist rounds. The unmodulated ecstatic microphone voice belongs to a young blabbermouth who lets flow an unending stream of uninflected narrative. A somewhat numbing hum resounds in my ear.

This is the Prinzenstrasse checkpoint!

Barbed wire in front of the Wall. Barbed wire on top of the Wall. Barbed wire on the other side of the Wall.

The lower part of the Wall consists of cement slabs, also used for house construction in East Berlin.

I stare at the Western cars, parked with their grilles kissing the barbed wire. Here people post themselves face to face with the East and honk their horns in protest. There between two utopias Fechter bled to death, trying to escape. On the other side a tall building displays a neon moving belt. The letters are four yards high, so people on the other side can read the news. The ugliness of hate. The ruin over there in the East used to be a famous nightclub, Fatherland House.

Now ladies, would you please get out of the bus for a moment. We are at the intersection of Linkstrasse and Potsdamerstrasse. You have ten minutes to view the Wall. Please take turns on the wooden observation platforms. From there you can see over the Wall. And be back promptly. We trot obediently out of the bus.

Damn these pilgrimages! Tomorrow I'm going to take off and go dancing!

Hannelore nibbles a licorice snail smaller. Refreshment stand. Wall snacks. Postcards. Ice cream stand. A little sign on the wooden platform. Proceed at your own risk. *I climb onto the gallows. Numb, as if my blood were flowing out at my feet, I stand there and stare.* Freedom must not end here! Down with the Hallstein Doctrine! *I feel as if I were stuck in an elevator. Both sides stare at each other from silent peaks of noncomprehension. Such effort. Such suspicion. Such a waste of time.*

It's so sad that one can only take pictures of it, the girl next to me murmurs. Two of the Wall is plenty, Cornelia exclaims, and tucks her camera into her wicker basket. Just in case the first is out of focus.

An out-of-focus wall. Come on, young lady, we want to see, too, bawls a group of young men, and forces me down off the platform. The film has already begun. Golden sandals are buying postcards and ice cream. Some of them are so moved that they cannot tear themselves away. Clutching their popsicles, they scramble onto the platform once more. To catch the last scene again.

Ladies, ladies, our time's up!

And already the bus is off again, in the direction of the Brandenburg Gate. It was constructed as a copy of the Propylaea. The chariot is by Schadow. The Avenue of June Seventeenth. *Art historical politics. A human voice can get over anything, survive anything. Graduating seniors lean back comfortably in an upholstered embrace. Contentment and satiety.* There you see the Congress Hall. The Berliners call it the pregnant oyster. *I doze off. A fence cuts me in quarters, divides me in four parts, laid out with painful precision, partitioned. What does Berlin mean to me?*

I found jewelry and furs. Protruding stomachs. Drooping cheeks, rosy cheeks, children and pets, overbred, distingué, ethereal. *Neurosis in size nine proffers an invitation. Yes, certainly, madame. The Wall is a happening. When you go, wear* Courrèges, *geometrics and straight lines.* Have you ever heard of the district called Red Wedding? *City of dead-end streets. Cemetery walls form the border between the sectors. Threshold to the other world. The street ends at the Wall.* Get out. Fifteen minutes for viewing. We have to be back early for lunch. *Shards of glass sprout from the stone.* The Church of Reconciliation behind the stone forest is being torn down. For the death strip. The houses are painted in light colors so anyone fleeing can be seen more clearly. *Border guards crouch on the roofs. Floodlights. The light shoots. A bare, gray, sun-swept street, broad like a dusty surrealist dream. Hands flutter toward us like waving handkerchiefs.* Get in. *Back into the big-mouthed bus. The microphone quotes headlines.* Flight. Nets to break the fall. Ropes. No wonder when you consider what things cost over there. Twelve marks for a pair of stockings. Ten marks for a pound of coffee. Everything is more expensive. And the wages are lower. *And rent, and fuel, and books, and university tuition, and railway tickets. Naturally that's reason enough for jumping out of an Eastern window.* Ladies, can you hear me back there? *Compulsory money exchange. Artificial rate.* Thanks to an almost completely successful boycott by the West Berliners the East Germans have racked up a huge deficit with their elevated railway. You know—political reasons; we're standing firm. *Standing firm. The former capital of the Reich is standing firm. Berlin will remain German.*

Vacation in a city of ghosts. Closest to the Wall are the shadows. They crouch on the stones in the sunshine and flutter away in the light of their times. On the Western side the potato wholesaler Grensing has a red amaryllis behind the bars of his window. On the Eastern side the windows have been bricked up. The walls stare at me with sightless eyes. Blind houses beat down on my head. They still bear the signs of yesteryear. Butcher, Frame Shop, Borkowski's Dairy Products. *On a lonely balcony railing dustcloths flutter in the blue. The East walled up the houses. It forgot two dustcloths, which now daydream forlornly into the West.*

SCENE 55. EXTERIOR. DAYTIME. HAMBURG'S GERHART HAUPTMANN SQUARE. AN INFORMATION BOOTH WITH LARGE SIGNS. CROWDS OF SHOPPERS. SCENE OPENS WITH A CLOSE-UP OF A SANDWICH BOARD CARRIED BY LOHMANN. ITS MESSAGE: GERMAN NATIONAL PARTY IN OUR TOWN—WHAT A COME DOWN! LOHMANN is proud of himself. Lohmann painted the signs. Lohmann set up the booth. It was Lohmann's idea. My study group on the schools came up with the idea, says DR. HAUSWALD. His study group on the schools, RAINER GEBHARDT thinks, and looks down the busy street. This opportune shopping street, where one can get out and talk with the people. Where one can make the people aware, says LOHMANN, That those guys are holding a rally here. In their own town, says MATTHIAS HAUSWALD. Again, RAINER GEBHARDT thinks. I'll take a hundred fliers. LOHMANN is unpacking. Lohmann has printed whole mountains of leaflets. These are for Dr. Hauswald. And these are for me. And Herr Gebhardt will stay here at the booth to talk with anyone who has questions. GUSTAV LOHMANN is handing out assignments. Organizing his campaign. Assigning positions. And GEBHARDT is counting, counting the number of crumpled-up fliers around the booth. In people's hands and out. They won't even take leaflets, LOHMANN exclaims. The leaflets are poisoned, LOHMANN calls. And GEBHARDT stands behind his table heaped with literature and waits for these evasive passers-by. Heads lowered. Don't slow down. Their pocketbooks step on the gas, GEBHARDT thinks. These briefcases can fly. They are afraid of discussion. Just like at election time, GEBHARDT thinks. And then someone stops. A fat little man. Say, can you explain to me why. And GEBHARDT launches into his monologue. GEBHARDT delivers his solo speech and thinks, the big one costs four-fifty. Take the big one. It will last longer. And the passers-by pass by even more quickly. For a person is standing there. A person is talking. Ladies and gentlemen. Fellow citizens. This is your opportunity to voice your opinion and ask questions. And LOHMANN calls out, The citizens' action movement will get rid of the apathy. And GEBHARDT waits for people to buy his answers, now that the fat little man has already gone rolling on his way. Between oppressive and repressive. One purchaser rolls on his way through Denicke's masses. And LOHMANN comes back to the booth and says, I can hardly get anyone to take these. Those philistines. They're afraid of a sheet of paper. And LOHMANN pounds his fist on the table. They don't give a damn about anything. Just so long as they have their peace and quiet. And while LOHMANN stacks his leaflets, HAUSWALD comes back, too, and says, All they're good for is writing in a tiny X. And even that only every four years. And GEBHARDT looks down the shopping street. GEBHARDT thinks, we're going about it all wrong. We want to explain. We have to try something else next time. The best thing would be to show a film. A picture book for illiterates. Beep, beep, a car. Ladies and gentlemen. Here you see a big gray elephant. And here you see a mean wild bear who wants to gobble up the little duck. This teeny-weeny duckie. Quack, quack. Can you follow me? Everything clear? My dear ladies, thinks GEBHARDT. My revered ladies and gentlemen. Why don't you just open your mouths for a change. I want to hear you say loud and clear a-a-ah!

With Limited Legal Responsibility, and Spared

The first day in East Berlin. Go through one by one, not as a group. Otherwise you might be arrested. Suspected. One girl a minute. Obtrusive in our very unobtrusiveness. The battle plans of a neurotic. We'll meet over there, on the other side of the Wall. One by one. So we won't be seen by those who are watching us and see everything. We have until six o'clock. But we arrange it so we can be sure of getting out of here. *One item on the program of hate is checked off. Eyes open! Mouth shut! Curtain up! Reality.*

I look down at the curb. I'm looking for all the raped women, the brutality of communism. The enemy of the working man, ruthless system, the concentration camp of today. *I am visiting the city we studied in civics.* Communism, a threat to the world. *The problem that is as old as I am. Where are the inferior beings? The prison garb? Why isn't everyone wearing a uniform? I go looking for reality in East Berlin. And a black and white image becomes a film in color with political shadings.*

We sacrifice the morning to the Museum Island and the Berlin Cathedral. *I have to take a look at the wooden organ. Down below a floor covered with stones, war rubble. Above me birds flying about in the dome. The National Gallery. Menzel's* Iron Foundry. *I see Christian Wolf's* Forest. *Yellowish brown life, yellowed birch trunks. My teacher hastens alone through deserted halls.*

Do look at the bust of Goethe by Schadow, she says, turns, and yawns into the emptiness. Middle-aged loneliness, hiding in a museum, speaks to white sculptures, freezes into white marble, and experiences East Berlin at the Pergamon Altar. Our itinerary reads Visit all the museums. We dash into the Bode Museum. Three thousand years before our times. Cosmetics spoons, hairpins carved of bone, a crouching skeleton in an animal pelt. The morning trickles away in museums.

Noontime, inevitable mealtime: you I mean to skip. I run away from the group, from its blockheaded spitefulness. I run away. First separation. An East Berliner with waving octopus arms points in all directions.

You're standing on Unter den Linden. That is Marx-Engels Square. Where are you from? Oh, yes. The Hamburg Sailors' Revolt. Just keep going in that direction. You'll come right to the Cross of Penitence. The prior of Bernau was stabbed to death there. When it rains, the white cross turns green. Have you already been to the Museum of German History? Over there you see part of the Berlin Castle. Liebknecht spoke from that balcony.

Who is Liebknecht? What sailors' revolt? I look them up under Bismarck. I don't find anything. We never got past Versailles.

And if you turn left there . . .

I walk past the honor guard. Museum of Bourgeois Revolution. Hitler Period. Twenty Years of Liberation. Their death is a sacred charge to us. In these barracks served our comrade Just, murdered by West Berlin soldiers . . . Long live the Socialist Unity Party. All with the people. All by the people. All for the people. Our gratitude to the heroes of the Soviet Union who liberated us from fascism. I flee into the past.

Museum of German History 1933–1945. Two or three other visitors join me in the midday stroll past torture apparatus, yellowed letters, SS uniforms. Twelve years preserved in historical formaldehyde. He who did not surrender/was killed/He who was killed/did not surrender. I read Brecht's words and look down at my soft, unscarred skin. Warm white hands. He who was killed. My skin breathes silently, unscathed. I see myself reflected in the glass cases. A postwar child who was spared, who learned in school about Roman history, the painting of Spitzweg, and literature. Where do we have a museum like this? Are there any teachers who take their classes there? The political development of the National Consortium coincides with wishes that I myself and the Board of Directors have long cherished. Krupp writing on behalf of the Consortium of German Industry to Hitler, April 25, 1933. The Concordat with the Catholic Church. Dr. Hans Litten. Carl von Ossietzky,

177

editor-in-chief, who died in a concentration camp. My eyes swim over unfamiliar names. The next room, and the following. My gaze is speared. I see the murderers' weapons. Full of pride in their deeds, the National Socialists photographed their own crimes and sold the pictures as postcards. Letters. Orders for transport to camps. Newspaper clippings. Clothing. Erich Mühsam, writer, murdered on July 11, 1934. He has a sign around his neck: Concentration Camp Oranienburg 2651/Feb. 3, 1934. Around my neck hangs a pearl, set in gold. Spared. With his words he wants to gas the world. A photo montage by John Heartfield.

Hitler = Enslavement of the People

Enslavement of the People = Increased Profits

Increased Profits = My Ideal

Therefore Hitler = My Ideal

Where is there a museum like this in the Federal Republic? I race through rooms, pass things by, turn and go back. My eyes are taking pictures. Picture books call out with teddy bear voices. The Jews are our misfortune. In my head I am developing hazy photos. Everything is underexposed, spared. Ernst Thälmann, imprisoned eleven years, Buchenwald Concentration Camp, 1944. Spared. Me. Walter Ulbricht. Heinrich Mann. Lion Feuchtwanger. Arnold Zweig. Proclamations. Numbers. Statistics. What do the statistics mean to me? There are two of us at home. My school has 600 students, Hamburg 1.9 million inhabitants. Four million people died at Auschwitz. The Warsaw Ghetto resisted from April to June. With the help of ninety billion Reichsmark Hitler succeeded in preparing Germany's downfall between 1933 and 1939. Four million soldiers fell. Ninety billion Reichsmark were spent. How much does that make per capita? How much? One corpse cost 22,500 marks. The walls display the present-day map of Germany. The concentration camps are all marked. Leprosy. Acne in the atlas, in the dotted Third Reich. Where is there a museum like this in West Germany? And are there any teachers who take their classes on field trips to them?

In the last room the timeless instrument of torture. I turn my head to the right. I turn it slowly to the left. I am 5 feet 5 inches, have blue eyes, and am young, interested, quick of grasp, sensitive, with limited legal responsibility for my actions, and spared . . . I swivel my head and go to stand, helplessly compassionate, before the immortal guillotine, a wooden bed with water floating underneath. The cut through the throat,

178

and a shiny tin basin catches the blood. Spared in the year 1965. Spared. Spared.

Yellowed pictures. Hitler with the monopolistic bosses Thyssen, Borbes, and Vögler. Hitler and Himmler. Hitler and his SS. Upright uniforms stand at attention in the glass cases. Helmets perched on imaginary heads of air. I imagine they must have looked like, looked like . . . I run down the broad staircase of the past. Grab coat and shopping bag, open the door, Unter den Linden, sunlight, spared. Two o'clock. I hurry to the Pergamon Altar. The sun is hot. My thoughts are melting. Stockings off, stuffed into the basket. The catalogues are getting crushed under a pound of East Berlin apples. They are not poisoned, but Zirkel refuses to touch them. A man comes up, a retired East Berliner, says helpfully, I'll show you around. Alexanderplatz, St. Mary's, the Cross of Penitence. And I join the crowd. I listen. The herd trots along.

The old man explains: Here the Huguenots . . .

Back, back, before it gets dark and the East Germans cut the girls up in their scrambled eggs!

Come along! There's nothing to see here anyway!

I think Frank said something about the Big Apple and the Monkey. Come on, girls, let's go dancing!

We'll meet at six at the latest!

My class gallops back to West Berlin. I stay. Stay until six. Take the elevated to Alexanderplatz. For the first time I see people who don't come from Hamburg or hang in picture frames, who are not called Goethe, with oil paint in their veins. Where should I go? With whom can I speak? And what am I after anyway, and what am I seeing? Am I blind? Can I hear? Am I incapable of absorbing, merely a packer and storer of impressions, who straps life onto her back and only exhales? Will I report that I rushed through the streets of East Berlin; there are people there, too, and everything is more expensive?

I go past state-run stores and cafeterias, time circling on my wrist. They speak the same language and have different meanings in mind. I stumble along in my little-girl dress. Where is Bertolt Brecht buried? People don't know. Finally, amidst gray piles of stone, in the Dorothea Cemetery, his marker. The name covered by chrysanthemums. A bare slab waiting for use. Tin cans and carnations in honor of Brecht. Heinrich Mann and Becher, Eisler, Hegel, and Fichte. Worth a tin can carnation. One cemetery long and four top hats high. This blade of grass

179

grew on top of Brecht, and Treptow lowers its flags from among the stones of the Reich Chancellery. A soldier with a child is there mastering the past.

In a side street my eye is caught by a poster, Religious Art. Chagall, Rouault. *I enter the exhibition. A dead church, a dead Christ. Rouault painted death in black India ink, ten past five in late summer, in a side street, in a storage area called a church. A thirty-five-year-old woman sitting in the porch of the church gives me the catalogue to the exhibition. Entrance free. West Germany? Yes.*

Do you like the paintings?

Yes.

An art student from Poland was here today. He had never seen pictures by Chagall. It was hard to put together the exhibition. I think people didn't even realize what they were letting us have. You understand, religious pictures. No. No new churches are being built, but there is no ban. Yes, children are put in kindergarten at three. You know, there are two clocks on television. A West German and an East German one. One can tell that way which channels the parents watch. The children go straight to the familiar clock.

And otherwise? Standard five-day week. And day care centers right next to the factories. Vacation every year. The rent freeze of 1938 is still in effect. But . . .

There's a young man in our congregation. He was in the Free German Youth for fifteen years, then he resigned, against his parents' wishes. His father is very active politically. But now he works for the church. Nothing bad has happened to him. Of course there is a certain degree of freedom. No chance for advancement, naturally. Not to speak of university studies. Only Party members get that sort of opportunity. Is your teacher back in the West already?

Yes. She didn't want to stay here.

I look at the eastern clock—five-thirty. I have to be going.

Do come back. All it costs you is twenty Pfennig for the train. That's not much.

Back to Prinzenstrasse, unscathed. Papers, please! Through a slit behind the dark curtain, behind the iron curtain. Identity check. Eyes scratch my skin. Two members of the People's Police smile at me. Flirtation at the Wall. I slip through a crack. Behind me, behind my back, I can feel the concentrated gaze of the People's Policemen, who stand in their watchtowers and whistle after me. Unscathed and spared. The discomfort of a new truth, without Plotzensee, without the murderers' memorial.

West Berlin. Instead of an execution machine for eighteen thousand Reichsmark, a return to the rehabilitation center. Only until ten—it's all your fault! Now we can't dance the shake at the Eden Saloon—all because of you! Today we wanted to, today we were going to be allowed to. Now we're under arrest again. Petit bourgeois despair. How does one go about defending East Berlin? How does one explain to the Max Factor-obsessed crusaders that one set forth to find the truth? How am I supposed to explain that Life itself is at stake. Never again must Germany cause a war. What are you doing? I myself have barely grasped that idea.

SCENE 56. INTERIOR. EVENING. A DIGNIFIED, MIDDLE-CLASS RESTAURANT. SUBJECTIVE CAMERA. GEBHARDT ENTERS FROM THE STREET, LOOKS AROUND UNCERTAINLY, THEN HEADS FOR A TABLE AT WHICH THREE MEN AND A WOMAN ARE WAITING FOR HIM. They told him to meet them here. He let them tell him. So the atmosphere will be pleasant, HERR BRAMMER said. More dignified, said BRAMMER. All right, see you at nine. There they are, all four of them in the corner, GEBHARDT thinks. Pleasant and dignified. All four of them at nine o'clock. Good evening, BRAMMER calls out to him. Good to see you. He has brought along three other Brammers, GEBHARDT thinks. May I. Tesch from the BDD. Herr Pagel, from the German Peace Coalition. And this is our Frau Priess, also from the BDD. And you know me, of course, Gebhardt, old man. Gebhardt, old man, thinks GEBHARDT. Yes, him I know. Herr Jürgen Brammer. Political pensioner. With slow-breathing turtle face. The head buried between round shoulders. Stumpy, crooked gait legs. With a snapping mouth, emitting little bubbles, clapping shut. Herr Jürgen Brammer from the Peace Coalition. A wham with a ham sandwich. What'll you have to drink? What'll it be? A pool to swim in, thinks RAINER GEBHARDT. Be our guest. A beer, GEBHARDT says, and FRAU PRIESS smiles. Smiles red-painted and gently powder-dusted over at him. Smiles for four. Two times Peace Coalition. Two times BDD. Now I'm playing four-handed, GEBHARDT thinks. I'll deal in a minute. Really nice of you to come. We're so glad to see you. And have an offer, a suggestion to make. HERR PAGEL smiles. HERR TESCH smiles. Herr Gebhardt, how would it be if you joined us? FRAU PRIESS smiles, and HERR JÜRGEN BRAMMER solemnly lays down knife and fork. Herr Brammer abandons his sandwiches. His pleasant, dignified sandwiches. The wallpaper is green and the tablecloth blue. A primrose blooms next to the ashtray. Join us in the GPC, says HERR BRAMMER, and pokes his little head out from between his shoulders. His gray little snapping head. With droop-lidded sleepy eyes. Or us, chirps FRAU PRIESS softly, for BDD or GPC. For GPC or BDD. Well, GEBHARDT thinks, many children can have many names. Many children can have many names, but a common father. And then you could come along, says HERR PAGEL. Come along to meet him, GEBHARDT thinks, the children's father. Have you ever been in East Berlin? Well then, come along to the conference. You of all people, you who are trying to promote rapprochement, should not allow your energies to be absorbed entirely by this young people's club. Nothing can come of it, puffs HERR TESCH. Small in his suit. With vest and Dunhill pipe. As a tie a lizard-green suede bow. Well, how about it, says HERR PAGEL. Now it's your turn to say something. What do you think? What do I think, thinks GEBHARDT. How about a sandwich? Another ham sandwich, calls PAGEL. And what we wanted to ask you was. We're planning a big evening for next week, for the liberation of the Vietnamese people, for Vietnam. It so happens that a man from *Pravda* is going to be here at the same time. Perhaps you could. Just a little speech, says HERR BRAMMER. Without a fee, of course. For the liberation of the Vietnamese people, says GEBHARDT, And for the liberation of the Greek people. I'd be happy to talk on that, even without pay. How so? says FRAU PRIESS. I don't understand, says HERR TESCH. He understands perfectly well, thinks RAINER GEBHARDT. With his vest and bow tie, perfectly well. After all, why only Vietnam? says GEBHARDT. That could be combined very neatly with Greece. And then with the man from *Pravda* here, we can have a discussion afterwards on why the Soviet Union is supplying the Shah of Iran with arms. That should interest the students, too. That won't interest anyone, says BRAMMER. That has nothing to do with the subject. I don't know what this is all about, says FRAU PRIESS. They all know perfectly well what this is all about. Perfectly well, GEBHARDT thinks. They have divided freedom up neatly for a monthly salary. A piece of apple strudel for Vietnam and dogfood for Greece. Whichever way it is

182

convenient. And they were there in Mexico City. Twenty-one gun salute for sixty people executed. For sixty students shot dead. But cheerfully present in Mexico City. There for the Olympic Flame from Jaros. Viva Trotsky, RAINER GEBHARDT exclaims, Here comes my sandwich. The revolution has gone sour. You just don't understand, says a turtle glance. The socialist countries maintain contact with the Greek people. Precisely, says GEBHARDT. And why not with the South Africans? Are dark-skinned people worth less than Greeks? Or do you distinguish between one people and another? Could you please explain to me, says GEBHARDT, Why they continue to maintain relations with Greece? On and on. Supporting by their presence a regime that is bringing up a new generation as fascists, in the shadow of the camps? I really don't see, says HERR TESCH, Why you have to get so violent and worked up. Yes, worked up, says HERR PAGEL. I must say, you are getting everything balled up. After all, green is green. But white is not white; and red is not red, thinks RAINER GEBHARDT. For there is a new economic system. And a New Man with a suede bow tie and an Opel sedan. Slippers on the hearth. And for a professional politics hustler Vietnam is really worth its weight in gold compared with Greece, is good for a nice fat salary. You misunderstand. Believe me, Herr Gebhardt. I want to tell you just one thing, says the puffing HERR TESCH. We are concerned about the Greeks, too. I know, says GEBHARDT. Right after the coup, the Greeks invited everyone to a discussion. But only foreigners showed up. The Third World people were there alone. Iranians and Greeks. All young students. They invited you, too. Invited everyone. But where were you then? Where? Yes, where were we? HERR PAGEL reaches uneasily for his coat. Come, Wiebke, let's pay. What a dreadful misunderstanding. No misunderstanding at all, says RAINER GEBHARDT. All I want to know is, where were you then? I'm sorry, says HERR BRAMMER. Really sorry, says HERR BRAMMER. Maybe you just happened to be in East Berlin at that time, thinks GEBHARDT. It was nice talking with you, says HERR PAGEL. Good-bye, says HERR TESCH. Thank you. Don't mention it. Good night, says GEBHARDT, And let me know when the man from *Pravda* gets here. I have a few questions I'd like to ask him.

Rust on the Bars

Before you. After you. The Spandau Prison outside my window. Look to the right, girls. There you see the Wilmersdorf crematorium. Cremations take place here. Still? We are driving right through the autumn in our vacation bus. Where almond shells like urn fragments/lie cracked in the brittle grass of the path,/the spiders scurry, the threads fly./And still summer's Sibyl will not die. *Ladies, the Freedom Bell in the Schöneberg City Hall rings every day at noon. Over there, the pink and white structure, is the Sports Palace. You know, six-day races.* They built it up again. It was bombed, but they rebuilt it. The same old dream. *I don't know what to say to the American hippie who asks me why we rebuilt Hitler's sports tomb. Hitler was gone, Germany was gone. The Berliners brought it back to life—the six-day bicycle race. I'm not a Berliner.*

High school seniors in Berlin. We hold our cameras to our mouths to keep from whispering. We smile at the bus microphone, Over here, over there, smile, smile. Lunch. *It is twelve-fifteen, and the plates are steaming in the heat. Every mouth seeks its plate. Take your knife in your right, your fork in your left. And the left-handed people do it the other way around. Look how she cuts her meat, my neighbor Petra trumpets out, staring at my left-handed knife. And I, my face behind the steaming plate, look up foggy-faced:* Where almond shells like urn fragments, *please all look over here to the right, look, she's left-handed, she eats with her left hand. And for dessert ice cream at the Wall. The Langnese ice cream flag flutters red, white, and brown over the city's bowls.*

Midday break. Berlin, a city with artificial respiration, sleeps hot and warm. It is just a few steps from the hospice to the Wall, and I traverse them. Past rubble, over patches of pavement, from which camomile and grass sprout. I remember childhood games in bombed-out Altona. Boys are hunting a fat gray rat with stones. I hate this game. I don't want to be a hunter, or the hunted. The scent of camomile reaches my nostrils. Here stood, here occurred. A murder in the Landwehr Canal. Rosa Luxemburg. Who is she, who was she? I am racing through the Land of the Great Wall. Somewhere, between happenings and Courrèges, words in my head. September. Rocky gardens at the Wall. Quince-yellow autumn in Berlin. Rust on the bars. Rusty grapes. The hanging grape leaves of a frontier-city legend. The giant balloon Germany collapses on a rubble-strewn lot. Get in. Get out. Somewhere along the Iron Curtain. I gather up autumn with my face. Berlin, the biggest small town in the world.
184

Behind retirement pensions lurk the dreams of yesteryear. The Greater German ghosts have turned sixty-five. The future is twenty. The second-class values of a freedom flame are dancing away their fire in the Eden Saloon. Berlin remains Berlin, a burned-out skeleton of the West. Subsidized territory of a lost cause. Sunflowers and autumn marigolds. Somewhere, between flat, overstuffed fingers. Banana hands grope for the throat, into the mealy autumn. Palate and moon melt on the tongue. Oil melts in the mouth. Sparrows pursue the canary, because it is yellow. Spiderweb on railings, a dead leaf the booty. Summer excess curls around the neck, leaps at the Kranzler throat of this city of old people. Life itself is at stake. Never again must Germany cause a war . . . What are you doing?

SCENE 57. DAYTIME. DINING ROOM OF THE PALACE HOTEL IN MONTREUX. THE ROOM HAS GIGANTIC DIMENSIONS. ONLY ABOUT TEN PERCENT OF THE TABLES ARE OCCUPIED. IT IS STILL PRESEASON, AND OUTSIDE RAIN IS FALLING. GEBHARDT IS SITTING AT BREAKFAST. SCENE OPENS WITH AN EXTREME LONG SHOT. DURING THE OFF-SCREEN NARRATION A SLOW, ALMOST TORTURED TRACK-IN TO EXTREME CLOSE-UP. GEBHARDT is here and doesn't know what he is supposed to be doing here. He might just as well be on the moon. The loneliness is the same. A pain; it would be good to be able to scream. At least to cry. GEBHARDT cannot do either. He has forgotten how. He has a skin made of tissue paper. Usually it is completely exposed, irritated by any contact. A competition is taking place in Montreux. Three exceptional radio series are to be selected. Ten whole days. From ten in the morning to seven in the evening. The experts must formulate their judgments. The dead experts. Or is he the dead one? That must be it. The experts are alive, while he died at some point. Didn't even notice. He is staying at the Palace Hotel. Best hotel in town. Room with a bath. A bathroom so big one could play cricket in it. How much does it cost? The company's picking up the tab. He is living like dozens of other creatures. Dozens. It is still off-season. Soon hundreds will be living this way. Hundreds. Living human beings. It is comforting to be rotting away in the preseason. To be the dead one among dozens, not hundreds. Why did he let himself be sent here? He knew in advance that it would be the wrong train. Too late. One of those accidents. If it weren't for the options, everything would be so much easier. But the options are there. And accordingly the need for laws, ordinances, coercion. Marriage and jobs. Such things restrict. Limit. Make everything clear, simple, comprehensible. A deception, but it gets rid of the anxiety. Erases, rocks to sleep. Creates a life that is bearable, digestible. Eliminates contradictions. At least temporarily. Inside Gebhardt, chaos reigns. And all around him is chaos. His conclusion: he must fight his way through the chaos. He can't close his eyes to it. He just can't. Only sleep helps, nonbeing, with a pension plan for waking up. One day. Round trip. For a handful of brain, frayed from one-day lies. No hospital will have him. Psyche-plumbers and botchers can cut out the cancer, but the disease continues to spread. Gebhardt has a short distance ticket, from station to station. A streetcar named madness. He rides along, doing time for life. Reads the newspaper. A paper umbilical to connect him with the world. With his gross and net world. Gebhardt world. He is dripping away. Gebhardt flirts with a girl. Signposts, there and back. Last stop. And the whole thing again from the beginning. He dozes gently. He is squeezed in beside a crowd. He elbows his way through to a seat. If you are sitting down, you don't see the others. You look out, and nothing belongs to you. Nothing but a sweaty scrap of paper. Crumpled in your hand. Paid for and punched. Next to you waiting faces. And then their station comes. They get out. *Rien ne va plus.* And new ones continue the game. Once there and back. They still believe in the green-red-yellow of the traffic lights. In the and-yet, and-yet. Why does he avoid the truth? This simple equation? This childishly simple truth? Lie number one. Going, going. Why is he afraid? All the time, permanently? And what about love? These hapless leaps across thin ice? Love is the best of all lies. Still. Even if it is nothing but two solitudes rubbing against each other, leaving the empty spaces untouched. And they do remain untouched. One can't stack that many boxes inside each other. Maybe that's the principle? He tries it again and again. Sex, what a paltry word for this ghostly recycling process. Eyeless, nameless. With senses dulled to the feel of carrion. Gebhardt sits over his breakfast eggs in Montreux and thinks about love. About his anxiety. About his panic, his flight. But what good does it do? Just bear it. A brilliant form of therapy: pain to counteract pain. No alternatives. Except madness. For him and all those whose skin was peeled off, an amen before birth. Marriage. The feeble forfeit game of monogamy. God

186

as the all-blessing glue for empty spaces. A hallelujah as background music to cover up the rattle. To life's end. 'Til death do. What a mix-up. As if the last insane despair, this mad attempt to cancel solitude through physical contact were a fitting subject for an amen! And if one were to love? If it were this one person? This one and only this one? Plucked out of anonymity. Bracketed and underlined. Hope. A long drawn-out experiment. Not calculable like the everyday dead ends. And solitude overflows. Always. Sooner or later. The sink of love is stopped up. The faucets are blocked. Dying off while still alive. Gebhardt stood on the scale before he came down. In his cricket field. One hundred fifty-four pounds of old newspapers in Montreux. In the experts' Montreux. They sit around in their soft plush coffins. She holding his arm, but already on her way. With fluttering lids. Let's have one of the next, there and back. Torn by anxiety, endlessly divisible. Anxiety over loss of sparkling tiled security. Dance along. In the hope twist. With the silver wedding anniversary bow in her hair. Hand in hand with Daddy and the childish excuses. With glittering reptilian eyes. A gesture is enough. A hole in the chicken wire. And already a bargain has been brought home to roost. Haggle and know the market. The standard household candle from the Sex and Flesh Recycling Company. And another great opportunity. For ten days. From ten in the morning to seven in the evening. He can't help it that he is forty-three. From ten in the morning to seven in the evening. Forty-three. That will change soon. The little everyday Galilei is not going to give up lying. He likes his food too well for that.

At the University Feeding Trough

Let's dance. *Purring in silk. Powdered armpits, hair spray on the soles of the feet to keep one's gait upright before the leap from three yards of beer ends in a four-legged belly landing. They call this the university, with Japanese lanterns. A summer party of academic hairdressers, with topknots, shoe polish in their eyes.*

Wow, is he good-looking. Like Alain Delon.

Cool. Wait and see, he's going to ask me to dance.

Two seniors at a student ball. Hannelore and I in our good jersey knits, with snuffling schoolgirl brains and highly polished awe in the halls of one hundred percent learning. Do I look better in the gray or in the green? The eyeshadow troubles me. My Elizabeth Arden conscience is beating. So this is the university! One gigantic bar—great! Everywhere you look, Coke students who have already passed their rum exams. Everywhere young people. Young people hopping up and down. Not forward, not backward, always in place. Standstill on wheels. It isn't we who move with the beat, the beat moves us. The girls, double-decker lashed with vermilion looks, ask the men for a dance. Every contact an accomplishment. The men, mini-gentlemen with masculinely teased hair, wearing big flowered ties, are dragged away by soft little girls in pink shirts. What is there to recommend us except our youth? Young. We are just celebrating our year-and-a-halfth birthday. Knee bent inward, finger in the mouth, heart on a pacifier. We all think the same and buy the same and throw the same things away. Uniform look. Today it's still voluntary. But what about tomorrow? Dance of thousands. Liberated youth with pale pink pearled evening bag and Ph.D., a hand's breadth above the knee. The steps of youth. At the university feeding trough. Among standing drinking cuddling staring gabbing young people. Among students. One really should work that out, get to the bottom of it. One should make more careful distinctions. That is oversimplifying. I disagree. That's an unscientific argument. Aggression. Repression. Marxism no longer is applicable in today's world. Democracy is going to fall by its own weight. It will be destroyed by its inner contradictions. A beer please. Make that two. One really should do something. One could have. One might. Academic stick-in-the-muds discussing action. The future in plunging décolleté. Crushed, mangled, beaten, squeezed. Dead set on youth. Impaled on the spit by their schools. Roast youth. Three-quarters of us see a lucrative job as our highest goal. Would you care to dance? I'm Jens.

He has a little chip missing from one of his incisors.

Still in school?

Why, what do you do?

I'm studying medicine.

Oh, one of those. With long black bangs. Domesticated Beatle bangs. His nose takes a slight academic turn to the right. He has large hands, I am carried along on shovels. It's fun to flirt alongside him. Black hair and sky-blue eyes. We don't speak to each other; we are still looking

188

around. Over his shoulders, near the string of Japanese lanterns, I spy my second victim. More dashing. More machismo. A Lincoln student. My powder cake dusts toward him. He comes over, taps me away. My med student opens his shovels in confusion. But a bird in the hand. Perhaps the other one really is too swinging. I'll stick with my med student. Safe is safe. In the trap, out of the game. I have not managed to fulfill my academic-based Playboy dream. My world, I realize more clearly from day to day, is not a world of adventure, of rebellion, of defiance. We are so well bred, vaccinated with an A in conduct. Bandbox happiness. Neat little people, programmed and structured from here to their sweet mini-end.

His name is Jens and he likes three square meals a day, just like me. We stroll through the Coke groves of Young Academe. He drives a battered Volkswagen, smokes a pipe like the fellow I flirted with under the Japanese lanterns, and will be taking his final exams next year. The subject of his dissertation, his summa cum laude, is already taking shape in the curlicues that issue from his pipe bowl. He is smoking up a nice little future. I am student-crazy. Students—now there are people for you! Scholars, their heads in the clouds, their pockets empty from sheer love of the spirit! Superior beings, ruled over by Titans, professorial chiefs, the feather of truth stuck behind their ears. Old, sixty, and venerable. When one curtseys to them, one's knees scrape the ground. The university, cultic center of the zealous. Stand fast, O Fatherland. Training for life. A life of teaching and research. That's where one should go. That's where one should be.

Let's dance!

The academic spirit of tomorrow sloshes in the beer mugs of today. What a marriage! If Jens marries me, we'll take a vacation trip every summer, kiss our children from top to toe, and treat ourselves to chocolates with liqueur filling when we retire. I will bring Mary Quant and Twiggy, Donald, Dave, Dee, Dozy, Bicky, Mich, and Tich into the marriage. And Jens will bring Bob Dylan, five pipes, and a mortarboard. And what if an arm or a leg insists on sticking out, instead of fitting in tidily? What if some irregularity crops up? In that case two nice old gentlemen will appear with a paper cutter and standardize whatever interferes with the design. For the adult world takes everything off our hands. Even life.

189

SCENE 58. INTERIOR. EVENING. LOBBY AND WORKROOM IN THE LATE NINETEENTH-CENTURY VILLA. THIS SCENE IS STRUCTURED INTO THREE EPISODES THAT TELL A MINI-DRAMA. DIRECTING AND CAMERA SHOULD CONSCIOUSLY EMPLOY STEREOTYPED ELEMENTS. SCENE OPENS WITH A CLOSE-UP OF LUTZ WOCKER. Unexpectedly LUTZ WOCKER is also here. One of many who turn up. Who suddenly appear in the door saying Hello, is there anything I can do? Hello, folks, I want to do something for a change. Lutz Wocker is twenty-eight and getting a Ph.D. in philosophy. LUTZ WOCKER wants to launch something. He waits for GEBHARDT by the bulletin board. Right next to the entrance. Next to STEERING COMMITTEE = BULLSHIT. Next to HANG GEBHARDT, STOP THE WAR IN VIETNAM. He is small and delicate. His pressed ochre yellow velveteen suit bells out stiffly pressed around him. He looks like a sofa doll. LUTZ WOCKER stands there with freshly washed horsehair bangs. His face covered in white linen. Two red cheeks painted on. Two sparkling round brown India ink eyes. If I lift him up, RAINER GEBHARDT thinks, the price tag will be stuck to his soles. Lutz Wocker, factory made with hand painted features. Hello, he says politely, like the stiff and proper little doll he is. I've already been to see Dieter Biehl, LUTZ WOCKER says. I'm going to head up the study group on INFORMATION AND RESEARCH. I'm putting up the lists on the bulletin board, and Tuesday we'll get started.

TILT WIPE. INTERIOR. WORKROOM. SCENE OPENS WITH A LONG SHOT. GEBHARDT can hardly count the heads. More than thirty people are sprawled on chairs or leaning against the walls. Thirty-two, says LUTZ WOCKER, and proudly strokes his paintbrush-red cheeks. We're going to accomplish a great deal. Here! I'll take it! Here! Hand that over here! *Die Welt*? Here! *Die Zeit*? I'll take it! *Die Rundschau*? I want that! The *Zürcher Zeitung*? Give it here! LUTZ WOCKER is handing out reading assignments. The *Times*? For me! *Le Monde*? Mine, too! LUTZ WOCKER is passing around his scissors. He has bought forty pair. One for each newspaper reader. And I'll have takers for the last seven, too, LUTZ WOCKER assures GEBHARDT. When the first results come in. When our project really gets underway. LUTZ WOCKER is making out a list. I made out lists once, too, GEBHARDT thinks. LUTZ WOCKER is labelling green file folders. TASK FORCE ON DOMESTIC POLICY. TASK FORCE ON FOREIGN POLICY. Green magic marker. Blue magic marker. I labelled file folders, too, once, GEBHARDT thinks. Study group on the church. Study group on trade unions. Folders for minutes that no one ever wrote. For presenta-
190

tions that no one ever made. WOCKER's India ink eyes are gleaming. WOCKER says, In two weeks. Starting today I want you all to read everything you can lay hands on. We will set up a comprehensive information bank, WOCKER says, and is already eagerly sorting names. And GEBHARDT thinks, now everything will run smoothly. At last a study group that is functioning. At last thirty-two members snipping away. At last, GEBHARDT thinks.

TILT WIPE. INTERIOR. EVENING. LOBBY. CLOSE-UP OF LUTZ WOCKER. He is lying in wait for GEBHARDT by the bulletin board. Right next to the entrance. Next to STEERING COMMITTEE = BULLSHIT. Twenty-eight years old. Lutz Wocker is getting a Ph.D. in philosophy. LUTZ WOCKER wants to terminate something. Except for Biehl and Schusters, no one was there, LUTZ WOCKER says. I just don't understand it. He hands GEBHARDT his long list. He points to Friedhelm: *Le Monde* and the *Times.* Uwe Gerber: *Spiegel.* Walter Burkhart: *Frankfurter Rundschau.* Alex Sommer: *Le Combat.* I just don't understand it, says LUTZ WOCKER, and shows GEBHARDT his library of file folders. And GEBHARDT understands it perfectly. Understands empty folders with magic marker labels. Green magic marker. Blue magic marker. Empty folders for briefcases. All that organization just for show. All that organization in vain. And suddenly LUTZ WOCKER is gone. Turns into one of those who vanish, leaving a mess behind. A mess for fellow club members to clean up. An insuperable mountain of newspapers for thirty-two new pairs of scissors. For thirty-two illiterate pairs of scissors. Who is Uwe Gerber? Who is Walter Burkhart? The time before last only Biehl was there, and he had forgotten to do his clippings, because his exams are coming up very soon. *Time* and *Life*? Not here! *Süddeutsche Zeitung*? Absent. *Der Stern*— Not here. *Frankfurter Allgemeine*? Absent. For suddenly Lutz Wocker is also gone, absent, disappeared without a trace. Suddenly Lutz Wocker, factory made with hand painted features, packs his empty study group briefcase, departs, and announces that he is pulling out. On a Tuesday.

Attention! Final Exams!
Thirteen years of having to be at the school gate at seven fifty-five. Tardiness recorded in the attendance book. Thirteen years of having no book in which to record the teachers' tardiness. Thirteen years of supervision, Lesbian supervision, Folk-and-Führer supervision. One

learns to crawl. One learns to stoop. One learns that progress is achieved by compromise. One creeps from one compromise to the next. If you have a D in Latin, you can become a nurse or a social worker. Iron yourself out a C-minus, paint a red cross on your brow. To become a Protestant nursing sister, you'll need a C. A future nun gets a B.

My blouse is white, my skirt a little too long, my hair restrained in a braid. Lipstick only lowers your grade. Attention! Fasten your safety belts! Mouth shut! Two by two into the wringer, across the hall into the holy of holies, the teachers' lounge. The grading machine is rattling. Fall in! 'Tention! Final exams!

Good morning, Frau Oberschulrätin!

Facing me a chain of highly polished glasses, Chopin in their shoes and Goethe in their pockets. This room with its coffee pot. Off limits for thirteen years. For thirteen years no one was allowed a glimpse of these wooden chairs and tables. The lawn outside the window is hallowed ground. Why did Mozart stop off in the teachers' lounge on his way to Prague? What do you think, child? We are taking our maturation exam, but are still treated as children. They call this part discussion. Actually an interrogation. The high court is in session.

Zirkel searches for a blackboard. When she does not find one, she scribbles in chalk on the masonry. No objections raised. Everyone has heard—mental hospital, twice, with the walls closing in. We, the school board, are not concerned. Teacher shortage. Good-bye, wrong number!

The path to Mozart leads past the inkwell, through lies and curved daggers. Dance of the D's. I help my mother wash the dishes. Mow the grass. I make mobiles and stuff toy animals. I have never heard of the stab-in-the-back legend. I don't know who Papen is, or Hugenberg. The only one I know is Hitler, and he was to blame for everything, no one else. Brecht—Brecht never existed. And even if he did exist, he is not to be mentioned at the final exam. I refuse to examine you on that kind of writer. The line is drawn at the nineteenth century. Communists and Jews keep out. The True floats above the treetops. Man. The Good. I have been raised as an absolute hero, in no way inferior to the Maid of Orleans. All I have to do is speak the truth, so they can identify me quickly, unmask me, hand me over. Just ask what you want to ask. Say what you think. Bite right into the bread knife. A small loss of blood will just drain me smaller. That way I can duck better, creep along the corridors, reach the gate by 7:55, and never be late. That way I can learn *by heart. But anyone who does not put on this model heroic mask, who questions the concepts of the Good, Man, the Truth—such a person comes up against a phalanx with streaks of gray, broken here and there by courageous young teachers, who are called Siefert and emigrate to Canada, who are called Frl. Plath and protest in silence, keep silent on the Truth. Who envelop their lives in silence. With time, such things make a dent. With time, one begins to grasp what is expected. With time, one puts things in perspective. Gets smaller and smaller. Loses half an inch every day in order to get a little bigger, and a little bigger still, as big as prescribed.*

Cornelia is wearing blue with white polka dots. Like my grandmother's. Her essay on her educational development was written by her brother. And Hannelore has reinvented the words prayer and contemplate, insight, and all in flux. Dear Lord, if I should die before I wake, be sure the school my soul doth take. The tribunal questions me about Mozart. It is important that I washed my hair this morning. Everybody washed her hair, trimmed her nails, brushed her little teeth.

And you, please!

Questioned in rows of three, we return to our classroom, where we have a catered lunch and coffee made by the lowerclassmen for the seniors in their delicate condition. The teachers eat in the music room. Everything tastes better when they are by themselves; after all, even a mealtime has to have some significance. Then Phoenix the school director appears and reads off who will be dispensed from taking the oral examination. Precondition for this freedom: first you have to quake with anxiety until one o'clock in the afternoon. Polish history drops from Cornelia's fork, Catullus falls out of Margret's pocket.

Let's put on a record!

The Beach Boys. After all, we have a swinging school. We actually dare to put on a barely tolerated Beach Boys record. One-thirty. Cicero hurls his oration against Cataline. Two-thirty. In what century was the Hanseatic League founded? Three-thirty. What is vegetative reproduction? Four-thirty. Insufficient living space is Japan's chief problem. Just step up nicely two by two. Congratulations. Good luck. Congratulations. Good luck. Congratulations. Good luck. Everyone shakes everyone else's hand. In the holy of holies the first teacherly tears begin to fall. My seniors, my girls, how fond I was of you.

You plan to become a social worker?

Why a social worker? Fashion model Doris says good-bye. Television announcer Petra dabs 4711 Cologne behind her ears. Hannelore starts up the Opel and drives to the Academy. Only our teachers trudge on foot down well-raked garden paths and weep their eyes out. Twenty-one fewer compositions. More free time. Cross your fingers and hope that the new class will write compositions in advance, so the excessive work load is restored without delay. Lots to do. Lots to do. For every ten pumps there is one man's shoe, and he is already married.

SCENE 59. MONTAGE OF ADVERTISING CLIPS USING ATTRACTIVE YOUNG PEOPLE AS BAIT FOR THEIR PRODUCTS. OVER THEM A RUNNING TEXT OF PHRASES FROM THE REPUBLICAN CLUB'S LEAFLET. THE MONTAGE IS OVERLAID WITH SHORT INSERTS SHOWING GEBHARDT AND MARQUART ALONE IN A STUDY IN THE LATE NINETEENTH-CENTURY VILLA. Alone together in a back room. A storeroom. One leaflet high. One plenary session wide. ROOMS SHOULD BE AVAILABLE FOR DISCUSSIONS ON POLITICAL ISSUES. One promise too short. YOU ARE INVITED TO JOIN AND LEND YOUR SUPPORT. Not even worth an evening. OUR DEMOCRACY. Not even there and back. Once every two weeks. What a burden. What unbearable regularity. COULD MEET INFORMALLY AND TALK. Three of them. WHERE DOES ONE MEET? By two's. For today there are only two left. Two in a back room. Two in a study group. GEBHARDT and MARQUART, MARQUART and GEBHARDT. Alex Sommer is absent. Sommer was supposed to keep the minutes. Sommer had promised to come. Ten little Indians. ROOMS SHOULD BE AVAILABLE FOR DISCUSSIONS ON POLITICAL ISSUES. Two little Indians. I think we should dissolve the study group. One adult plus one adult makes two adults. IN SUCH A PLACE REPORTS COULD BE PRESENTED. Too bad, says MARQUART. Really too bad. But we cannot accomplish anything unless we work. Who is we, thinks GEBHARDT. If everyone keeps the minutes. Who is everyone? When people reach an agreement. Who are people? When everybody, MARQUART says. If everybody, says GEBHARDT. Ten little minutes. Nine little minutes. Then there was only one. Who wants to give the report next time? No one. I don't have the time. You don't have the time. He, she, it doesn't have the time. OUR DEMOCRACY. THAT HAS TO CHANGE. Study group on the German National Party—two. Read through a program. We don't have the time. Read through a newspaper. You don't

194

have the time. Read through a book. Draft a pamphlet. No time. No time. No time. YOU ARE INVITED TO JOIN AND LEND YOUR SUPPORT. It's like at my place, says MARQUART. Like in my quarters, says MARQUART. Volunteer groups. I see groups formed, but none voluntarily. They can't even make themselves read a newspaper regularly. Rudolf Marquart. Stale white skin between two shoulder blades. He places his rooms at other people's disposal. For two. For two solitary members of a study group. PERHAPS NOT ONLY WRITERS, JOURNALISTS, STUDENTS, MINISTERS, TEACHERS, SCIENTISTS, TEACHING ASSISTANTS WOULD COME, BUT MORE AND MORE. I don't think Sommer will be back. BUT MORE AND MORE SHOP FOREMEN, PROFESSORS. RUDOLF MARQUART stuffs his report into his pocket. MORE AND MORE WORKINGMEN, HIGH SCHOOL STUDENTS, UNION MEMBERS, AND PERHAPS SOME DAY, PERHAPS EVEN. PERHAPS. Where does one go in this city, MARQUART asks. Home, says GEBHARDT. The best thing is to go home.

Secret Society with Mixed Fruits

Medical student, two bunches of carnations high, two yogurt containers wide. The evening begins with "Blowing in the Wind." Bob Dylan froths the dessert into our mouths. We are celebrating my final exams. With a little hair spray and Chanel No. 5, with My Mixture and a twenty-mark bill. My conquest is taking me out. The path leads down into a cellar. Tearoom, says the prospective doctor with the chipped incisor and the VW beetle, my 1200 de luxe model friend.

Congratulations, says Bini. Her hair grazes her ankles. How's my Jens? The waitresses are actually experts on Kierkegaard. The lords of yogurt creation remain glued to their chessboards, long hair, already showing a few threads of gray, falling forward. The house slippers of the future dance ring around the rosie about played-out students, the artists and thinkers of today, the TV grandfathers of tomorrow.

Hi, Jens! A puff on the pipe. Hey, hey, greetings! Hail Marx! How're things? What're you up to? What've we got here? She's cute. I'll drop by some time.

Youth is a sect, a secret society with mixed fruits. Tearoom. Jens feels at home here. His pipe puffs his image into the air, in perfect harmony with Joan Baez. They all know Jens. Jens knows all of them.

Call me Hans.

Let's have some Beethoven. Cheers!

Petit bourgeois bliss. Still smooth-skinned, still size nine, still thirty-two inch hips. But with protest hang-ups, with rock habits, with beer bottle weaknesses. Here in the cellar everyone is a big wheel. Bernt is an architect and knows Gropius personally. Werner's TV plays get turned down for political reasons. Marian is a painter, deeply interested in new materials and the poetry of Paul Celan. Avant-garde underground. My final exams take me down twelve cellar steps. To the tearoom moles. When they see daylight, they turn blind. Another beer!

Congratulations on getting through with school. Free at last!

He has on a gray suit and a small-buttoned vest. A twenty-five-year-old vest. When it comes to Vietnam, he sees the whole situation differently. Every issue is knottier, has more nuances. You can view it this way—but also this say. No need to get so excited. Over beer Jens is for Black Power; when he steps on the accelerator he's betting on Godard; facing his exams he counts on his tutor. When he shakes hands with me, his shoulders fold toward the ground, and his head follows. A round back. A heap of humility hunched over its Django dreams. He seems to be looking for his potato chip and frankfurter youth on the floor. Jens is already standing with both feet on it.

SCENE 60. INTERIOR. EVENING. CORNER OF A LITTLE BAR. GEBHARDT AND KONSTANTIN ARE SITTING FACING EACH OTHER. CLOSE-UP OF THE BEER GLASS THAT KONSTANTIN KEEPS ROLLING BACK AND FORTH BETWEEN HIS HANDS. BACKGROUND MUSIC FROM THE JUKE BOX: THOSE WERE THE DAYS, MY FRIEND. I think, GEBHARDT says, I won't bother teaching my daughter how to talk. It won't do her any good, anyway. He sits there over his beer, those were the days, my friend. He looks intently at KONSTANTIN, the Greek who knows all the political groups. Who comes and goes in the SDS, who sometimes spends an afternoon with Rosa L. What can we do? That's what I want to know. Come on. Say something, Konstantin! GEBHARDT stares at KONSTANTIN and thinks, so this is how the story ends. In a bar. Over a couple of beers. Like with Willy Stiebler. And ZISSIS KONSTANTIN looks at him, rolls his beer glass between his hands, says, I don't know either. Should, could, might have, would, actually! I can't stand to listen to that any more, GEBHARDT says. They are planning for what will come after socialism. After the revolution they dream of. Always three against two. They are in such disarray that they theorize to death anyone who happens to drop by. GEBHARDT orders another beer. A contented beer. He thinks of Neubüser. Konrad Neubüser in his comfortable chair. Comfy, comfy. These young people go about everything differently, better. Much better. GEBHARDT blows the head off his beer. GEBHARDT says, Young cowards are simply young cowards. They differ from old cowards only in being young rather than old. ZISSIS KONSTANTIN draws something on his beer coaster with a felt tip pen. Says, They aren't just students. There are apprentices in the group, too. Three, says RAINER GEBHARDT nervously. Three. And they just withdrew. They said the club was just a bunch of bull artists. There are others, says KONSTANTIN. Where are they? GEBHARDT asks. Where do they go? It's their club, after all. It's not called a socialist or an antiauthoritarian club. Republican, says GEBHARDT. Re-pub-li-can. Why don't they come? Why don't they ever open their mouths? Why don't they defend themselves against these Rosa L. people, who spend all their time making things rough for us. Who disrupt only our meetings, not the German National Party's. You're pretty done in, says KONSTANTIN, and paints flowers into his hand. You sound like you've about had it, Gebhardt. Yes, GEBHARDT thinks, I've had it up to here. He winds his watch. He is sitting over his third beer. Those were the days, my friend. He hears himself talking. He thinks of Frauke. He has already begun to sound almost like his wife. Except that she makes no effort at all. Except that she folds her manicured little hands in her immaculate lap, like almost all of them. And is proud that she isn't involved, since it's all useless anyway. And that's why it's going to fail. As she knew from the outset. As Pantenburg knew from the outset. Clever Herr Professor. Oh, my colleague Schlesselmann is not interested? And Hesse hasn't joined either? But otherwise, an excellent project. Highly commendable. I think, says GEBHARDT the beer drinker, I think there are only outsiders left. From the right and the left. In all shades of the rainbow. But democrats? Real live democrats? People who do more than believe or feel or talk. GEBHARDT interrupts himself. GEBHARDT thinks of Bachhof and Hauswald. GEBHARDT is sick of speechifying. Like Pantenburg. About the Germans and their understanding of democracy. And that unfortunately all is not as it should be. Yes, it's bad, says KONSTANTIN. I know that. You don't have to tell me. And ZISSIS KONSTANTIN drinks his third beer.

197

We Greeks are all at each others' throats. Each man forms his own party. And the colonels are the ones who benefit. He taps his felt tip pen against the table edge. Those were the days. He says, My people are cut off. They have no leaders. The entire avant-garde is shut up in the camps. And yet, says KONSTANTIN, And yet we have something you don't have here in your fat, contented Europe. I mean a passion for freedom, says KONSTANTIN, and paints flowers into his hand. GEBHARDT thinks, he's a European, but he doesn't consider himself one. He no longer considers himself part of Europe. Athens, Lisbon, Madrid—they're already Third World. Africa. Latin America. Vietnam. And ZISSIS KONSTANTIN drinks his beer. Drinks a beer with felt-flowered hands and says, We've got to shake free of Europe. And GEBHARDT understands what he means. He understands it over beer and Mary Hopkins. And it doesn't help him at all that ZISSIS KONSTANTIN tells him, Here in Europe it's not a question of socialism. You're too well-off for that. It's only a question of democracy. You must not allow yourselves to become a Greece, stabbing the Third World in the back. It's bad enough that you exploit us. GEBHARDT thinks of Bachhof and his information services. And he thinks of the passengers in the elevated, of the men in bars, of the hundreds of thousands in soccer stadiums, crisply ironed, freshly shaven. All living off the fruits of colonialism. Coffee at sinking prices. Raw materials snatched cheap from colored hands. Oil from Iran. Gold from South Africa. The wedding bands of oppression. Check please, calls KONSTANTIN, and smoothes out a smooth ten-mark note. You Europeans scare me, says ZISSIS KONSTANTIN, and helps GEBHARDT into his coat. But perhaps you're right. Perhaps this club was a mistake. Perhaps there really is only manipulated democracy left. Perhaps it's already too late. Perhaps, GEBHARDT thinks, perhaps, and pushes open the door for KONSTANTIN. For this Greek who says, The greatest sin is to stand idly by. Amen, GEBHARDT thinks. Hallelujah. Amen. Amen. What does my father confessor look like, actually? Here we've been sitting together for two whole hours, and all that comes to mind is black hair, brown eyes. What did you say you're studying? Medicine. His socks are much too short, GEBHARDT thinks. He is studying medicine in too-short socks. KONSTANTIN calls out, See you tomorrow at the club. He runs to catch the streetcar, in worn-down brown loafers. He just makes it to the streetcar stop. GEBHARDT remains standing on the sidewalk. He wants to wind his watch, which he wound just a few minutes ago. It's eleven o'clock again. Another eleven o'clock discussion. Another six beers. Six beers. Still. Six points for Willy Stiebler.

Flottbek Teachers' Altar, 1966

Stand Fast, O Fatherland. *1914–1918. Carved gray in stone over the sandpit in the schoolyard.* MY FATHERLAND *leering down at every broad jump. For thirteen long years. I pass under it. Up, up, to the heavenly ascension of graduation. Between coats and posies of lily-of-the-valley. Black is the color of solemnity. Tailored solemnity or pleated solemnity, but black solemnity it must be. Nicely two by two. No gray, no red blouses. A white blouse. Official humility. We step up before the sacred body of teachers and parents, who rise in our honor, for the first and last time, in honor of the graduating class. Bach, let's hear you. Beethoven, play as loud as you can. How solemn and festive—Goethe's words lisped out by trembling lowerclassmen.*

The school orchestra in graduation minor. The cantatas of our future ripple gently. All paths lie invitingly before us. But for each of us there is but one door, small and nervously open just a crack. Do not stray from the path. Look neither to right nor left. Happiness lies in the middle. Frl. Hübner is delivering her valedictory address. She speaks of the Golden Mean, recommends the middle path that she herself has traversed. For thirty-four years, unmarried, from composition to composition, from the present to the imperfect. Frl. Hübner was young once, when she was studying Latin. She will never be young again. The future of a middle way, with buckteeth. Horse's teeth, we called them four years ago. Horse's teeth, we thought as seniors. Her permanent wave is brushed stiffly back from her forehead. Dear graduating seniors! I see you through my thick glasses swimming off into life. Remain as mediocre as I am.

Clutching my lily-of-the-valley, I see before me the triptych of my youth. Frl. Dr. Rautenfeld's Rise for the Graduates. Centerpiece for the Gymnasium Altar in Hamburg. Worm-eaten faces. Carved wooden planes from olden times, with severe bishop's creases. The faithful servants of power. Little regulations with permanent waves and black men's socks. A tomb monument. I take leave of Judas, the unbeliever, the apostles of the law.

The guardians of my values sit enthroned before me. On the side wing Herr Hillmann, the drinker, model for a figure in the Flottbek Teachers' Altar, 1966. On class trips, he stumbles into the girls' bathroom, into the showers. He looks like his house. The mortar is crumbling from his face. Soon his eyes will fall out. He really should oil his heart; it creaks when he breathes. Next to him Frl. Stege. White haired, stern as a Spanish grandee. English for inquisitioners. At her side the Scriptural authority Frl. Reiser. Religion for the sick and dying, neutralized compassion from old legends. Infantile paralysis for life. Frau Koske, geography for tea drinkers. Giggling, a married teenager who visits old friends 365 days a year and demolishes mounds of pastry. Russia, Japan, just so long as you learn it by heart or doze inobtrusively during class—everything stays comfy, nothing changes. Next to her the magistrates. Frl. Dr. Rautenfeld, pupilless lizard, stealthily agile, a mass of flesh that rolls over the classes, until the last hump of rebellion has been smoothed out. You must all. You must! She also teaches religion: Christianity for businessmen. Faith is hawked like the students. Anyone who helps others does so stealthily. Solidarity is treason. In the foreground Herr Dr. Hartwich, the local cynic. Anyone who cannot work out $x = 4$ will not find shelter under his raised eyebrows. Will be sent back to arithmetic class. Girls are numbers. At the age of twelve he trained himself not to look. Now he lives in a state of resistance. Everything is neuter; he and she no longer exist, only it. $Y =$ it. At his side Frl. Dr. Zirkel, the high tomb. The whole Third Reich has settled in under the folds of her chin. She teaches history with folkish consciousness, German struggle for living space, Freedom and Unity, 1943, Moritz Diesterweg, publishers. She still teaches history, and she still trusts in Moritz Diesterweg. Bender's German Reader, the section on Fatherland and World, On Reverence, will do the trick, too.

Perhaps someone utters a protest. In the last throes of her youth (29), biology for troublemakers. But when Rautenfeld crows three times, even Frl. Biereichel's courage ebbs away, falls silent, is trimmed and graded; a school newspaper is spied on; if necessary the light is switched off.

School: a pilgrimage shrine. Here the lamentation of freedom takes place. Little coercions. No bigger than one page in a notebook. But for thirteen years life itself is no bigger than a page in a notebook.

Hannelore Bastian. Congratulations. Karin von Fröbel. Congratulations. Congratulations. Congratulations. Congratulations. The final re-

200

port card, filled with imaginary grades. *C's become B's. C-minuses become D's. C's become C-minuses. Do you have any questions about your grade? Do you mean you are a better judge than the examiners?*

Cornelia Thiele, congratulations. We prevented you from improving your grade on the oral? I refuse to discuss this with you! Out of the question! Go to the school board! I have nothing more to say on the subject.

Sabine Finke, congratulations. Clandestine grades. Bow to them. But of course you are incapable of humility!

Then why does the girl next to me have a C?

You're trying to make things unpleasant for someone else again! Congratulations.

A settlement. As a send-off gift, Feininger's Mouth of the Rega *for the bedside table, with Picasso's* Woman Reading. *In half profile,* with light, delicate strokes, absorbed in her reading. *Explanations for the blind. A gift from lily-of-the-valley bouquet to lily-of-the-valley bouquet.*

Farewell to the pedagogic court. Dear teachers, who have guided us to this proud moment. *The legend of our schooldays, supposed to be our* happiest days, *is already being hatched in the nests of tradition, just turned twenty.* You, as our teachers, will have sensed a certain gratitude in the efforts of individual students who caught fire for your subject. *Farewell requiem of a graduating senior who is* entranced by the magic of the new.

What kind of a language have we learned, a language which senses, captivates, and enchants? With dear parents, *and* dear members of the faculty, *and* gratitude from your daughters? *The world of the school triptych knows no social compulsions. Praise and rebuke flutter around the educative portals of my inner values. The pedagogic band raises its baton. Hallelujah. Stand fast, O Handel Fatherland. Now we are leaping into the sandpit of life. We take a running start for the broad jump. Industrial society is waiting for our offspring, is waiting for us, life's ten commandments chalked on our brows.*

Embrace humility and modesty. Congratulations.

Introspection is the true path to critical understanding. My best wishes.

Man is good. That is as indubitable as belief in the Good, the True, and the Beautiful. Congratulations.

Man is made for a higher task. Freedom gives us the opportunity to serve. Best wishes. *If each person would unceasingly work on himself, the world would soon be perfect.* Congratulations. *Freedom is the value that distinguishes us in the West so positively from communism.* Best wishes. *There is no such thing as society, only community.* Congratulations. *Criticism is essentially destructive and as such should be rejected.* Best wishes. *The middle path is not the path of compromise, but of truth.* Congratulations. *He who does not reach the top has only himself to blame.* Best wishes. *To take one's place and serve the community, to work for the positive on a small scale and preserve order and tranquillity are cardinal virtues.* Congratulations. *Solidarity with a second person against third persons is treachery.* Best wishes. *Preserve your individuality and integrity and affirm the whole.* Congratulations.

Heavenly ascension of graduation. Over at last. The philosophical compositions have formed us into golden meaners. The future lies in the middle. In the middle, where my fatherland stands fast. In the middle, between Sachsenhausen and the Rabbit by Dürer, we take our stand. Between Jews and colored not wanted, *between Vietnam and the* Knight of Bamberg *I erect the monument to my* inner values.

SCENE 61. MONTAGE OF PHOTOS FROM A FAMILY ALBUM, SHOWING WOLFGANG KNOPKE IN PRIVATE LIFE, THAT IS, IN HIS GARDEN OR ON A VACATION TRIP, AT A NEW YEAR'S PARTY OR WITH THE NEW CAR. ADD OFF-SCREEN NARRATION. Wolfgang Knopke has assented. Has agreed to take in the Schrader Bookstore. Little lawyer Knopke has told Gebhardt, That was a good decision to take Schrader. Knopke whispered to Gebhardt, Your steering committee has a quorum even without Fromm. Even without calling a membership meeting your steering committee is legally empowered to pass resolutions. And Denicke did turn you down, after all. In the end even Denicke was in favor of Schrader. And when he left he himself said that he understood our position. At any rate Schrader is the best of all our options, says little Attorney Knopke, tips his hat, and slips back inside his mechanical clock, raising one little porcelain leg high to the tinkling of little bells. For club member Knopke is fragile. Wolfgang Knopke is only allowed out once an hour. When the clock in the tower strikes, Attorney Knopke has his office hour, turns once in a circle, and gives information to the tinkling of bells.
202

On Board the 1919 Jet Clipper

Research. Instruction. Education. Nineteen hundred nineteen incised in stone. I continue on my course, passing under the immatriculated motto, without a sandpit, but with the graduate's sophistication. University of Hamburg. An alphabetical listing. Professors multiplied by students. Civil service careers lined up according to the ABC's. Abels, Ahrens, Aichle. Seminar on Structuring and Evaluation of Living Space and Equipment. Readings in Selected French Texts. Seminar for Doctoral Candidates. Fasten your seatbelts, up we go! Ladies and gentlemen, we greet you on board our 1919 jet clipper. We are cruising at a height of twelve stories and will cover a total distance of twelve semesters. Please extinguish your thought processes. We wish you a pleasant lecture.

Skyscraper atmosphere. They call this the Philosophers' Tower. On the Broadway of learning the elevators ring their way with illuminated green arrows from department-story to department-story. Bungalow corridors. Ceiling and floor almost touch. Windows focused on the building that houses the main auditorium, the Auditorium Maximum. Waiting benches for office hours that are not observed. In these corridors the electric light bulb is reinvented, a career thoroughly ventilated, a suicide plan hatched. These benches, modern equivalents of the rack, are located just outside Helsinki. Their clocks tick differently. If one sets one's watch at ten-thirty when it is eleven-thirty, one is there in time to catch Herr Professor Gümpel at eleven-thirty. For him a thousand years are as a day. Here one learns the meaning of detention. Here, outside the professors' one-room homes away from home, with their coffee makers and Encyclopaedia Britannica.

The servants' quarters for hollow chested assistants dressed in atrium style are strung along on a leash. The telephone becomes a dictaphone into which one reads one's desires. Yes, Herr Professor, I'll be right over. The boss, he whispers, and flies into his jacket as fast as his shortness of breath will allow.

Here, where the brewing of a cup of coffee becomes an unforgivable petty luxury and one has a guilty conscience about eating cookies because it implies succumbing to the desires of the flesh, here where knowledge is concretized, differentiated, analyzed, here in this four-walled cage, where one hopes one can write the two dissertations that qualify one to become a professor if one is good and obedient and studies diligently, here, where one's head grows so large that the body *shrivels and the legs wither to stumps, here old Alma Mater inhales and exhales student fodder. Instructors speak* pro domo. *I am an educational resource to be exploited. I must overcome perceptional barriers. I must consider my own viewpoint critically. Ladies and gentlemen. We have reached subsection Roman numeral three of our fourth chapter.*

When the academic bellwether arrives, the herds thump on their desks with their hooves. When he leaves, they thump with their hooves on the desks. When they like something, they thump. When they do not like something, hissing sounds, protest condensed into one syllable. A code of taps—cave language. One can give up speech altogether if one has two strong fists and a hissing, steaming set of teeth.

Captain Professor and his crew. Two young, scrupulously well-brushed gentlemen two steps behind His Holiness. Hauling books, carrying the briefcase, holding open the door, shutting the window. The Bobbsey Assistants. As their professor trots along, they support him like the two long-tongued lions on Hamburg's door-to-the-world crest. University crest 1919. It not only crowns the course catalogue, it also lives on in the atrium corridors of the office-hour bungalows. Except that the lions are no longer rampant. Their claws have long since been clipped. You can find them in their bosses' scholarly works, bound into the chapters. Trotting on all fours through the lecture halls. And always behind, never in front. Whisper the cues. Alma Mater's prompters. Stick it out. Warm your little niche. And at noon a bit of gossip stew to refresh you.

Fasten your seatbelts! You are cruising at an altitude of nine stories. History Department. Entombed history. I raise the lid and peep inside. I have to check how far gone the corpse is at playing dead. I never got past Bismarck. I can only spell Hitler, and I don't know the Civil Code. I am an historical illiterate, a monkey in the coconut tree of the past. When I vote in my first election at twenty-one, I will look for the name Goethe among the candidates. My vote, a whole life long, for Suleika. That will be where I put my X unless I lift the lid to get a glimpse of an entombed National Movement.

SCENE 62. MONTAGE OF PHOTOS FROM A FAMILY ALBUM THAT SHOW WINFRIED BÖHM IN PRIVATE LIFE. ADD OFF-SCREEN NARRATION. Winfried Böhm has assented. Has agreed to having the Schrader Bookstore. Has thought over his probationary year. Has counted his children's little socks and his distant wife's clothes and has agreed. He has agreed because the Vessel Publishing House does not want to cough up any money. Because the editor, Dr. Brenner, has told him, We won't give Rosa L. an advance. Not a penny for the anarchist Denicke. We don't finance people who are going to go bankrupt. Böhm has checked over his starting salary. Has subtracted the weekend flights, the daddy flights to home and children. Has counted his fourteen blue hundred-mark bills, made piles, one for Hamburg, one for Berlin, and discovered that he does not have a single bill left over. Winfried Böhm hopes to move to the Mövenring area, soon. Böhm thinks about the move, about his promotion, and about installment payments that have to be made. Böhm doesn't even have two hundred marks left over for the Rosas, not his two hundred. Not even one hundred, or fifty. Böhm officially and on behalf of the steering committe gives Herbert Denicke the final decision. Böhm says, We have decided definitively in favor of Schrader. You understand our position. Yes, says the voice on the other end. Yes, we know. We didn't expect anything different. And Böhm smiles and buys a handful of striped tulips for his weekend, for his daddy weekend in West Berlin.

A Fortress Wreathed in Peasant Flowers
She is blond. One eye a little smaller than the other. Are you going to the orientation tea, too? she asks, and holds the elevator door open for me. Are you a history student, too? she asks, and realizes from my festive five-o'clock eye shadow that that must be the case. Professor Jäger is supposed to be there. Maybe it's a good idea to have an introductory gathering like this for first-year students.

A broad back, I think. A house wall in lightly flowered cotton, I think, a good unit of measure. One quickly sees one's own place. On slips under the chin, makes oneself comfortable under the shoulder. Starting with the tea, it is no longer accidental that she sits beside me. From now on we always sit together.

Her name is Helga. She stands beside me like a tower. She draws me along behind her like a child's toy on wheels. I have made friends with a fortress. This fortress lies wreathed in peasant flowers, near the spreading village oak. Helga came to the city barefoot, to big Hamburg, her wooden clogs in her hand, the lawn of her childhood meadows under the asphalt streets. She studied for her graduation exams under a linden tree, did her reading on a wooden farm bench. Neighbors passing on the way home to milking. She never lifts a finger! The less time spent in school, the more hard working a village child is considered. Work on the farm. Contribute to the family income. The farm has shrunk so. All the pigs had to be sold; they weren't worth their feed any more. It's different with the big farms, of course, but my father. Helga's father. At six o'clock his eyes fall shut, at five they fall open again. No vacation for twenty-six years. Just once when he was in the hospital for an operation and got fourteen days of rest. Farm machinery is too expensive. You have to borrow. And if it rains, you stand there helplessly while the owner of the equipment gets his harvest under cover in time. Maybe you are number five on the list, so at least you earn your seven or eight hundred marks per month. Stick it out. Wait and see what eggs bring this year. You haven't been able to afford a hired hand for years, so you become your own hired hand. And Helga, the bonded offspring, sets forth to the city to learn how to earn money. To become a teacher. Prospective subsidy for the family. Their retirement pension is all of twenty years old. Soon she will be cherishing dreams of the farm as it once was. In those days everyone still pitched in at harvest time, and Helga's aunts had a German blood-and-soil orgy. But who wants to stay in the country nowadays? They all marry city boys. They take the six A.M. bus to the county seat. The village tavern dismisses its children.

Brandt's Children's Zwieback, I think when I look at her. Her hair is wheat blond. She spent too much time in the fields. Her eyes are unpracticed, only skilled at picking out ripening gooseberries. Her artistic taste is shaped by the local housewares shop. Franz Marc and Schumann, Berlioz, Kleist, and Genet all fall under the designation good. But she knows her Latin. English and French for advanced students, recorded on fresh, new tape. Her head is well-aired and smells of fresh paint like a new housing development on the outskirts of town. Still unfurnished, without an academic past, and inherited library, a ship builder as father on her left, a Ph.D.'s mortarboard as a springboard under her feet. Helga comes barefoot, her wooden clogs in her hand.

SCENE 63. MONTAGE OF PHOTOS FROM A FAMILY ALBUM SHOWING DR. FRENZEL AND HIS WIFE IN PRIVATE LIFE. ADD OFF-SCREEN NARRATION. Dr. Frenzel and Frau Irene have assented. Have agreed to having the Schrader Bookstore. Frenzel asked Irene, and Irene asked Frenzel, and Frenzel asked Irene again. She reckons up their debts in beer bottles. Reckons up their sons, plus interest. Reckons gymnasium plus university divided by childhood. Reckons apartment times pension divided by four. Reckons rent plus political sympathy. Reckons rent plus Rosa L. Reckons rent stays rent. One chair less is one chair less. One table less is one table less. One coatdress less. One vacation less. One semidetached house less. One full house less. One house in the country less. And no matter how Irene reckons it, less remains less. Politics, says Irene. Naturally, Rosa L., says Irene. Really cool comrades. But not out of our pocket. Sympathy divided by house in the country leaves house in the country. Irene Frenzel keeps both cashboxes under lock and key. Not a penny for sympathy without house in the country. Not a penny. Not a penny for Rosa L. And Frenzel thinks, Irene's right. We're saving ourselves rich. One more chair is one more chair. And because that's the way it is, Dr. Frenzel agrees, too. Agrees to taking in Schrader. Doesn't think it over again.

Earthworm Existence

Read the Spiegel regularly. Enjoy a good cup of tea. Leaf through Die Zeit religiously, clipping articles, mounting them in a looseleaf notebook, buy a new Spiegel, and have another good cup of tea. That's the pattern in his little room. A room that for all the world resembles a grandfather clock. Except that the old furniture has been painted orange and blue. Except that Jens wears velveteen trousers and drinks Pepsi. Except that he sleeps on a sofa and sits on the floor. Except that he gobbles up record after record of Aragon chansons. Yet all these things do not make Jens any more youthful, any more hopeful, any freer.

His life is regimented like the life of a sixty-year-old. Be there punctually, be back punctually. Every week the same. Living a whole life as if he were almost ready to retire. Lecture-hall senility. Interminable earthworm existence. If you cut off a piece at the front, it grows back on the other end. Others provide big adventure; he clips it out with his scissors. The newspaper scandals, the miscarriages of justice, the Nazi atrocities, protest actions against the Vietnam war. He snaps Norman Mailer, Rudi Dutschke, Abendroth into his notebook. His father collected stamps, his grandfather coins. Jens collects sensational revelations and protests. He applauds daring deeds. He discusses such things with his friends. Makes minute distinctions. Instead of his father's skat games, Nolte's fascism theory and a little Marcuse with smoked ham. But beyond three marks on the beer coaster to keep track of the drinks, the talk does not show much in the way of results.

Perhaps it is the ten-Pfennig tip that distinguishes Jens from his father's twenty. Perhaps it is also the big undertaking, the VW 1200 audacity, the proud spur-of-the-moment trip to the Baltic, where he lies regimentedly in the sand, regimentedly eats his smoked eel, and feels like Columbus because it is Monday rather than Saturday. Jens's great discovery consists in displacing his days of rest to fall on two weekdays. But this professional student only allows himself this luxury of youth once a year. Foot on the accelerator for an hour and a half. Strenuous ocean. Better to stick to buttering crusts of bread and buying tickets for the university cafeteria. Build up a supply. Busy, busy, scrimp and save yourself a Ph.D. Civil servants at work. With linen shopping bags or briefcases, at a stroll or an energetic, just slightly late, pace. Like at the post office, the students slam shut their notebooks. Six on the dot. The chairs scrape. Closed! The only one left in our queue is a professor. But we don't want to wait to hear the last sentence about Pestalozzi if it is going to drag on until 6:01. Sandwich into our six-o'clock mouths. Glass window lowers with a snap. Little sign propped up. This window closed. Finished! Time to go home!

SCENE 64. INTERIOR. EVENING. LATE NINETEENTH-CENTURY VILLA. FIRST THE ENTRANCE DOOR, THEN THE STAIRWELL AND THE BIG ROOM WITH THE PARQUET FLOOR. THE SUBJECTIVE CAMERA ENTERS FROM THE FRONT LAWN, PAUSES FOR A MOMENT WITH OTHERS IN FRONT OF THE BULLETIN BOARD, PUSHES ITS WAY THROUGH THE CROWDED MEETING HALL TO THE TABLE AT WHICH THE STEERING COMMITTEE MEMBERS ARE SEATED. People, people, people. In the halls, on the stairs, in the parquet room. Everywhere people, ashes, and Coca-Cola close at hand. Study group on the German

National Party—three people, GEBHARDT thinks. Study group on the unions—six people. Study group on the press—five people. Plenary session—two hundred. And what people, GEBHARDT thinks. The Denicke crowd. BIEHL, blast furnace Dieter Biehl, is steaming with excitement. They all came and joined up yesterday. They heard some rumor about a membership card check. Maybe Frenzel mentioned it to them. At any rate they all showed up here yesterday. BIEHL is delivering a situation report. And GEBHARDT reads from the walls, DOWN WITH MOTHERFUCKER GEBHARDT. And GEBHARDT reads from green leaflets, WILL YOU LET THE STEERING COMMITTEE LIE TO YOU? And GEBHARDT, motherfucker Gebhardt, thinks, well, let's get on with the evening's entertainment. With Ringo Böhm and Irene Zappa. The shit's going to start flying, yells DENICKE. Watch this thing explode, shouts a HIPPIE WITH A RED MOP. The steering committee's going to be blown sky high. One, two, three, four o'clock rock. Clear the table up front. Round one. Let's beat these liars to a pulp. I think, BÖHM says. He doesn't think, yells DENICKE, He lies. We can get started now, BÖHM continues. Shut your trap, yells a BLOND YOUNG MAN. As we informed you in our letter, DR. FRENZEL says, We have decided to take in Schrader. Because our debts, BÖHM says, Our debts. You fools, yells DENICKE. You just want to pull the wool over our eyes. You promised the rooms to us, and now you're trying to lie your way out of it. Manipulation, screeches the LITTLE BLOND GUY. We members are being manipulated. That's right, bawls a GROUP ON THE RIGHT. Let's hear Denicke, not just these morons on the steering committee! Man, what a happening! Crazy. One, two, three, knock-out. People, people, people. Between the university and the corner bar. Between the office and the movies. Way station Republican Club. Now two of them are quarrelling, GEBHARDT thinks. That's great. What a joke. What a joke if the club is blown sky high. Something different for a change. Not just talk all the time. Let's have a real blow-up. Come on, let Denicke speak, yells GEBHARDT, and sits down again. In front of him, BIEHL is perched on the edge of the table, chewing his fingernails. FRENZEL is standing there struck dumb. IRENE is sitting there, not saying anything. Not a single word. And WINFRIED BÖHM's smile has faded.

Uta

I am her friend, and we use the familiar form of address. Twenty-two hairdresser-pampered years. Penthesilea over lunch at the cafeteria. Will you listen to me go over my lines? *Ever since I met Uta, I have been listening to her go over her lines. A whole year of Kätchen von Heilbronn. A whole year spent with Juliet. I sit with Uta over the pudding they give us for dessert. Gretchen stirs the muddy mess.* Kätchen says, Oh, German literature. Juliet, already in her fourth year of university, explains, Sure, but really I'd rather be an actress.

She does not finish her pudding. She leaves scraps of meat on the plate. Three spoonfuls of applesauce to be thrown away. Four spoonfuls of bean soup for the garbage pail. Uta can't manage any more. *She can't force down another spoonful of German literature.* Uta is full. Full of Penthesilea, with diction lessons planned for some day. Ma-me-mi-mo-mu. Brush your teeth. Rinse out. *Ma-me-mi-mo-mu gets washed down the sink.*

Uta, it's noon already!

Uta, overslept, chokes on her toothbrush. Gracious me! She was too lazy to wind the alarm clock last night.

Uta, it's one o'clock already!

She sits there honeyed and cheerful over her breakfast. Good gracious! She lives around the corner from me, twenty gardens down the street. Ever since she discovered that, Uta has used the familiar form of address with me. Ever since she discovered that, she's been saying, Why don't you come and wake me, and we can go to class together. *We set out at a quarter to one.* Uta in her dressing gown. Sweet little Uta. *Uta in her nightgown.* Poor, tiny little Uta. Stroke, stroke. *A kiss for herself in the mirror.* Uta is late, twenty-two years late.

Three spoonfuls of acting school. Four spoonfuls of German literature. Uta is full. Fed up with family. *She simply had to go to the university. Father went to the university. Mother went to the university. And Ulrich is studying in Freiburg. Little brother Ulrich. Actually she wanted to become an actress. But it's her parents' fault. Her education's fault. Her bourgeois surroundings. It's simply expected, that's all.* The solution Uta has found lies between getting up around one—actors need their beauty sleep—and going to a lecture around five—let's check to see if the university has burned down yet. *Lies between Max Factor's Lucent Make-Up and dinner around the midnight witching hour.*

Black hair sprouts from her head. Pony face with malnutrition cave-ins. She sucks in the world around her. An Uta polyp. My function is to wake her and take notes. Couldn't you get to the class at eleven-fifteen? Just one lecture, just one hour? Could you get a course catalogue for me? Could you get this novella Xeroxed, since you'll be at the university anyway? We all work for ma-me-mi-mo-mu. Her mother buys rolls and Swiss cheese for Uta to nibble on. Her father parks a birthday car in front of the house, so Uta can spare her little feet. A lemon, says Uta, and slams the door. Boy friend Gert buys her a dress for her birthday, a pocketbook, shoes. What a moron, says Uta, and hangs the dress in her closet, plops the pocketbook down on a shelf, takes the shoes to the shoemaker. Gert has a Ph.D. in business administration. How he sweats when it's hot! Listen to the way he talks! He can't even characterize Woyzeck. Uneducated fool. Can't even express himself.

Talk. Talk. Talk. Off with your head. On with your hat. Uta's world consists of talk. I'm against that. I don't see it that way at all. One really should. If one could, one would have done it long ago. Beer in a student mug. Uta brandy. Let's talk our heads off. Against the filthy war, yes, yes. Against the filthy yes-yes war; one really should be opposed to it. Write an article some time that never gets written. Take part in a demonstration some time when it ended hours ago. Play a role some time for which there is no play. Live a life some time when it is already over. Uta with the temperament of a cigarette. Instead of fire, everything dissolves in ashes. Taped poses. Uta cannot get past the tearjerk issues. Still a teenager at seventy. None of her questions answered satisfactorily. No roles properly learned. No semesters finished out.

Even her complexion is dissatisfied with itself. It rejects nourishment, refuses to bloom. Hills and dales. Ambition with acne. Cover it over. Powder it out of sight. Makeup it out of existence. At the first sign of a wrinkle, night cream to the rescue!

Don't sit scrunched up in that chair! I mean to inherit it some day. When my parents are dead. Uta calculates. Unsentimentally. Headstone by headstone. Since father and mother are both trained in the law, it should be possible to arrange everything. Ulrich and Uta. The fork is mine, the push button is yours. Don't wear out the carpet! Use paper cups so you won't break the good set. When Father dies. Straight, ambitious legs support broad, angular hips. One hundred twenty pounds of indolence, puffed out with acquisitiveness. Have, have, have. Jurgen won't be able to offer me anything. As a teacher. Really, not bad in bed, but in the long run? I think I would make a good wife for a great composer. Or conductor. Me, the wife of a director. Pablo and Uta Picasso are happy to announce their marriage. We have married. Uta and Luchino Visconti. Gilded castles. Palaces with twenty-four rooms, in which she would like to live. I'll put the sofa here, and over here maybe a baroque dresser. The path to the castle is easy. It doesn't have to be a real castle, just so long as it is gilded. Just so long as others believe in it.

Her black lashes stare straight ahead. Each one a little index finger stretched out to grab me. Two well-sharpened eyebrows, two flashing black sabers. Horizontal declaration of war. A slim, mown façade wraps itself in silk, cuddles into soft wool. And changes its character with its dress. Slips from disguise to disguise, because no one guise belongs to her. In jeans to Vietnam. Silken pleats for a summer resort under heat-crackling skies. Oh, could you get me? Oh, would you hand me? Isn't there anything to eat here? Who is going to cook something for me? Who is going to buy something for me? Three spoons of gold for Uta's little tummy. A secret, clear as water, camouflaged as transparent glass, which fills the vacuum even more transparently. Uta lives on an advance. She hopes for permanent credit. She has no hiding place. Airport of the life-lie. On board, emptiness flies over the two-hill chain. Comes in for a landing over the hungry upper lip. Corners turned down. Uta wipes away the creases around her mouth, wipes lost time from her eyes. Another night and another day. Uta is twenty-five and she's learning Japanese.

SCENE 65. INTERIOR. EVENING. PARQUET ROOM IN THE LATE NINETEENTH-CENTURY VILLA. ABOUT HALF AN HOUR HAS PASSED. CLOSE-UP: HERBERT DENICKE. CAMERA OBJECTIVE AGAIN. We don't contest that. But when we offered a hundred marks, when we said we could get a loan, we were given a firm promise. Everything was settled. And then Herr Gebhardt, who manipulates this whole operation, simply forced us out. That's how it was, shouts DENICKE, and sits down. Put-up job, bawls the REDHEAD. A fucking injustice, yells a RED SWEATER, joined by a GREEN SWEATER and a BROWN SWEATER. Denicke's thousand and one nights, GEBHARDT thinks. For yellow and black sweaters. He hardly knows any of the people here.

Only the SCHUSTER COUPLE, squeezed into a corner in the back; they once helped paint the walls. Only DR. HAUSWALD, the gymnasium professor Dr. Matthias Hauswald, who directs the study group on the schools and looms out of the crowd like a tree. Amidst striped sweaters and checked sweaters. Who looms and keeps silent. K.O., thinks GEBHARDT. K.O. after the first round. No, now BÖHM is standing up. BÖHM is shouting, I told you no. You couldn't get a loan. I talked to Brenner myself beforehand. And he said no. Absolutely no. And then I told you no. But, DENICKE shouts, Dr. Brenner is here! He granted us a loan right off. And besides, shouts DENICKE, No one told us no. And then, says DR. BRENNER, a tweedy herringbone gentleman, And then, says a GENTLEMAN, I never, at any time, spoke with Herr Böhm. But I can prove it, BÖHM exclaims. I called from Knopke's office. I spoke with you on Friday. And then BRENNER takes off his horn rimmed glasses and says, And who is Herr Knopke? And says, Oh, so that was Herr Böhm? And says, Well, I didn't know that Herr Böhm was Herr Böhm. Yes, we didn't know that Herr Böhm was Herr Böhm, shout the PATTERNED BOXCARS, shouts LOCOMOTIVE DENICKE, and GEBHARDT searches for witness Knopke. And GEBHARDT calls out, Where is Wolfgang Knopke? But Herr Knopke isn't there. No one is willing to say anything about Wolfgang Knopke. We're not in a court of law, shouts the BLOND YOUNG MAN. I move we hold new elections! The steering committee here can't tell us anything. We're through. They're too authoritarian. And four men don't make a quorum, shouts DENICKE. Fromm is missing. They pushed him out, screams the REDHEAD. A vote, bawls the BLOND YOUNG MAN. A vote! GEBHARDT counts the hands. 82. 83. GEBHARDT counts the votes for Rosa L. 174. 175. GEBHARDT hopes that HAUSWALD will say something. He himself has nothing more to say. There is nothing he can say. GEBHARDT hopes that Frenzel, that Grützmann will insist that Knopke should be heard at the next meeting. That Knopke can witness to the previous discussion, in which Herbert Denicke said no. Said no again and again. But Hauswald keeps silent. And Frenzel keeps silent. And Grützmann keeps silent. And the sweaters clap their hands. They don't want to hear Knopke. They are happy to see the project going up in smoke. Happy that this operation is being blown sky high. They want their Denicke to yell, We don't want Schrader. This Schrader who manipulates everything with his fancy little books! We're going to set things up our way. With our books. And we're going to pick the books.

We're going to mount campaigns. So that's what we're here for. So they can manipulate the membership, GEBHARDT thinks, so they can silence their political opponents and terrorize the club. And that's what we puppets are here for, to let ourselves be lied to, because we can't get our mouths open. Because we can't put ourselves across. Because we let ourselves be steamrollered. Because we capitulate before the extremes, right or left. Because we are too feeble for democracy. Because when you come right down to it, we don't believe in democracy. No one in this room believes in our republic. No one, GEBHARDT thinks. They are glad to be lied to. That relieves them of having to lie to themselves. They are happy that this operation is being blown sky high. That no one knows that Herr Böhm is Herr Böhm. That someone dictates an opinion to them, so they don't have to come up with one of their own. And BIEHL is chewing his fingernails and will come up afterwards and say, We should have sent for Knopke. We should have thrown Denicke out. We should have. And Dr. Hauswald will say, It was perfectly evident that this Herr Brenner was lying. That he only came to an agreement with the Rosas right before the meeting. That could all have been set straight. And Frenzel will say. Afterwards. Afterwards, GEBHARDT thinks. Afterwards, when no one is listening; that's when they'll speak out.

He Doesn't Mean It That Way
An afternoon, an evening at Heidelinde's. How's ballet? An afternoon, an evening at Heidelinde Cramer's, twenty-two years old, with a profession clearly in mind: gym and ballet teacher to piano accompaniment. From a smoothly running family. From the family of Cramer and Wife. Cramer, Rudolf, owner of a lighting supplies store. Owner of two villas. One in the suburbs along the Elbe, right next to the golf course. One in southern Carinthia. Owner of a vineyard in the sunny south of Carinthia. Owner of a wife in a dirndl, who also owns a lighting supplies store and two kinds of villa. One in a Hamburg villa paradise, the other in southerly Carinthia. Frau Cramer, who owns a husband. Herr Cramer, who also owns a daughter, who in turn owns a mother, Frau Evelyn Cramer, from a well-situated family.

Heidelinde, a glasses wearer with the face of a picture-book gnome. With a hard, knobby forehead, wooden painted eyes, and a sharp, crookedly carved gnome's nose. Heidelinde Cramer. Slightly stocky.

214

Classmate with crooked legs to piano accompaniment. Hobbies: not wearing glasses, collecting art calendars, reading fashion magazines, sewing pleated skirts and patterned blouses with puffed sleeves. For summer in care-easy Trevira. For winter in care-easy Trevira.

And how are our two students?

Herr Cramer shakes my hands amiably. Frau Cramer shakes Jens's hand amiably. Still in a dirndl, just as when she was a schoolgirl. In summer in a dirndl. In winter in a dirndl. In a care-easy burial dirndl. In a death-time dirndl subject to recall. Hello. How nice of you to stop by.

Herr Cramer fetches out the cognac. Herr Cramer must be about fifty now. With gray temples and crewcut. Burned brown by the winter sports sun. By the summer lake sun. Full-bodied and care-easy and sturdy. And that was already the case when he was a schoolboy. Rudolf Cramer looks better and better with the passing years. Broad, tall Rudolf, who fills the cognac glasses and asks, What's on television tonight? Sit down, pull up chairs, turn off the conversation. Until this moment I never realized that Fanta orange soda was the key to happiness. Have a seat. Swallow some cake. Chew some little sandwiches. Until now I never realized that Bayer's Aspirin would save my day. Buckle up in your easy chair jet, tamed by pumpernickel and Swiss cheese. We are flying at an altitude of 0.00 news. Please do not smoke. We are approaching a thriller landing and wish you a pleasant death. Potted pink geraniums, luxuriating out of a copper kettle. Which Jens and I find lovely. Lovely lovely. Just lovely. Which Frau Cramer likewise finds lovely. Which Herr Cramer finds lovely. And Heidelinde finds lovely, these brightly polished geraniums in the copper kettle on Evelyn Cramer's Channel 4.

Brightly polished and sandwich spread. Lean back. Please have a seat for the housewife's afternoon dinnertime in front of a polished walnut baroque chest which has swallowed up Channels 1 and 2. In front of an antiqued old-time German chest, crowned by a wooden madonna, the mascot of luxury Christians.

Jens and I sit down because Heidelinde is sitting. And Heidelinde is sitting because Frau Cramer is sitting. And she is sitting because Rudolf Cramer is sitting. We all lean back together, together staring at Hudson quality pantyhose, at super silver Gillette blades. We attend to the philosophizing of a thickly spread salami sandwich. We make ourselves comfortable. And an hour from now, says Cramer the announcer, his beer bottle microphone held close to his mouth, We'll see the Fight.

And in an hour we saw the Fight. With I'm the greatest. With Cassius

Clay. With Turn up the sound, let's have the picture lighter so the nigger looks white. *Rudolf Cramer, the greatest. He yells,* Evelyn! *He yells,* Heidelinde! *Fix the focus! Turn up the sound! Owner Cramer herds his women onto the screen parade ground.*

Give it to that Jew!

Cramer urges the tube on.

Give it to him, that nigger Jew!

But Daddy!

An evening at Heidelinde Cramer's.

But Daddy, the nigger is not a Jew.

But Daddy, the kike is not a Negro. Daughterly protest. And Mother Cramer passes the sandwiches. Once around the circle of chairs. Once to stuff her daughter's mouth shut.

But Daddy!

And Daddy, this broad, tall, full-bodied, well-nourished Daddy, confronts this but with his Dachau. His broad, care-easy fifty-year-old Dachau.

But of course he's a Jew! You can see it by the hooked nose. It's obvious, a Stone Age mixture. Some Jew gets involved with a nigger woman, and out come these little vipers. Come on, give it to him! Beat that kike into the ground!

They should have all been smoked out, shrieks Cramer. Dachau was a recuperation station, bawls Cramer. And Jens sips his beer. And Jens tries not to listen. When an adult is speaking, one keeps one's mouth shut. When an adult is speaking, one doesn't contradict.

Knock the nigger's teeth out!

And I try not to listen. I don't look up when I know that Herr Cramer is speaking. For when Herr Cramer is speaking, I don't contradict.

Knock him dead!

He rolls his chair right up to the screen. Pushing with his heels, the beer bottle in his fist, his head thrust forward, his forehead reaching right into the ring. I see Cramer out of the corner of my eye. I see his shadow slowly inching toward the screen.

Hit that Jew, Cramer yells. We only gassed half of them, says Herr Cramer. And Frau Cramer keeps silent. And Heidelinde keeps silent. And Jens keeps silent. One keeps silent. One. Because one is polite, one does not contradict. For one is here as a visitor. One doesn't want to call attention to oneself. One doesn't want to get hurt. One keeps very quiet.

216

One waits. One does not argue, although one is embarrassed. One thinks one's own thoughts, but steers clear of trouble. It's hopeless anyway. Hopeless. Hopeless. It does no good anyway. No good. No good.

One tries not to listen. That's the best method. One knows about Jews only from not listening. One knows about niggers only from not listening. About the past only from not listening. The one past. When one kept silent. When one did not contradict. When one steered clear of trouble. When one tried not to have anything to do with such people. Take your seats. Finished. Dead. The weather prediction: Hitler and muggy. And Herr Rudolf Cramer falls beer-soothed asleep. Because his boxing match is over, his Second World War is over. Falls fiftily asleep, his bottle between his fists. Owner Cramer sleeps between the fenders of his easy chair. The Minotaur is getting a good rest. Has been doing so for twenty-two well-foddered years. Sh, sh, says Frau Cramer. Sh, says Heidelinde. I'll see you out, says Heidelinde. He always falls asleep, says Frau Cramer. He doesn't mean it that way, says Heidelinde. Sh, says Frau Evelyn Cramer. Sh. Tiptoe. Take off your shoes. Sh. Take off your socks. Sh. Take off your clothes. Sh. Break out your teeth. Sh. Pull out your hair. Sh, says the Minotaur. And Jens and Ariadne put their fingers to their younger generation mouths. And Jens and Ariadne sneak away on tiptoe and steer clear of trouble. But it is embarrassing to them, and they think their own thoughts.

SCENE 66. INTERIOR. EVENING. PARQUET ROOM OF THE LATE NINETEENTH-CENTURY VILLA. IT IS APPROACHING ELEVEN O'CLOCK. THE MEETING IS APPROACHING ITS FINAL CLIMAX. SCENE OPENS WITH A LONG SHOT. BÖHM has lost his self-control. BÖHM is shouting, is shouting, too, now. You elected us! We rented this house for you! It was we who did the dirty work for you, for months and months! Who helped us with decisions? Where were our members then? And who knew the financial situation of this club, anyway? Who knows about the debts Nikolaus Hopp racked up? Which of you just come here and vote for the fun of it and never appear for the study groups? And don't write a single pamphlet? And never hand out leaflets, and don't do a blessed thing? Is Nikolaus Hopp here? shouts DENICKE. Hopp is not there. Is Schrader here? Schrader is not there. Is Knopke there? Knopke is not there. All right, HERBERT

DENICKE shouts, Then it's our club! If these people don't come to the plenary sessions, the club doesn't belong to them. The club is our club. Their club, GEBHARDT thinks. Everything is theirs. And the thirty-nine-year-old schoolboy WINFRIED BÖHM loses his patience. I explained it all to you. I will repeat it one more time. I explained to you that we need the hundred marks' rent and for that reason are taking Schrader. And you said yes. You said yes because at that time you didn't have a penny to your name. I know that, because I talked with Brenner beforehand. All right, comrades, I'll repeat it, too, shouts DENICKE, Because Herr Böhm keeps lying to us: There never was any preliminary discussion. And we didn't know that Herr Böhm was Herr Böhm—Brenner told you that already. And GEBHARDT promised to let us have the bookshop for a hundred marks' rent per month. That's all old hat, shouts the BLOND YOUNG MAN. The only question is, are we sure of getting the loan? I can vouch for that, exclaims DR. BRENNER. I am the editor at Vessel. I personally approved the credit. There, you see? says DENICKE. So we can pay two hundred marks, too. Just as much as Schrader. And later more than two hundred. Maybe even two hundred fifty. He'll raise the price to three hundred in a minute, GEBHARDT thinks, so the sweaters will have something to hurrah about. Because today they have taken things into their own hands. Have raised their hands, shaken up the steering committee, and had a damned good time at it, too. Come on, let's vote again, while we're at it! Isn't Schrader here? No, he's still not here. Still not? No, still not. All right, then, hands up! One, two, three, all for Rosa. The LITTLE BLOND FELLOW collects hands. One hundred fifty. One hundred fifty-one. One hundred sixty-nine. Everything fine. GEBHARDT and BÖHM vote no, of course. DR. FRENZEL abstains. DR. HAUSWALD likewise. The BLOND YOUNG MAN grinningly storms the front table. From today on, we're in charge here. From today on, things are going to be democratic around here! You really shouldn't have done that, the REDHEAD tells GEBHARDT. You really shouldn't have lied, says a GREEN SWEATER to GEBHARDT. You must have something against beards. What's wrong with two hundred marks' rent per month? You must have something against antiauthoritarians; you must have something against money, says a BLUE SWEATER, a BROWN SWEATER to GEBHARDT, the motherfucker. BÖHM reaches for his briefcase. Demoted to third grade. BÖHM makes his way through the sweaters, past FRENZEL, past the SCHUSTERS. Past DR. MATTHIAS HAUSWALD, who is also forcing his way

218

through the crowd, who is saying, This could all be changed. We need a committee. An investigative committee to get at the truth. Made up of nonpartisan members. Of independents. Of the young people here. That's right, says the BLOND YOUNG MAN. Good, let's form a committee. I'll propose it to the membership. We'll go over the whole business again, says the GREEN SWEATER. Good-bye, says DR. BRENNER. Good-bye, DR. BRENNER says to GEBHARDT, That business with Böhm was really most unfortunate. It was probably a misunderstanding. But still. I must tell you this. You really shouldn't have done that. The whole thing behind our backs, and then saying yes to Denicke! That was really unfair, says a PEOPLE-PERSON, say PEOPLE-PERSONS to RAINER GEBHARDT. Well, the blond guy will straighten everything out. The meeting is adjourned for today. We'll go home for today. Denicke and his crew go merrily on their way. It is already approaching midnight. And for midnight the Hamburg film makers' coop has scheduled nonstop underground films. And BIEHL will sweep up the leavings, so everything is nice and tidy tomorrow. For the study group on the press, all three or four of them, really nice and tidy.

In the Meat Grinder of Connections

Rolf knows Uwe and Uwe knows Gert and Gert knows Uta and Uta knows me. There's going to be quite a party tonight, why don't you come along, says Rolf to Uwe, Uwe to Gert, Gert to Uta, Uta to me. I know one of the editor's secretaries; she'll get us in. Fantastic villa. Cool people. If we get there an hour late, no one'll notice. Rolf wants to be a journalist. Uwe wants to be a journalist. Gert has to go into publishing, for that is Uta's wish. Uta herself wants to become a journalist. Travel, get to meet new people. Escape from this deadly student life. Nothing but lectures. Always in jeans. Seminars. The future teachers are rebelling. Forty years before retirement they take one more deep breath, and breathe in a rotary press and an editor-in-chief.

Hello, Darling, Rolf says, and sweeps us past a girl who lets him in with a kiss on the brow. Okay, Uwe, in we go! Fantastic villa. So that's how these people live. Guests standing around with glasses in their hands. In velvet suits or fitted silk shirts. Like him over there. Like her over here. Important people conversing under a porcelain chandelier.

Really important people. When I look at them, I can hear them swelling with importance. Gert has disappeared, Uta is missing in action. Rolf is standing back there and talking with some blonde. A reporter for Stern? *Almost looks that way. Take courage, move a bit closer. No! Yes! Why, there's Professor Pantenburg! What is he doing here, his dark blue jacket stretched tight across his back? He bends his head like a doorkeeper accepting a tip. Who can that be, the person he's talking to? Except for that fellow in back, no one is drunk. If only I could join in the conversation. If only I could bring myself to say something. Here I am, alone with all these important people around me. Press, radio, television. These nebulous concepts, these anonymous monsters—in private for a change. Heard, seen, read by millions, as Rolf always says, as Gert always says. Now I, a millionth reader, am here, face to face with the sources of my intellectual manna, who let fall their utterances from heaven above. I have my image of them, all with gigantic houses like this. A pound of airplane, two pounds of New York. I recognize that man over there from television. He reads off editorials, solemnly clutching his script. No question about it, this party is Channel 1, news and analysis.*

Man, get moving! Now or never!

Uwe hands me a canapé spread with delicate asparagus and pea salad.

That's the host. Editions of 500,000. Snow-white Porsche. Houses in Kampen and the Ticino. In addition editor-in-chief of Pardon, *the satirical monthly. That one over there works for* Die Welt, *the one behind him's from* Spiegel, Zeit, *or* Stern. *That tall man has close business connections with the Hamburg Senate. Over there, the little guy, is from Rowohlt. And him? Don't know who he is.*

Uwe's index finger takes soundings of his future.

This is your big chance to wiggle your way in. All you have to do is say something that'll call their attention to you. Just a dash of piquant opposition, not too little, not too much. You're young, and these old codgers have a weakness for youth. Younger generation, that always draws. Hello. Pleased to meet you. A pretty young demonstrator, says a gray haired fifty-year-old, and digs his melted-butter hand into my hair.

How are things? What's your student government up to? Heard about that business recently. Maybe we'll run something on it.

Uwe is making rollmops. Twisting his tie around and around his finger. How do you do? I could write that article for you.

Uwe stammers his way bravely to the front.

220

I mean, so you get something out before too much more time goes by.
Editor Uwe at nine-fifteen. Uwe is already looking for his job at
nine-fifteen.

I mean, it was four weeks ago already.

Yes, yes, says old Butter-fingers, Something should have been brought
out right away.

The light goes out around two chandeliers. The fifty-year-old switches
on the whiskey lamp. Time rolls on. The twittering beauties, the
thoroughbred ladies, dig into the men-salad. The TV news commentary
has already flopped, overcome, into his girl friend's rocking chair. In
place of subdued conversation they now put on records. This eroticism
mill is called soul. People move closer to each other, their armpits damp.
And all these big people turn very small. A teenagers' party for aging
would-be's. Ordinary pawing by perfectly ordinary people.

Have another romantic Scotch?

The fifty-year-old drinks. He is working on two glasses at once. Left
hand. Right hand. Alternating. And Uwe pants along beside him. Uwe is
out of it. His future is talking to him! The subdued future of eight-thirty
can barely stand upright at half-past nine. Fifty and stoned. With puffed
throat and double-chin dike. Uwe's future. It is going bald.

Another drink?

Fiery red woolen socks approach the tips of my shoes.

Teetotaler?

The little pearl around my neck appeals to him. Hello. He fumbles
around me, while Uwe tries to nail down their conversation. Ah, if only
things would stay just the way they were! But Uwe's future turns away.

Excuse me.

Here comes my professor, the doorman. His head bowed very low. He
stumbles inhibitedly toward us. So many famous people and only two
hands for shaking. Uwe's feet are melting. In a moment he'll be unable
to breathe. If the fifty-year-old exhales, Uwe will be blown away. Here
one creeps one's way forward, like the dancing cuddlers under the
wooden Madonna.

My professor wants to know if I have any questions. Whether he can
be of use to me in any way. To think that I'm here, too, comments my
professor. How nice, says my professor, his head bowed low, although he
usually carries it so high.

Another drink and yet another. Hello. The ceremonial introduction to

221

drunken indulgence rolls up its sleeves, throws its jacket onto the sofa, digs in. An arm here, a leg there. The butchers select the calves. Female calves with parsley in their mouths. From the one-yard diving board of their spectacle right into the décolleté. That's how it's done here, between Madonna and leather couch. Hugging the Oriental carpet, they slither under the skirts. From skirt to skirt. From room to room. Just do a backward crawl along the belly and knock over the lamp. Lights out! The artfully madeup spouses are making out with husbands who've made it. Uta backed up against a coat rack. Uta behind the kitchen door. Uta, the literary camp follower, giggling in the broom closet. A gentleman of the press well along in years pokes his hand down her blouse. Uta slops over gin number three. And Uwe is talking politics under the last light bulb. The public. And the circle around him grows. The masses. How sweet! An angry young man! People hurry over, barefoot.

See if you can do anything for this sweet young man!

Wife number five or six, her hair piled high, her face somehow cut wrong, implants a coy kiss. From the rear. All the way up the neck. And the mountain of butter grunts, Yes, something should be done.

Look here, old boy. That was a nice little attack on me recently, a nice little attack.

The publisher hangs there from his glass. Sealed in velvet from top to toe. Fortified in silk, his mouth a smudge, his eyes strung crookedly across his forehead like a mobile.

I'll do penance in my next little column.

The fifty-year-old grins.

Let's fraternize. Let's drown ourselves in drink. First you drown me, then I'll drown you. Hello. Weeping whiskey tears, they fall into each others' arms, these rival giants of the press. They are eating the same canapés. They have both had more than their fill of the same little scandals and news stories.

I want to publish the next article directed against me!

Agreed. Agreed.

The publisher thumps his circulation rival on the back. The friends shake fists. Objective reporting and controversial editorials have taken off their collars and ties to meet in the sauna of private congeniality. Here one hand washes the other, washes the one next to it, washes mine right along if I wash yours. If that fellow lends me his wife for breakfast,

I'll come out in favor of the added-value tax, too. For the duration of one column; after that I'll oppose it again. As long as the villa remains standing, as long as controversy still sells, we'll cut each others' throats and sew them back together again tomorrow with sherry and salmon canapés. Settled. Agreed. Ten newspapers—one newspaper. Fifty people—one publisher, with sofa bellies you can scramble over, with newsprint smudged around their eyes, with royalty gout in their limbs.

Rolf knows Uwe and Uwe knows Gert and Gert knows Uta and Uta knows me. If you look out for my interests, I'll look out for yours. Cheers! There's still room for us in the meat grinder of connections. Let's hop in. Jammed in tight. Slowly lick up the floor. Round and round the publisher. Up his toes, down his heels. We want to get somewhere, too, in this club of if-one-could's, one-should's, one-really-ought's, in this yes-yes club. Everyone with his bedsheet in his briefcase. Everyone a potential suicide. From the rim of the glass down into the cognac, push your opinions down deep until they drown, and bubbles well up for a month's salary, for a line-by-line fee, for a Christmas bonus. The really big fish, the medium big fish, and the little big fish. I know Uta and Uta knows Gert and Gert knows Uwe and he knows a fifty-year-old and he knows a professor and he knows a newspaper publisher. Let's lie down flat in front of the desks of these gentlemen, who determine our fate at a booze party after ten P.M. We can do that, too. We'll go along with that. Hope at your sides, head up. Youth hash, available in tins on the cold sandwich market. Let's hiss a wild miaow. Once, for the last time, before we defect to the pâté canapés, to the white Porsche, to the wooden Madonna. But let's write, let's write just as we don't please, and pass our articles around, from private rival to private rival. Dotted on the inside, checked on the outside. Hello, Gert, we say. I'll do penance next time. Hello, we say. Here's a little column attacking you. Take a look at it. Make any changes you feel are necessary. Hello, we'll say. Hello. Hello, for our future's sake.

SCENE 67. INTERIOR. EVENING. GEBHARDT'S LIVING ROOM. FRAUKE IS SITTING IN FRONT OF THE TELEVISION SET. GEBHARDT COMES INTO THE ROOM WITHOUT SAYING A WORD. STANDS IN THE DOORWAY A WHILE, LOOKING AT FRAUKE AND THE TELEVISION. THEN HE WALKS OVER AND

SWITCHES OFF THE SET. FRAUKE SWITCHES IT ON AGAIN. GEBHARDT SWITCHES IT OFF. FRAUKE SWITCHES IT ON. GEBHARDT SLAMS THE DOOR SHUT AND GOES UPSTAIRS TO HIS STUDY. PANTOMIMIC ACTION WITH OFF-SCREEN NARRATION ADDED. SCENE OPENS WITH A LONG SHOT. Gebhardt is almost drunk. Just now that is his usual state. He knows he is being weak. He is. He has had to take a lot of blows recently. Actually a whole series of them. A whole collection of Frauke marriages. And he is tired, beaten down, discouraged. He is well on his way to becoming a zombie. He finds it disgusting. He believes in something worthwhile. Something better than this. But the obstacles all around him are growing more and more insurmountable. He feels helpless. He has been banging his head against a wall for years. The wall has proved stronger than he is. What can he do? Give up? If things were only that simple. Swim with the current? That would be detrimental to his self-image, to his reason. That would gnaw away at his very substance. But decisions have to be made. It is unpleasant to have to think about them. He has had too much practice in not thinking about things. He is petrified of coming face to face with himself. The longer he lives, the more his fear of life grows. To the casual observer, everything seems amenable to rational thought. Calculable. Accessible to analysis. Subject to the laws of logic. But that is nonsense. Bergman has the right idea. He perceives the anxiety. His films exude angst. Gebhardt sees a great divide here. Anyone who does not like Bergman does not speak his language. Frauke doesn't speak his language. Doesn't understand. Is not alive. Is merely passing through. Gebhardt would like to go to bed and sleep and sleep and sleep. But he is wide awake. Wide awake with a bottle of cognac for company. A swig from the bottle. Life is so alarmingly primitive. Much more primitive than even a dyed-in-the-wool cynic would like to admit. Food. Drink. Sex and money. Those are the basics. Anything else is just window dressing. He has tried to get that through his head. This stupid, simple realization. Disappointments hit him brutally. He has tried to stay clear of them. But his world is not the world at large. And other human beings cannot be kept at bay. Not even if he puts on friendly faces, a grin from the rack, and pretends to be someone he isn't. Hands up. He does not trust the parachute on his back. Hands down. He's caught in the trap. He no longer loves his wife. And for the past year or so he hasn't even been able to hate her. But it isn't easy to loosen bonds. It is difficult, even if one is not ready to compromise. An infinite void has opened around him,

224

and on its rigid stage grotesque gyrations are performing for the millionth time the ceremonial dance of the happy marriage. The applause is as conventional as the audience. The situation is as predictable as a simple equation. A child always becomes an inhibiting factor in the dissolution of a marriage. Gebhardt is right not to brood over this more persistently. Transport planes are poorly suited to stratospheric flight.

Someone Like Me

Someone has been shot. His name was Benno Ohnesorg. He wanted to study at the university like me. Ladies and gentlemen. I ask you to join me in a moment of silence. *Well, that's something, at least. He's the only one to say anything. At least he's showing some courage. Pretty good for a professor.* Yesterday my dear and respected colleague, Professor Burnes, died in a tragic automobile accident near Tubingen. *Main auditorium. Heads bent. Stare at your hand. His name was not Ohnesorg, it was Burnes. He did not demonstrate against the Shah of Iran; he filled a bookshelf with his works. He will help us move on, past 1780.* Thank you. *We thank you.* We will continue with the lecture. *History takes its pedagogic course. After 1815 the world is in order again. Dip your head as deep as you can into the formaldehyde of history. Knuckles tap respectfully. He has on a good suit, a good formal dark blue suit. It fits faultlessly. Simply fantastic. He has never had so much as a brush with the police. Not him. He rides on horseback into the nineteenth century.*

At least put on a pair of pants!

My mother. She fetches my equipment for the battlefront from the closet. Laced-up tennis shoes in which to make a quick getaway. She has read the papers. She has seen it on television. Blood-drenched pictures, dissected out on the terrace with her glasses. Don't go! Don't get into the line of fire! Why do you insist on being so stubborn?

She reaches for a piece of toast. She licks the honey from her fingers. She wipes the meal from her lips. All right! Go ahead and let them beat you up!

The sugar explodes in the tea. The blood explodes in her blast-furnace head.

Let them kill you!

She is fifty-eight. She sits across from me, the gym shoes on her lap. Tattered, for I am staring at her past. My mother. None of her clothes are whole. And that is the fault of her guilty conscience. Her conscience, slightly to the right.

Yes. Being a doctor does constitute a political stance!

That's not the issue. They sent in the tactical force, used the liverwurst formation. They never even apologized for killing him!

I'm shouting at her. It's the first time I've shouted at her, the first time I say, If I don't open my mouth today, we'll have the thirties all over again. I'm shouting at my mother's youth. Bystander. Accessory to murder.

Or were you unaware of the human shipments?

I want to torture her, and at the same time I feel sorry for her, seeing her sitting there, agitated, stammering for an alibi. She did not take part in the things that went on. She buried herself in her profession. Retracted her head. Kept quiet. She escaped unscathed, bent double. She escaped with her hide. She did nothing, either for or against. Privacy, off-limits. And now she clatters with the dishes and exclaims, You can't change things; human beings just are that way! She sees herself confronting the same situation again. She sees me lacing up my tennis shoes, and the recurring cycle of televised brutality proves to her that you can't change things. The present offers an alibi for the past.

And what did you do to prevent them from shooting Father?

My mother doesn't answer. Fate, she is thinking. Go ahead and let them beat you up, she says. She slams the door behind her. She goes from the breakfast table to her profession. She is preparing her flight, digging her private tunnel under the reality of the news reports, in the face of which you can't change things. But the rest is not silence; the rest is scorn, with hair tightly braided, in pants and tennis shoes. She is a doctor. She performs an operation. She aborts the guilt she once incurred by not incurring any. The shy, anxious shadow of my mother turns the corner to the station. She is leaving politics to the politicians. They must know what they are doing.

She will never understand that she belongs to the generation of gravediggers, I think, one train later, half an hour later. We are travelling separately in the same direction. But I travel farther. Three stations farther. A lifetime later. Twenty-two years later.

The streets are broiling. Quivering tar jelly. Oily June oozes into our armpits. People must be filling the whole area up to the post office. A black wall, storming the opera house. Telescopic perspective. Barricaded anxiety. There are too many people who want to see the Shah and can only get as far as the mailbox. The fences of security, a loafing pen for the curious, dotted with black flags. The Prince of the Orient parades between police lines. He is pushed quickly into the oven of the Opera, like an early morning batch of bread. No more torture of political prisoners! The first shout. Ohnesorg! Ohnesorg! Scattered chants. Sweating silence. The protest movement is in black. Dew drops of anxiety cascade down foreheads. Murderer! Murderer! Pressed in tight. I don't know any of the people around me. I only recognize the police, hardly lines around their mouths, the same age as me, behind the barricades. Visors deep down over their eyes. Right in front of me. I hear only a Hup!, and they leap over the barricades. No warning. My own flight drags me backward. They are coming, their nightsticks, the extended arms of violence, forming a victory sign, the V of law and order. One blow. Left. Right. The nightsticks swish down like the legs of a chorus line, mowing forward in a rhythm of blows. That officer is feeling the heat. He mops his hat from his head. A person like me. My age-mate on the police force. Why is he beating this guy next to me? Will I beat others, too, if the order goes out tomorrow? The steamroller is advancing. Next to me a woman falls to the pavement. And behind us they are already pressing forward. In a moment I will be trampled underfoot. I won't be able to get out of here. I can't be of any help to anyone, and no one is helping me. Me. Me. Me, I think. This is what they call fear. An arm is beating my back in two, grabbing wetly at my throat. Let me through, yells a sweat-drenched old man, and shoves me aside, although there isn't any side left, no room, no air. We choke our way forward. To the Botanical Gardens, someone shouts. No, sitdown strike! Here one has to be twenty years old. Otherwise there is no escaping. I'll get you out of here! A starched white shirt. He seizes my hand. I am almost the only girl. Here one has to weigh no more than one hundred pounds. The old and fat will be squashed, will never make it. Now we're on the other side of the street. The chain of white helmets is shoving us ahead of it. Sit down! my escort shouts, lets go of me, sits down, with thirty, forty, fifty others. The chain comes to a halt.

    But I don't sit down. I keep on running. I am feeling physical fear.

Pure panic, for the first time. My breath is rattling like a tin can. What was I doing here, anyway? Did I want to see the Shah, or demonstrate? My eyes are weeping from the heat. Now they are sending in mounted detachments. Gallop straight into the ranks of the sitdown strikers. Just like that. What are we? Animals? Don't we count at all? The blue flasher of the ambulance is waiting for victims. A false peace, until our skulls split. Go ahead, let them beat you up, she says. Stay away, she says. Peep out behind the curtains. Crouch behind the blinds. Don't look. Turn your head away. Go home. Cowardly, with soaking pants and tightly braided hair. At the Dammtor station, warm, good-hearted people. Flower vendors and candy stands. One calmly gets in line for a ticket, with tightly laced tennis shoes for making a quick getaway.

SCENE 68. INTERIOR. EVENING. THE PARQUET ROOM IN THE LATE NINETEENTH-CENTURY VILLA. HANGING FROM THE CEILING IS A GIGANTIC BANNER: THE EXTRAPARLIAMENTARY OPPOSITION. SITTING BENEATH IT, SPREAD OVER THE ENTIRE ROOM, SEPARATED FROM EACH OTHER, ARE REPRESENTATIVES OF THE VARIOUS EPO GROUPS. EACH IS MARKED BY ITS OWN SIGN, LIKE A BIB. THE CAMERA EMPHASIZES THE GROTESQUE SCENE FURTHER BY MEANS OF WEIRD ANGLES AND UNEXPECTED CUTS. ESG, SDS, SHB. Gebhardt invited them. LSD, HSU, KSG. If the SDS comes, we're leaving! GSG, CAMPAIGN, DFU. If the DFU comes, you can't count on us. The CAMPAIGN is a cover for the illegal CP. If the CAMPAIGN comes, we're joining forces with the SDS! AUSS, FALCONS, FRIENDS OF NATURE, YOUTH WING OF THE SOCIAL DEMOCRATIC PARTY. We'll only come if the DFU isn't coming. If the CAMPAIGN isn't coming. If the SDS isn't coming. If the FRIENDS OF NATURE aren't coming. CITIZENS' LOBBY. PEACE LOBBY. Is the SDS here, too? We won't speak to the PEACE LOBBY. But why don't you call the SB. The LSB. The USG. They're good people. LYNX CLUB? Here! INTERNATIONAL NEUENGAMM COMMITTEE? Here! EMERGENCY POWERS TASK FORCE? Here! This is the HASA. BDD, I'll connect you. VAN! Are those people from the VVN? No, those are the ones from the VAN. If the VVN people show up, we're walking out! Man, I'm telling you, those are just people, I mean the old folks from the VVN! PAS, HSP, COMMITTEE FOR RACIAL JUSTICE. The COMMITTEE ON COORDINATION will see you now. Clear the ring for self-criticism.
228

GEBHARDT is sitting over his list of groups. Checking off the WOMEN'S PEACE MOVEMENT, the SCHOOL REFORM MOVEMENT. He is looking for the SOCIETY FOR CHRISTIAN-JEWISH COOPERATION. Unfortunately only three members of the CHRISTIAN RADICALS CLUB could come today, because unfortunately the other three couldn't make it today. Unfortunately only one person could come from our movement, because there are only two of us. And there are eight of us. But we have a thousand card-file corpses. A thousand yellowed card-file corpses. We only work on Vietnam. We only work on disarmament. We're directing all our efforts against the German National Party. Unfortunately only. We exclusively. Is someone from the SDS in the room? In that case I'm going home right this minute. They sit spread out over the whole room. And everyone represents the opposition. DIETER BIEHL has waxed the parquet floor. Frenzel conveyed Böhm's regrets for this evening when he called to say he himself couldn't make it. For weeks now, Böhm has been writing articles every evening. And Frenzel still has work to finish at the hospital. Gebhardt will be able to handle it. The RC's intention, GEBHARDT says, Is to provide a democratic gathering point, a center from which to coordinate the opposition. We must learn to communicate with each other even if we differ in our positions. We should. I refuse on principle to discuss with clandestine communists! You expect us to find a common basis with fascists? To side with leftist democrats against rightist Ulbrists? Throw out the Stalinists! That's all we need, a bunch of old Nazis! Death to the, GEBHARDT thinks. GEBHARDT says. GEBHARDT speaks. BDD, VAN, SDS, DFU. He is marching through the streets with his squad. He is shouting, Jews! And the squad shouts back, Down with the communists! GEBHARDT reads from his prepared notes. We should be able to unite at least for limited campaigns. He reads, For Greece, for Vietnam. He reads, Not allow ourselves to become fragmented. In the past that led to. Think of 1932. He reads, Not be isolated. We're in the minority in any case. Let us consider the things we have in common. Not the things that separate us. It is crucial to maintain and preserve democracy. That is in your own interest. Because unless. The Greeks are planning a campaign right now. We shouldn't leave them in the lurch. We should join with them. Just for this one campaign. But with the unions. With the parties. It is a question of alerting our citizens to the threat of fascism. Immunizing them. The time has come for them to learn practical democracy. For them to take to the streets. So it's not always just us. And the Greek question. Why don't we have a single Greek speaking here? Yes, where are the Greeks, anyway? Aren't the Greeks here? No, the Greeks aren't here. They don't even speak up for their own cause. We can't do anything for the Greeks anyway! We're so busy with Vietnam. We already told you, against the German National Party. Exclusively against the GNP! If the FALCONS come, we're through! Not even for Greece. Not a step. Not a step! If they are here. If he so much as coughs. If more than three are here! The only way to handle that is with a counterdemonstration. For a socialist Greece! I thought this was a republican club. GEBHARDT thought, this is a republican club for a democratic Greece. Greece must go communist! SHB, DFU, KSG, LSD. If they, then we. Only with you against them! If he leaves, we're going in. And GEBHARDT folds up his notes. And GEBHARDT thinks, they can't even take to the streets for a democratic Greece. Well-paved, clean streets. They are splitting the future in three. My arms disagree with my head. If my leg joins in, my foot will unfortunately have to withdraw. If my eye won't join in, death to the shoulder! And not a step for Greece if your eyelashes go along!

One Lisbeth, Going, Going . . . !

Mink jacket to the hips. The Mercedes star through her nose. How successful has who been? The fancy dishes roll in on breath-polished patent leather. Petra as a caracul caramel flan, flambé with diamonds. Cornelia, a silken ragout with sliced garnets around the wrist. Annette, a little goose, roasted, takes her seat between a tweed pâté de foie gras, stuffed Bärbel. A few Scotch eggs for garnishing, Irene and Margot.

It's a question of possessions. We bring everything with us. We drag all our loot along, as if going to a robbers' ball. We tow our Othmarschen, our suburban villa, our balcony apartment with Elbe breeze along behind us on a string. We park our living room decor right by the fence. We knot our strings of pearls to the garden gate. The Group is gathering. Kirsch-torte Corral. Class reunion with whipped cream. A semester has passed since our last pilgrimage to school. The affianced bosoms are well nourished. The graduation casserole has been ready in the refrigerator for some time. And now it's on to the dessert! Use the puff paste years well, while you are still warm, fine skinned, and delicate.

One Lisbeth, going, going, gone! We all want to auction ourselves off as best we can. A cruise with Neckermann Tours. Caribbean. I earned the money modelling. Mars chocolate bars, hmm. He asked if I would be interested. So of course I jumped at the opportunity. Anecdotes. Illona on the rocks. Adventures in the chocolate past of a Bounty student. Why is one at the university? Because one is at the university!

I tell you, I've had med school up to here!

Why don't you simply quit? If I only could. Like a flash! All I'd need would be a man, a proper one, like Lisa's. Forty. That would be cool. Neat. That'd be something. A guy like that has something to offer. But students? What a waste of time!

Well, Lisa's is really fantastic! Genuine pigskin, the whole apartment. Now that's elegance, I'm telling you. When she gets back from Beirut she's going to hold the reunion there. It's already settled.

He drives a Ferrari, doesn't he?

Oh, no, that's hers! He has the red Porsche.

Yes, that's right. Well, how about another piece of Sachertorte?

No thanks. Not until after the wedding. Have to keep in shape. Someone may turn up.

And how are things with you?

Irene smiles a shriveled smile. Allotment garden and a bank teller father—out of place, of course. But one does have to ask. It can't be avoided completely. The few black sheep have to receive their cake, too. Although they really should have the decency to stay home if all they have to show for themselves is one semester of theology. Breakfast. Pack your briefcase. Cartridges for the pen. Department library. A poppyseed roll for lunch. Fruit flavored yogurt. Lecture. Work in the library. Back home to bed. And breakfast again. Pack the briefcase. Cartridges for boredom. A requiem for lunch. Single with fruit flavor. One-room cemetery. Virginal work. What'll become of Irene? Not even a gold bracelet. Not even a boy friend. Nothing whatsoever. Susi, now, is just the opposite. She's going to be marrying this man—just listen! What a story that is! It just happened from one minute to the next. Snap! He's a surgeon. A friend of her father's. It was all pretty hairy at the beginning.

Heads together. Display your hips, display your knees! Well, if your throat is smooth, you are better in bed. Who wants to be forty? Twenty is trumps, with little white sweetmeats. A student marriage? Why not? But not for me! Well, I would insist on some of the—how shall I

231

say—financial dainties. A tender little university bouillon with a dash of first-semester seasoning.

That's enough of your stupid politics!

Typical Irene!

Why did Ohnesorg have to show up there, anyway?

Gert always says, Clyde always says.

Bonnie is tired. With a delicate mouth and a fine little tongue she licks at the university. Isn't there some nice little assistant professor who needs a sweet little kitten? A perfect little graduate kitten? We can purr and cuddle all around the porridge. Until it is ready, academic ready, male ready. Twenty-one marriage filets à la Goldfinger, if we had our way.

SCENE 69. SPECIAL EFFECTS. MONTAGE OF STILLS WHICH PROVIDE ABSURD ILLUSTRATIONS TO THE OFF-SCREEN NARRATION. He just dropped in. He has written a play. Agitprop. He is sitting across from GEBHARDT. A mixture of jackal and weasel, with long legs. With blond and yellow sideburns. A hundred eyes on the steppe of his skin. Tiny blackhead eyes. BRUNO GRIMME has written a play. He hunches in front of GEBHARDT's desk. Just dropped in. Just needs a little help. Just needs a captive audience for his words. Just needs a functioning street theater. Couldn't Gebhardt, for tomorrow? Ten actors would be plenty. Only ten. No, he hasn't been to see Pechstein yet. It would be better if Gebhardt called. Better if Gebhardt did everything. Better if Grimme kept out of it. He'll stop by again some time. Has written a play. To shake the workers awake. To create class awareness. To release slumbering forces. Not his forces. Everything but Grimme's forces. Anyone but Grimme in the club. Anything but taking an active part. Urging others to join. Grimme has written a play. Will stop by again some time. No, he hasn't been to see Pechstein yet. Has already been working on a new play for some time now. Perhaps Rainer Gebhardt could call. Call Pechstein so he can call Donner and ask him. For Grimme has written a play. A play for the workers. A play for guerilla theater. Ah, so Donner isn't coming. Thought it over. No. Grimme hasn't spoken with Pechstein yet. He just dropped by. He is sitting across from Gebhardt. He wrote a play six weeks ago. Yellow and blond. He is crouching by Gebhardt's desk. Needs some help. Does Gebhardt know of a publisher? Tomorrow? The best thing. The best thing would be if Gebhardt acted as agent for the

232

book. It's better if Gebhardt takes the whole thing into his hands. Biehl can run it off on the machine. It only has to be stapled together. Not more than two hundred copies. For a start. Grimme will stop by again some time. When the new play is finished. When the guerilla theater starts rehearsing. For Grimme has written a play. A play? Yes, now that was really something.

In the Valley of the Songbooks

His head had the shape of a spindle. Narrow and pointed, rearing up out of his black Sunday-go-to-meeting jacket. An oval atop a thinly wrapped neck. Quick to swivel. Flexible in all directions. Like a pecking bird ready to turn in any direction at communion time.

He has a sharpened pencil nose, I thought in the valley of the songbooks, and tried to imagine him writing out invitations. Crowded close onto the paper. With hard, sharp nose strokes. Invitations to divine worship, to confirmation class, to the study group on the Third World. Little absorbent white Christian slips. And all written with our minister's nose.

The Rev. Bachhof. Thirty-six years old. Married. One child. When he looked from his pulpit, that three-stepped elevated lectern on which he stood, unmarried, without children, upright as the figure on a ship's prow, when he stood there, with tiny black pinhead eyes, little mouse-eyes that gnawed away at the empty pews, when he stood there with his tight sickle-mouth, sharpened nose, and dizzyingly narrow swaddled head, I felt sorry for him. Sorry for every Sunday morning on which he pronounced, In the past week our congregation lost—Frau Elisabeth Streicher, aged 82 years, Herr Dr. Ernst Brauer, aged 71 years. The funerals will take place on Monday . . . *And then he presented them all in order. One coffin at twelve and another at two. And then he could catch his breath until the next Sunday and wonder, while we recited* Our Father which art in Heaven *whether it would be Herr Kramer or Fräulein Wunderlich. Bachhof was actually a gravedigger. His pastoral duties consisted in closing eyes, measuring out a shovelful of earth, day after day, visiting old-age homes and hoping from one ten o'clock to the next that there would be at least four people in church the following Sunday, not three.*

That I came at all was due to the study group. That Frl. Wicherstädt came was due to the study group. If I came on a Sunday now and then it was because Frl. Wicherstädt had said on Wednesday evening that one really should go on Sunday, and the Lindemanns agreed. When I came now and then and counted the little old Christian mothers who had all outlived their husbands, who would die at 82, instead of at 71, when I saw them, always one of them alone or three in a row, and here and there an old man knotted into their midst, when I looked at them, those Sunday Christians, and observed how they folded their hands, their boney, knotted old hands, I was frightened by their black Sunday flowerpot hats, those men's felt hats of belief, their religious achievement society, which near- and farsightedly sang We are the lambs of Jesus.

We want a war memorial in the church again!

We don't feel at home in this modern church!

It's not cozy here.

We want a cross on the wall, a picture of Jesus above the altar, and runners on the stone floor. In the old church we had runners, a Jesus, a war memorial. We want to be reminded of our heroes again, as we were in the old church, in the old days, as we always used to be.

And—Bachhof looked up ministerially—Our Father and and and. Something was brewing under the flowerpot hats. The inquisition slipped out from under the felt.

What do we need with a study group!

Why should we contribute anything for the Negroes!

We don't want an information service. Why should we contribute to the forty million who starve every year!

We don't want posters in our church!

We don't want to have to look at these swollen hunger bellies anymore!

Communism doesn't belong in our church!

We want peace!

Bachhof looked down at his lambs of Jesus for four whole verses, for a whole Our Father. Bachhof looked down at the churchly peace, at the regimented Christian club existence, sheltered from responsibility. They praised their Jesus so high to heaven that they forgot about themselves. They had monopolized the Bible and their potted geraniums for themselves. Between Moses and Samuel there was only room left for habit, which slithered along the pews like a fat cat and thought anything that moved was a mouse.

234

His head had the shape of a spindle. And Fräulein Wicherstädt and Herr and Frau Lindemann, watching this spindle from week to week and listening to it believingly, felt like slaughterers in the study group on the Third World. Slaughterers of an old German hymnal peace, which had choked hard on a cross which it had swallowed one well-heated Sunday morning when the lambs of Jesus were singing joyously because their cozy Jesus was going out into the bog with a shovel.

SCENE 70. INTERIOR. NIGHT. GEBHARDT'S STUDY, AS IN SCENE 1. IN THE HARSH LIGHT OF A DESK LAMP GEBHARDT IS GRUBBING OLD PHOTOS OUT OF A SHOE BOX. MONTAGE OF THESE PHOTOS, PICKING OUT DETAILS, PERHAPS WITH ANIMATION. OFF-SCREEN NARRATION. GEBHARDT is cross-examining his youth, trying to reconstruct it. He grew up in a lower middle-class hell. Tightly chained to his mother, estranged from his father. Child observer of a tragic comedy with a lethal ending. A chaotic father. Sensuality that reeked of pea soup, preserved in not too brilliant intellect. Unfounded artistic ambitions. Aspirations to stratospheric flight without wings. An unflagging determination that even lasted until his death, an almost brutally pursued desire to catch his wife at marital infidelity so he could force her to give him a divorce. No courage to ignore petty-bourgeois taboos and thereby gain a breath of freedom. Freedom which would not have done him any good anyway. He would never have been capable of shaking off his mentality. Resignation must have taken root early. At forty his struggle had long since been decided. And not in his favor. At thirty-five he must have begun to drink. A few years later he reached for stronger poisons. At forty he was a morphine addict. His sturdy constitution held up for years. He was spared becoming a wreck. A stroke got there ahead of slow decay. Father cut his wrists, fell into the bathtub, and drowned. Gebhardt was nineteen when his father died. He said DIED because it was no well thought-out suicide. Not even a self-destructive gesture growing out of despair. It was simply a physiological short circuit. Gebhardt never had much contact with his father. Father was a person he saw every day, who provided him with food, clothing, and pocket money. And whom he despised, because he was still too young to understand him. As a nineteen-year-old he had a horizon little broader than that of a sixteen-year-old. Perhaps his ruined

235

home life was responsible for his inability to develop paternal feelings, a sense for family, his incapacity for keeping up a pretense of affection. Familial joys. A youth embedded in morphine. Growing up wrong. His mother was hardly less of a stranger to him than his father. But a common need linked her and Gebhardt. Camaraderie vis-à-vis the father. Gebhardt remembers evenings when his father came home drunk and he and his mother locked themselves into a room because he threatened to kill them both. Gebhardt remembers one Christmas Eve when he and his mother sat up for his father until midnight, and he did not come home at all that night. Gebhardt remembers miserable evenings when his father lay down on the couch after dinner, drank beer, read the newspaper, and paid attention only to Alex. Alex the fox terrier. Why don't childhood experiences act as a deterrent? Why didn't they prevent Gebhardt from trying three marriages? Three marriages which all went sour? The result of a childhood experience? In a certain sense, yes. The fear of being an actor in *Virginia Woolf.* The almost physical panic at generating lies, day in, day out, to guarantee the survival of something which is visibly falling apart. In a certain sense, no. Childhood experiences cannot be made responsible for one's own behavior. Conditions and behavior can be explained rationally. Gebhardt does not see any reason for seeking psychiatric treatment in order to find something to blame for his mistakes.

Annette's Rise and Fall

Annette's belly is swelling. Come around eight. Annette's belly is swelling. I know that long before eight, even before the engagement.

She's having a baby, but that's not so bad. The news travels. With pill protection, with feigned well-so-whatism, but flickering curiosity. So now she has to marry him. A baby, really? Yes, a baby, really. Around eight. In the housing development. With spiral staircase and burning albino engagement eyes.

I'm the first one there. I catch the mother's handkerchief and spilling-over eyes. Annette, she calls, Come down here, and licks the tears from her mouth. And he comes down the stairs. I spot him in the mirror above the bureau, surrounded by gilt plastic angels. He is blond and pallid like a haystack. Dried out and left behind. My name's

Flemming, he says, and conducts me to the sofa cushions and the pretzel sticks.

Punch or champagne?

I'd really prefer a glass of gasoline.

Annette, what's keeping you? Pink Annette pompom. Little Annette. She spills champagne on her dress, a festive pink silk garment, a rigid sack on blurred legs. That can't be Annette, can it?

Do have a pretzel stick, child.

Annette runs teeteringly on whitened leather to the gift table.

How cute! A silver fork from Aunt Friedel, to stick the baby with. We'll have baby in aspic.

Horst. Hold this for a second, darling!

Salted darling which cringes like a lap dog.

Annette, the doorbell!

Sabine appears, and with her Dorothea and Margo. No, Wiebke didn't want to come. I don't know why. To the young couple! Clink. You're looking so well! Cheers! Nette, the doorbell! Aunt Herta is here, now there are ten of us. With each guest who arrives, it grows more empty and silent.

An engagement party is always so lovely, yes, yes.

One-two-three-four. Sabine is silently counting up the gifts. Engagement presents. Three more towels than I received. Three fewer gold forks. No diamond, hmm. But good dishware. About twenty-five marks apiece for the cups.

Dorothea shoves me in behind the towels and whispers. His parents didn't want to come. They're dead set against the marriage, of course. With him studying theology! Horst, please pass around the canapés! Salami, cheese dip, salt crackers. The guests stand reflected in the china cupboard, nibbling shinily in the panes, among the Meissen porcelain. Twenty-four, twenty-five. Sabine is counting the dishtowels. Cheers. Best of luck. Well.

The child is bringing shame on the house. Father grits his teeth, compresses his lips, clenches his fists. Petra did not want to come. I can't imagine why. Saltines, cheese dip, salami. Annette's rise and fall. Tied to the cradle at twenty, surrounded by bottles, a husband. Her shoulders hunched, slightly cramped, the baby blanket of humility in her eyes. You'll always be grateful to me. Hand knitted.

Have some more shaving cream?

No thanks, I'll stick to floor wax.

Potato salad with franks. How nice. Clattering dishes. Knife and fork conversations. Porcelain conversations. Thirteen table settings have been invited. They are tinkling at each other. The champagne glasses are gossiping. The mustard pot is humming. The water sighs bubbles. The franks burst. Thirty-two, thirty-three. Sabine is counting the last handkerchiefs. Annette has an engaged belly. Around nine o'clock in the Saltine development. By the way, Hannelore couldn't make it. She didn't say why.

SCENE 71. INTERIOR. NIGHT. AT GEBHARDT'S. LIVING ROOM, LATER ENTRANCE HALL AND STUDY. CLOSE-UP: THE TELEPHONE. OFF-SCREEN SOUND EFFECTS: A TELEVISION PROGRAM. CAMERA OPENS OUT AS SOON AS THE TELEPHONE RINGS THE SECOND TIME. He rings FRAUKE away from the television. He rings GEBHARDT out of his photographic past. For you, FRAUKE calls. Take it on the upstairs extension. It's for you again. It's Biehl, FRAUKE calls. Don't talk so loud, Tanja's in bed. Tanja's been asleep since six. Dieter Biehl, FRAUKE calls, and wakes up her daughter by calling RAINER softly up the stairs. There's no way to turn her off, GEBHARDT thinks. She doesn't even have a third channel. A third channel in her head that you could switch to. Not even three buttons to choose among, GEBHARDT thinks. My wife is a nonstop slapstick program. Across the hall the child is crying, crying red and white checked baby tears. Yes, Biehl, says GEBHARDT, and pulls the telephone closer. So late? Man, Biehl, you woke up Tanja. You're going to turn that child against me. There, listen to her bawling, says GEBHARDT, and holds the receiver in the direction of the disaster area. Oh, you're sorry, says GEBHARDT, and closes his eyes, so he can doze off over the caretaker's bedtime stories. Well, Dieter, what is it? I'm sorry, BIEHL stammers. Really sorry. But listen, the fire department was just here. I had to call the fire department. When I got home, just after eleven, our club was going up in smoke. The whole lobby was filled with smoke. And in the room behind it, right next to the beer bottles, there was quite a big pile of paper on fire. The first chairs were already red hot. And with a tax consultant upstairs! With all his files in the office. Biehl gasps for the sequel, takes a deep breath. That could have been a real mess, a real mess. I had to call

238

the fire department right away. I couldn't possibly have put it out myself. And everything turned out all right. One more time, says DIETER BIEHL, the concertgoer Dieter Biehl, who lets the study groups meet while he checks out Beethoven and experiences Bartók through the program notes. One simply can't leave the place unattended, BIEHL says. Today Rosa L. had a meeting at eight, the study group on the army. About nine people in all. They promised faithfully to be there until eleven. And now this fire. And all the paper in a heap. Biehl rushes along, delivering his eyewitness report. Our man on the scene. Dieter Biehl of Hamburg. I had the key with me, the one we lock up with. I was counting on eleven o'clock. But the place was already empty. Everything was already going up in flames. We're going to have to make one person in every group responsible. Right from the outset. Before every meeting. With our debts, says DIETER BIEHL. With our high rent, says BIEHL. Because if I had gone to have something to eat after the concert, the whole house would probably have burned down. All the files, says DIETER BIEHL, And our club. I just wanted to report it to you. Without accusing anyone. Without expressing any suspicion. The political caretaker, subject to recall for exams, who wants to defect to the establishment soon. DIETER BIEHL dictates a few more details and experiences to GEBHARDT, says good night, and hangs up hastily. And GEBHARDT, Rainer Gebhardt, thinks, where does one go in this city, of an afternoon or an evening, when things have reached that point again? Where one can exchange political views and information? And GEBHARDT, Rainer Gebhardt, thinks, we need a place. A place to burn down. A coffee on your left, a beer on your right, a steaming pot of hot onion soup on a system-inherent antiauthoritarian burner.

Because There's No Braque on the Wall

Uwe had discovered them, fished them up, ferreted them out. That'll make a nice little newspaper feature, says Uwe the discoverer, the fisher-upper, the ferreter-outer. That'll bring in a tidy little two hundred fifty marks again. Simple as that. The party led to something after all. Of course just on trial for the present. But old granddad is okay. Something'll come of it. I'm going to make a go of it.

Student Uwe had taken clever advantage of the whiskey. Now it was just a matter of making the transition. From academic drudgery into journalistic drudgery as a freshman reporter.

Come along, why don't you, Uwe says. A girl sweetens the atmosphere. Come along. Show a little curiosity. You don't know a soul. Come on, let's go.

I went along. I was a little curious. I had never seen one, after all. Except for Herr Zabori. But he probably wasn't a real one. The real ones, the monsters of my school days, raped German women, separated children from their mothers, dissolved families, expropriated one's house and garden, one's freedom and one's car, and all just to enrich themselves. Visions of a bloody Hieronymus Bosch. Civics drummed into schoolgirl heads. I am afraid of this visit. Physically afraid. And I get into Uwe's car as if it were a train in a house of horrors. Rendezvous at eight-fifteen P.M., in the underworld. Located in a newly developed area, one of those piled-up eggboxes that spread across the landscape. One square yard of window and twenty-six blades of grass for each resident.

Rendezvous at eight-fifteen. Up through the tiled stairwell, like swimming up the bathroom wall. The little plaque on the door says Jakob. The plaque next to the bell says Jakob. Actually it sounds perfectly innocuous. That's the last name of my old classmate Johanna, too. Uwe rings the Jakob bell. Steps that halt before they reach the door. If it's a woman, she'll be taking a quick glance in the mirror, running a comb quickly through her hair. What if it's a man? The steps resume. The chain is unlatched. Good evening, says a crack in the door. Good evening, a man says.

My name is Jakob.

Herr Jakob. In scuffed brown slippers. His gray pants stretched tight over a large belly. A tieless white nylon shirt, open a few buttons too many. His thinning gray-blond hair greasy, combed around the bald head in strands. A bullish red face. Herr Jakob.

Watery handshake. Bull's neck. He looks like Menzel's working man in the Iron Works. He is sweating from physical effort. Even on Sunday. He sweats even in a white shirt. Description of a painting. Class 13. Museum in East Berlin. I am describing Herr Jakob. Herr Jakob, painted by Menzel, with sleeves rolled up, stuffed into his suspenders, a tattoo on his right forearm. A blue stamp on his forearm. A blue pattern on his arm. A number on his arm. The man with the numbered arm is called

240

Jakob. Like a sheep out to pasture. Branded, like an animal, I think. What is that number on his arm, I wonder, watching this man in worn brown slippers who goes on ahead of us, traversing the bare hallway that reeks of new paint. Fresh, newly painted white walls.

Come in. Join us. Hello. Hello. Round the circle shaking hands. Hello. Hello. No one is skipped. No one wants to be left out. We squeeze ourselves around chairs and cupboards. There's someone else sitting by the window. Sitting there with hand outstretched. Hello, Uwe says. Hello, I say. Have a seat. Hello in this spanking new eggbox. Not a picture on the walls. Only ten books behind glass, concealed by department store china. White dogs with gilded ears to be dusted in the best china cupboard. And with the glass at its back, the discussion group. Cushioned with youngish women's-magazine wives, all packed onto the sofa, their fresh piles of hair towering above them. Whispering. Just let the men be men. Fingernails painted. Eyes mascaraed. Lips freshly lipsticked. How are your kids, my kids, his kids? Coffee-time chat. Sofa gossip. Interrupted by feminine distrust, lids dropped in pistachio green secrecy. Lips pressed together. Eyes pressed together. What do these two want? Whisper, whisper. Oh well. Quick glance at the fingernails. Beautifully filed and polished. My kids, your kids. Now they are chattering away again.

Visions of Bosch ebb away amidst the routineness, dissipate between beer glass and suspenders. The young man next to Uwe looks like Uwe. And Uwe is a student. The young man next to Uwe looks like a student. And he's the one who got Uwe into this. He's a locksmith's apprentice. At a student teach-in, at a Vietnam rally, he said to Uwe, You should come over some time. I have something to show you. The young man next to Uwe approached Uwe. Approached him, Uwe says.

All right, let's get going, says Jakob, the boss. He doesn't want this to drag on too long. He and the others have to leave for work at six tomorrow morning. King Jakob looks around the circle.

We have to discuss these leaflets.

There's a family in the neighborhood who can't pay the rent. The man has been sick a long time. The woman can't manage by herself. A man and five kids. Now they're supposed to be evicted. Uwe is taking notes. Stenographic fate in a spanking new eggbox. We've got to help them, Jakob says, and shoves a mighty thumb under his suspenders. There's no day care center here. No playground. No supermarket. No doctor. No

241

drugstore. And the rent gobbles up a third of your income even if both husband and wife are working.

The young man next to Uwe clasps his hands behind his head. Leaflets in the mailboxes, Jakob says, Either in the morning at five, before work, or after you get home in the evening. Jakob offers his apartment as headquarters. Jakob calls for solidarity, discussion, getting the word out.

We have to get people to help themselves, says a silvered little man. White hair and delicate gold-rimmed glasses, a delicate voice. He could be a teacher. He is every bit the match of my Herr Professor, the expert on the Ottonians. He chooses his words slowly, though by thought, tasting each of his sentences. A careful chef. He arranges and flavors his little voice like fine spices.

A little man jumps up. Wrinkled like Rumpelstiltskin, withered and tiny. He exclaims, We of the German Communist Party. He exclaims, I as an old Communist. He doesn't want to hear about citizens who merely gab and grumble, who don't do anything. We always do all the work, he exclaims, crumpled and embittered. Jakob tries to soothe him. Oh, come on. You know we always end up doing all the work. They don't lift a finger.

The little man is so gray and tiny, so grim and frustrated by every hour of his life. The little man, a postwar ruin in a department store suit. With bomb craters in his face. With watchtowers behind his shoulders. With concentration camp soup in his belly. It's true, he keeps stammering, like the old men on the park benches. He can't keep his mouth still any more, or his feet.

They messed him over in the camp, Uwe whispers to me. Uwe, my beer neighbor on the left with the stenographer's pad, who is getting involved. Great idea, this leafletting plan, Uwe says. Strike while the iron's hot. Public housing and a citizen's organization. That's good. That'll show results. I'll see that something comes of it. Uwe accelerates. And father Jakob grins. He sits there enthroned like a great bull, one fist clenched, in his checked easy chair, turquoise and purple, purple and turquoise. Neutral. On ice. Jakob, Herr Jakob, switches on his at-work grimace, sits there on his flashily checked chair and says nothing, the dark blue number on his forearm. Stamped on, like the entrance tickets at the Rock Barn.

What would I do if they asked me now whether I would be willing to distribute leaflets, leaflets for day care centers, for lower rents, for

242

solidarity? I would say no. No, no, no. I feel too good for that sort of thing, too busy. I don't want any part of this, don't like it. It's embarrassing to me, as every deed is embarrassing, every involvement. I, an armchair democrat, capitulate in the face of people whom I was educated against, because they are concerned with activism, because they want to do something. Perfectly normal people, sitting here like the first Christians in their catacombs. Still involved, despite concentration camps and persecution. Still active. Not for themselves. For their neighbor in Block 93a. Communists. What they are doing here in the desert of a housing development is actually right. Actually one should get involved, too. But what if they asked me now?

The little man cannot keep his mouth still. The little man is shouting, We were the ones who got sent to the camps. We, the workers, always us! The little man throws up his arms. The student apprentice. The silvered man. Boss Jakob. Around the circle. Around the circle. What sort of people are these? They are workingmen, completely unfamiliar to me. People who go to work in shifts. Who have never read Gottfried Benn and don't know Latin or French. Simple people, my mother would say. Proletarians, my aunt would say. Simple people, uneducated, my professor would say. Primitive, Dr. Vera Zirkel would say.

Paul was with us, too. That is, not with us. We women were sitting apart. But Paul, says Frau Tempel, Paul said we should work together with all democrats.

That's very true.

Uwe smiles at her. And Frau Tempel, who is not sitting on the ladies' sofa, who does not have her hair piled high, who wears no makeup, Frau Tempel smiles back. With tiny burst red veins, she sits there massive and obese. Plastered down white hair, her pills next to her beer glass. Her hand always lying on her bosom. A swollen white hand, always laid on her heart to warm it a bit. To keep it beating a while longer, Frau Tempel says. Old Frau Tempel. Ancient Frau Tempel.

He thinks it's still the twenties, my beer neighbor to my right whispers, a colorless forty-year-old, pointing out a scrunched-up little man who can't keep his mouth still, whose hands tremble, whose knees tremble. They did him in, says a colorless forty-year-old. One of those you find in every group. Pale. Gray. Silent. Paler and paler from meeting to meeting, paler, grayer, more silent.

New egg carton. Not a picture on the walls. Only ten books behind glass, concealed behind china dogs with gilded ears. An educated member of the middle class looks around. An intellectual's daughter, who does not feel comfortable unless there is a Braque on the wall, unless there is a statue by Arp on the bookshelf, a volume of Celan among the books. I don't feel comfortable unless there is a Chagall on the wall. This Frau Tempel was in a concentration camp. But my imagination cannot reach as far as Dachau, never reached as far as Auschwitz. Those are just names to me. Secret ciphers of my schooldays. This Frau Tempel was there when Jews were being gassed. Maybe she was in Dachau along with Judith's parents, while my teacher, my final examination teacher, was doing what she is still doing today: instructing children. Indoctrinating children. Against Frau Tempel, for instance. Against the communist Berta Tempel, about whom the children know nothing and whom they do not understand. Just as I don't know anything about her and don't understand her. My schooling placed communists among the dungbeetles and rats, in the category of lower living creatures. In biology class we examined skeletons and skulls, stuffed seagulls and mounted butterflies. But we never did see a preserved and stuffed communist, a wolf who attacks our free system.

Me among communists. Me among workers, about whom I learned nothing in my world of academics and business people. Me, me. Looking for pictures, from wall to wall. Upset at every grammatical slip. Me, smarter by all my lectures, more developed by all my front lawns, am sitting here in a cushioned discussion circle with a strong-smelling white-painted entrance hall. They can't even fix up their hall. They have to buy everything on the installment plan, buy their lives on the installment plan. And while I'm going to a concert or reading Death in Venice, they're sitting here, writing professor with two f's, and drafting flyers. I am looking for Tapiés on the walls. While they need kindergartens. What if they asked me to help distribute leaflets? I nodded my assent to the contents. What if they ask me now? Uwe read it aloud. Uwe made corrections. Cut out one f, an and. Uwe and I said, That's right, that's how to put it. What if they ask me now when I'm coming to help distribute . . .

Uwe snaps shut his notebook. Uwe says good-bye. All around the circle. Someone is sitting over there by the window. Good-bye, I say. Good-bye, Uwe says, going from hand to hand. What is that number on his arm? This Jakob, who is going on ahead of us in his scuffed brown slippers, with his sleeves rolled up, stuffed into his suspenders?

244

'Bye Jakob, says Uwe, thumping him in comradely fashion on the shoulder. Bye, Jakob. Stairs. Car door. Step on the gas.

Those sad sacks!

Uwe, the discoverer, the fisher-upper, the ferreter-outer, grins. I just said those things to put a little sparkle in them, says Uwe, the ferreter-outer, who is earning two hundred and fifty marks.

Or do you really want to help distribute leaflets?

And I sit there next to Uwe. I am embarrassed for Uwe. And Uwe is embarrassed for me, because we would both say no. We would both say no to communists. Because our parents said no to Jews. And our grandparents said no to Social Democrats.

Uwe and me. Raised for the royal hunt. For we are better people than the communists. As our parents were better people than the Jews. And our grandparents were better people than the Social Democrats. Because Christians are better than Moslems. Because white Christians are better than black or yellow Christians. Because German white Christians are better. If they had asked me, I would have said no. I would have said no because they are communists, because the sky is blue and the meadow green, and because there are no Braques on their walls.

SCENE 72. INTERIOR. EVENING. PARQUET ROOM OF THE LATE NINETEENTH-CENTURY VILLA. ABOUT ONE HUNDRED MEMBERS AT THEIR WEDNESDAY DISCUSSION MEETING. SCENE OPENS WITH EXTREME CLOSE-UP OF DENICKE'S SHOUTING MOUTH. Gebhardt sent a telegram of congratulations to Brezhnev about Prague! Frenzel told me, HERBERT DENICKE is shouting. We've got to get rid of Gebhardt! Should've been done long ago! GEBHARDT is sitting next to BIEHL. Gebhardt has already heard all about it from Biehl. Gebhardt is supposed to answer the charges. Come on, let's go, shouts the LITTLE BLOND FELLOW. I'm waiting for Dr. Frenzel to get here, GEBHARDT shouts. I want Dr. Frenzel to answer first. To Brezhnev, GEBHARDT thinks. That was probably Herr Brammer. Gradually they are all starting to work against each other. And at one time we wanted to work together. At least I wanted to. What kind of rumors are you making up? HAUSWALD shouts. Let's throw out the communists, DENICKE shouts. Down with the communists! Down with Brammer, SCHUSTER shouts, the usually silent Schuster. Brammer approves of the Soviet intervention! That's true, BÖHM says, Schuster's right about that. I must admit that Joachim Schuster is right. Since Prague a number of things have looked very different. The chairman sent a telegram in the name of the RC to Brezhnev! ALEX SOMMER intones.

GEBHARDT does not answer. GEBHARDT is waiting for Dr. Ludwig Frenzel. That's bourgeois anticommunism! We should work with them if only not to interfere with Brammer's emancipation. And the person who shouts this is—of all people—DIETER BIEHL. Biehl at a Wednesday discussion meeting. It would have to be Biehl, GEBHARDT thinks. A motion, shouts SOMMER. I move we exclude both the GCP and the SDAJ! Right! shouts Denicke. We have to acquire the trust of the people, just like in France. Acquire, GEBHARDT thinks. Have to acquire. And SOMMER shouts, We have to move forward with antiauthoritarian policies, not authoritarian tactics! What I associate with the concept RC, shouts BÖHM, Is a broad platform! Well, your association is wrong! What we're concerned with here is getting rid of the Stalinists! DENICKE shouts. We have to create revolutionary momentum, the way Sommer suggests! There's nothing at all new in what your group proposes, says DR. HAUSWALD. You never were very effective politically. And we have to confront the question of whether this club is capable of functioning. Whether we can accomplish anything through it or whether it is just wasting our time, Herr Sommer. That's the question, Herr Denicke. Not Prague or France. What's important here is whether we're contributing anything to our democracy. That's the decisive issue! Old fool, SOMMER shouts. That misses the point entirely! We have to break through to the dependent masses, like in Berlin. And we have to do it, shouts DENICKE, By spontaneous operations, just like in France. Like in France, GEBHARDT thinks, with two hundred people. Man, here comes Frenzel, shouts SOMMER. Now we'll get to hear something! Come on, Frenzel! What do you mean? How so? DR. FRENZEL says, and shrivels, becoming whiter and smaller. I don't know, FRENZEL says. About the telegram, FRENZEL says, I must have gotten everything all wrong. Why to Brezhnev? FRENZEL asks. I don't know. I didn't have anything to do with it, FRENZEL says. I probably never said that. He probably never said that, GEBHARDT thinks. Probably never. Things can't go on this way, DR. HAUSWALD exclaims. Enough! What we need is coordination. A place for discussing important issues. That's what the club is supposed to provide. Not a place from which people are excluded or to which they are admitted. What we need, SOMMER shouts, Is a weekend workshop on

246

Prague and the left. We have to clarify the problem. We need a love fest, the REDHEAD shouts. Shut your trap, shouts ROSA L. Now the Denicke squad is interrogating Cassandra, GEBHARDT thinks. Now it's coming, HAUSWALD says. What do you think? Denicke shouts. What does the SDS think? And FRÄULEIN OHST exclaims, People only show their true colors in action. I'm of the opinion we should see how it goes with Herr Brammer. Why are they so set on Brammer, GEBHARDT wonders. That turtle, who doesn't say anything, who just goes creeping along the wall? What nonsense, DENICKE shouts. Only all the members together can decide who's a communist. A resolution, BIEHL shouts. Let's forget about right or left. The RC is supposed to be independent and nonpartisan. Resolution two, shouts HERR STIEBLER. Our RC is for peace and culture. Resolution three. Let's vote, shouts KNOPKE, On who is for the Soviet intervention and who against. That's manipulation, SOMMER shouts. The motion is worded all wrong. The question is, who sees this RC as an antiauthoritarian socialist form of organization. So from today on, the RC will be an SC, GEBHARDT thinks. An SC because Herr Sommer is shouting, Let's vote, right now. FRÄULEIN OHST stands up. Resolution four! shouts DÖRTE OHST, The steering committee is nothing but a paper tiger! Let's adjourn until next Wednesday, SOMMER shouts. We're not going to get anywhere today. Always on Wednesday, KNOPKE shouts. Why does it always have to be a Wednesday? These people can't come up with any plan, WINFRIED BÖHM remarks. This can't go on. With the GCP or without Brammer, BIEHL says, This bickering has got to stop. Down with the steering committee, ROSA L. choruses. Gebhardt sent a telegram to Brezhnev. Send him to Moscow.

Hunger in Cloth Covers

There are more and more of us. From Wednesday to Wednesday we are increasing in number. Every increase in number means winning over one more lively, healthy, real human being. He is plied with tea and cookies so he will stay. We are all plied with tea and cookies, so we will stay when the Third World is brought up for discussion. From Wednesday to Wednesday. Around eight. After supper.

Hunger in cloth covers. Hunger for one mark eighty. Hunger in Rowohlt's Current Issues series. Christian flight from responsibility, padded with Bread for the World, is subjected to the dissecting scalpel of us readers. Bachhof sharpens it daily on his Bible. He wants the blade sharp, he wants to see the innards. Jesus shows us all the opportunities we've missed, the spindle says, and disinfects our eyes with the New Testament. And the Old Testament is served along with the cookies, so everyone can have a piece and we can all digest it. He is so earnest about knotting the noose of consistency that I can imagine his head dangling slightly over the teacups. He urges us on from week to week. From book to book. He takes out his impatience on our eyes. He wants us to tell him something he has known for a long time. But he wants to hear it from us. Only from us.

Heads between the pages, among the statistical graves of the Third World! We read about land in the hands of just one family, a white white company. We read about Peace for me and napalm for you. *About* Cheese, ham, eggs, and canned goods for me and a handful, a bare handful (if you're lucky) of rice for you. *When Fräulein Wicherstädt says,* Outflow of profits and interest on profits, *when she speaks the two new concepts slowly, slower than the Our Father, when Herr Lindemann says* Prices for raw materials, *and Frau Lindemann, maliciously coiffed and powdered, speaks of the* Dictatorship of monoculture, *when we exchange our guilty conscience for an even guiltier one, our spindle sits before us at the upper end of the table, trots out his Bible knowledge, and explains, mouse-eyes shining with insight,* My Sermon on the Mount does not increase Siemens's or Krupp's profits, but it helps make them known.

Every hymn sung by our congregation has twenty deaths on its conscience. At issue is a change in existing conditions. When the spindle explains this to his Wednesday revolutionaries, bald-headed postal supervisor Lindemann and his plump, sturdy little kitchen fairy, when Bachhof says that, and Fräulein Wicherstädt blows her thirty-year-old, still unmarried nose, we know, with the cookies in our stomachs, that we have become involved with a truth which Herr and Frau Lindemann only dare think about from Wednesday to Wednesday. But these two hours of study group, during which I sit there with my tea, are more fruitful than another Wednesday, when I again sit there with my tea, and Esso's profits for the preceding year are discussed; they are more fruitful than a circle that spawns pity. These two hours of study group demand that something be done. It is a matter of changing existing conditions,

248

the spindle says, and we, paralyzed by neatly bound insights, cannot get beyond the book covers of our knowledge. We sit there and nod and cannot formulate any plan against apathy other than these Wednesday evenings on which we confess that now that we know more than those who know less on Sundays, we will stick with knowing more than those who know less from Wednesday to Wednesday.

SCENE 73. EXTERIOR. NIGHT. A DARK STREET DOWN BY THE HARBOR. SHOOT THIS SCENE IN THE STYLE OF A GROTESQUE SPY THRILLER. Don't tell anyone, says WINFRIED BÖHM. Last night he slept at Dr. Raake's. Don't tell anyone, says DR. GRÜTZMANN. Tomorrow he will sleep at Hermann Knauer's. He is at Knauer's now, says SOMMER. He was at Raake's, says DÖRTE OHST. But don't tell anyone, says WOLFGANG KNOPKE. Of course not, says HERR HOPP. Of course, says HERR LOHMANN, It has to be kept secret. Absolutely secret, GEBHARDT thinks. The only person I can tell is Lohmann. Because Gustav Lohmann has known for a long time that the police have been looking for Dietrich Wetter for weeks. That Dietrich Wetter spent the night at Raake's. The fugitive demonstrator. The student Dietrich Wetter. The student Dietrich Wetter who blocked the street with his sitdown strikes and spent last night at Gebhardt's. But don't tell anyone, GEBHARDT thinks. Just don't tell anyone that last night Dieter's fellow student Agnes Paulsen visited the fugitive. With a red hat on, like Little Red Riding Hood, and bread and wine for poor Herr Wetter. Unobtrusively in a big basket, while a car unobtrusively followed Frl. Paulsen, a car which has been following her unobtrusively for weeks. Dietrich Wetter's girl friend Agnes Paulsen. Even Winfried Böhm has already noticed that. Because when he was at my house—don't tell anybody—there was also a car like that. Well, well, says BÖHM. Well, says GEBHARDT, and thinks about the fugitive, Dietrich W. The fugitive guerilla fighter who is eating liverwurst sandwiches in the cellar, drafting his revolutionary diary and writing messages. To everyone. Your Comrade Dietrich Wetter. Stand firm. Get your cadres organized. Hold out. Your W. Ever your W. Your Wetter, the red fist. We are stronger. I am always with you. Your Wetter. Don't give up. Well, says FRENZEL. Well, thinks GEBHARDT, and thinks of Herr W. who sits in the cellar, drinking red wine, Herr W., of whom no one knows the whereabouts.

Except Böhm. Except Böhm and Raake. Except Frenzel and Ohst. Except Sommer and Knopke. Except Knauer and Lohmann and Grützmann and the friendly gentlemen from the secret police who always drive a few yards behind a red hat bringing bread and wine. From Raake to Kranz. Who amiably use up gas so they can fulfill Dietrich Wetter's youthful visions—LENIN IN PETROGRAD BEFORE THE KORNILOV PUTSCH—before he later turns himself in. Dangerous Ché from licorice Samboland, who has disappeared with a red wine lifejacket on. Herr Dietrich Wetter, always in flight. And when he arrives, the car is already there ahead of him. So the conspirator can feel persecuted. Just like in the old days. Romantic. In the dead of night. Like Mao and Torres and Uncle Ho. Hunted by the friendly gentlemen who very amiably know that Herr Wetter has been at Böhm's and Raake's and Gebhardt's and will spend tomorrow night at Hermann Knauer's. But don't tell anyone, the gentlemen whisper. Let's keep it to ourselves, says trapper Grützmann. Not a word, says Agnes the squaw. It has to remain a secret, thinks RAINER GEBHARDT. Indians know how to keep a secret.

The Three Holy Monkeys of My Childhood
The business on page 174. The business in my history book. The business there in the bookcase. The business that reminds me of Judith. The business on page 175. Not in the course catalogue. No seminar you can register for. Two or three lines. A stale business. As deep as an original source. As old as an original source. A business to be interpreted. A business to be analyzed. A business to write commentaries on. A business from the old days. A once-upon-a-time business. From father's fairy tale hour. From mother's bedtime stories. An and-if-they-are-not-dead business. This third business. This third business on the bottom of page 5 of the newspaper. Room 231. My business. The they-are-still-living business. The business with Alfred Bauer on page 42. On page 1942. Fifty-eight years old. Public school. Gardener's apprentice. Volunteers for the police. Rises to inspector. Dismissed from the force on 1947. Later reinstated in the state police of Schleswig-Holstein. The business with Heinrich Steinhof. Police captain, retired. Served with the Hamburg police. Kept on until retirement. Until 1964. My friend and helper. My friends and helpers. The business with my friends and helpers. Mr.
250

Policeman will help you cross the street. The business with Mr. Policeman, who helps little girls across the street.

The business with Werner Hagemann. Fifty-one years old. Graduate of a humanistic gymnasium. Instructor at a police academy for the offspring of his past. The business with the settled future. Cordon off the Soapbox Green! Werner Hagemann's students stand there staring at me. All I can hear is hup! and hey! They leap over the barricades. I won't be able to get out of here. Go ahead, let them beat you up, my mother says. And I count to fourteen. Count to fourteen. Bauer, Steinhof, Hagemann. Go ahead, count them. One, two, three. Take a deep breath. Four, five, six. Faster. Seven, eight, nine, ten. That's good. Eleven, twelve, thirteen, fourteen.

Fourteen on trial. Not in the course catalogue. Not a seminar for which you can register. The business with the fourteen in Room 231. Citizens whose deepest secret has been exposed. All between fifty and seventy-five. All fathers, grandfathers, who help little girls across the street. All members of the former Reserve Police Battalion 101, constituted in Hamburg and dispatched as a special operations unit to Zamosch in the district of Lublin, pursuant to an order of June 20, 1942. All the then-they-are-still-living business.

Herr Bauer. Herr Bauer. Herr Bauer. Herr Bauer! The generation without memories is sitting in the audience, behind pillars and barriers. The generation without memories. As old as the armistice in Germany. The generation with the name of me wants to hear Herr Bauer. Wants to hear the then-they-are-still-living tales. I cut them out of the newspaper. I have decided to skip a class. I am skipping Otto the Great in order to hear Herr Bauer. Our parents never testify. Our teachers never testify. Our history books never testify. The three holy monkeys of my childhood crouch above the portals of my youth, hearing, seeing, and speaking no evil. But Herr Bauer will explain to me why I am so fascinated. Why I want to hear all this firsthand, not read it. Why I want to hear why Else Kohn, why the tramp-tramp-tramp of the marching column, why my father.

I knew that refusal to obey an order was punishable with death. But there were no women and children present.

But the court transcript shows that you testified: I realized immediately that women, children, and old people were supposed to be killed, too.

When you were questioned the first time, did you realize you would be indicted?

No, absolutely not.

Fischer's Fritz fishes fresh fish. Fresh fishes are fished by Fischer's Fritz. One, two, three, don't look at me.

In your original testimony you did not even think to mention that you were under compulsion to obey orders. In contrast to today, when you are suddenly no longer certain whether women and children were supposed to be shot. Did you testify voluntarily because you believed you would not be indicted, whereas today everything appears in a different light, and you give us a completely different version?

The Bauer opera. Gardener Bauer. Arias sung before the footlights.

I don't quite follow you. I was not to blame for the expulsion. I was just carrying out orders. If they had told us straight out that we were killing them—

If they had told Bauer straight out that he was killing them.

—then some of us would have resisted. I would have, too.

Then some people would have resisted. The three holy monkeys as well. Otto the Great would also have resisted. Now go ahead and shoot the rest.

Bauer, shoot the rest. Bauer, go and check whether all the Jews are really dead.

They said something about medics. We were supposed to handle the so-called body check.

And what did the word body check mean to you?

I thought it meant a check to see that everything was all right. For humanitarian reasons. So no one would lie there shredded to bits and still alive.

To make sure not a single foxglove dies of thirst. That not a single pansy wilts. For gardener Bauer grows flowers. Even in Zamosch. Even in the Lublin District Gardener Bauer waters his roses. Fresh Jews. One-fifty a bunch. And my mother says, There was Käthe Levi. She was especially interested in literature, my mother says, and I listen to her. Black milk of morning. Mor-ning. Pronounce the r distinctly, child. Pronounce it distinctly. Pronounce the past distinctly. Black milk of morning. Pronounce this unique poem about a unique past distinctly. Morning. R as in Himmler. N as in Eichendorff. In class 12 we go over the past. The past, reduced to a black milk, reduced to the boiling-over point, to death, the maestro from Germany.

252

One, two, three. Take a deep breath. Four, five, six. Seven, eight, nine, ten. That's good. Eleven, twelve, thirteen, fourteen. Death, a maestro from Germany, has on fourteen gray suits. His hair is thinning. He is a grandfather now. He helps little grandchildren across the street. Little ride-a-cock-horse grandchildren. The business with the fourteen. The anonymous fourteen. Fischer's Fritz fishes fresh fish. Press table. Press table. They have excused themselves. They are off by ship to cloud-cuckooland. Who's interested in the black milk of morning, anyway, the sour milk of the past. The past! Going, going, gone!

Empty spectator seats. Not a single school class. No students. The final solution is settled in a line and a half. It set up its nest somewhere not too far from Potsdam. And no more than one hundred people knew anything about it.

Heinrich Steinhof, there is no need to be agitated. We're going to make this very short. What was your assignment in the village of Josephus?

Your Honor. I damn well have to make some changes in my former testimony. I was supposed to attend to the cordoning off of the village so that no one could get in or out.

But the transcript of your testimony reads: I supervised the firing squad.

Your Honor! That can't be right!

But that was your testimony.

No. No. I just didn't know what had happened to my column; I rode to the execution grounds and left again after five minutes.

In 1965 you testified at your interrogation that all the Jews were supposed to be shot in a clearing in the woods. Do you recall that?

Herr Steinhof wearily shakes his head; I don't really recall. My mother wearily shakes her head. Now we wearily shake our heads; we don't really recall. The whimpering past tries to cut off the lies' head. But the past is full of lies. Every time one is cut off, a new one grows in its place.

I final-solution, you final-solution, he, she, it final-solutions.

My client was vomiting all night. Today he can only listen. My client asks to be excused today.

Hunched over the towers of files, behind the Manhattan of the German past, is a court-appointed defender. Two court-appointed defenders. Four, five, six, faster, fourteen court-appointed defenders. On Forty-second Street, the one-way street to Zamosch.

253

He is wearing a pinstripe suit. He is smaller than a garden dwarf. A sixty-seven-year-old dwarf. His name is Karl Sonntag, and he remembers the operation in Josephus. He is first. The only one among fourteen defendants. The worker Sonntag, dossier no. 5, twenty-fourth story, can remember that business.

We were awakened at three. We were supposed to go to Josephus. We got there around six-thirty. Didn't know what was going on. There were little children standing around the square. About eight or ten. We couldn't see what was in the third boxcar. Suddenly we heard a kind of whistling, and then in the woods I got hold of an old woman. I fired. I wanted to get it over with. I thought, how can you shoot an old woman.

I twist my ring. My little golden ring. I twist my innocent ring, my Jewish ring. Innocence twists a ring of Jewish tooth-crown gold. I twist my Jewish tooth-crown-gold ring once around my ring finger, and Sonntag fires. Then the shot went off, he says. A shot went off. It went off. It is the twin brother of people.

And Herr Grimme and Herr Kulowski also fired. They both began to laugh. I had white stuff all over me. White bits of brain from the bad shots; it splattered all over. I wiped off my hands on some leaves. I thought, what a nasty mess you've got yourself into.

Who gave the order for the execution?

Don't remember. But Steinhof said, You take care of the rest. I didn't get to see any of the higher officers.

How long in your opinion did the shooting last?

Until noon. Then we went home. There was pea soup with hambone for lunch. A good meal. But I couldn't get any of it down. There was no alcohol. Back at the barracks we were trained to be decent. It was only out there that we turned into monsters and murderers. When I tried to get the white stuff off my fingers, the others all laughed.

The bell rings. I shut my book on page 174. I get my sandwich out of my briefcase. I go out into the schoolyard. It is recess. The lawyers' black robes flutter down the corridors like bats being shot at. The green courtroom guards look like hunters. Is the no responsible for the yes? Or the yes for the no? After the hambone has cooked for three quarters of an hour, add the peas, thoroughly rinsed and drained. Cook one more hour. Stir flour and butter into a paste and add to the soup to give it a creamy consistency. Sprinkle the soup with parsley and serve with the ham. But I couldn't get any of it down.

254

The courthouse cafeteria is serving liver with vegetables. But I can't get any of it down. The waiter is fifty. He says, They got their material from the East Zone. And he says, Young people shouldn't worry their heads over such things. And he says, We have to leave the past alone. And he says, There's got to be an end to revenge and reprisals. And he says, If those fellows in Bonn don't get around to declaring a general amnesty pretty soon, people will have to show them with their ballots. That's what he says, my waiter. The fifty-year-old waiter. A waiter from the adult world. From this world which consists only of fifty-year-olds. Who have gone underground. Fathers whose offspring lack access to the wealth of material needed for uncovering their criminal past.

Everywhere they are hard at work. Heinrich Peters, commercial artist, with ink-red fingers. Winfried Grubbe, welder with a quick-on-the-draw past. There is a little blood sticking to our engagement announcements, to our front-door keys. The blood of the fifty-year-olds, the sixty-year-olds. Our aunts and uncles. Honor the aged. They are all still busy and industrious. Serving us in candy stores. Weighing out butter and cheese. Teaching us history and teaching us the little verse posted next to the continuous-chain elevator in the courthouse:

If you fail to disembark at the right moment you may continue on without risk through the attic or the cellar and wait until your stop is reached.

Did you ever discuss these things with your wife?

Workingman Sonntag withdraws into his sixty-seven years. He is riding on a continuous-chain elevator. He will be riding through the attic or the cellar for the rest of his life.

My wife said to me, You've never shot a woman. Never.

Herr Sonntag does not get out. For his wife knows that anyone who eats her homemade chocolate pudding cannot be a murderer. Liver with vegetables. The liver must be larded finely on the upper surface like a filet and rolled in flour. Use fresh garden vegetables. Germany's women have only one history book, Dr. Oetker's Cookbook.

At the indictment microphone stands Herr Denker. Businessman. Upright, still military in bearing. Herr Tietze, retired, on a pension. Learned trade: baker. What does he remember about the execution of Jews in Josephus? Nothing. Or almost nothing.

The Jews had to lie down with their faces to the ground. Then they were shot in the back of the neck.

255

Attention! Notes from the diary of a baker. How many people did he shoot?

Three or four. But no women. No children!

Herr Tietze, you testified earlier that women and children were also among them.

It's always the same. Now I am sitting here and already thinking, it's always the same. One contradiction covers for another. One untruth replaces another. And when there is no more possibility of evasion, they fall back on orders. That's the case with Tietze. That's the case with Bauer. He was only in the market ˋsquare, not in the forest. He can't remember. He can no longer say exactly. He never was at the execution site. Not even when it was cleared. Transcript 3625 of May, 1966, documents the opposite. I took part in the clearing operation, also in the execution. My assignment was to divide the Jews into six or eight groups. But Bauer contradicts. Bauer contradicts Bauer's testimony. Bauer accuses Bauer.

I was only involved in the cordoning off!

But Herr Bauer, Company 2, to which you belonged, was charged with the clearing operation. *It's hopeless. Bauer insists he was not Bauer.*

I was there for the cordoning off! And last week, your Honor, my father-in-law gave me some photographs I had sent him during the war. He said I had turned to him in my spiritual distress. It went against my grain. I remember that very clearly. We had a Jewish family doctor, Dr. Weiss. I was raised as a democrat. My brothers and sisters also never felt at all close to the new movement.

Keep your ears open. Everything is in order. Keep your eyes open. Everything is in order, your Honor. Dr. Weiss went up the chimney. In order. And Else Kohn, dumb Else Kohn from the Jewish lower class. Everything followed its prescribed order, with Else Kohn as well. Behind the curtains everything was in order. Everything went up the chimney in order. In orderly order. A broad, care-easy fifty-year-old Dachau. Beat up the Jew, Herr Cramer yells. Beat that Jew!

And I sit there without memories, facing the jury. The dozen from the past. The orderly dozen. They are fifty, fifty-one, fifty-two. Like the people in the spectator seats. Fifty-three, fifty-four. Their arms are still charley-horsed from the German salute. Fifty-six. Their heads are still ringing with Horst Wessel's marching columns. Sixty, sixty-one. Like the men in the defendants' box. Sixty-five, seventy. Seventy in a country

256

where for a thousand years everything was done according to order. Where for a good thousand years everything was ordered in orderly fashion.

I personally never volunteered for such duty, Bauer says.

I personally, Bauer says. And the group interrogation of January 5, 1965? The group interrogation indicts Bauer against Bauer.

Our company commander asked beforehand who wanted to volunteer. Members of a firing squad were always volunteers. No one was simply ordered to take part. That was true not just in Josephus but on other operations as well. And that was your testimony, in contradiction of the testimony of Herr Trost.

Bauer against Bauer. He does not know any Herr Trost. He cannot explain how the testimony came to be made. How our past came to pass—no one can explain that to me. Not even John Maynard, our pilot, can explain it.

Herr Bauer, you have given us a statement on the question of volunteering. A very precise statement. We can prove this is your signature.

John Maynard! You have given us a statement on the question of volunteering. On the business on page 174. On the business in our history book. On the business about the gigantic toys. This once-upon-a-time business from father's fairy tale hour. From mother's bedtime stories. Off with his head. Off with his hat. All in order. The gentle moon is rising. The Auschwitz stars glow bright and clear in the sky. And Bauer, Adolf Bauer, puts on the white gloves of snow-white innocence and begins to dance the Josephus waltz on the gleaming floor of forgetfulness. One-two-three, don't look at me. Eeny-meeny-miney-mo, catch a yid by the toe. Three times round, then out you go. One two three, they didn't look at me, for Bruno Lohse, Herr Bruno Lohse is next.

The past forms a bloody puddle when Bruno Lohse the dock worker, sixty-two-year-old Bruno Lohse, comes next. He was only assigned to the cordoning off. The Jews were driven up in a truck. A clearing. Fixed bayonets. Shot in the neck. He himself shot three or four. The whole thing took a good hour.

Each one picked his target and fired.

Each Lohse picked his good target and fired. Each good father picked his good target and fired. He does not remember whether Adolf Bauer gave anyone the finish. Two years ago he remembered. Two years are a long time. Back then it was recorded in the transcript. Today he can only remember that he felt sick to his stomach after the execution. After the good execution in the good year 1942. When he was thirty-seven, union member Lohse. Good union member Lohse.

What does Herr Lohse have to say today to the shooting of women and children? What does Daddy Lohse have to say?

It was an ugly business, your Honor. And inwardly it went against the grain.

Inwardly, he says. For in the well-tended herb garden of German inwardness, the truth is mowed and innocence is harvested.

You know, fifteen years ago I suffered a concussion, and since then my memory has been going. Though I don't forget to go to work in the morning.

The past is free on its own recognizance. Daddy Lohse is free on his own recognizance. The court only sits on Monday-Wednesday-Friday. Only on Monday-Wednesday-Friday do I catch up on my lectures on reality, on good old reality. Gather information about my father. Gather good information about my good father. About my family, Germany. About my cradle full of blood. My baptismal dress was put together out of watchtowers. Six million were stitched in cornflower blue into the hem. My mother lifted me out of a bloodbath into the air. I came up out of my cradle, my good cradle, Germany. The child did not drown, my mother exclaimed. The child is alive, my family exclaimed, and pumped me up. This future balloon of fresh flesh. Pumped me adult.

Germany must die, even if we must live, Bruno Lohse tells me. In your places, finished, dead, Bruno Lohse says one Tuesday. Says Bruno Lohse on Thursday, when Bruno Lohse goes to work. When Bruno Lohse is free on his own recognizance. When Bruno Lohse is free on his own recognizance on Saturday and Sunday and eats his soup for lunch. His nourishing soups cooked by Emmi Lohse. Uncle Bruno Lohse watches television. Citizen Bruno Lohse holds open the elevator door for me. Ladies first, says Herr Lohse. Future first, says old Lohse. Defendant Lohse says:

Mr. Prosecutor. At first I said I was there for the clearing operation. But I wasn't. I was assigned to the cordoning off. Yes, I was only involved in the cordoning off.

Bruno Lohse was assigned to the cordoning off. Bruno Lohse made a mistake. And Granddad Lohse never heard anything about refusal to
258

obey orders. Grown-up Lohse is a Stone Age man. For if anyone had told him to go ahead, he would have murdered all of Lublin. Gone right ahead and murdered, against the grain. Against the inward grain. But it is in order. It's been in order for a long time already, says the waiter. Says the fifty-year-old waiter in the courthouse cafeteria.

Everything is in order if Max Sturm, the police sergeant, the seventy-five-year-old police sergeant, has been in retirement since 1952. Sturm draws his full pension. He distinguished himself. Honor the elderly, for they have distinguished themselves. Fresh flesh honors age, for it has distinguished itself. He shot ten or more people. Max Sturm shot a thousand or more. He doesn't remember. Max Sturm no longer remembers. The parents no longer remember. The teachers no longer remember. The professors no longer remember.

I don't remember anymore.

Didn't know anything. Didn't say anything. Didn't do anything. And the seventy-four-year-old locksmith Grubbe, who is still trying to file his master key of forgetfulness into shape, the good locksmith Grubbe, the good master tradesman Grubbe, never heard anything about the shooting of Jews.

You know, your Honor, with your helmet on and the wind at three in the morning you hardly hear anything.

Sturm one, Lohse two, Steinhof three. Don't look at me. The generation without memories, eeny-meeny, is sitting in the spectator seats, eeny-meeny-miney-mo. It is sitting in the one-two-three in the morning, out you go. Sitting behind pillars and barriers. Behind pillars and barriers sits Germany's fresh flesh. A generation without memories. As old as the cease-fire. A generation without memories is marching against you, Herr Lohse. A whole generation, Herr Lohse, is marching against you. Marching from the soapbox greens, from the universities. Marching from the schools, a children's crusade, marching against you, the thousand-year-olds. Against the three holy monkeys of my childhood.

SCENE 74. INTERIOR. EVENING. PARQUET ROOM IN THE LATE NINETEENTH-CENTURY VILLA. THE MEETING HALL IS CROWDED. SCENE OPENS WITH A CLOSE-UP OF A CAT WITH A COLLAR, THEN ZIPS TO A LONG SHOT. THIS SCENE IS OVERLAID THROUGHOUT WITH PORNOGRAPHIC INSERTS,

POLITICAL AND SEX POSTERS. He leads his cat by the collar. He leads his cognac-soaked cat on a six-foot green leash. PETER BRUHNS is here. Even Bruhns is here. Is Irene here? Yes, Böhm is here. Have you seen Hopp? the LITTLE BLOND FELLOW asks. He's talking to Denicke, says the student ALEX SOMMER. Alex Sommer, who could never make it again. Says WILLY STIEBLER, who didn't have the time anymore. Are the Schusters here? Yes, the Schusters are here. Are already here. RAINER GEBHARDT is sitting on the windowsill. Sitting next to BIEHL and WOLFGANG KNOPKE, both of whom have come today. Like the REDHEAD from the book committee. Like the BLOND YOUNG MAN from the investigation committee which up to today has not yet come up with anything. Nor has Hopp come up with anything yet. Still has his debts. Has not explained anything. Sexy like a plenary session. Always a good hundred and fifty. Always something cooking. Now this is a decent number for a study group, says the LITTLE BLOND FELLOW. And WOLFGANG KNOPKE, Attorney Dr. Wolfgang Knopke, gently pulls a magazine bosom out of his coat pocket, to the tinkling of little bells. A bosom on which he has drawn in a pair of glasses. So it can see the Vietcong better, KNOPKE giggles. So it can shoot better in the jungle, KNOPKE gurgles, quiet little Knopke, and hands DIETER BIEHL his framed art work, so he can look at it grinning, and hand it on to STIEBLER. Who comments, Bare as an ass, but highly political, and sticks it into GEBHARDT's pocket. Rainer Gebhardt, the mother-fucker, who is still perched on the windowsill. Who knows that today a Godard is showing at the university, but Alex Sommer is here in spite of that. Who knows that today Kattelbach is coming to see Dr. Grützmann, but DR. GRÜTZMANN is here despite that. They're all here today. Another beer for Herr Hopp. Quiet now, comrades! Let's get started. Dörte Ohst raises a red-laquered hand. And HE leads his cat around by the collar and sits down on the sofa, the sofa which has been here since yesterday. For Biehl sees to it that things are kept orderly. Tomorrow the beds are coming. Tomorrow the beds are coming, says RAINER GEBHARDT. And then we'll have some proper fucking, KNOPKE giggles softly. KNOPKE searches for the bosom. Knopke wants his spectacled bosom back. And GEBHARDT thinks, the revolt of the petit bourgeois. The fattened young petit bourgeoisie, which confuses the civil rights struggle in the USA and the jungle war in Vietnam with their own well-cooked problems, their satiated, contented, good-housekeeping country with Guevara's freedom struggle. And GEBHARDT thinks, what peaceful children. What an

260

overfed, spoiled youth, which stuffs itself on picture magazines and newspapers. Waving the flag. Fists in the air. And bellies full. Today they are all here. They barely know the platforms of the parties they despise as bourgeois. They don't know even one of the millions of workers whom they plan to win over tomorrow. They don't even want to pay their dues, but they want to change the world around them. In the study group on the unions, which has folded. In the study group on information, which has folded. In the study group on the German National Party, which has folded. In the study group on the church, which has folded, even though two people are still meeting. Has already folded because the young men and women plan big political campaigns which never get off the ground because each political group has opposing goals. Because no one can get together with anyone else. Because each is out for himself. And to this day there has been no study group on the Third World. No study group on Greece. Damn this club. What did he imagine when Böhm came to him months ago? What images did he have of students and republican clubs, like the ones in Berlin? The study group has been cancelled. The one like the one in Berlin. The legend of Berlin, which they keep frozen in their refrigerators. These land-of-plenty big-city kids, full of Django and undigested Marx, full of soup and dessert. GEBHARDT sits there. On the windowsill. A windowsill thinker. He sits there and is fed up. Fed up with these Indian silk scarves, wholesale. Sick of this youth, wholesale, which confuses its consumer society Jungfernstieg with Bolivia and Harlem, its beret down over one ear. He is sick of these smart young people, who talk and talk and never do anything, because everything falls through. Fall through, happy ice cream, into a big hole of canned thirty-year-olds. And GEBHARDT thinks of Bachhof and Lutz Wocker. And GEBHARDT suddenly feels sorry for Dr. Hauswald, good school-teacher Hauswald, who is sacrificing his time for an impulse. For the big fad of democracy, for which no one down below lifts a finger because those up above. For whom no one. Just in joke, just for fun. And if possible only two or three times a year. DÖRTE OHST rings out crescendo. Dörte Ohst, a political bluestocking in linen and hand carved wooden beads, is conjuring up antiauthoritarian day care centers. Where the little ones become acquainted with sex early. Where the parents also get to know each other. Where everybody can, without pressure, repression, with plenty of tolerance. For the main issue is finding new forms of social organization, in which everything, in which. I'll give you a baby first, so your day care center runs better, DENICKE shouts. And DÖRTE OHST squeals with contentment. And ALEX SOMMER wants to contribute one, too. And PETER BRUHNS distributes free promotional copies. One ticket to Chicago, round trip. I'm the only leftist magazine. PETER BRUHNS distributes striptease documentations and sprawls on the sofa. Rests next to HENNING, the comrade from Kiel, who couldn't make it anymore because of classes and work and so forth. And the student with the self-determination utopia, who shouts, We need a love fest. So parents and children can get closer to each other. Who shouts, which of the ladies wants to have a baby? And DÖRTE OHST reckons up her years. For Dörte Ohst does not have much time left. And DÖRTE OHST claps her hands. And IRENE exclaims, Let's ask the caretaker. So our day care center can get off the ground soon. Yes, it has to be soon, whispers Attorney KNOPKE. Really funny, says BIEHL. The student Dieter Biehl, who is joining the establishment tomorrow. But today once more. Once more is here, to experience something, so Daddy and Mommy both won't see it. And don't have to worry if he was here once more today. Like all of them, once more. We are petty bourgeois, RAINER GEBHARDT thinks, petty bourgeois from Daddy's land of milk and honey, practicing for a revolution against Mommy over a beer.

Sunglasses Glittering with Memories
He shouted to the students, You all belong in concentration camps! *He had been thinking that for twenty years. For the more than twenty years he had been living in the underground. A resistance fighter. A partisan who hid behind democracy. Slightly stooped and ready at any moment to. It was something one couldn't mention out loud, not yet. But one could think it. As a partisan of fascism in a neat, double-breasted democracy, pressed, brushed, combed back. One could cross the street just like other civilians, also neatly pressed, brushed, combed back. Their briefcases in their right hands. Their car keys in the left. Wife and children in the back seat. One looked like so many other couples. Many younger couples. Except that one was older. Twenty or thirty years older. And one also took vacation trips, ate rolls and knockwurst, ate ice cream and drank beer. Unrecognizable and secretive, one did all the things the others did. One stayed undiscovered, undiscovered after twenty years,*
262

twirling one's spaghetti in one's spoon like the wops when one was in *Filetto. One was not identified as one wandered around the meadow at Dachau, sunglasses glittering with memories.*

He had stripped off the external markings. And he knew many who had done the same. But the inner markings were there to stay. *A thin layer of scab from many evenings with the boys, from evenings at the club, had grown over them. But at the unexpected sight of hooked noses, at the slightest curve over a foaming head of beer, one thought of miscegenation. One mixed the Jewish joker in with the skat cards. One* said Cheers, Karl, *and thought of Leningrad. One said,* There's got to be law and order, *and thought of Auschwitz. He had many friends from those grand times in these petty times, and when he shouted that sentence, when he shouted at the students in the main auditorium,* You all belong in concentration camps, *these petty times turned into grand times again. Grand times, which could draw breath again after twenty-two years of silence. One could say it out loud now, again, still.*

When he was disciplined by the institution, he divided the punishment up into a semester's leave among little friends from those grand times. And then he returned. Well rested, recuperated. A relaxed Professor Sprengler, who no longer lived in the underground, who no longer had to hide, who could now say what he thought without his past's coming to harm.

Professor Sprengler had once told the protesters, the academic vermin, what he thought of them. It made him proud of his country once more that this action cost him no more than a semester of paid leave, a few months of sabbatical. Gave him hope that great times were once more in the offing. The external signs confirmed his internal markings. And the evenings with the boys grew more noisy and the evenings at the club more rousing. For one could say what one thought now. Again. Still. Once more.

SCENE 75. INTERIOR. EVENING. IN THE LATE NINETEENTH-CENTURY VILLA. LOBBY, STAIRWELL, BIEHL'S ROOM. CAMERA CLOSE-UP OF A BLACK POWER POSTER, WHICH ZISSIS KONSTANTIN IS TACKING TO THE BULLETIN BOARD. They went and got their gold medals! He is standing next to GEBHARDT at the bulletin board. He is tacking Black Power onto the bulletin board. Reddish purple, designed by Herr Denicke. He is sticking next to GEBHARDT, sticking up demonstrations for Greece, proclamations of rallies. He tells GEBHARDT, Yesterday I spoke with Brammer. That overfed warrior. That petit bourgeois tendency to settle down. Always full and contented. And I asked him, Well, how was it in beautiful Mexico? Are you proud of the shiny medals for your social forces of production? Of your Mexican earnings for a socialism of production figures, balances of trade, and investments? He mounts the stairs at GEBHARDT's side. He says, You should have seen him. That mirage of socialist solidarity. With a whole Ave Maria of verbal assurances on tap, just to save his fat belly. He goes upstairs with GEBHARDT to see BIEHL in Biehl's little bull session apartment. Where there is always hot coffee. Even when the caretaker Biehl is not there for a change. When Dieter Biehl is visiting his parents. Even then, GEBHARDT says, There's good tea. Tea or coffee, Zissis Konstantin? A cup of tea: to Comrade Brammer, KONSTANTIN says. To the warrior Brammer, GEBHARDT thinks. It's really nice you're here, GEBHARDT thinks, and we have an offer to make you. To Herr Jurgen Brammer, KONSTANTIN says. To this wash-out of consolidation. He drops six cubes of sugar into his cup. He sugars the tea for Brammer, this brackish water of a revolution, of which nothing was left behind in Europe but a few rills and puddles and well-paid Brammers, says KONSTANTIN. And GEBHARDT thinks, what would you like to drink? On a blue tablecloth. We're paying, says a Frau Priess. A red-painted one. We're grateful to you. Have some milk? GEBHARDT asks. But KONSTANTIN is stirring. Stirring his sugared tea. KONSTANTIN is saying, They leave us to our own devices. We're supposed to go on selling goat cheese for the next thousand years and greeting dictatorship with cries of joy. And GEBHARDT thinks, they stay in touch with the Greek people. They stay in touch. When they go to bed, Brammer thinks of Herr Pagel, and Herr Tesch thinks of Frau Priess. And they never appear at a demonstration, unless they themselves are staging it. And don't listen if a Zissis Konstantin says that peaceful competition with the Western economic systems is forcing us into a hopeless position. If a Konstantin asks, What ever came of internationalism besides a clear-blue-sky slogan of declarations of socialist solidarity. For the trauma, says ZISSIS KONSTANTIN, The trauma of the prosperous socialist citizen is not only to be found in the German Democratic Republic or in the

USSR. Everywhere in Europe the twilight of the gods of the petit bourgeoisie is celebrating its resurrection, while in Greece, Africa, India. All at our expense, says KONSTANTIN. All at the expense of the Third World! For the more the productive capacity of the socialist bloc develops, the smaller becomes the gap between it and the capitalist countries. ZISSIS KONSTANTIN is talking to himself. To ask him questions now would be fruitless. Ludicrous, GEBHARDT thinks. In this setting, with Biehl's brightly polished furniture around him, this Konstantin seems ludicrous. In these waxed surroundings, in which Herr Konstantin is drinking tea, in which ZISSIS KONSTANTIN drinks hot tea and says, I hate all the socialist countries of Europe. Without exception. Without exception, GEBHARDT thinks. For white is not white. And red is not red when ZISSIS KONSTANTIN tells him that, compared to the material misery of the Third World, people in East Europe live like kings. For the comrades have turned bourgeois. Well-fed, selfish, and bourgeois, solving our problems and their own questions of conscience schematically and administratively. For believe me, Gebhardt, the gap between them and the peoples of the Third World, the gap between them and us is growing and growing. For, GEBHARDT thinks. If Konstantin did not have the word FOR, what would his future look like, without a FOR? And Europe's without a BUT? Konstantin's sugar is taking on a brown tinge. He is coloring the cubes. One after the other. He is playing at relaxation. He is playing at casualness while he says, What has come of it all? Where is the New Man, who is not to be undermined by the new economic base and can point to a new, more humane form of awareness? The New Man, who is not just after a little luxury, a little distraction, a lot of peace and quiet, and a relatively easy conscience? GEBHARDT looks at KONSTANTIN. He is still wearing those worn-down brown shoes, this new man. Has black hair, brown eyes. At the main railway station Gebhardt would not notice him. If this is the New Man, Gebhardt would not notice the New Man. He would not notice Zissis Konstantin, who says, All I can find are old revolutionaries in retirement. Brammers, Teschs, Pagels, who think all problems will be solved by the automatic processes of economic laws. A comfortable belief, RAINER GEBHARDT thinks, and a well-remunerated one. It is more comfortable to believe that history follows fully automatic laws, GEBHARDT says. And KONSTANTIN affirms the thought for him like a teacher. KONSTANTIN says, That's very true, Gebhardt. And GEBHARDT thinks, A, you can sit down now. Very true,

ZISSIS KONSTANTIN repeats, And that produces a nice socialist Franken-stein to ride the backs of the forty million who starve to death every year. An automatic fat Herr Brammer. Why do you have to get so worked up? RAINER GEBHARDT thinks. You're getting everything all mixed up. Why do you have to get so excited? For green is green. And a completely automatic Tesch is a completely automatic Tesch. Just as adjusted, says KONSTANTIN, Just as opinionless, just as businesslike and smooth, as ruthless and selfish as his political opponents. For this New Man of socialism, who occupies a qualitatively new stage of morality, as it says so inspiringly in the encyclopedia, this New Man permits himself everything which his ancestors permitted themselves. Nationalism. Anti-Semitism. Militarism and provincialism. Uncritical acceptance, blind obedience, and an intact world. But, GEBHARDT thinks, you misunderstand us. A well-groomed ham sandwich is a well-groomed ham sandwich. And GEBHARDT thinks, there were four people sitting in a corner. Four intact worlds. Four uncritical people who do not hear the way Konstantin is issuing commandments. The commandments of Zissis Konstantin. Of the prophet in the worn-out old shoes, who is dyeing his sugar. Who says to GEBHARDT, It is time to break out of these unimaginative automatic patterns. Time to put an end to this unbridled egotism, this inhumanity on both sides, preying on the corpses of the Third World, our, my, First World. Time for this world to be changed, in accordance with a distinct socialist ethic which will create the men of the twenty-first century. And not merely reproduce those of the nineteenth century or the decadent, rotting ones of the twentieth century, as Ché Guevara says. Ché Guevara, GEBHARDT thinks. Ho-Ho-Ho Chi Minh. What a pity, GEBHARDT thinks, that you are getting so excited. We give thought to the Greeks, too. The transformation, says KONSTANTIN, The transformation of man must be idealist in nature. Beyond material reward, extreme dogmatism, and smooth scholasticism, which is merely intended to isolate human beings in the infinite, says ZISSIS KONSTANTIN. The founder of a religion, GEBHARDT thinks, who hopes his way from transformation to transformation. Who says, We have to find practical proof, not just theoretical, that human beings can be changed. That the New Man need not remain unprofiled, a mere specialist. For, KONSTANTIN says. But, GEBHARDT thinks. For, THE GREEK says, up to now the New Society called only for adaptation, not for transformation. But, says KONSTANTIN. For, thinks GEBHARDT. But, says KONSTANTIN, This
266

transformation must finally take place. For changed conditions call for new ways of approaching problems, new answers, new practices, if one is not to declare bankruptcy, the betrayal of hope. For the change in the relations of production, the entire economic transformation, is and can only be a first step, never the final goal. Amen, GEBHARDT thinks. Like that time in the bar. Hallelujah. Those were the days, GEBHARDT thinks. What if Biehl could hear that. Biehl, who is joining the establishment. What would he say to Zissis Konstantin, who teaches that the new society has not answered for us the question of the meaning of life? Biehl would not say anything. Biehl would stir his tea, just like GEBHARDT. He would think, our club is well heated. It is already seven-fifteen, RAINER GEBHARDT thinks. And KONSTANTIN says, Executors of a will who are only interested in hanging on to their power will never educate their fellow human beings to take over the government themselves. Will never create conscious individuals who can make the leap, in the name of solidarity and internationalism, from the realm of necessity into the realm of freedom. The realm of freedom, GEBHARDT thinks. We can't even manage two hundred. For the two hundred can't govern themselves. That's the way it appears, RAINER GEBHARDT says. And ZISSIS KONSTANTIN says, You don't understand me. I was not talking about them. You haven't been listening to me for the past hour.

Just as Well If They Die
Could you spare a little contribution for Biafra?
  Why should I give anything for those Negroes?
  Please, can you make a little contribution for Biafra?
  Leave me alone with those niggers!
  Could you spare a little?
  Where's that?
  A collection for Biafra.
  Lazy dogs!
  Could you perhaps?
  Send them the pill!
  Might you please?
  Let those niggers starve, then we'll be rid of them!
  They have a famine there.

We don't have enough to eat either.

As long as the people behind the Iron Curtain are unfree, you won't get a penny from me.

Something for Biafra!

You want me to feed those slit-eyes so they can come over here and kill us all? That's what it's going to come to. Just wait, miss, those Negroes with their golden beds. What do you mean, war! They just want us to pay for everything. I've seen those fat bellies on TV. And they're always after our white women.

A collection for Biafra!

Just as well if they die.

A little contribution!

I won't give a penny for Jews! Don't bother me with your Jews. You want me to feed those Jews? They just want us to pay for everything. Down with the Jews! Down with the Negroes! A little contribution. Give them an A-bomb!

A little A-bomb for Biafra.

SCENE 76. INTERIOR. DAYTIME. DR. NEUBÜSER'S OFFICE. GEBHARDT IS SITTING IN AN EASY CHAIR. SCENE OPENS WITH A CLOSE-UP OF NEUBÜSER, WHO IS PERCHED ON A CORNER OF HIS DESK. Nice of you to stop in, says NEUBÜSER. Karin will bring us a bourbon in a minute. Konrad Neubüser, contributing a bourbon, says, Why don't you call your wife so she won't worry if you're late? Worry? RAINER GEBHARDT asks. I mean, if she has steaks turning to charcoal under the grill. But we won't be here that long. I really liked your manuscript. Revolt in a consumer-oriented society. A good topic. Well, Karin, can we expect a little one soon? KARIN ANDERS in a green mini-dress and wooden clogs stares past GEBHARDT. KARIN ANDERS pours bourbon into the glasses. KARIN ANDERS groans a determined no. With her wedding ring pressed firmly around her finger, Karin has already passed the plumpness border. At twenty Frau Anders is spilling over her woolen dress. Cheers, exclaims NEUBÜSER. And GEBHARDT thinks, here's to our youth. For Herr Neubüser has contributed a bourbon. Comfortable in his chair, KONRAD NEUBÜSER (60), who does not support and participate, but places his bets on youth. Who hopes for babies and always says, What a good topic. And Susanne did

268

an excellent job on the narration. To think it was her first time. Really splendid, NEUBÜSER says. Almost as splendid as that time Neubüser was so enthusiastic over Menck's manuscript. At last an uncompromising approach. At last an unequivocal statement. For two thousand marks. But it was never produced. Is still lying around somewhere. Splendid, GEBHARDT thinks. Konrad Neubüser's opinion on the rocks. An opinion, GEBHARDT thinks, which says, My dear Rainer, I'm not old-fashioned. I am very willing to put up with your views. After all, I represent your scripts. I am tolerant. And GEBHARDT waits for what is coming. Waits for Neubüser's world LIBERAL. I am tolerant and liberal. You are a grown man. You must know what you are doing. But, says NEUBÜSER. But, GEBHARDT thinks, he has been avoiding me for weeks. Leaning against the windowsill, chatting with Karin. But, says GEBHARDT. Well, I mean, NEUBÜSER says, I don't claim that you're a communist, but that club you're in. My dear friend. I place my bets on youth, too. But those fellows? It verges on criminality. Or am I wrong? RAINER GEBHARDT tries to explain. You don't quite understand, Dr. Neubüser. We are attempting to put democracy into practice. To set up a small model of self-determination, in which each individual. Frenzel and Böhm, not just young people. And everything from the bottom to the top. Getting away from party structure, GEBHARDT explains. And what about the fire? NEUBÜSER asks. The fire Karin told me about. The fire in your, ah, soviet? Oh, the fire, GEBHARDT says. That didn't have any significance. A cigarette butt in a waste basket. You know yourself that people blow such things up out of proportion. When the glass is empty, the good mood will dissipate, GEBHARDT thinks. Drink it up quickly. Neubüser is not paying attention. NEUBÜSER is saying, In every party one needs people like you. Opposition within the party. Only that way do you accomplish anything. Really splendid, GEBHARDT thinks. Really splendid. That's how Weinberg got kicked out. And Neubüser didn't say a word. We've go to do something. We've got to express our solidarity with Weinberg. Gebhardt declares his support for Weinberg's program. And Neubüser says, The station director will handle it. And tells Menck, There's really nothing I can do. And basically it was perfectly legitimate. His contract had expired. And that's the way a conservative, or a liberal, gets kicked out if he's unlucky. Political parties are outmoded, GEBHARDT says, or at least ours are. Institutions force one into false positions. Well, what do you know, NEUBÜSER says, And at forty, too! Half-past six,

GEBHARDT thinks. Six thirty-two already. And forty-three. Forty-three already. He looks at NEUBÜSER. I'm on his track, GEBHARDT thinks. He has found out a lot from Karin. From some Frenzel. Perhaps from Pechstein, too. GEBHARDT knows Frau Anders. She is saving. Is already saving up credits for a farewell gift so she can devote herself to washing diapers in her cozy little pop household. All she needs is a generous retirement bonus. Makes her report daily: another study group folded. The house went up in flames. Final reports to my calm boss, GEBHARDT thinks. To my boss with his calm political party. Only two hundred, GEBHARDT says. There are only two hundred of us. Thinks, soon it will be all over. Says, The study groups are functioning well. Says, We're really getting somewhere. Not just blind activism. Says, Why don't you drop by some time? Thinks, I hope he doesn't drop by some time. Neubüser won't drop by. Sitting there comfortably in his chair, comfortably drinking his bourbon, saying, All right, all right, a case of belated youth. Belated democracy, GEBHARDT says. A small beginning. Without instructions from higher up. Free to sweep the floor, GEBHARDT thinks. Free to mail letters. Free to pay the rent. Hang Gebhardt, that motherfucker! A model, GEBHARDT says. Just a model. Just as you say, NEUBÜSER says. Just as you say, says DR. KONRAD NEUBÜSER. I'm liberal about such matters.

On a First Name Basis with the Sharks

Impossible! You mean he's teaching again? Professor Schlesselmann exclaims. The Herr Professor Doktor, political scientist and sociologist. A head full of scholarship, pumped up to the forehead with methodology and facts, with facts and methodology. It took him years to get where he is now. From a starched-shirt assistant with white cuffs to assistant professor. Always sticking to the rules of the game. One marble after the other. First a toss, then help it along with his finger. Closer and closer. And closer still. Pop into the promotion slot of success. Next, please! Another toss. Better than the others'. Farther than the others'. My career-marble rolls faster, smoother, gets closer to the hole. Now! Congratulations, Herr Doktor! Herr Professor Doktor, congratulations!

He walked on ahead of me. With gray temples and the sharpened smile of a deep-sea diver who had seen many algae and was on a first name basis with the sharks. He walked on ahead of me, always with this

270

smile on his face. Now he was smiling at the hall walls or the office-hour waiting bench. I could see from behind that he was smiling again, my professor, the diver, smiling along the course of the Second World War. Silent as a fish. Inhale, exhale. Today he no longer had to dive deep down. That was past, past. Now it was only a matter of raising the wrecks and bringing the past up to the surface. He was a good professor. He discussed and analyzed a society's obsessions. Various groups' stereotypes. Hidden links, marginal phenomena, results. He was a good professor. He revealed things. Brought things to light. He could pronounce the word socialism and only blush up to his neck. He was a good professor. He wanted to transform social learning into creative momentum. A good professor. Not subjective attitudes but objective social relationships. A professor with a program for democracy. Against rigid systems, for self-determination. He was a good man, a Herr Professor, a good Herr Professor. From a working-class family. And whenever Herr Professor mentioned that, he blushed up to his neck. He had shut off his cheeks long ago. He had reached that point long ago. Today he could afford it. Only up to the neck and no farther.

Well, he said, and smiled at me. Well? He left the office door wide open during office hours. Have a seat, he said. Well, he said, and sat down. Well? Professor Sprengler, I said. Impossible, he said, you mean he's teaching again? Yes, I said. Incredible, he said. Yes, I said. Good heavens, he said. And, I said, we're starting a campaign, Herr Professor, and I'm collecting signatures. I see, he said. Yes, I said. That's the right thing to do, he said. Yes, I said. Only it would be good if you, I said. It's good, he said, That it's being done by students, that the young people are doing it on their own initiative, yes, that's good, because if I, for instance. Yes, if you, I said. It would carry more weight, I said. And, he said, it's right that the students are doing it on their own. And he leaned back slowly, and said, It's good that you are doing this, and smiled.

He was a good professor. He uncovered hidden connections. Uncovered himself. I saw how he dived down under the desk, in the middle of his office hour. How he swam under me, inhaling, exhaling. How the water rolled off him. Now he swam up the side of the desk and rolled over the edge into his chair. No, he said, and smiled at me, and praised my list, the list with the anonymous names. Worth no more than a rally, a rally of all the students. A movement without a head. For no one could be found who was not for sending us to the concentration camps.

Your head, I said. Your social-minded, creative, democratic head, I

271

said. Your name, I said. Your self-determinative, system-free name. He smiled and swam out the office door and away down the hall. Moving in his Sprengler circles, around and around his colleague, up and around the soles of his feet. Keep under the soles, he said; One should do something about you, colleague, one should do something about you.

And you say he is teaching again, Professor Schlesselmann said, and left his office door wide open; That's unthinkable! I folded my collecting list. I inhaled. I said, It may not be thinkable, but it's experienceable. And my professor, my good creative Herr Professor, blushed. But only up to the neck.

SCENE 77. EXTERIOR. EVENING. ON THE SOAPBOX GREEN. ABOUT ONE HUNDRED DEMONSTRATORS, MOSTLY YOUNG PEOPLE WITH PLACARDS, STANDING AROUND A SMALL VAN, ON WHICH A TEMPORARY LOUDSPEAKER IS BEING MOUNTED. SCENE OPENS WITH A LONG SHOT, THEN ZOOMS TO MARQUART AND GEBHARDT, WHO ARE STANDING SOMEWHAT TO ONE SIDE. What sort of people are these? MARQUART towers next to GEBHARDT. Broad, blocky, massive. MARQUART was there again. MARQUART joined the march. Through the downtown area, accompanied by police detachments. With his pupilless, creamy gaze, which is getting creamier and creamier. From protest march to protest march. His eyes are growing shut, GEBHARDT thinks. And MARQUART says, Why are there fewer and fewer of us? Why do we look like so many only on television? Crowded into a threatening mass for the viewers? Why do people read their *Stern?* Why do they stare at the pictures of the concentration camps while chewing away at their morning rolls? They know all about it. They know from their magazines what freedom for Greece implies. But nothing ever happens. Absolutely nothing. From the sidewalks: You hippies belong in a work camp! Send the student whores to a brothel! MARQUART is blowing off his demonstration steam. MARQUART hurls his leaflets to the ground. He is standing next to GEBHARDT, whitewashed by the spotlights. He says, You were lucky, Gebhardt. At least you weren't in the march. But I was. And now this ridiculous speech I'm supposed to give. What kind of democrats are these, anyway? After all, I'm thirty-eight already. I'm not a student anymore. MARQUART shakes his head. See you later. He pushes his way through a gap. The microphone is on. One, two, testing. He turns the sound up high. MARQUART is speaking for the hundred listeners. The unions have called out their members. Perhaps there are only ninety. Turn off the sound! The Social Democrats have also called out their members. Reluctantly, but nevertheless. The Christian Democrats are also speaking today. Leaflets were distributed at the university. And now there are about eighty standing here. Turn off the mike! MARQUART is standing on the van. Shut your mouth, dear Jesus! People are being tortured in Greece. I'm cold. Let's go home! Now Rainer Gebhardt will address us. You traitor, come down from there! You and your Christian Democrats! You sign their proclamations! Shut your bourgeois trap! Beat it, fascist pig! Turn off the mike so the motherfucker can't talk! We've had it with Gebhardt! Boos and whistles. Get down off the truck! The CDU and the SPD are as dumb as the RC! CDU and SPD are pure bullshit. Bull-shit! Bu-u-ull-shi-i-i-t! Well, old blabbermouth finally shut up. Watch it! Don't let the SPD up on the trucks! Cut off the mike! SPD! Out of here! Someone is storming the truck. He seizes the speaker by the shoulders. He is shouting at him. A Greek. They're both Greeks. Friends and foe roar. Three parties. Four parties. Ten young Greeks. Ten parties. We want Konstantin! We want Konstantin! And GEBHARDT thinks, how can you reduce eighty demonstrators to twenty? How can we disband this group? How long will it be before we are no longer speaking to each other at all? How long before it is all over? Before the patrol cars turn off their flashers? Before the police detachments finally go home? Before the bystanders turn out to be right? The cowards behind their shopping bags, who want to go home to bed and dream about the camps, with their magazines and two good TV programs to regulate their emotional life?

Subway Tunnels of the Past

Freedom for Greece! *I shout in unison with Helga, and Helga shouts in unison with Jens, arm in arm and running. The Republican Club—ten people. The YMCA with fifteen. The SDS with fewer. A dash of Campaign and Youth Wing of the Social Democratic Party. Student cocktail. Three hundred marchers. Four thousand were supposed to come. Four thousand are marching in their heads, not on their feet. A meager procession, with a feeble voice.*

Through rush hour. Down Monckebergstrasse, the main shopping street. We are marching to City Hall, past department store after department store. Police barricades and flashing lights. Security detachments on either side. Police vans patrolling. The side streets are closely guarded. Paddy wagons and horses' hooves between us and the after work crowds. Who is behind the barriers? Who is being cordoned off? Who is being protected against whom? Walkie-talkie troops. Over here, over there. Jogging in space helmets. The Martians of power, keeping an eye on every slogan. There are at least as many of them as there are of us.

Jens unhooks his arm. Now we are dragging ourselves along, our feet tired.

To City Hall! To City Hall!

Those must be Greeks at the head of the procession. Greece and the EEC—no siree! Greece and the EEC—no siree! *Slogan-caffein.*

The CDU has called out its members.

I know. Only one of them came. Like all the rest. Man, this is my last demonstration. You never accomplish anything, anyway.

Two-three-four! Fellow citizens, don't just stare. Come and join us, show you care! *Protest with a marching permit. And the good citizens stand watching the children's crusade with their bald-shaven faces, armored with gray hair and Ajax in their gaze. They are simply scrubbing us away. The delivery men of law and order stand in rank and file.* Commies! Lazy bastards! You belong in a work camp! That's right! You parasites!

Come on, comrade, join with me. It's never too late for solidarity!

An elderly gentleman pushes past the barricades. Well-groomed gauntness. What they call distinguished, with dimples and white locks. The older gentleman attacks people like a tiger in the zoo. You punks, he yells, I'll teach you how to run. You can run straight to a concentration camp, that's what you can do, every last one of you! We huddle together. The police! Where are the police? Hippies! Good for nothings! Criminals! *Our information bullhorns wobble toward the barricades.* Do you know what's going on inside Greece? *Shut your trap! Three dock workers.* Ladies and gentlemen! *Shut up! Forward! The police get us moving again.* Stand back! Stand back!

Fellow citizens, don't just stare! *You should be gassed! The woman who says that is one of those types who enjoyed the harvest-time orgies with Helga's aunts. One of those types. One of many.* Ratatatat! Mow them down with machine guns! These student whores! *Housewives with*
274

menacing shopping bags, with lettuce bombs wrapped in newspaper, garnish the sidewalks, the subway tunnels of the past clenched in their raised fists. My fellow citizens. This is our youth. This is democracy, what we are seeing in action here. Commies! *They yell at us. They stand, scissors and comb in hand, outside their hairdressing salon, giggle behind the windows, laugh us dead.*

We're going to win over the masses, the demonstrator next to me says, and shouts at two office workers. Listen, man, in Greece people are being tortured; listen, you silly geese! Wow, isn't he a riot? And we pay taxes so they can go to school! *Construction workers yell down from their scaffoldings.* Lazy bastards! Commies! Morons! But in Greece! *Who cares about Greece, says a young girl, says a young man, says the young past. Final rally. Mike on. Whistles.* Down off the truck! *Ten Greeks, ten parties.* We don't want to hear the SPD! Shut off the mike! *Social Democratic youth wing, Maoists, Falcons, Spartacists, socialists, communists, liberal fascists, anarchists. Solidarity is shouting itself hoarse.* Down off the truck! *Bourgeois bullshit!*

Come on, let's go get an ice cream. It's all nonsense.

You deserve a good hiding, an old man yells after me. He looks like my newspaper vendor, my grocer. He looks like the waiter. And I stuff my Greece into my pocket, my leaflets and make love, not war, *so he will bring me the ice cream I ordered. Ice cream with whipped cream topping. Sitting in the station restaurant in my summer dress I feel safe.*

SCENE 78. EXTERIOR. EVENING. ON THE SOAPBOX GREEN. ABOUT TEN MINUTES LATER. THE FINAL RALLY HAS DISSOLVED. EVERYWHERE LITTLE GROUPS ARE STANDING ABOUT, ARGUING HEATEDLY. SEMI-CLOSE-UP OF GEBHARDT. GEBHARDT pushes his way through the gaps who did come after all. Except what does after all mean? He pushes past the BLOND YOUNG MAN. We'll get you next time! We've really had it! Anyone who cooperates with the parties is finished as far as we're concerned. You secret fascist! Why don't you turn yourself in at the sanitation dump! That's where you belong! You can sign all the proclamations you like! GEBHARDT is already past him. He has stopped listening. Freedom for Greece. Freedom for ten splinter groups. For twenty different Greeces yelling at each other under the loudspeakers. Man, Gebhardt, what a missed opportunity! MARQUART is standing beside him again. Booed, whistled at, booed off the podium. MARQUART asks, Whom are we supposed to be representing, actually? Whom are we taking to the streets for? For these stuffed-animal democrats? For these gross-and-net cowards, who won't even march for Greece when their parties give them permission? And then this bickering! These ridiculous campaigners, who just make fools of themselves. Constantly arguing among themselves. Waging their protest all alone. MARQUART scuffs the ground with his toes. MARQUART says, Tell me, Gebhardt, what are we doing here? With families at home who cling to our coattails and plead, Daddy, don't go! Leave the young people be! Don't go there if the police are coming! Stay home! He looks at GEBHARDT. With his creamy gaze. With boiled milk in his eyes. He says, I'm fed up. A total waste. A wasted opportunity to get a discussion going with the two major parties. To question them. Damn, what an opportunity! MARQUART pulls his toes out of the sand. His anger puffs him up. His shoulders expand. He pulls up his coat collar. His metal button clicks into its lock. Rudolf Marquart withdraws into the citadel of his age. The bear has had enough. He trots back to his lair. And DENICKE pokes GEBHARDT in the ribs. We don't speak to CDU bosses. We're through with you bastards from today on. And GEBHARDT thinks, on behalf of the steering committee, on behalf of the absent but still operative steering committee, I signed a proclamation. A proclamation entitled FREEDOM FOR GREECE. That was going too far. Turn off the mike. Turn off Greece. Turn off freedom. We're not speaking to you anymore. We're just going to hole up in the hospital, like Dr. Frenzel, the woolen-socked reformer. Like Winfried Böhm, the pen pusher. I'm not going to do anything anymore. Will just be forty-three, stay home, and play demonstration down in my basement. A rally with a single spectator. A rally at which no one speaks. At which everyone keeps silent. At which everyone keeps silent for freedom in Greece. From the jam jars to the frozen strawberries, silent, silent, silent.

Please Pass Me the Sugar

Dear Hannelore, On the 14th, hurrah, I will be seeing all of you. So be it! And *justement* in the Christmas season—when in Munich the little puppy dogs run around with smart little caps on their little heads—will you girls also come prancing along in thrilling costumes, or even masked? Will I be able to recognize you? Hoping that this is the case, and thanking you all for your invitation, Your old Zi.

You old Zi. Your old Zi arrives late. An hour and a half late. Arrives late in a taxi, cannot be punctual. Because Zi has no children and no Herr Zirkel, because Zi is all alone, Zi cannot be punctual. Not as punctual as her letter, the bubbling Zi letter, hurrah. Despite all the German classes wearing smart little caps. Despite all the history classes, Nazi brown to the core, Zi cannot be punctual.

Will you have another slice?

Yes, I will have another slice. If you'll have another slice, I'll have another slice.

Another cup of? Yes, I'd like another cup of. If you'll have another cup, I'll have another cup.

And we'll set this slice aside for Frau Zirkel. And we'll set this cup aside for Frau Zirkel. Yes, yes, we'll set this aside, between instant coffee and thick white whipped cream. I'll pass you the sugar, and you pass me the milk. Thank you. You're welcome. Ah, lovely forest of candles. We are celebrating Christmas with our teachers. Each one a Fräulein Mary. Thank you. You're welcome. Fat and thin. Assiduous cake eaters gaze expectantly in the direction of the goodies.

Coffee: good.

Eclairs: satisfactory.

Atmosphere: adequate.

Pre-Christmas coffee klatsch. Each person has a candle shining over her plate. O silent night, a whole Mardi Gras late. Class reunion with the mighty of yesteryear, our teachers, to whose hems our curtseys are still clinging. Good morning, Frau Dr. Rautenfeld. Good morning, Fräulein Plath. Respectful greetings, embarrassed attempts at banter. What did I get on the math test? Oh, please tell me, Herr Dr. Hartwich. Oh, please tell me, Frau Stege. One only asked if one knew one had done a good job. Otherwise one sat there, pale and well-behaved, at one's numbered desk, and worried one's way down through the alphabet. Bastian, C-minus. Brasak, B-minus. And now, with a sharp D, a blow on the throbbing head, loud and clear. The grade executioner goes down his list.

And we set aside this slice for Zirkel. And we set aside this cup for Frau Zirkel. A life counted out in grades. Thirteen whole years. Always with a running start. The leap from one grade level to the next. Dress

277

neatly. Behave properly. Thank you. You're welcome. There was always the possibility of paying it no mind. Good. One could laugh at the D's. One could scratch away at one's violin instead of learning Latin vocabulary. One could take drawing lessons instead of being tutored. One could act carefree and cheerful, leaf through D's as if they were a bore. Yet when the school year ended at Easter, there stood the gallows. The school machine rejected everyone whose parents were not in the position to pay for extra tutoring, or for other things. For this or that. The school spewed out those whose parents weren't in the position. Either the father was a locksmith, and one crammed one's way painfully to the top, or one was better off, with a well-groomed mother in the PTA and a father who was always ready to contribute a little extra. Who paid for a lawn party, who offered trees to be planted around the school. Thank you, you're welcome. Running start. Leap. From grade to grade. In training for thirteen long years. Now we function smoothly. Uniform students on the assembly line of secondary school. Stamped out flat in one and only one format.

Dear children, your old Zi is going to sit down!

She arrived late. She could not be punctual.

Here you are. Thank you. Your old Zi will eat a piece of leftover cake. Your old Zi will drink a leftover cup of.

Would anyone else like another piece? Frl. Plath at the cookies exchange. Frl. Plath auctioning off the leavings. She was the most human of them all. Always personally pleasant. Always personally friendly. Always personally pleasant and friendly. Thank you. You're welcome. I'll pass you the milk, and you pass me the sugar. Justement. Hurrah.

Zi had grown whiter, older, as they had all grown older, all those women who had nothing to say but Please pass me the sugar and So what subject are you studying?

Oh, I see. How nice.

Oh, I see. Yes, yes.

Oh, I'm glad to hear that.

Our teachers had come. And since there were no compositions to assign, no grades to hand out, they sat there and were at a loss for anything to say, since they had had no experiences in their scheduled meantime except C's, C-minuses, and D's, and three square meals a day. Now, between fork and cake, when I was not even afraid of them any-

278

more, they shrank to a mere buttoned-up heap, whose faces and names I would never have remembered, had they not been my red-inked judges, tyrants over a youth which they now sat facing and to which they had nothing to say but Please pass me the sugar. Thank you. You're welcome. They passed everything on to me, everything, that is, but a future. We'll set aside this slice for the young people. And we'll set aside this cup for the young people. Thank you. You're welcome. Please pass me the cream. Oh, yes. Yes, oh, I'm glad to hear that. Teachers. Teachers. Teachers. Wiebke is studying to be a teacher. And Sabine is studying to be a teacher. And Petra is studying to be a teacher. Teachers for the next forty years. Teachers who will likewise sit there, between instant coffee and thick white whipped cream. Who will also say, Please pass me the sugar, the cream, the milk, the cake, the cookies. Thank you. You're welcome.

Nothing changes between Coke and soul, between mini and maxi. Youth is just a transition. Youth is a quality. My, your, our quality. Youth is not a quality. Only six wrinkles younger. Thank you. You're welcome. Youth and a quarter-pound of hope.

Hamburg, February 7, 2000. Dear Gisela, On the 16th, hurrah, I will be seeing all of you again. And *justement* in the Mardi Gras season, when in Berlin all the puppy dogs run around with smart little caps on their little heads—will you girls also come prancing along on the 16th in thrilling costumes, or even masked? Will I be able to recognize you? Hoping that this is the case, and thanking you all for your invitation, your old Ha.

SCENE 79. INTERIOR. EVENING. GEBHARDT'S HOUSE. HALLWAY, KITCHEN, LIVING ROOM. OPTICAL AND STYLISTIC ALLUSIONS TO SCENES 5, 6, AND 8 SHOULD BE CONSCIOUSLY AIMED FOR. SCENE OPENS WITH LONG SHOT AS IN SCENE 5. RAINER GEBHARDT GOES TO THE DOOR. The good men are coming. Their shadows loom up behind the glass door. GEBHARDT hears their footsteps. He opens the door for the good men when they ring. They stand there behind the door, glass-ribbed and wood-latticed. Good evening. Hello. Well, finally. The best-looking coat belongs to Dr. Raake, FRAUKE says. Moss-green loden with leather buttons. GEBHARDT fetches beer from the kitchen. The best-looking beer for Dr. Raake. He drags a case past the moss green. He is providing a case, for today all the good men are there. And all the good hats are hanging on the hook. Leather for Bruhns. And poplin for Biehl. Biehl has a hard road ahead of him, GEBHARDT thinks. BIEHL holds the door for him. Hmm, a case probably won't be enough. A club won't be enough either, GEBHARDT thinks, for the apostles are gathered together. The apostles of the republic are conferring on what finally is to be done after five long, week-long months. GEBHARDT looks at BACHHOF. He knows the tale of the apostles and the cockcrow, GEBHARDT thinks, he knows it perfectly well. He knows what it means to be sitting in the flowered chair in which Böhm once sat. With its glued leg. Bachhof knows what it means when KONSTANTIN says that talk by itself is just another form of alienation. Talk by itself won't get us anywhere. But, but, dear friend. RAAKE leans back, exposes his chalked white leisure teeth. Don't jump to conclusions. After all, we're here to reach a decision. And since Herr Böhm invited me here, I want to say something, too. And I hope from the bottom of my heart that our meeting proves meaningful. For as Winfried says, things have become chaotic. Very true, says BÖHM. Our Winfried, GEBHARDT thinks. As I already said, BÖHM says, Rosa L. is taking over. They manipulate every meeting. And we can't even rely on Knopke anymore. Although he was against it at the time. He didn't want that book business, either. And now? He and Sommer, says HAUSWALD. And not one of the study groups is functioning. And only three of us show up to hand out leaflets downtown. And Gebhardt tries to hold the pieces together and writes letters. This has got to stop, HAUSWALD says; I agree with Böhm. And the worst of it, says DIETER BIEHL, Is that only the Rosa L. people always know what is going on and ap͏ ear en masse at every meeting. And only BIEHL says, Because they have so much time and can tyrannize over the others, because most of the members don't grasp what is happening. Because the others, says BIEHL, Only appear sporadically and never act as a group. That's it, says BÖHM. We never have the time. That's why next time all seventeen of us, as a bloc. Dr. Raake, too. Of course, says DR. RAAKE, If it's absolutely necessary, of course. But of course, BRUHNS says. How can you even ask? It is in all our interest that this undertaking should succeed and not be manipulated to death. Manipulated to death, GEBHARDT thinks. Here are seventeen people. Ludwig Frenzel and wife. Falcon Frenzel, small and hunched, clinging to Irene's leather fist. Who flies out for prey and brings it back to the babies in the nest. The little birds from Sheriff Bonanzaland. There are

280

seventeen of us, GEBHARDT thinks. With Herr Dr. Raake, who stands with both feet firmly in the air. With his after-shave tongue. Sweet seventeen, GEBHARDT thinks. With HERR DR. GRÜTZMANN, the tobacco puffer, who lets FRAUKE serve him. Plays a pasha with a chimney and eyes KONSTANTIN with suspicion. The only person who has something to say. Who understands that the club does not exist for its own sake. Who says, We cannot reduce democracy to theoretical utterances. Who says, We need action, living commitment, Herr Bruhns, not just written manifestos. One must live as one writes. BRUHNS smiles. He smiles with boredom. My magazine, BRUHNS says. You need money, too, Konstantinus, or am I mistaken? It's not enough just to be a Greek and bewail the status quo in your country. Tasteless, BIEHL says. But true, BRUHNS exclaims. Besides, I'm doing my best. I'll call Knauer first thing tomorrow. I know he sympathizes with your cause. If you want to rescue this undertaking, fine, let's rescue it. Oh, come on, says RENATE. Give a kiss, says JOACHIM. Sh, Joachim, says RENATE, No, please, stop it! And is already tossing her blond curls, laughing and swirling, in HERR RAAKE's direction. Yes, GEBHARDT thinks. Yes, Herr Raake. We are rescuing the club, while two turtledoves play at marriage. She offers him for a pigeon shoot. Please, take my husband first. Putting love aside for a moment, HAUSWALD says, I can't come on Monday. We have conferences at school with the parents. But it's important that the others come. That's no catastrophe, LOHMANN exclaims. I'll talk for two. We have to nose these troublemakers out. Some time this has to stop. Some time we have to get moving. My opinion, BÖHM says. Hopp never did pay up. And Kranz, FRENZEL says. I simply don't understand it. He always said he was going to get something from Rudi and Buci. What's the situation with the dues? HERR MENCK inquires. Rudolf Menck, there for the first time, invited by GEBHARDT, to join in rescuing the club. Rudolf Menck, GEBHARDT thinks. Actually he was the one. Not Grützmann. Not Böhm. Actually it was Rudolf Menck. FLASH-BACK.

Ring-around-the-Rosie of Solidarity

A comprehensive examination would be childish, said the Herr Professor in the midnight blue suit, and placed his hands, clasped for the academic invocation, on the point of his crossed right midnight blue knee. It would be psychologically unwise, childish, and irrelevant, said the Herr

Professor, who handed out seminar certificates with the formula Herr/Frau/Fräulein . . . from Hamburg/ . . . participated during the first/second semester in my seminar on . . . His/her performance was excellent/good/satisfactory/adequate. He/she completed an excellent/good/satisfactory/adequate paper on. . . .

There should be no need for an examination if you are performing satisfactorily in your classes, as I have no doubt you are doing, said the Herr Professor, and placed his hands, folded for the academic invocation, carefully on the point of his crossed right midnight blue knee.

He smiled benevolently when the student Köhler declared, All right, then we'll disrupt it. He smiled as brightly as his desk when the student Reiche said, All right, then we're going to see that this exam gets changed. His smile faded when the student Kümmel pulled a flier out of his pocket. A little white flier, no larger than a seminar certificate. Unsatisfactory, unsatisfactory, said the Herr Professor, and left in a huff because the student Herr Kümmel had taken him at his word.

Kümmel had broken the rules of the game. Everyone knows that things should not be the way they are, and no one changes the way things are in order that it may continue to be true that things are not the way they should be. Certainly the Herr Professor spoke of change. But was that any reason to act on his remarks? After all, for fifty years he never acted on his own remarks, and here he had become a successful midnight blue professor.

No, this action of Kümmel's is not one bit to my liking, the blue professor remarked to his moss green colleague. Not a bit. Absolutely not. No. And the moss green professor in the Bavarian hunting outfit with an academic stand-up collar, the green-dyed Mao professor from Hamburg's Sachsenwald, nodded. Nodded like a poplar that bends with every breeze. That bends and stoops at the slightest movement. Bends adequately/satisfactorily/well/excellently.

But these young people are totally inflexible, said the midnight blue butterfly, and thought about his own backbone. Yes, yes, said the moss green professor, and took fright at the banner declaring Down with the Comprehensive, and took fright at a democratic vote, and took fright at himself.

They want to make the proctoring stricter, the student Kümmel shouted into the microphone. We refuse to let ourselves be treated like babies any longer, shouted the student Reiche, and bit into the mike. The

282

professors have already admitted that this exam should be disrupted!
Thumping applause pounded its way along the rows of seats. During the
exam we'll have someone read the answers out loud, Kümmel shouted.
Who votes in favor? Kümmel shouted, and could not even begin to
count all the hands that were for the proposal. And my friend Helga, one
eye a little smaller than the other, poked me in the ribs and stuck up her
arm. Almost all of us stuck up our arms. We expressed our solidarity
with the call for solidarity which our fellow student Kümmel was
pumping into the mike. Louder and louder. Sol-i-dar-i-ty!

When we entered the lecture hall, exam tension between our thumbs
and index fingers, when we entered the lecture hall, ready to write down
the answers learned by heart, when we all appeared and took our seats in
a sudden failure of solidarity, and when half of us wanted to start writing
after all, and when the boycott unexpectedly tasted defeat, our fellow
student Kümmel dashed in, and Reiche yelled out the answer to a
question, and the professor in the midnight blue suit broke off the
examination and stormed out, rage-red, followed by his assistants,
fluttering along behind him like a concert pianist's coattails.

Meetings. For? Against? Posters. Discussions. Delays. The ring-
around-the-rosie of solidarity. One should. One might have. One must.
And then came the letters. The blue letters sent to every examination
candidate. The university issued private invitations to the examination.
Everyone received one at his home address. Everyone read, This letter
must be presented at the examination center. Everyone read, 9 A.M. at the
Langenfort School or the Eichkamp School. Located far out on the out-
skirts of Hamburg. Selected for strategic reasons, as one of the
instructors let slip. In case there are clashes with the police, as an
assistant let slip. And Kümmel shouted, Boycott! We refuse to write
under police guard! And Reiche shouted, Boycott! We refuse to write
with paddy-wagon escorts! And Köhler shouted, Boycott! We refuse to
write with police dogs at the doors!

We won't let ourselves be reduced to prisoners, Köhler said. Academic
freedom is in danger, Reiche said. The professors have assumed police
powers, Kümmel said. The assistants are being made into stool pigeons,
Kümmel said. As spokesman for the SDS, Kümmel said. We categori-
cally reject these extrauniversitary methods, Kümmel said. The radical
student Kümmel declared.

Jens drove me to an industrial park, a deserted strategic area where the

*building superintendents had been questioned as to the political
reliability of the tenants. Jens drove me to the Eichkamp School. To a
deserted summer-vacation empty school with a dark red brick factory-
type gateway in which my Herr Professor was standing. My midnight
blue professor. Like a doorman at the Palace Hotel. He stood there
checking off the invitation letters against a list. He admitted one student
after another. They had all scrubbed off their solidarity in the bathtub.
None of them found it shameful to take their exam with police dogs at
the doors. They walked through the gate like breads into the oven.
Molded into shape. Well kneaded. Ready for the heat.*

*And my professor stood there like a railway conductor with a face
dusty from many years of service. Opposite him a police sergeant.
Behind him three patrolmen. And at his side a police dog. And in front
of the school two paddy wagons. And in the schoolyard two riot vans.
And my professor was standing there, protected against Reiche and
Köhler, both of whom showed up for the examination. Radically
opposed but there nonetheless. And my professor stood there and
protected the childish, psychologically unwise, irrelevant comprehensive
examination with a detailed police-intervention strategy. With policemen
peering out of the upper windows of the school building like puppets.
Shouting, Are you all here? Yes, we were all there. And Köhler
whispered to me, It would be to our disadvantage if. The revolutionary
Köhler, who had called for a boycott and did not even answer his own
call, the student Köhler whispered, I spoke to the professor, and he said
it would be to my disadvantage if. He said, Don't stand in the way of
your own future. You're a sensible person, Köhler. I'm counting on you,
Köhler.*

*And Köhler, on whom a professor was counting, our fellow student
Köhler, stood ahead of me in line and whispered to me, his beard as long
as his hair, but the rest of his face shaved as close as a bald head. Shiny,
full of blemishes, and bald. So you're not going in, Köhler said to me.
That's the right thing to do, Köhler said. It's shameful to take the exam
under police supervision in a grade school, Köhler said. That's the right
thing to do, Köhler said, and pulled his briefcase from between his
legs and went inside. Went up to the oven gate, showed his letter, let
himself be stamped like a package, strolled past the police dogs, slunk
into one of the little classrooms, and did not stand in the way of his own
future.*

284

I left the Köhler citadel, the strategic Reiche fortress, and Jens drove me to Helga's school, where Helga was waiting for me, one eye a little bigger than the other, Helga, who also did not want to take the comprehensive. And as we drove up to the police-protected school, far outside the city, where the riot vans were standing, we saw Kümmel run across the street in front of the car. Kümmel came panting up. Kümmel, who had knitted his red flag into a red turtleneck. Kümmel who hurled the Third Reich in his professors' and our fathers' faces. Kümmel the agitator, who was unwilling to sacrifice even a meager semester for his cause. Kümmel, who had no job to lose, no family to feed, who spat at his parents for not belonging to the Resistance. Our fellow student Kümmel dashed across the street, clutching the letter of admission tight in his right exam-hand. So you're not taking the exam, Kümmel called out, and came over to the car. So you're not taking the exam, Kümmel said, and thought, wait 'til I have my degree safely tucked away, and said, Tomorrow we're going to take over the departmental library. He leaned far into the open window of the car and said, It's no good simply refusing, and said, when his father asked him why he hadn't simply refused, as he had not refused in the bad years, It's no good simply refusing.

SCENE 80. INTERIOR. NIGHT. IN RUDOLF MENCK'S CAR. IT IS RAINING. LITTLE TRAFFIC ON THE HIGHWAY. THE RADIO PROGRAM IN THE BACKGROUND OCCASIONALLY EMERGES INTO THE FOREGROUND. CAMERA: LONG SHOT FROM THE REAR. Are you comfortable? MENCK asks. Have enough room? MENCK asks. Everything okay? MENCK asks. Everything's okay, GEBHARDT replies. NOT ONLY IN THE AREA SURROUNDING CUZCO. No, leave the radio on. THE CITY OF OLLANTAYTAMBO BY VIRTUE OF ITS SIZE. You aren't sorry you came along, are you? GEBHARDT isn't sorry. First edition, MENCK says. Berlin 1967. That's our first edition. And the rest, GEBHARDT thinks. No more wreaths. No more bows. THE ROYAL GRAVES WERE PAINSTAKINGLY CONCEALED. BUT THEY WERE NOT SO DEEP THAT ONE COULD NOT RETRIEVE THE MUMMIES. MENCK passes his tongue over two narrow, faded streaks. Menck always does that when he is nervous. He looks like a bird, RAINER GEBHARDT thinks. Eyes close together. The nose like a red beak. In a moment he will blow away through the vents. PARAMONGA. A HEAVILY FORTIFIED CITY. Very interesting, MENCK says. But my script will be even better. Much better. Neubüser won't have anything to laugh at then. GEBHARDT closes his eyes. The wreaths in the Lichthof. NEAR CUZCO. THE RUINS NEXT TO THE GRAND THRONE ROOM. A little black-flagged convoy. A silent march past rows of onlookers. Hanover and Django. His breviary was a Colt. Why, GEBHARDT laughs. Why won't Neubüser have anything to laugh at? Why? GEBHARDT asks. Killing time with questions. The rain is dripping down over the landscape. GEBHARDT looks out through the glass. Three abreast. A school field trip, RAINER GEBHARDT thinks. Directed by the green-red-yellow of the traffic lights. Only a field trip, RAINER GEBHARDT thinks. Keep nicely three abreast. That will be hard to take, MENCK says. Just like the ribbon on the wreath: To the first victim of the emergency powers act, MENCK says. The smile will die on his lips. MENCK blinks, passes a car. THE SPANISH CONQUERORS SEEM TO HAVE SNEAKED UP ON THE NATIVE BUILDERS AT WORK. IN THE INCAMISANA AREA. Idiot, MENCK shouts, Doesn't even signal! Eight professors, GEBHARDT thinks. Eight. No more. Like the Monopoly game on Tanja's birthday. It was like an exercise in organization, RAINER GEBHARDT says. Like a dry run. Just a moment, MENCK exclaims. I've got to get past this guy first. All right, now, says MENCK, What do you mean by that? Dry run at a grave? It was depressing, GEBHARDT says. That's all I can say. You needn't say any more, says RUDOLF MENCK. One thing is clear. It was an attempt at physically exterminating the student opposition. HUMAN SACRIFICES WERE THE EXCEPTION. USUALLY ANIMALS AND CORN BEER WERE OFFERED UP. AND WHEN THE LAST INCA RAISED HIS EYES TO THE SUN GOD BEFORE THEY STRANGLED HIM. A good program, RUDOLF MENCK says. Turn off the preaching. Turn on the preaching. This calm is unbearable. TERRACES, WELLS, AND AQUEDUCTS. Usually, GEBHARDT thinks, usually animals and corn beer were offered up. As Duensing so appropriately remarked, students as liverwurst, MENCK says, and pats his jacket pockets. Do you have a cigarette on you, Gebhardt? Menck with a menthol filter. The rain has stopped. MENCK turns off the windshield wipers. Up with the flag, GEBHARDT thinks. In our booths, at the control console, thinks RAINER GEBHARDT, almost like me. Earned their spurs in the Third Reich. Big and small. Their ranks still tightly closed. CULTIC ABLUTIONS AND CONFESSION ARE CUSTOMARY. And what now, GEBHARDT says. MENCK signals. MENCK passes a truck. MENCK says, Excuse me, just a moment. MENCK is already writing his script. Writing his script in his head, RAINER GEBHARDT thinks. About the aridity of theory. From theory to practice. What Habermas gave his talk on. MENCK is already making his outline. The general population resents minorities. Suspects them. Page eleven. Menck is already on page twelve, GEBHARDT thinks. Is sketching out the conclusion. FOR THE SAME PROCESS TOOK PLACE IN ASIA. SHIPS WERE REPLACED BY CAMELS. I've got to turn this off now. MENCK presses the button. Now he has silence. The silence of the Lichthof, GEBHARDT thinks. Was your son there, too? Yes, my son was there. He's studying under Flechtheim, in Berlin. His name is Benno. Benno, of all names, MENCK says. I don't find that funny, RAINER GEBHARDT says. What does that have to do with it? Nothing, MENCK says. He's simply called Benno. Aha, GEBHARDT says. What is this all supposed to mean? GEBHARDT thinks. What is going to become of those five thousand students? Those Coke-drinking, yogurt-eating five thousand? People were beating up the students for a good three or four minutes before the police even stirred. Benno told me that over the phone. He was there, too. Law and order at any price, GEBHARDT thinks. They have still not learned to live with minorities. With liverwursts, GEBHARDT thinks. I can spell you for a while, RAINER GEBHARDT offers. I'd like to drive a bit. He drives much too fast, RAINER GEBHARDT thinks. That's all right, says RUDOLF MENCK. The main thing's that you're comfortable. Very comfortable, GEBHARDT thinks. As comfortable as our population has been for centuries with its WHAT DO YOU WANT, its Philistine WHAT ARE YOU AFTER, as Frauke Gebhardt would say. Our population, RAINER GEBHARDT thinks. You have to be able to picture the world as a different place, if you want to. Hentig said that, the professor of education from Göttingen. If you want to change it. Point four, GEBHARDT says. No one followed as far as point four. They were supposed to discuss practice under point four, RAINER GEBHARDT says. Just a moment, MENCK says. Is it all right if I let you off here? Right by the subway. I have to turn off here, and Wellingsbüttel is the wrong direction. Like the whole day today. As you say, point four, the question of practice, was never dealt with. The opportunity was missed—for good. For human sacrifices, RAINER GEBHARDT thinks, human sacrifices were the exception. Practice led to theory, not theory to practice. Good-bye, says MENCK. IN THE AREA AROUND CUZCO. Only three hundred came, out of twenty thousand students, twenty thousand students, MENCK says. Thank you for the ride,

287

GEBHARDT says. Good-bye, GEBHARDT says. That was really a good lecture, GEBHARDT thinks, to think they have things like that on that station.

I'm Counting on Easter

Christ said I am the truth, not I am habit. Bachhof said so. Bachhof the figurehead. And I stood there, up to my ankles in lawn, on the Soapbox Green across from the station. We stood there, and I held out my collection can to him, my collection can for Vietnam, and I popped ten Pfennig for Vietnam into his collection can. The Lindemanns had not joined us. It was Tuesday evening, not Wednesday, so only Fräulein Wicherstädt came running across the rally lawn, her leather shoes rimmed with dampness. I glimpsed her through the gaps. Her can rattling, she ran from person to person, for this demonstration was full of holes; you could take it all in like a logged-over wood lot.

We cannot be satisfied with dogmatic statements. We have to reformulate them, give them new content!

Bachhof stood there, his lids blinking nervously. During the past week there passed away. Bachhof stood there and said, If all we do is preserve tradition, our profession of faith will be at an eternal standstill. We must remodel the world, for the world is here for human beings, not human beings for the world. He stood there, stood on the grass, twisted and slight, shifting from one leg to the other, facing his responsibility to the world with a collection can, not taking refuge in his hymnal. I always wonder, the spindle said, To what extent suffering is caused by our institutions. I keep wondering whether I shouldn't give up my congregation if I ever want to become creative again. Give it up, give up everything, so my world does not disintegrate into a mere environment.

A contribution! A small contribution for Vietnam!

I don't want to look at Bachhof when he is contributing again. Contributing alternately to his can and the others'. Saying again, Who will do it if I don't. In the middle of the green, right in front of me, Bachhof wants to storm the status quo with his ten-Pfennig collection can, on a Tuesday without tea and cookies. I was ashamed that I had no message for him but: I'm collecting, too. I did not have an answer for him when he said, I have compared the claims and the truths of this
288

world with each other, and find myself sitting in a gulf, alone with my church, excluded from all the shuntings in the life process, responsible only for religious club activities. But: What counts is moving beyond the world around one into the world of the future.

Bachhof paused suddenly. Like the founder of a new religion, he was seeking his anchorite insights on this Soapbox Green, where his Christmas Christians declared, We're not giving anything for Vietnam, we're not giving anything for slit-eyes. Living Christianity had emigrated into club activities. It was hastening past us, carrying thin briefcases, Judgment Day neatly wrapped next to the sandwiches. Hasty steps, from one calamity to the next. These people were regimented maggots, white maggots in black bacon.

There are so many freedoms that we haven't even begun to make use of, Bachhof said, And this crowd, these masses, are not just an undifferentiated lump to me, they are a challenge. Take flowers and grass, for example. They are not merely a rash on the face of the earth. There is a purpose. These people must learn to get involved, must learn that history is worthwhile. Their history. Their mass history, in which so far they have only been living mechanically, with ulcers. Man is not here just to adapt—as in nature. He must take things into his own hands and move forward. He must not let opportunities slip by him. Life has to be lived aggressively. Security, order, calm, and the whole accursed tribe are not all there is to life. Life's pots contain much more. Life has so much surplus to give. The world's imperfections are not due to lack of regulation, but to lack of emancipation.

Fräulein Wicherstädt came up to us. Came up to us in soaked shoes. This collecting is for the birds, she said. These overfed citizens can't be budged, said Fräulein Wicherstädt, and dived up to the surface with the experiences she had gathered while collecting. She stood silently beside us, a touch of thirty-year-old puberty on her brow. She stood beside us, her collection can half full. Bachhof was shifting from one foot to the other, from one sentence to the other. Bachhof was growing thinner and thinner, the more he spoke. More and more like a Giacometti.

We were just talking about.

I hesitated. I tried to think. About problems.

I hesitated. I tried to think. About life's problems, I added softly, to initiate Fräulein Wicherstädt into our silence. The soundless silence that had descended since she arrived. Oh, I see, she said gratefully. I see, life's problems.

We are talking about.

I mean, I went on, We are talking about. I mean. I had forgotten how to express myself while the spindle was speaking. And although Fräulein Wicherstädt did not even ask, I felt the need to inform her of the essential details. The essential details that I was now unable to express. Only clichés occurred to me. And the more I pondered how to convey the content of our discussion in words, the closer I advanced toward the abyss of proverbs, where speech, and silence, and silver, and gold. I looked helplessly at Bachhof, that churchly bulwark who wanted not to abolish the commandments but to fulfill them. The church contained creative minorities who wanted more out of life than pious phrases and a safe preserve fenced off into areas of duty. The creative minorities could always cite the Bible as their authority, said Bachhof, For the Bible is an inexhaustible source for Christian provocateurs, not only for the functionaries of brotherly love. The Bible is a dynamic process. We must not fall back on the Bible; we must learn to listen to it in a whole new way. For what does Jesus signify, what does holiness signify today, but fulfilling one's proper role in life? Finding the right relationships. We must liberate the captive Word. We collect for Vietnam. We support black America. We lift the anchor of the Occident on the shores of the Stone Age. We must find a solution to the sin of commission, to the discrepancy between what I am and what I can be.

And what about the sight of God, said Fräulein Wicherstädt, suddenly remembering her confirmation classes and questioning Bachhof, her minister, about faith and eternity. And what about the sight of God?

The spindle burst into flames. Bachhof shot up before me like a pilot light. His pointed oval head pierced the heavens. The boundaries of the discussion blurred into the evening, which flooded over the afternoon and our discussion like an exploding temple.

The sight of God is a comforting, comfortable cliché for Christians, said Bachhof. But don't stay comfortable, Fräulein Wicherstädt. Don't stay comfortable. Our society will not be home free even when it learns about solidarity. The socialist world is not yet home free even when the means of production have been taken over by the state. There is no economic structure that can transform human consciousness. For what is at issue is more than exploitation or increasing production or fulfilling a quota. What is at issue is transforming our human substance. Democratization, socialization, the transformation of social structures, must go
290

hand in hand with the emancipation of man. Otherwise progress is meaningless. For our life process, the presentness of what is to come, must hold out hope. Hope for what is to be, not for something that will never be because it is impossible. We need a new religion, a new ethics. A new dialectical way of listening. Certain individuals struck out in this direction long ago. But the whole society has to get moving in this direction. It is not society that should shape the community, but the community that should shape society. Our domestic hearth, our European life style, will be politically impotent once Asia begins to revolt in an escalation of bitterness. The Third World does not hate us in the abstract. It hates us for our actions. What we need is a new form of awareness, not a history of phrases. Jesus was one of the first to face up to responsibility for the entire world. In our religious achievement-oriented society we must find a new Jesus and disciples who will storm our institutions. Instead of fighting against the Sabbath, interpretation of Scripture, and temple cults, they must fight against exploitation and humiliation. Against the new institutions that create new suffering.

Bachhof looked at Fräulein Wicherstädt. She had been shrinking more and more, while he grew larger and shot up higher. He looked at Fräulein Wicherstädt and said, I know it is difficult to discover Jesus in the missed opportunities of one's own life. But Christ, the agent provocateur of a new religion, must be capable of action, of assuming responsibility. Plunge into life, Fräulein Wicherstädt. Think about it, but don't forget that thinking must never be an end in itself. Don't support the oppressors with your collections for Vietnam, for the Third World. The time for alms is past. The time has come for us to have our fill of justice. Social revolutionary groups need the money more than an underdeveloped country that is completely dependent on the West or the East, and where every penny just lands in the pockets of a small corrupt class. Let us prove that Europe is not a dying rat. Let us be resurrected. Let us celebrate the resurrection of Europe, not our Good Friday, our entombment. What was Jesus' resurrection but a proof that he was not forgotten in men's minds, that he had not died, but lived on. What will and can Europe's resurrection be but that it does not die, but lives on. Not as an oppressor but as a liberator.

We should collect a bit more, I said.

Yes, said Fräulein Wicherstädt, We're standing around on the lawn here and don't even have our cans full.

I looked at Bachhof, the little founder of a religion in our midst, who had so much energy that he could consume himself in flames, that he was ignited by the friction of his own life. I'm going over to the central station, Fräulein Wicherstädt said.

Then we'll take care of the area around City Hall, I said. Or, Herr Bachhof, do you perhaps want to do the downtown area?

He turned very pale at our questions. The street lights around our Soapbox Green illuminated him from behind. He stood there transparent, the halo of a street light behind his head. No, he said, and dropped another fifty Pfennig into his can. No, he said, We can't just stand by and watch Europe be buried. Good Friday is an ending. But Easter is our beginning. He turned toward the street lights. He said, We'll take the downtown area. He shook his can with the tinny rhythm of the future. He said, I'm counting on Easter.

SCENE 81. LIKE SCENE 79. SCENE OPENS WITH A CLOSE-UP OF RUDOLF MENCK. OFF-SCREEN: I don't understand. There are over two hundred members in the club. Half of them pay. That half is made up of those of us who don't show up. And the other half don't pay, and vote on the fate of those of us who pay. How can a good cause be so perverted, BACHHOF asks. I don't understand. Yesterday I talked on the phone with the Rev. Börne. He doesn't want to come, either. Not to mention Wocker, BÖHM adds. We are forcing the good people out. You mean the democrats, ZOBEL says. Dr. Zobel of the Protestant Academy. Whom Bachhof brought in. Whom Bachhof brought along. Dr. Zobel, cautious as a smiling nun. His thoughts polished to a satiny sheen. Thoughts that say, But today we are here. Zobel smiles. Pure tact. Pure St. Matthew's Passion. And Fromm, says RAAKE. In any case we still have to convince Fromm. An extraordinary young man. He is editing a book we're going to bring out. The theories of Camillo Torres. Simply terrific. Yes, we need every vote, that's correct, BÖHM says. One should try to understand the state of mind of the doubters and the hesitators. It's a long march, as we all know, says KONSTANTIN. And the club is not enough. Going through the motions of democracy is not enough. Yes, we have to give the form a human foundation, says BACHHOF. We have to commit ourselves. That's right, says MENCK. The institutions are there for human

292

beings, not the other way around, like our club now. With the club just gobbling up your efforts, but you not getting anything out of the club. There's nothing else we can do now. That's just it, says BÖHM. That's what Pantenburg thinks, too. The movement has to come from within, as he always says. As he said in his last interview, in fact. The very people who are always talking about movement never get anything moving, says KONSTANTIN. I think it's time we got down to basics! DR. RAAKE displays his teeth. DR. RAAKE lectures. But KONSTANTIN says, The people who talk most about principles are always those who don't have any principles. Well! I beg your pardon! RAAKE exclaims. You, says KONSTANTIN, I have never seen you out working. What do you do with your free time? That's enough; let's not quarrel, says DR. HAUSWALD. That won't get us anywhere. We've decided on next Monday. I can't come because of the parent conferences. And Herr Bachhof has to go to a meeting of the deacons, as he mentioned. But there will still be thirteen of us. And if Knauer can come, and Frau Gebhardt, that makes fifteen. Of course, says FRAUKE. Of course, GEBHARDT thinks. She had no idea how chic this club was. That we had important people like Raake. Bound in moss green. She'll come next Monday. She'll come straight from her visit to the hairdresser. She had no idea that a club like this was a social event. Before we close, I just wanted to ask, says BÖHM. Who is that little blond guy who is in charge of the book committee? I was thinking we might win him over, BÖHM says. Because up to now Denicke hasn't paid a cent, hasn't even set up the bookstore. Unless we do something immediately, BIEHL says, Set up a program, find a solution, unless we can work together with all the groups and all the parties, we might as well close up shop tomorrow, says BIEHL. Yes. Then the club will have to dissolve, WINFRIED BÖHM adds. So, fifteen of us, BRUHNS says. Monday. We'll leave it at that. Good-bye. See you Monday. Really nice. Really nice, FRAUKE remarks. You never told me. Really brave, GEBHARDT thinks. What brave warriors. And now Menck is with us, too. I'll come along, FRAUKE says. Next Monday, GEBHARDT thinks. Next Monday Father Frenzel will bring along fifteen revolvers. Fifteen revolvers from his children's Sheriff Bonanzaland. And Rosa L. will be shot dead. And Sommer will be killed. And Herr Stiebler murdered. And Knopke done in. And Herr Grimme and Herr Kranz, while Irene busies herself arranging the corpses and Ludwig Frenzel weeps softly: We really like all of you much better. We didn't mean it that way.

Ah, to Be Young

What does being young really mean? Jens asks. It means, I say, that one still has everything before one. What does having everything before one mean? Jens asks. That means, I say, That you can become a doctor for instance, or a lawyer, or—well, you can choose, you can make a free decision. But once I made my decision, Jens says, Everything was decided. Now I've become something that a friend suggested, that my mother suggested, that my father suggested, that my teacher suggested. I could have become anything, but I didn't have any choice. Because if one doesn't know what one is choosing, one doesn't have any choice. One just does something.

And you don't like what you are doing?

I've passed the exams. I've passed them all, says Jens. And what I have before me is a life in which I've passed all the exams and am going to pass all the exams, and my children will pass all their exams. Maybe I have a few hobbies. Once I thought I might become a pianist. So I still play the piano a little. My mother once wanted to be a singer. Now she sings while she's setting the table. My friend once wanted to be a painter. Now he paints my bookcase for me. What does it mean to be young and pass one's exams and play the piano? Jens asks. And if I ask him what he believes in besides his exams, he just laughs.

Jens laughs. I think, Jens says, That people always find me nice because I always am nice. Never contradict. Once I said afterwards, Don't get involved in that. But when I wanted to say that loud and clear, I ended up being nice. I think I'll probably always be nice. I think I'll earn money, and more money, and still more money. Perhaps it'll be enough money for me to buy a house, with nice neighbors, who are nice because I'm nice. Because if I'm not nice, I won't earn so much money. I'll read books and go to the theater and say, This play was good and this one wasn't good. And the next day I'll buy the papers and compare the reviews and nod or shake my head. I'll take a trip once a year. And after twenty years of making money, I'll take two trips a year. On vacation I'll have breakfast, lunch, and supper and lie in the sun. And after four weeks I'll pay the bill, pack my bags, and go back to work. Enlarge my practice and earn money and more money. For a wife, or two wives, for a child, or two children. There's just room enough in my life for a five-room apartment in a quiet neighborhood. I'm young now. And later I'll get older and older and older. Hmm.

Hmm, I say.

Something should be done about that, Jens says.

What, I say.

There should be a way of getting away from all that, says Jens.

Where would you go, I say.

One should do something original, something new.

What you can look forward to, what we can all look forward to, I say, is being employed, getting integrated, adjusting. Someone will always have gotten there ahead of us. Fifty-year-olds, sixty-year-olds, who will tell us about yesterday and advise us to steer clear of today. We'll do as they say, and they'll pull us up to their level. Leaning on the covers of their coffins, they'll tell us how nice we are, how cooperative and hard working. And then we'll wait for them to die so we can move up and take over their world. Theirs, not ours. For when we reach the top, it'll be too late for our own world. We'll have used up all our energy. We'll have helped their world remain static. And we'll raise our children to carry on the world of yesteryear. The world of the old and dying, who will be at the top, like us.

One should be like Uwe, Jens says.

He's just slaving over his newspaper columns, I say. Learning about style. Learning to write what he doesn't really think is true. And soon he'll believe it.

One should be like . . .

Even if one breaks away, that doesn't change the basic set-up. And if one stays, one gets changed oneself.

I'm young, Jens says.

Yes, I say, so am I.

What are we waiting for? Jens asks.

For me to pass my exams, I say. To become a teacher, with a nice retirement pension. With two people earning, we'll be better off. Young people are better off if they're both earning.

Oh, to be young, Jens says.

Yes, I say. Oh, to be young.

SCENE 82. INTERIOR. DAYTIME. IN THE LATE NINETEENTH-CENTURY VILLA. IT IS SUNDAY. THE SUN IS SHINING. THE SUBJECTIVE CAMERA WANDERS THROUGH ALL THE CLUB'S ROOMS, WHICH ARE IN A SHOCKING STATE. WHEREVER ONE LOOKS, DIRT, BROKEN CHAIRS, SCRIBBLED-UP WALLS.

OFF-SCREEN NARRATION. I should hand out seminar certificates, GEBHARDT thinks. Or give marks in democracy, which would have to be stamped officially, so Herr Stiebler could draw his salary. So Alex Sommer could get his scholarship. The best thing would be to organize voluntary participation. Give out dessert as a reward. Anyone who comes to a study group would get a hot fudge sundae. Anyone who keeps the minutes would get a trip to Majorca and back. At half pension, GEBHARDT thinks. At full pension if he comes twice and keeps the minutes twice. Participation in a demonstration would be rewarded with free beer. The union distributes chocolate. And the political parties hand out apple strudel to anyone who marches for freedom in Greece. And for anyone who speaks for Greek freedom a basket of goodies from the delicatessen and a luxury cruise on the heavenly blue Mediterranean. Payment of dues will of course also be generously rewarded. Punctual delivery of at least two marks fifty assures every remitter the right to spend two weeks in the Canary Islands at the club's expense. That way we will be able to put together a voluntary mass demonstration now and then. Get volunteers to volunteer voluntarily. But, GEBHARDT thinks, even without that things are working themselves out. Things are right as they are. It's just a question of time, GEBHARDT thinks. In due time Nikolaus Hopp will work himself out. Herr Hopp, who promised weeks ago to pay off his debts in installments. Herr Hopp, who has not yet paid a single installment. Not today, and he won't tomorrow. That'll straighten itself out, GEBHARDT thinks. Like the building superintendent, who complained weeks ago because of the fire. And who has now written us a letter because he found two doors bashed in. Even a building superintendent straightens himself out eventually, GEBHARDT thinks. Given time. Given time, GEBHARDT thinks. Like Herr Denicke, who to this day has still not paid any rent. Who to this day has not set up his bookshop. Who has still not. It'll die down, GEBHARDT thinks. It'll straighten itself out. Just like the bookshop committee, which hasn't had a single meeting. Not so far. As Herr Fromm hasn't yet. Given time, everything will come out even, GEBHARDT thinks. A club like this will straighten itself out. Will just run down. Given time, GEBHARDT thinks. Everything takes care of itself, given time.

Hello, Hope!

We are shoving our way in. Just take your place on line. Soon the political entrance tickets will be sold out. The short subjects have already begun. Push your way forward. Nine, eight, seven, six. Come on, close up! Central station Republican Club. Hello, Central! The University of Hamburg passenger car is pulling into Track Mao. Sardine-packed meeting. Bump! Take a quick jump toward the ceiling and then soar over the heads like a jet.

If you don't shove over, I'm calling up Django!

Send a message in a bottle to the front. So they know I'm stranded!

Plenary session. Everybody out. Everybody out. Your political opinion, please. Thank you. Your connecting train is on Track Ché. This is Peking. Please pick up on the other line.

Come on, shove over. Fifty more people want to get in here!

One hundred more people want to get in here. They all want to get in. All the I's want to get in.

It's too physical for me in here!

A young girl forces her way into the villa and unbuttons her blouse. One button after the other. Takes a deep breath. Heavily polluted political air. Hamburg's political bungalow with a chandelier hall and parquet floor for the beer-bottle minuet. Here in this cigarette-butt court I am risking my two ears. I'll take a look. Going, going, gone.

I squirm my way flat along the wall. Slouched in the chairs are the counts of the proletariat, with swirling velvet capes and silk blouses. Dangling at their hips are their little countesses. Long-maned, white-powdered ladies, delicate as transparent bacon strips, their heads full of campaigns.

The project groups should act as political cadres!

I disagree completely!

The project groups are task forces and as such determine political practice.

That's manipulation!

Bullshit! Shut up!

In my opinion the club's executive council consists of an operations council and a political council, and we should merge the two.

I won't let myself be made impotent by your fucking council! We have to divide up into cadres!

What's the difference between a task force and a cadre?

Well, for instance there is a cadre on culture but no task force on culture.

Cle-ver! Cle-ver!

How should the cadres be divided up?

What kind of cadres do you mean?

I consider this motion unnecessarily complicated.

Bravo!

I would like to ask whether this concept isn't too awkward.

Have you heard the new album by the Mothers of Invention? We're only in it for the money? That's telling it like it is.

Next to me against the wall, in the vicinity of my powdered chin, a human juke box begins to hiss assimilated albums through yellowed teeth. The base is singing. The base is swinging.

Christ! Up front, where the steering committee is sitting, a chair has collapsed. What a laugh!

Man, it's sweltering here! Get that window open!

Let your pants down!

The chorus of two hundred beer drinkers is swinging. The chorus of emancipated youth is singing. Hands in the bosoms. Hands on the flies.

Why don't you get an antiauthoritarian day care center going, a blond Ophelia shouts. Go ahead and practice group sex first, her Orestes shouts, and takes over the microphone, the Bastille of individualism.

First we have to be able to live freely with each other, before we can explain all the bullshit to our kids. I mean, as long as we're still schlepping bourgeois habits around with us, this shit will never get cleared away.

Laughter-applause. With the hands go clap-clap-clap.

I don't know that this is all supposed to mean.

With the feet go tap-tap-tap. Someone pushes Orestes away from the microphone.

Who's he?

Oh, a Greek. All right, give the Greek a chance. SCENE 83. INTERIOR. EVENING. PARQUET ROOM OF THE LATE NINETEENTH-CENTURY VILLA. SUBJECTIVE CAMERA (GEBHARDT'S POINT OF VIEW) OPENS WITH A SLOWLY PANNING LONG SHOT. GEBHARDT is sitting at his observer's post. The club and him. In front of him. Separated by a wooden table. Buckshot back and forth. Facing him a mass of brightly colored splinters. Splinters that are chatting, clinking. He doesn't know how many are there. Chairs have sprouted all over the playground. The middle distance blurs. GEBHARDT can only see the foreground clearly. He sees LOHMANN's face as enormous. It would have to be Lohmann, GEBHARDT thinks. Gustav Lohmann. He can keep silent for two. Is there as a representative for four. Lohmann from the student government. Where is Dr. Raake, BÖHM asks. And Bruhns, BIEHL asks. In Lohmann, GEBHARDT thinks. They are standing behind Lohmann's knees. They are sitting in his heels. They are all keeping silent inside Lohmann. These dear distant relatives from the Republic family. The saviors, GEBHARDT thinks. These comforting bandages, which do not stay stuck. Beer doesn't stick, GEBHARDT thinks. Today he is going to decide on a separation. He has lost faith in his script. In these grocer's measures. A pound of tolerance and a pound of Civil Code. GEBHARDT passes. That is his situation. He is already getting himself accustomed to distance. He hears KONSTANTIN. But the chaff of his experiences is up to his neck. Konstantin is just collecting the last gleanings from the stubble fields. CUT. *I don't know where this will lead. If you want to achieve anything, you have to work concretely. Papandreou's son is buried, and in Athens seven hundred thousand people march in the streets. Seven hundred thousand, not a couple of thousand. A spontaneous demonstration of popular opinion. That shows that the Greek people want freedom. And when the battle begins, we will need democracies here in the West. Because if you can't keep democracy alive here, then you will some day have not only Greece but the entire Third World on your conscience! If that happens, one day fascism will be on the march here, too. Against a free Greece and against the Third World. So you must do something! Call on your fellow citizens to show solidarity with a free Greece. Explain to the man on the street what such freedom means. Explain your basic position, don't just always talk about it!*

Man, get out of here!

Orestes moves in for the attack. His chains jangle. He bites into the mike. He shouts, Discussion—that's revolution. Clap-clap-clap. Tap-tap-tap.

I think we have to become much more flexible.

We must. We should. One must. I look at the ceiling. I would like to be up there. Up there is plenty of room. Up there it would be nice. We can. We will. I play compost heap with my toe. I push together ashes and butts, bits of bottle and movie tickets, apple cores and leaflets. SCENE 84.

INTERIOR. EVENING. PARQUET ROOM IN THE LATE NINETEENTH-CENTURY VILLA. ABOUT FIFTEEN MINUTES HAVE PASSED. CAMERA REMAINS SUBJECTIVE. IF OFF-SCREEN NARRATION IS PREFERRED, THE ON-SCREEN DIALOGUE BLURS INTO BACKGROUND SOUND. GEBHARDT sits hunched behind his table. He thinks, the accidental details are peeling off gradually. The trains are on the sidings, all the signals are on red. And he thinks, as long as there is enough fuel. He snaps his manuscript shut. The measles of hope have been survived. The beginning was better than the middle, GEBHARDT thinks. It shouldn't be allowed. A Konstantin shouldn't be allowed. A Konstantin has to get out of here because a Denicke is shouting at him. A republican club cannot exist, because there are too many Denickes. And Konstantin's bursts of energy don't accomplish a thing. Finished. Anyone who picks up an apple core from the floor is counterrevolutionary. Finished. GEBHARDT renounces this alternative. Renounces Herbert Denicke and a mush of motions. Renounces a bookstore for two hundred or two hundred fifty marks per month in rent. Renounces a lie that moves mountains of members. This disorganized mishmash of waving arms and half-truths. All little everyday Galileis, who prefer to guzzle and take precautions. Who always make sure they are on the right side of whoever is the best, the fastest. Who are always in Django's favor. GEBHARDT is too tired to talk. To convince. He is fed up with trying to make a straw tasty. CUT. *I move we have discussion of Herr Belinsky's motion. I, too, am of the opinion that all the members should participate regularly.*

Who's Belinsky?

Send him up to the mike!

Belinsky to the mike!

It is my opinion that.

He looks like an old man who has been snowed in. He is of the opinion that there is no more steering committee, that direct responsibility belongs to the base.

My proposal is an antiauthoritarian proposal!

He takes a deep breath. A cold, windy breath of the tomb. He has fallen from his flesh. He is not allowed out until midnight.

Get rid of the steering committee. Then this place will get moving at last!

And what if we have to make a decision in a hurry?

The Greek creeps through the microphone. He sends his message out via echo. He says, This is the last time I'm speaking for Greece. For

Greece and the seven hundred thousand who are marching at this very hour in Athens. What do you mean here by antiauthoritarian? It is your duty to combat fascism. Why doesn't any mass movement get going in Greece? Why don't the seven hundred thousand have leaders? Because there is no vanguard left. No steering committee, if you will. There has never been a successful movement, a successful uprising, a successful revolution without a vanguard. And that is not what authoritarian Bolshevism says, Herr Belinsky, but your antiauthoritarian hero, Ché Guevara.

That's not true!

Belinsky jumps up. The stone guest storms the microphone. He shouts, Every vanguard ruins things. The steering committee cannot make decisions for all of us. We the members will meet, spontaneously if necessary.

He's right!

A gangling spinster jumps up. With slit, fringed skirt, a kerchief around the hips, and lemony smiling charm.

Right now, when I'm busy trying to set up our antiauthoritarian kindergarten, I would like to emphasize that right now the membership as a body has an enormous importance.

That's too abstract for me!

The person who shouts that is sitting way in front. At the antiauthoritarian steering committee table. The person who says that is the oldest one present, next to the song of the tomb. The only one in his forties. The only solid citizen. The only one who does not have to get promoted to his third year of university study. What does it mean to call on the membership? Who will do the work? Who will pay the postage? Lick the stamps? Draft the letters and duplicate them? Who will speak for the RC and conduct its business? Who will speak on its behalf in public? We will become incapable of action if no one assumes the responsibility. We won't ever get to do anything, because we'll spend all our time in debates. What did you elect us for, anyway?

I never elected you, Belinsky shouts.

Because you were never here! Because you just turn up and settle in when the nest has been prepared by others. Because you don't like to get your hands dirty; you just turn up today to transform everything. You want to change the base?! You weren't even capable of showing up for the membership meetings.

Shut your trap!

Authoritarian shithouse! SCENE 85. LIKE SCENE 84. CAMERA REMAINS SUBJECTIVE (GEBHARDT). GEBHARDT is shouting. He finds it easy to let out his rage in words. He has reached an impasse. He knows it. And the louder he becomes, the more he stands to lose. But he wants to lose. He does not want to try to understand this impasse, as Böhm does. He does not want to whisper like BIEHL, who is now standing against the wall next to the SCHUSTERS and doing everything differently because no one can hear him. GEBHARDT is shouting loudly. He is shouting for Bachhof and Hauswald, who are at the deacons' meeting and the parents' conference discussing the problems with problems in order to get the evening over with. GEBHARDT knows that in a moment the new elections will begin. In a moment the steering committee will be dissolved. In a moment everything will be transformed into a happening. For FRENZEL is keeping silent, and HERR ZOBEL is keeping silent, and HERR MENCK. Another of the red numbers. Of the red numbers, who from today on will be worth twice as much. For no one will be able to balance the club anymore. Bachhof and Hauswald have taken their leave. And Gebhardt has no more credits in his asset column, because BIEHL and FRENZEL, because BÖHM and GRÜTZMANN are going to put themselves up for election again. Have themselves voted down and then voted in again. Dismiss. Delay, because the SCHUSTERS and LOHMANN want a period of delay which will provide relief only for the moment, but which GEBHARDT does not want. GEBHARDT does not want to continue on with ALTHOUGH's and BUT's. All or nothing. And he wants the nothing. CUT. *The political camp followers cross their black net stockings, think about the antiauthoritarian children in their anti-bellies, and shut their eyes. Membership meeting nap.*

That's utter nonsense!

A deus ex machina appears. He comes flying in on an Attic cloud. He flies over our heads. An angel in a suit with a vest. He lands gently in front of the microphone-Bastille and flutes cultivatedly, classical learning in his buttonhole; We do need a form of organization, comrades.

Clap-clap-clap. Tap-tap-tap. The camp followers open their pale eyes. The tallish spinster shouts, Don't forget the women!

Brothers and sisters, the angel flutes. I don't think we should vote out the steering committee every time. We should simply keep it under strict control.

How?

Tombstone Belinsky questions his male and female ghosts.

302

The steering committee meetings should be open, brothers and sisters. And the decisions of the steering committee should be submitted to a vote. That would make for a perfectly functional model.

Angelic serenade. Please, could ze points of order be a little louder and ze motions a little more lifely, vould you please? One, two, three. Wait for me. For me here, where events form a continuum. Where time consists of action committees and project groups. The exact time. It is now eleven-fifteen. The exact antiauthoritarian time. Where a year passes like a day. And one hour has a hundred minutes. The exact membership meeting time, where one hundred points of order pass like one membership meeting, and one membership meeting has a hundred points of order. SCENE 86. LIKE SCENE 85. CAMERA REMAINS SUBJECTIVE (GEBHARDT). OFF-SCREEN NARRATION AS BEFORE. This meeting is actually just like any other, GEBHARDT thinks. It has many antecedents. It's always the same, he says to BÖHM. I'm through. But BÖHM does not hear him. BÖHM is in the process of repairing his burned bridges. BÖHM has thought it over again. Just as all of them have thought it over again, GEBHARDT thinks, and looks at FRAUKE's fresh hairdo. Way up front. First row, third seat. She is brooding now under her topping, GEBHARDT thinks, and stares at FRAUKE's festive hairdo. And next to her, behind her, up and down the rows, what are their names? Are they all called Denicke and Sommer? Have they all dolled themselves up for the Hollywood death? For the funeral with colored tinfoil? A waxworks funeral under the direction of Irene Tousseau? GEBHARDT is no archivist. No collector. He does not mount corpses in the album pages of his days. The leave-taking is going to be fragmented, GEBHARDT thinks. It is high time I put an end to this. I don't want to see Camilla Hauswald wearing the funeral bow, GEBHARDT thinks. Later Grützmann will rake the graves. He knew ahead of time that it would turn out this way. But what good does that do him now? CUT. *Motion on the agenda. The study group on the church is bullshit. Let's get rid of it!*

The girl next to me spits on the floor. Right into the middle of my compost heap. Right into the middle of the movie tickets. Dripping over the apple cores. A brownish liquid. The girl spits Bini liquid. My neighbor Bini. Bini from the tea room, who has now become politically active. Who has just arrived. Bini spits a point of order. She has pushed her way through to me.

I saw you right away. That's a neat blouse you have on.

303

She mutters, Nothing going on here. I'm going to split to the establishment. She murmurs, All this democracy bullshit, and starts to gnaw on her nails.

Countermotion. The study group on the church should be kept. One, two, three, four. Discussion. Let's have another beer. Speeches pro and con.

Bini should open her mouth more often. That's really cool.

A tired messiah stands up. He bunches his hand into the fist sign. He waves like a medicine man.

Really outstanding!

He sits down. A kitschy souvenir Jesus with corkscrew-curled beard and colorful sweater. The china Jesus sits down. Speeches for and against, and smoothes his velour pants. Titian blue. A Politjesus you can take with you. Put it on the bureau. A souvenir of the Republican Club. With long curried black hair. I have long curried hair. I have activated politicized debated hair. I wear velour pants. We wear velour pants. I wear, you wear, he, she, it wears velour pants. We wear velour pants. You all wear velour pants.

The steering committee is a paper tiger.

Pass around the future. The future is a paper tiger. For we are in motion. We are in motion toward the door. Let's get out of here. The movie tickets were sold out long ago. The main feature has already begun. Hope, hello, hope! SCENE 87. LIKE SCENE 86. CAMERA SUBJECTIVE AS BEFORE (GEBHARDT). OFF-SCREEN NARRATION AS BEFORE. You can make up many lies with the ABC, GEBHARDT thinks, and lays his files on the table. The files of the circulars and the study groups. The documents of good will and good persuasion. He places half a year in a pile. The time has come. His time is up. GEBHARDT is waiting for a collision. He finds it. He slams his files down on the table in front of FRENZEL. He passes a wave of effort on to a wading pool, to feign a last bit of motion. But now his time is no longer dependent on the crazy notions of a Willy Stiebler or a Denicke, who have declared all the study groups dissolved as of today. Who from today on. Who from today on. No. Gebhardt has no intention of becoming a wading pool reptile. With a thick protective skin. With scaly small all-seeing eyes, dozing lazily. Which children drag along behind them, only to stomp on it some day. Gebhardt is not going to let himself be stomped on. Not by them. He has definitely had enough. CUT. *Now he is resigning his post. To great whooping and hallooing.*

304

*Hope. Hello, hope. Tap-tap-tap. Clap-clap-clap. He is forty. He shouts,
Just go on standing with both legs firmly in the air! He takes his
briefcase and goes. Simply leaves. Brushes the butts from his shoulders.
Kicks the leaflets off his shoes. Shouts, I've had enough!*

*But the children do not go and stand in the corner. The children
cannot be forced to eat their spinach. They open up the list of nominees.*

That old fool is gone at last!

Now I'm going to elect this guy.

Who?

You know, him.

Do you know who he is?

Naw. That doesn't matter.

Well, at least we're rid of that motherfucker.

At least we're rid of that old moron.

Come on, you're supposed to pay for your beer.

Up yours. I'm not a capitalist!

*At least we're rid of the cashbox. At last we're rid of the base. Hope.
Hello, hope.*

*It is now twelve-fifteen. The politvilla is exactly twelve-fifteen.
Clap-clap-clap. I'll give them some more room. Tap-tap-tap. I'm getting
out of here. Tap-tap-tap.*

*I had enough long ago. Four hours of debate. Twelve motions and
twenty-four amendments. My name is Konstantin.*

*I don't look at him. He is standing in the lobby-car number hope. I
already know him. Have known him since eight-fifteen.*

It's the same thing every day.

He says, The same thing every day.

Is this your first time here?

He says, The same thing every day.

*The only thing that unites the people here is that each one has two
perpendicular legs. Believe me, they have no goals. This is an intellectual
mob, mixed in with a few well-meaning people who don't understand
what is going on. They want freedom? What for? To rot away in. To rot
away in antiauthoritarian bliss? Their freedom is comfort, sheer surfeit.
Some day we are going to have to fight in Greece. But we aren't going to
wait for these petty-bourgeois revolutionaries, these elitist academics
who don't even understand their own language of arrogance, to hand out
three leaflets. Three wretched little solidarity leaflets. We Greeks will go*

it alone. Will have to go it alone. For the big question is whether those people sitting in there and swilling beer even have a future. SCENE 88. INTERIOR. EVENING. INSIDE GEBHARDT'S CAR. CAMERA OPENS WITH LONG SHOT FROM THE BACK SEAT. THE SCENE SHOULD END WITH A CLOSE-UP OF GEBHARDT, SEEN THROUGH THE WINDSHIELD. You don't have to drive so fast, FRAUKE says. He doesn't have to drive so fast, GEBHARDT thinks. He just has to drive home, raise Tanja, and water his cozy home with salary. He just has to make it through. Don't take it so hard, FRAUKE says. Bruhns and Raake probably just couldn't. He's not supposed to take it so hard. Certainly not. But his life doesn't consist just of feelings. He did want to do something. Something more. Something for later on. We'll find a solution, FRAUKE says, and strokes his hair. Strokes Gebhardt the body. The part of me, GEBHARDT thinks, that she lives with. With which one can conceive children. Perhaps a second one. To care for us in our old age. The other half, GEBHARDT thinks, the other half will digest all this without any trouble. If Neubüser just rattles out his proverbs, if Neubüser says he knew it all along, if he just says, We've all made our mistakes, the other half will calm down. And when Frauke switches off the light he will read another page of possibilities, before he, too, goes to sleep, tired and full. For Gebhardt, Rainer Gebhardt, will go back to just reading the newspaper. Gebhardt, the television viewer. Gebhardt, the head shaker. He looks into his rear-view mirror. He thinks, it is not enough. I'm not enough. And he is sorry and suddenly ashamed that he did not speak to Konstantin. For now he is sitting here in the car with FRAUKE, and Tanja will ask some day, What did you do when, when. And now he is sitting with his spouse in the car and driving toward the eiderdown quilts of his future, but he did not speak to Konstantin. Did not even say thank you to that man Konstantin. CUT. *He stood there. Leaned against the bulletin board. Leaned against Biafra. A little contribution for Biafra. I'm not giving anything for Negroes. A little contribution for Greece. I'm not giving anything for Greece. He leaned against the Negro poster. He was wearing Black Power on his shoulders. We're not giving anything for Europe.*

He held the door open for me. He stood there, transparent as the spindle. Pale as the spindle he went out toward the street light, the halo of the gutter. He silently nodded good-bye. And I nodded back. Twenty-four years of future nodded. Twenty-four years of hope, encrusted under the nails, nodded back.

306

I thought, this is not the end. I will tug the rat by the tail to keep it from dying. I thought, Bachhof, this is not the end. Youth is more than a cigarette stub which goes out pointlessly, leaving nothing behind but ashes. Youth is more than that, I thought. More than an under-thirty passion, that disintegrates into a pension. More than a belly without wrinkles.

Is it more, I thought. Hope. Hello, hope. I took two ten-Pfennig pieces out of my pocket. I hammered out the second verse. I hammered out the Groschen-rhythm of the future to the second verse. I rattled Easter. I wrapped the rat's tail tightly around my wrist. A political hope. Thank you. You're welcome. Connecting train on track zero. I turned toward the street lights. I shouted, I'm counting on Easter. I shouted down the empty street, my rat's tail tightly under my arm. This is Station Easter! Please identify yourself! Come in, please. Easter, please come!